◆ THE FIFTEENTH CENTURY SERIES NO. 4 ◆

COURTS, COUNTIES AND THE CAPITAL

IN THE LATER MIDDLE AGES

EDITED BY
DIANA E.S. DUNN

SUTTON PUBLISHING • STROUD
ST. MARTIN'S PRESS • NEW YORK

First published in the United Kingdom in 1996
Sutton Publishing Limited
Phoenix Mill · Far Thrupp · Stroud · Gloucestershire

First published in the United States of America in 1996
St Martin's Press • Scholarly and Reference Division
175 Fifth Avenue • New York • N.Y. 10010

Copyright © Diana E.S. Dunn, David Mills, Tim Thornton, David Tilsley, Deborah Marsh, Carrie Smith, Penny Tucker, Caroline M. Barron, Hugh Collins, David Rundle, Rachel Gibbons, 1996

All rights reserved. No part of this publication may be reproduced, stored in a retrieval system, or transmitted, in any form or by any means, electronic, mechanical, photocopying, recording or otherwise, without the prior permission of the publishers and copyright holders.

British Library Cataloguing in Publication Data

A catalogue record for this book is available from the British Library.

ISBN 0-7509-1149-2

ACKNOWLEDGEMENT

The editor and publisher gratefully acknowledge the assistance of the Marc Fitch Fund and Chester College towards the cost of publication.

Typeset in 10/15 Baskerville.
Typesetting and origination by
Alan Sutton Publishing Limited.
Printed in Great Britain by
Hartnolls, Bodmin, Cornwall.

Contents

Contributors	v
Abbreviations	v
Introduction	vii
1. *David Mills*	
The Chester Mystery Plays: Truth and Tradition	1
2. *Tim Thornton*	
Local Equity Jurisdictions in the Territories of the English Crown:	
The Palatinate of Chester, 1450–1540	27
3. *David Tilsley*	
Arbitration in Gentry Disputes: The Case of Bucklow Hundred in	
Cheshire, 1400–1465	53
4. *Deborah Marsh*	
'I See by Sizt of Evidence': Information Gathering in Late Medieval Cheshire	71
5. *Carrie Smith*	
Medieval Coroners' Rolls: Legal Fiction or Historical Fact?	93
6. *Penny Tucker*	
Relationships between London's Courts and the Westminster Courts in the	
Reign of Edward IV	117
7. *Caroline M. Barron*	
The Education and Training of Girls in Fifteenth-century London	139
8. *Hugh Collins*	
The Order of the Garter, 1348–1461: Chivalry and Politics in Later	
Medieval England	155
9. *David Rundle*	
On the Difference between Virtue and Weiss: Humanist Texts in	
England during the Fifteenth Century	181
10. *Rachel Gibbons*	
The Piety of Isabeau of Bavaria, Queen of France, 1385–1422	205
Index	225

The Fifteenth Century Series

Advisory editor: Ralph A. Griffiths, Professor of Medieval History, University of Wales, Swansea

THE FIFTEENTH CENTURY SERIES is a tribute to the vitality of scholarly study of the later Middle Ages (and especially of the fifteenth century) and to the commitment of Alan Sutton Publishing to make its conclusion widely available. This partnership, which Charles Ross did so much to encourage, has been extraordinarily productive in the quarter-century since the pioneering colloquium on 'The Fifteenth Century, 1399–1509: Studies in Politics and Society' was held in Cardiff and presided over by S.B. Chrimes. The proceedings of that colloquium edited by S.B. Chrimes, C.D. Ross and R.A. Griffiths, were published in 1972 (and reprinted in 1995). Since 1979 Alan Sutton Publishing has published a number of papers, invited especially from younger scholars and discussed at further colloquia, which have become a notable feature of the academic landscape in Britain. Aside from the encouragement given to talented young historians, noteworthy features of these volumes are the breadth of topics addressed, the novelty of approaches adopted, and the participation of scholars from North America and the European Continent. The volumes have proved influential and informative, and there is good reason to include future volumes in this major new series, both to recognize the achievements of the present generation of fifteenth-century historians and to consolidate the interest in later medieval history which they have undoubtedly generated.

This fourth volume in THE FIFTEENTH CENTURY SERIES arose from a colloquium held at Chester in 1994. The papers invite novel comparisons in matters of aristocratic and urban culture, social behaviour, and the practice of the law between the capital and the provinces – and with particular (and appropriate) emphasis on Chester and its palatinate.

Contributors

Caroline M. Barron is Reader in the History of London at Royal Holloway, University of London.
Hugh Collins is a research student at Balliol College, Oxford.
Rachel Gibbons is a research student at the University of Reading.
Deborah Marsh is currently working for the Stafford Castle Project.
David Mills is Professor in the Department of English Language and Literature, University of Liverpool.
David Rundle is College Lecturer in Early Modern History at Mansfield College, Oxford.
Carrie Smith is currently employed by Cambridge University on a Leverhulme Project on medieval taxation records at the Public Record Office, London.
Tim Thornton is Lecturer in Late Medieval and Early Modern Political History at the University of Huddersfield.
David Tilsley is researching aspects of the Cheshire gentry.
Penny Tucker currently holds a Wellcome Institute Fellowship to research the history of Bethlem Royal Hospital, London.

Abbreviations

AN	Archives Nationales, Paris	*CPR*	*Calendar of the Patent Rolls*
BIHR	*Bulletin of the Institute of Historical Research*	*DKR*	*Annual Reports of the Deputy Keeper of the Public Records*
BL	British Library, London	EETS	Early English Text Society
BN	Bibliothèque Nationale, Paris	*EHR*	*English Historical Review*
Bodl	Bodleian Library, Oxford	JRULM	John Rylands University Library of Manchester
CCR	*Calendar of the Close Rolls*		
CCRO	Cheshire County Record Office	MS(S)	Manuscript(s)
Chester CRO	Chester City Record Office	PRO	Public Record Office
CFR	*Calendar of the Fine Rolls*	*RP*	*Rotuli Parliamentorum*
CLRO	Corporation of London Record Office	*TRHS*	*Transactions of the Royal Historical Society*
CP	G.E. Cokayne, *The Complete Peerage*, ed. V.H. Gibbs et al. (13 vols, 1910–59)	*VCH*	*Victoria County History*

INTRODUCTION

These papers, with one exception, were given at a conference on Recent Research in Fifteenth-Century History held at Chester College in September 1994. It was the fourteenth in a series of conferences dating back to that held at Cardiff in 1970, and the seventh with an aim of providing postgraduates, near to completing higher degrees, with the opportunity of presenting papers on some aspect of their research to a friendly and receptive audience. These have developed into a happy tradition of relaxed and often informal occasions, enabling the free exchange of ideas between historians whose individual subject specialisms are very varied but whose common interest is in the study of the late medieval period. The Chester conference was attended by fifty participants from all parts of the country, with about a third from the north-west, and others from as far afield as the Netherlands and Australia. Through the generous support of the Royal Historical Society, I was in the happy position to be able to offer six bursaries to postgraduates from the universities of Keele, York, Aberystwyth, Reading, London, and Western Australia.

In common with its six predecessors, there was no single theme for the Chester conference: a programme was put together after invitations had been sent out to a number of possible contributors. The response was good and the papers offered could be grouped together loosely under a variety of headings which I have tried to represent in the title of this volume. The local 'community', especially the gentry in their role as local administrators, set against central government based at Westminster, controlled by the Crown working with the nobility, provides the subject of the first grouping. The second focuses on the court and the capital as centres of culture and learning in the later Middle Ages.

I had always hoped that it might be possible to devote a part of the conference to aspects of local research and this hope was fulfilled by offers of papers from four people working on Cheshire and Chester history. Although

David Tilsley was not, in the event, able to present his paper on the Cheshire gentry at the conference, I am pleased to be able to include it in the volume together with contributions on related subjects by Deborah Marsh and Tim Thornton. I was delighted that David Mills from the Department of English Language and Literature at Liverpool University accepted my invitation to open the conference with his paper on the Chester mystery plays. As a former Director of the Centre for Medieval Studies at Liverpool University, David Mills has always been an advocate of an interdisciplinary approach to medieval studies: as an expert on the texts of the Chester mystery plays, he has much to share with historians on the use of the plays as historical evidence. Although the material for the fifteenth century is limited, he has been able to show how changes in the plays, especially the Corpus Christi play, can be linked to the development of the office of mayor of Chester in the first half of the sixteenth century when the civic authorities were taking over control of the plays and attempting to use them as a vehicle of civic power. He thus establishes one of the main themes of the conference: the frequent assertion of local independence in the fifteenth century and resistance to outside interference whether it be from Crown, nobility or the Church.

The debate on the distinctiveness of the county palatine of Chester has smouldered for a number of years,[1] and Tim Thornton now adds further fuel to the fire with his paper on the source of effective power in fifteenth- and early sixteenth-century Cheshire. He seeks to re-establish the very real importance of palatinate privilege as a force in the structure of local power-politics: palatinate office-holders played a crucial role in local government both as negotiators of taxation with the local community and as arbitrators in local disputes. Far from being redundant and powerless, palatinate institutions such as the exchequer and the court of equity based at Chester Castle, offered the chance of a more efficient administrative process and a much speedier execution of justice than

---

[1] G. Barraclough, 'The Earldom and County Palatine of Chester', *Transactions of the Historic Society of Lancashire and Cheshire*, 103 (1951), pp. 23–57; M.J. Bennett, 'A County Community: Social Cohesion among the Cheshire Gentry, 1400–25', *Northern History*, 8 (1973), pp. 24–44; *VCH, Cheshire*, 2, ed. B.E. Harris (Oxford, 1979), pp. 31–5; M.J. Bennett, *Community, Class and Careerism: Cheshire and Lancashire Society in the Age of Sir Gawain and the Green Knight* (Cambridge, 1983); D.J. Clayton, *The Administration of the County Palatine of Chester, 1442–85* (Manchester, 1990).

INTRODUCTION ix

the centrally-organised alternatives such as the Westminster Chancery. Local people chose to use local courts because they believed that it was to their advantage to do so.

The wealth of material for the study of the Cheshire gentry in local archives as well as in national repositories has long been recognised.[2] Tim Thornton stresses the importance of the part played by the local gentry in the administration of finance and justice in Cheshire. This view is reinforced by David Tilsley who revisits the subject of arbitration with particular reference to a section of the Cheshire gentry.[3] His quantitive analysis of the diverse records of arbitration leads him to conclude that the gentry in fifteenth-century Cheshire, in common with the gentry elsewhere in the country at this time, made serious efforts to resolve their disputes by mediation rather than resorting to the expensive and cumbersome processes of the law courts. In Cheshire, the cohesion of the gentry community, based on land-holding and inter-marriage, was reinforced by a common involvement in local administration and palatinate office.

A different approach to this subject is provided by Deborah Marsh whose research has been directed mainly towards one particular Cheshire gentleman, Humphrey Newton of Newton and Pownall. The fortunate survival of a cartulary and a commonplace book has made it possible to attempt to penetrate the mind of a man whom she regards as one of the earliest county antiquarians. The need to maintain control over his property, especially his land, prompted Humphrey Newton to undertake an extensive search of local archives for any

---

[2] D.J. Clayton, *The Administration of the County Palatine of Chester*, p. 2.

[3] 'Arbitration' has been the subject of numerous articles over the past ten years or so, including papers presented at earlier conferences on Recent Research in Fifteenth-Century History: see especially, I. Rowney, 'Arbitration in Gentry Disputes of the Later Middle Ages', *History*, 67 (1982), pp. 367–76; E. Powell, 'Arbitration and Law in England in the Late Middle Ages', *TRHS*, 5th ser., 33 (1983), pp. 49–67; C. Rawcliffe,'The Great Lord as Peacemaker: Arbitration by English Noblemen and their Councils in the Later Middle Ages', in *Law and Social Change in British History*, eds J.A. Guy and H.G. Beale (London, 1984); D.J. Clayton, 'Peace Bonds and the Maintenance of Law and Order in Late Medieval England: the Example of Cheshire', *BIHR*, 48 (1985), pp. 133–48; S.J. Payling, 'Law and Arbitration in Nottinghamshire 1399–1461' in *People, Politics and Community in the Later Middle Ages*, eds J. Rosenthal and C. Richmond (Gloucester, 1987), pp. 140–60.

material that might be relevant should he need to prove his title in a dispute. In tracing the methods employed by Newton in gathering his information, Deborah Marsh identifies many of the same difficulties faced by researchers today – problems of illegibility, language, dispersal of documents, and the reluctance of some holders of material to grant permission for its consultation, and even, on occasion, active concealment!

The vitality of local provision of justice and the failure of central mechanisms to usurp control is demonstrated in two papers on the operation of the law. Carrie Smith's work on the coroners' rolls for Wiltshire in the second half of the fourteenth century has clearly established that borough and county coroners presented a challenge to the power of sheriffs in the locality. She seeks to rehabilitate legal records as a source for the medieval historian and argues the case for coroners' rolls as having a particular value for the study of peasant life and society, in the absence of other types of evidence. In addition, the records of coroners' inquests inform us about community solidarity and the astuteness of local responses to interference by royal officials. Penny Tucker's paper on the relationships between London's courts and the Westminster courts in the reign of Edward IV reinforces this point in a different context. Despite changes in legal fashions and the growth of new equity jurisdiction provided by the courts of chancery and star chamber, the encroachment on city jurisdiction by the central law courts was only very limited. As in the shires, Londoners looked to their local courts for redress of their grievances.

London is also the focus of Caroline Barron's paper on the neglected subject of the education and training of girls. She argues that we need to revise our ideas on the aim and scope of education, away from a narrow definition which concentrates mainly on a grounding in Latin provided by grammar schools, to a broader view, taking into account instruction in reading and writing in the English Language and/or apprenticeship in a craft or trade. Although the evidence is sparse, it seems likely that there were, at least in the capital if not elsewhere, small informal schools outside church control and sometimes run by women, where girls could pick up the basic literacy skills necessary to equip them to cope with the demands of an increasingly 'text-based' society.

A number of papers examine different aspects of court culture focused on the capital, whether it be London or Paris. Essentially we are dealing with the preoccupations of the royal family and the aristocracy. In the context of a chivalric society, Hugh Collins examines the use of the Garter by the English monarch as an instrument of control, especially in periods of political crisis such as that immediately following the Lancastrian usurpation of 1399. Through a detailed examination of the recipients of the Garter between 1348 and 1461, he demonstrates its potential as a source of royal patronage in the important task of winning the support and cementing the loyalties of the King's most prominent subjects.

A very different aspect of court culture, that of literary patronage, is discussed in a challenging paper by David Rundle. Fifteenth-century England has traditionally been regarded as an intellectual backwater and the English aristocracy have sometimes been dismissed as too ignorant to embrace ideas associated with the wider European Renaissance movement. David Rundle argues persuasively that a number of Italians, including the eminent humanist Poggio Bracciolini, found useful and lucrative employment in the service of members of the English court. In examining the diverse and fragmentary evidence for Italian humanist activity in England, including manuscript marginalia, he comes to the conclusion that humanist texts on a wide range of subjects were in circulation, and that English readers were as capable of appreciating the ideas of Italian scholars as other educated Europeans.

Finally, we move from the English court to the French, for Rachel Gibbons' paper on the piety of the unfortunate queen of Charles VI, Isabeau of Bavaria. A consideration of the question of her religious practices and her patronage of the Church is likely to help in any attempt to rehabilitate a queen whose reputation has suffered as badly as that of her English counterpart, Margaret of Anjou. There are, however, real problems in attempting to interpret the evidence for her piety when it is acknowledged that her actions are as likely to have been determined by social convention as by personal preference.

The wide diversity of subject matter of these papers is indicative of the vitality of current research in late medieval history. They remind us that England cannot be studied in isolation from the rest of Europe, and that the tools at the historian's disposal should be widened to embrace literature, drama and political texts, as well as the more commonly used archival material.

Many people contributed to the success of the Chester conference and I owe sincere thanks to all those who assisted me in many different ways: to Ralph Griffiths, Tony Pollard, Michael Hicks and Rowena Archer, for their advice and help in the planning stages; to Graeme White, head of history at Chester College, and my medieval history colleagues at Liverpool University, for their support and encouragement throughout; to Robin Gallie, the Conference Manager at Chester College for his guidance and close attention to detail both before and during the conference; to all those who chaired sessions and contributed to the smooth operation of the three days; and to many people who were unable to attend but sent messages of good wishes in their absence. I am grateful to Roy Stephens, Director of the Marc Fitch Fund, and to Glyn Turton, Dean of Arts and Humanities at Chester College, for their efforts to ensure that the money needed in order to make the publication of this volume possible was forthcoming. The personal appearance at the conference of Roger Thorp of Alan Sutton Publishing went a long way to convince me that the papers delivered at Chester, as at previous fifteenth-century history conferences in the series, would ultimately be published. Finally my thanks go to all the contributors, who have responded promptly and efficiently at all stages of the publication. I hope that they will feel, like me, that their efforts have been rewarded.

Diana E.S. Dunn
Chester

1

THE CHESTER MYSTERY PLAYS: TRUTH AND TRADITION

David Mills

In the preface to his great two-volume work *The Mediaeval Stage*, published in 1903, E.K. Chambers defined the niche which he hoped his study would fill, resisting attempts to claim it for some autonomous world of English literature:

> More scholarly writers, such as Dr A.W. Ward, while dealing excellently with the mediaeval drama as literature, have shown themselves but little curious about the social and economic facts upon which the mediaeval drama rested. Yet from a study of such facts, I am sure, any literary history, which does not confine itself solely to the analysis of genius, must make a start.[1]

Chambers would, I am sure, have approved of the way in which early drama has of recent years become a meeting point between historians and those of us interested in 'how texts mean'. We have a shared interest in drama's origins and functions within social, economic and political contexts, in the circumstances of performance as well as in the internal construction of the few extant play-texts. We have come to recognise, too, the confusing compartmentalisations that can spring from projecting back upon the public activities of the Middle Ages not only late eighteenth-century generic terms such as 'mystery' and 'morality' play, but the very term 'drama' itself, a sixteenth-century loan-word more applicable to the text-directed activities of the Renaissance stage than to the diversity of public ceremonial and show that was a feature of medieval and Renaissance life.[2]

---

[1] E.K. Chambers, *The Mediaeval Stage* (Oxford, 1903), 1, p. v.

[2] The *Oxford English Dictionary* records 'mystery' in the sense of 'a name for the miracle play' from 1744; and 'morality' in the sense of 'the species of drama (popular in the 16th.c.) in which some moral or spiritual lesson was inculcated, and in which the chief characters were personifications of abstract qualities' from 1773; 'drama' in the sense of 'a play' is first recorded in 1515.

Within the then still largely literary sphere of medieval drama specialists, the formation of the Records of Early English Drama (REED) project in 1974 was a significant development.[3] The aims of that international project, stated at the start of each volume, are ambitious: 'To find, transcribe, and publish external evidence of dramatic, ceremonial, and minstrel activity in Great Britain before 1642.' To date fourteen volumes have been published and there is now a queue of completed projects awaiting publication.[4] The north-west has fared well in the early stages of this programme, with Westmorland, Cumberland, Lancashire and Chester among the published material.

The value of such external evidence for an understanding of Chester's plays had been demonstrated some twenty years before REED's foundation by F.M. Salter's lectures on 'Medieval Drama in Chester', which provided a powerful and at that time startling corrective to the image of mystery plays as crude popular performances on machines resembling farm-carts and which decisively exposed the myth that Chester's cycle was the oldest in Britain.[5] Although this point had been made before, notably by J.H. Markland, whose edition of two of Chester's mystery plays for the Roxburghe Club in 1818 represents the earliest scholarly edition of any of the mystery cycles,[6] Salter deserves full credit for his thorough documentation and clear exposition. By 1974, when REED began, a number of scholars had already begun working independently on the *corpora* of drama records for towns whose mystery cycles were wholly or partially extant. REED provided the opportunity to publish their findings, though the researchers had to widen the area of selection in accordance with REED's

---

[3] On the foundation of the Records of Early English Drama project, see Stanley J. Kahrl, 'The Staging of Medieval English Plays' in *The Theatre of Medieval Europe: New Research in Early Drama*, ed. Eckehard Simon (Cambridge, 1991), pp. 138–40.

[4] The volumes, in order of publication by the University of Toronto Press, are: *York* (2 vols, 1979); *Chester* (1979); *Coventry* (1981); *Newcastle Upon Tyne* (1982); *Norwich 1540–1642* (1984); *Cumberland, Westmorland, Gloucestershire* (1986); *Devon* (1986); *Cambridge* (2 vols, 1989); *Herefordshire, Worcestershire* (1990); *Lancashire* (1991); *Shropshire* (2 vols, 1994). Note should also be taken of REED's 'Studies in Early English Drama' series, and in particular of *Dramatic Texts and Records of Britain: A Chronological Topography to 1558*, ed. Ian Lancashire, Studies in Early English Drama, 1 (Toronto, 1984).

[5] F.M. Salter, *Mediaeval Drama in Chester* (Toronto, 1955).

[6] J.H. Markland, *Chester Mysteries: De Deluvio Noe. De Occisione Innocentium* (London, 1818).

remit. A young American academic, Larry Clopper, was going through the Chester material. His volume of Chester drama-records was published in 1979, among the first of the REED volumes.[7]

Nevertheless, Clopper's opening comments to his edition might suggest that there is little to be said about Chester's 'mystery cycle' during the fifteenth century:

> The city of Chester has retained large quantities of records, most of which do not antedate the mid-sixteenth century. These include the common assembly's ordinances, official papers of the mayor, the city treasurers' reports, records of the various courts, and miscellaneous papers such as petitions and letters to and from the mayor and council.
>
> Chester is also fortunate in having many medieval guilds still active, and some of these have documents relevant to this collection which reach back to the early fifteenth century; however, the majority of the records do not antedate the last quarter of the sixteenth century.[8]

In the 486 pages of records, pre-1500 records occupy a mere 20 pages. Since 1992 my co-editor, Elizabeth Baldwin, and I have been working through the records of drama in the county of Cheshire for REED.[9] We have found a significant amount of relevant material which, for a variety of reasons, did not find its way into REED's *Chester* volume and which does excitingly change our perspective on Chester's drama and ceremonial. (We have also found significant material to supplement that found in REED's *Lancashire* volume, including its appendix relating to the Isle of Man.) But comparatively little of this new material relates to the fifteenth century or earlier, and, although this paper incorporates most of our findings, its evidence is drawn largely from the records previously published.

---

[7] *Records of Early English Drama: Chester*, ed. L.M. Clopper (Toronto, 1979); hereafter, Clopper.

[8] Clopper, p. xi.

[9] I gratefully acknowledge a research grant from the Leverhulme Trust which enabled the appointment of Dr Baldwin as my Research Associate from 1992 to 1994 and funded work on the records. I also acknowledge the award to me of study-leave for 1995/6 by the British Academy to allow us to complete the project.

I want to look at the sparse evidence for Chester's fifteenth-century Corpus Christi play against the background of the city's economic and political development and in relation to the subsequent developments in celebration and ceremonial in the first decade or so of the sixteenth century. What I have to say is necessarily tentative, not to say tendentious. I wish to suggest that the changes in the plays and the development of a corpus of civic ceremonial in Chester may be related to the growing importance and public prominence of the office of mayor in the city and to a desire to promote commerce.

The earliest extant reference to Chester's Corpus Christi play is in a document found in the loose papers of the Coopers' Company, all of which have been deposited and catalogued in the City Record Office since Clopper transcribed them.[10] Internally dated as 1422, the document is the record of an inquiry into a dispute among the city's companies. I shall quote from it in translation from the Latin:

> Memorandum concerning the discord and legal controversy which arose between the Ironmongers of the City of Chester as one party, and the Carpenters of the same city as the other party:
> Whether one party or the other should have all the Fletchers, Bowers, Stringers, Coopers, and Turners of the same city as helpers in putting on the Play of Corpus Christi of the same city.

The decision was:

> That the foresaid [Flet]chers, Bowers, Stringers, Coopers, and Turners should not either undertake to perform or be participants with one party or another – the foresaid Ironmongers or Carpenters – in their pageants for the foresaid Corpus Christi Play. But they [the Inquirers] said that they [the

---

[10] The records of the Coopers' Company are all catalogued under G7 in the Chester City Record Office. The document is transcribed in Clopper, pp. 6–7 and translated on pp. 493–4. The document also appears in translation in R.M. Lumiansky and David Mills, *The Chester Mystery Cycle: Essays and Documents. With an Essay, 'Music in the Cycle', by Richard Rastall* (Chapel Hill, N.C. and London, 1983), pp. 204–5. I use the latter translation.

Fletchers *et al.*] should themselves continue to be responsible for their assigned pageant in this Play – namely, the *Flagellation of the Body of Christ*, with its accompanying material according to the 'Original', up to the *Crucifixion of Jesus Christ*, just as it occurs in the said 'Original' – and that the foresaid Ironmongers should be responsible for the pageant of the *Crucifixion* in the foresaid [Corpus Christi Play], and the foresaid Carpenters for their pageant according to the foresaid 'Original'.

The document shows that by 1422 Chester, like a number of other towns, had incorporated into its Corpus Christi procession a play-sequence performed by city companies. It is perhaps useful to remind ourselves that, although the feast of Corpus Christi was promulgated in 1264, it was established only in 1311, and that it is celebrated on the Thursday after Trinity Sunday, whose date can vary between 23 May and 24 June, depending on the date of Easter.[11] The earliest contemporary documentary evidence we have for any such play in an English town is from York in 1376.[12] Although we have no evidence for the content of Chester's play, it may be significant that in our sixteenth-century play-lists and our late sixteenth-/early seventeenth-century play-texts the Fletchers, Bowers, Coopers and Stringers are still responsible for the *Trial and Flagellation* (play 16) and the Ironmongers for the *Crucifixion* (play 16A); in the extant text the Carpenters are responsible for the *Annunciation and Nativity* (play 6).[13]

The Corpus Christi procession into which the play was inserted is usually held to have been established in Chester by 1398/9, for in that year a group of masters and men from the weaving and related trades gathered in front of St Peter's church, armed with a variety of weapons, and 'insulted' colleagues and journeymen, with the result that the whole city was drawn into a general

---

[11] On the Corpus Christi feast and its possible connection with cycle-plays, see V.A. Kolve, *The Play Called Corpus Christi* (London, 1966). Miri Rubin, *Corpus Christi: The Eucharist in Late Medieval Culture* (Cambridge, 1991) traces the development of the feast.

[12] *Records of Early English Drama: York*, ed. Alexandra Johnston and Margaret Rogerson (Toronto, 1979), 1, p. 3.

[13] The standard scholarly edition of the cycle is *The Chester Mystery Cycle*, ed. R.M. Lumiansky and David Mills, EETS, supp. ser., 3 and 9 (Oxford, 1974 and 1986), 1, *Text*; 2, *Commentary*.

affray.[14] The record makes no reference to a Corpus Christi procession as such, although it does seem likely that the intention was to ambush such a procession. There is, equally, no reference to a play or to pageant-waggons. Because guild records are, in the main, so late, we have no clear idea about when individual companies were formed and hence no real sense of the composition and scale of Chester's fourteenth-century Corpus Christi procession. Such evidence as we have, however, suggests that it is unlikely that Chester's economic and administrative organisation would have reached a stage at which it was able to mount a full-scale *Creation* to *Doomsday* play-cycle much before the early fifteenth century.[15] It may therefore be the case that the record of 1422 relates to a very early stage in the cycle's development.

Later records reveal no dispute that seems wholly comparable to that of 1422. Usually, a guild in the sixteenth century petitions that it does not have the resources to stage its play, typically because of encroachment by other companies or by 'foreigners', and the political purpose of such a petition is therefore to enlist greater protection. Companies do not seem to petition to have the responsibilities of other companies changed. Typical is the charter of the Saddlers' Company in 1472 which complains: 'how, because of unauthorised trespasses, settings up, and occupations of the same art within our aforesaid city by foreign persons, and out of the unruliness of people of obstinate disposition in not helping them to support the burdens and costs of the play and pageant assigned to the occupiers of the same art and city . . . they are not able to continue the same burdens'.[16]

There is therefore, perhaps, a sense in 1422 that the responsibilities of the companies are still negotiable in a way that they will not be later. But if that was the expectation of the disputing companies, they were to be disappointed by the outcome of the appeal, which upheld the allocation of plays and responsibilities set out in the 'Original' (*secundum originale*), a term that appears anglicised in sixteenth-century documents as the 'Original' or 'Reginal'. The exact reference

---

[14] Clopper, pp. 5–6, translated on pp. 491–3.

[15] I am grateful to Dr Alan Thacker, Deputy Editor of the *Victoria County History of England*, for pointing out this possibility.

[16] Clopper, pp. 13–14, translation on p. 498.

of the term has been much debated, but one of our recent discoveries puts it, I think, beyond doubt.

In 1572 the Puritan divine Christopher Goodman was at the forefront of a campaign to suppress Chester's play-cycle. To demonstrate the dangerous character of the plays to the Archbishop of York, he abstracted what he deemed 'superstitious material' from the play-text, which he describes in this way:

> And to that effect We have according to your G. request sent herewithall the notes of such absurdities as are truly collected out of their old originall, by the which your wisdoms may easily judge of the rest. For albeit divers have gone about the correction of the same at sundry times & mended divers things, yet hath it not been done by such as are by authority allowed, nor the same their corrections viewed & approved according to order, nor yet so played for the most part as they have been corrected.[17]

Goodman's remark, and his accompanying notes, indicate that in 1572 the 'old originall' was the master text that controlled the play and was therefore the key to power over it and to its censorship. It is notable that the 'originall' remained in Chester long after the last performance of the cycle, in 1575, since it was available to copyists until at least 1607, the date of the last extant manuscript; indeed, a comment by the Chester antiquarian David Rogers in his *Breviary* of 1620, which refers to 'the author in the prolouge before his booke of the whitson playes', seems to indicate that it was still in Chester at that late date and that the text was prefaced by a copy of the late (post-Reformation) Banns.[18] Goodman's comment on corrections suggests that the Original bore the marks of revision and was therefore a record of change over a period of time.[19]

I am not suggesting that Goodman's 'originall' was the same manuscript referred to in 1422, but it is plausible that the character and function of an

---

[17] From Christopher Goodman's Letterbook, Clwyd County Record Office (Ruthin), Plas Power MSS DD/PP/839, p. 121. I am grateful to the Clwyd County Archivist for permission to quote from the manuscript.

[18] Clopper, p. 326.

[19] For evidence of the effects of this process of revision in the extant manuscripts, see Lumiansky and Mills, 'The Texts of the Chester Cycle' in *The Chester Mystery Cycle*, pp. 3–86.

Original as an instrument of central control had remained unchanged over the intervening 150 years. In this early centralised control Chester differs from York, where the guilds seem to have had considerable freedom in determining the content of their assigned plays. York's extant records and register attest belated attempts by the city to impose greater central control and order upon an occasion that threatened to become increasingly expansive and diversified.[20] Beyond occasional references to guild responsibilities and the specific titles in the 1422 document, we have no evidence of the content and scale of the Corpus Christi play. Our most comprehensive list of companies in the city during the fifteenth century seems to be that of the nineteen companies that reached agreements with the mayor about apprentice fees in 1475/6, itself an indication perhaps of growing central control;[21] our extant text contains twenty-five plays, or twenty-four in the latest (1607) manuscript which marks no division between the plays of the *Trial and Flagellation of Christ* and the *Passion*. One company that certainly existed from at least 1399 was the Weavers, and in 1423 the masters of that company brought a claim of debt of sixpence against John Silcock towards their *interludum*.[22] This may well refer to their pageant, which in our extant texts is *Doomsday*, though 'interlude' is not the usual term for a component play in the cycle.

Although we know that the play changed over the years and that it is therefore unsafe to draw closely upon the extant texts as evidence for our Corpus Christi play, the 1422 document suggests that there was some continuity, at least of subject, from the earlier to the later period. A tantalising

---

[20] A useful summary of the problems of interpreting the development of York's cycle is given by Richard Beadle in his essay, 'The York Cycle' in *The Cambridge Companion to Medieval English Theatre*, ed. Richard Beadle (Cambridge, 1994), especially pp. 85–98.

[21] Chester CRO, MB6a, f.30. The companies listed are, in order of listing, the Mercers, Drapers, Shermen, Butchers, Hewsters, Drawers of Dee, Goldsmiths, Coopers, Bowers and Fletchers, Skinners, Bakers, Ironmongers, Fishmongers, Barkers, Barbers, Glovers, Smiths, Cooks, Weavers and Walkers. The document is transcribed in Rupert H. Morris, *Chester in the Plantagenet and Tudor Reigns* (Chester, n.d.), p. 443. The dates of incorporation of the various companies are contained in Brian E. Harris, Annette Kennett and Elizabeth J. Shepherd, *Brief Histories of the Chester City Companies or Guilds* (Chester, 1985), held in the City Record Office. See also Margaret J. Groombridge, 'The City Gilds of Chester', *Journal of Chester Archaeological Society*, 39 (1952), pp. 93–108, which includes a survey of the records of the city guilds made in 1950–1.

[22] Chester CRO, SR/145 (June 1422–3).

hint of this continuity is represented by claims for payment brought in 1448 by Thomas Butler, a baker, and in 1488 by John Jankynson, a weaver, against the Cooks' Company for money owing to them for playing a devil in the Cooks' play.[23] In our extant texts that play is play 17, the *Harrowing of Hell*, and it includes in some of our manuscripts a comic coda in which a dishonest Chester alewife is the first to enter Hell after the redeemed have been extracted. The alewife and her attendant devil, collectively known as 'the cups and cans' after the vessels which hung about her, were also part of the Cooks' 'show' in the sixteenth-century Midsummer Show, and the devils in the cycle are specified in the Banns as spectacular figures.[24] Again, it would be dangerous to project the later evidence back, but these fifteenth-century records demonstrate that some companies were already buying in players from other companies to act specific roles.

A further slight piece of evidence is afforded by rentals such as:

1466–7 The Mercers of the city for the house of their carriage	(blank)
1467–8 From the stewards of the Shearmen for accommodation for their carriage	4*d*
1467–8 From the Mercers of the city for a certain accommodation for the carriage	8*d*
1480–3 From Thomas Rokley and John Smyth, stewards of the saddlercraft within the city of Chester for a certain accommodation of their pageant	4*d*
1480–3 The Drapers of the city for the rent of another plot [of land] for their carriage [for] three years	2*s*[25]

---

[23] Chester CRO, SR/262 (February 1448) mb. 1v. and SR/356 (July 1488) mb. 1r. respectively. Butler claimed 2*s* 6*d* and Jankynson 8*d*, which may simply indicate the different amounts still outstanding or be a reflection of the relative importance of the roles, since the play provides for several parts for devils. I am indebted to Dr Jane Laughton for these references and to the Chester City Archivist for permission to quote from these and other documents not cited by Clopper.

[24] The alewife appears in lines 277–336 of the play; but this section is not in the 1607 manuscript of the cycle. The devil and the alewife in the Midsummer Show were objects of attack from the city's pulpits in the later sixteenth century; see 'The Diuell Ridinge in fethers before the butchars. A man in womans apparell with a diuel waytinge on his horse called cappes & canes', Clopper, p. 253. The late (post-Reformation) Banns refer specifically to the devil in their account of the *Temptation*: 'the devell in his feathers, all rugged and rente' (line 122). Banns quotation from the edition in Lumiansky and Mills, *Essays*, p. 290.

[25] Translations from Clopper, pp. 496–7 and p. 502.

These rentals augment our list of companies engaged in the production and can be further supplemented by other, less specific, rentals of land by other companies which are merely noted as being for 'accommodation'. They indicate that the specially constructed wheeled stages or carriages that are a feature of the sixteenth-century productions were also employed in the fifteenth-century play, though how they were employed is not clear. Although their use would seem logically to predicate processional production at a number of points in the city, Clopper, for reasons considered below, has argued that the play was performed in one place only.[26] We know that that procedure was adopted in Lincoln, where the carriages were part of the procession and the plays were performed at the west door of the cathedral where the procession ended; but Lincoln may have been a special case, conditioned by the problems of anchoring and moving waggons on a hilly terrain. York's cycle was performed at a number of sites, but the performance proved too disruptive for the procession and the procession was moved to the following day. There were undoubtedly practical problems in combining the very different performative genres of procession and play.

Perhaps the most significant feature of the fifteenth-century play, however, was the route taken by the Corpus Christi procession (see Map 1). This is first most clearly set out in an adjudication by the mayor, John Sotheworth, in 1474 between the Bowers and Fletchers and the Coopers companies concerning the order for the procession: 'from saint maire kirke opon ye hill of ye Cety aforesaid vnto the Colage of Seint Iohanne'.[27] If we supplement this by accepting that the 1398/9 record relates also to the procession, then the probable route ran from St Mary's, up Bridge Street, past St Peter's and into the Eastgate, and thence to St John's.

I have suggested elsewhere that a city such as Chester acquires a symbolic

---

[26] Clopper, p. liii.
[27] Clopper, p. 16.

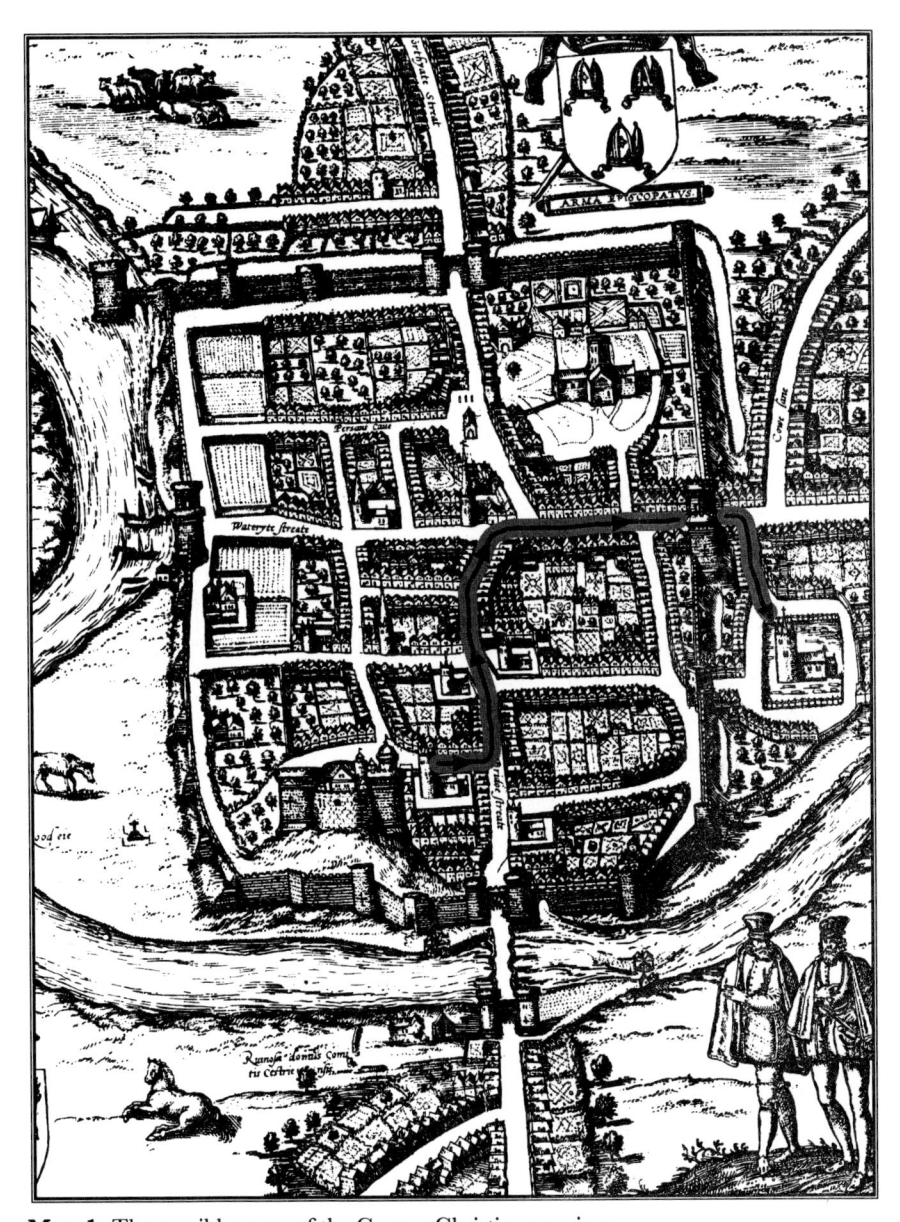

Map 1. The possible route of the Corpus Christi procession.

geography from the major buildings which reflect past and present wealth and power.[28] The Corpus Christi procession moved between two such sites. On the sandstone ridge above the Dee stood the castle of the earls of Chester, the centre of county administration and justice. St Mary's church, close by, was associated with the earls both by geography and by customary use. The Chester monk Lucian, writing in the 1190s, says that the earl, *caput civium*, 'the head of the citizens', with his court, customarily worshipped at St Mary's.[29] It remained a powerful church; in 1540 its rector received a stipend of £52 a year, far and away the highest in the city. The church of St John the Baptist was the largest of the Chester churches, excluding the abbey. It had been for a short time between 1075 and 1095 the see of the diocese of Lichfield, and as Husain states: 'When the see was transferred to Coventry in 1095, St John's reverted to its former collegiate status, but long afterwards was considered one of three cathedrals of the diocese, and retained nearby a palace of the bishop and the residence of the archdeacon of Chester.'[30] The bishop remained a powerful landowner in the county. St John's church itself was of impressive dimensions, and housed a famous relic of the True Cross which seems to have been a more famous relic than the relics of St Werburgh. Lucian says that on feast days the clergy processed from St John's to St Mary's; the Corpus Christi procession therefore reversed an established processional route. The feast in honour of the daily miracle of transubstantiation recognised the supreme power of the clergy, but the route also made a political statement about the centres of power within the city.

There was a further link between the two sites which should be noted, though its date is uncertain. The Dutton family of Chester had the right to license minstrels within the county. This right was certainly in existence in the fifteenth

---

[28] D. Mills, 'The Chester Plays and the Limits of Realism' in *The Middle Ages in the North West*, eds T. Scott and P. Starkey, (Oxford, 1995).

[29] *Liber Luciani: De Laude Cestrie*, ed. M.V. Taylor, Lancashire and Cheshire Record Society, 64 (1912), pp. 1–78. Unfortunately, the editor has distorted the overall shape and structure of the work by abridging the meditational passages.

[30] B.M.C. Husain, *Cheshire Under the Norman Earls, 1066–1237. A History of Cheshire*, 4 (Chester, 1973), p. 119.

century since a royal commission of 23 June 1476/7 authorised the convening of such a court of minstrels, *vna Curia histrionum*.[31] The tradition of the privilege is regularly rehearsed by later antiquarians: that Randle Blundevill, earl of Chester (1181–1232), was besieged at Rhuddlan Castle and sent to his constable at Chester for help. It being fair-time, the steward gathered what was available, a motley rabble of minstrels and whores, the sight of which put the Welsh to flight. The right to license minstrels was given to the constable as reward, and he in turn transferred it to his steward, a Dutton. The privilege had remained within the Dutton family thereafter. The licensing took place on the feast of St John the Baptist. We have only seventeenth-century descriptions of the arrangements for the court, which indicate a proclamation, a gathering at St John's church for a short recital, and a licensing at an inn in the city, during all of which the banner of the Duttons was displayed.[32] The occasion may well have become by then a sort of tourist event, but it had legal force; those so licensed were, for example, exempt from the Elizabethan vagabondage act of 1571. It also served to commemorate the authority of the earl and his officers and again pointed a link between the traditional *loci* of power within the city.

The latest extant reference to the Corpus Christi play is in the Saddlers' charter of 1471/2, to which I have referred. Our records contain no reference to plays on a particular date for the next fifty years. Then, in an agreement of 1521 between the Founders and Pewterers and the Smiths, the earlier formula of 'the play and light of Corpus Christi' has substituted for it 'whitson playe & Corpus christi light', the first indication that the civic play had moved to Whitsuntide.[33] Thereafter, throughout the sixteenth century Chester's civic cycle is known as 'the Whitsun play' or 'the Whitsun plays'. A list of companies and their pageants transcribed by Clopper under the year 1539/40 states that

---

[31] Clopper, p. 17, translated on pp. 500–1.

[32] The tradition is frequently repeated. Clopper, pp. 486–9, reprints the account from Sir Peter Leycester's *Historical Antiquities*. On the implications of the tradition for the local control of vagrants and entertainers, see G.R. Rastall, 'The Minstrel Court in Medieval England', *A Medieval Miscellany in Honour of Professor John le Patourel, Proceedings of the Leeds Literary and Philosophical Society, Literary and Historical Section*, 18:1 (1982), pp. 96–105.

[33] Clopper, pp. 24–5.

the plays were performed on the Monday, Tuesday and Wednesday of Whitsun week, but we may infer that this three-day production had been established earlier, since on 14 August 1531/2 three companies – the Dyers, the Vintners and the Goldsmiths and Masons – agreed to share the expenses and use of the same carriage.[34] Such a tripartite arrangement would have been impossible unless the three companies performed on different days. R.M. Lumiansky and I at one time felt that the singular form, 'Whitsun play', which appears in the records up to 1531/2, might have indicated a one-day production and that the subsequent plural 'plays' might have been suggested by the three-day division; but I am now less inclined to put that emphasis upon the morphology.

We have no idea of exactly when the move to Whitsun occurred, still less of why. But the immediate effect of the separation was to sharpen a distinction between the two genres of civic play and religious procession. We have one copy of a set of Banns for the Whitsun play which, though it cannot be dated exactly, is clearly pre-Reformation.[35] Its textual history is somewhat complex and we do not know how often it was revised or employed. But we do know from later records that it became the custom, whenever the plays were to be performed, for a herald in armour to ride out on St George's Day, accompanied by stewards of the city's companies and characters from the plays in costume, to read or ride the Banns (the verse announcement describing the plays) at the Cross.[36] Such Banns were presumably not needed when the play was an integral part of the annual Corpus Christi procession, but during the sixteenth century the Whitsun plays were not performed annually, as we shall see. The early Banns may suggest irregular performance even before the Reformation.

These early Banns announce both the Whitsun plays and the Corpus Christi procession and seem designed in part to reassure the populace that both events will take place in the same year. Probably they were first composed when the plays were separated from the procession. They indicate that although most

---

[34] Clopper, pp. 31–3 and pp. 26–7 respectively.

[35] In Lumiansky and Mills, *Essays*, pp. 278–84; the manuscript is described on pp. 273–4.

[36] The authority for this is David Rogers' *Breviary of Chester History*, first compiled in 1609 from the antiquarian notes amassed by his father, Archdeacon Robert Rogers of Chester, who died in 1595. See Clopper, pp. 238–9.

features of the procession are unchanged, there has been one significant modification:

> Also, maister maire of this citie
> with all his bretheryn accordingly,
> a solempne procession ordent hath he
> to be done to the best
> appon the day of Corpus Christi.
> The blessed Sacrament caried shalbe
> and a play sett forth by the clergye
> in honor of the fest.
>
> Many torches there may you see,
> marchaunty and craftys of this citie
> by order passing in theire degree –
> a goodly sight that day.
> They come from Saynt Maries-on-the-Hill
> the churche of Saynt Johns untill,
> and there the Sacrament leve they will,
> the south as I you say.
>
> (lines 156–71)

Though a play would still form part of the celebration, it would now be 'sett forth by the clergye', a church-sponsored occasion, though, I think, not necessarily clerically performed. This play must have been on a much smaller scale than the guild plays it replaced. It may well have been performed in the churchyard at St John's at the conclusion of the procession, since other plays were occasionally performed there.[37] It is this detail that might suggest that the guild play it replaces was also performed in one place only.

This brief description of the procession and the longer account of the

---

[37] The *Assumption of Our Lady* was played at the High Cross in front of St Peter's church in 1489 and 1499, and both it and the Shepherds' play were performed in St John's churchyard in 1515. See Clopper pp. 20–1, 23–4.

Whitsun plays that constitutes the bulk of the text share two interesting characteristics. First, the emphasis in both descriptions is upon spectacle. The account of the plays stresses the colour and richness of the production and the particular carriage and the way in which they reflect the wealth and importance of the company; for example:

> You wurshipffull men of the Draperye,
> loke that paradyce be all redye;
> prepare also the Mappa Mundi,
> Adam and eke Eve.
> The Waterleders and Drawers of Dee,
> loke that Noyes shipp be sett on hie
> that you lett not the storye –
> and then shall you well cheve.
>
> (lines 25–32)

The procession description, too, presents the 'solempne procession' as primarily a marvellous spectacle – 'there may you see' (164), 'a goodly sight that day'(167). And second, attention is focused upon the authority of the mayor and his brethren. It is by their authority that the Corpus Christi procession is permitted to take place (156–60), and it is they who have ordained the Whitsun plays:

> Our wurshipffull mair of this citie,
> with all this royall cominaltie,
> solem pagens ordent hath he
> at the fest of Whitsonday-tyde.
>
> (lines 9–12)

As if, perhaps, to underline this, the herald addresses most of his remarks in a jocular tone to the members of the companies, who perhaps are thereby called up before him to receive their commission. Alongside the later Midsummer Show, the play was the companies' major communal contribution and the two celebrations stand out as such among the companies' mostly internally directed orders.

But these Banns also endow the plays with a history. They claim that:

> Sur John Arneway was maire of this citie
> when these playes were begon, truly.
>
> (lines 176–7)

And this Arneway connection remains a recurring feature in announcements and descriptions of the plays throughout the sixteenth century.

Although the historical origins of Chester's mayoral office are obscure, a chronological list of mayors had been established by the sixteenth century and forms a preface to the city's first Assembly Book, begun in the second mayoralty of Henry Gee in 1539/40.[38] This list, which was copied by numerous annalists and antiquarians with slight variations, showed that Chester's first mayor had been Sir John Arneway in 1326. This was factually inaccurate; the city's first mayor had been Sir Walter Lynett in consecutive terms from 1257 to 1260, and Arneway had been mayor in consecutive terms from 1268 to 1276. But the error was revealed only in 1594 by the Chester antiquarian William Aldersey and even then gained only gradual acceptance. Historical truth, however, matters very little here. What is significant is that the beginnings of the plays become officially associated with the beginning of the mayoral office and that their production manifests the authority of the mayor over the companies. The late (post-Reformation) Banns even seem to suggest that the economic organisation of the city derived from the play-text itself:

> This worthie knighte Arnewaye, then mayor of this citte,
> this order tooke, as declare to yow I shall,
> that by xxiiii^{tie} occupationes – artes, craftes, or misterye –
> these pagiantes shoulde be played after brefe rehearesall.
>
> (lines 56–9)

The plays are seen to be ordained and constructed by the individual mayor, not by custom or by the collective will of the citizens. This may, perhaps, explain why the early Banns remind the companies of their obligations in the form of

---

[38] Chester CRO, AB/1.

imperatives – 'loke that paradyce be all redye' (26), 'loke that Noyes shipp be sett on hie' (30), etc.

The power of the mayor over the plays is clearly stated in a note to the play-list of 1539/40: 'Prouided Alwais that it is at the libertie and pleasure of the mair, with the counsell of his bretheryn, to Alter or Assigne any of the occupacons Aboue writen to any play or pagent as they shall think necessary or conuenyent.'[39] Thus, when Christopher Goodman complained of the 1572 production to the earl of Huntingdon, Lord President of the Council of the North, he laid the responsibility firmly on the shoulders of the mayor, John Hanky: 'Our Mayor of this city joyning himself with such persons as be thought of corrupt affection in religion, doth with great practise endeavour to cause them to be played here this next Whitsontide.'[40] Goodman placed similar personal responsibility upon Sir John Savage, in whose mayoralty the last production in 1575 took place, and significantly when Savage was called before the Privy Council, it was to face the charge that he had personally authorised the production in disregard of the wishes of his fellow councillors and citizens. In fact, the city council had voted in favour of the production and could certify to that; but it is the only such recorded vote and may indicate that Savage, recognising possible future charges, had called for the vote as a prudent act of self-defence.[41]

I am therefore suggesting that the shift at the turn of the fifteenth century from Corpus Christi to Whitsuntide correlates with the final appropriation of the plays as a celebration of mayoral office and that this represents the culmination of a process which we can see under way in the 1422 agreement. I have not space here to consider the extent to which the plays then came to serve the individual interests of the mayors, in particular through their associations

---

[39] Clopper, p. 33.

[40] Clwyd County Record Office (Ruthin), Plas Power MSS DD/PP/839, p. 119.

[41] The vote of 25 May 1575 is recorded in the Assembly Files as 33 for and 12 against; see Clopper, pp. 103n–4n. It is, however, not clear whether the vote was merely to authorise the performance of the plays or to authorise the change of date of the performance from the customary Whitsun week to Midsummer. The Whitsun performance had been cancelled because of a threat of plague, which subsequently receded. For the summoning of Savage before the Privy Council, his letter to Chester and the certificate provided by the city, see Clopper, pp. 109–10 and 112–17.

with the central doctrines of Catholicism and through the changing ascriptions of authorship and purpose, so that the significance of their performance changed. Rather, I want to conclude by noting that the plays constitute one component in an expanding corpus of civic ceremonial and pageantry which similarly combines the city's commercial interests with the celebration of the city and its mayor.

Chester's corpus of civic ceremonial developed from the end of the fifteenth century to include the city's Midsummer Show, the ceremonial privileges allowed under the great charter of 1506, the Calves' Head feast of 1511 and the reform of the Shrovetide Homages in 1539/40. Space permits me only briefly to summarise these last three ceremonies. The great charter of 6 April 1506 which created the city a county palatine with increased powers of self-government, granted to the mayor the right to have his sword carried before him point upwards except in the monarch's presence and to have the mace borne in front of him.[42] During the sixteenth century mayoral authority was displayed each week when the mayor, attended by aldermen, sheriffs and council in ceremonial dress, processed from the Pentice to worship at St Werburgh's or St Peter's each Sunday. In 1511, according to the annalists, the Calves' Head feast was begun by Sheriffs Hugh Clarke and Charles Eaton.[43] Held on the Roodee on Easter Monday before the mayor, it consisted of an archery contest between two teams of gentlemen, each led by a sheriff. At its conclusion the two teams returned to the Common Hall to breakfast on calves' heads and bacon, at the primary expense of the losing side. While providing entertainment and promoting archery, the occasion also served to point to the office of sheriff within the city. Finally, in 1539/40 Mayor Henry Gee reformed the so-called Shrovetide Homages into archery, athletics and horse-racing competitions on the Roodee before the mayor and his officers.[44]

---

[42] Chester CRO, CH/32.

[43] Clopper, p. 23, prints the entry from Mayor's List 9: BL, Add. MS 11335. See also Chester CRO, CR469/542, p. 54, which juxtaposes the inauguration of the Feast and the dispute between the city and the abbot of St Werburgh (presumably the continuing dispute concerning the transfer of privileges under the great charter).

[44] See Clopper, pp. 39–42.

The Midsummer Show, however, deserves more attention than the other civic ceremonies. The annalists who compiled the city's Mayors' Lists placed particular emphasis upon the mayoralty of Richard Goodman in 1498/9:

> 1498 In this year it appeareth the watche vpon mydsomer dawn beganne. also the northsyde of the pentice buylded. prince Arthour came to chester about the fourth of August. the assumption of our lade played before the prince at the abbaye gate. the xxvth of august the prince made mr goodman esquier. the xix day of September he departed from chester.[45]

The royal visit was of itself a special occasion, but it coincided with two important events. First, the north side of the Pentice was completed. The Pentice was the major civic building in the city, an annex on the south side of St Peter's church facing down Bridge Street. The completion of the north side, extending into Northgate Street, both completed the building and gave it a symbolic domination of all four Roman streets from the centre or Cross. The city now had its own *locus* of power which took its place among the other symbolic structures. Since the building was used for the entertainment of distinguished visitors, it is probable that the prince banqueted there.

Second, the Midsummer Watch was traditionally held to have been instituted in that year, although we have no contemporary records of the Watch before 1564, when some of its features were being reconstructed.[46] The Show was held on Midsummer Eve, that is, on the evening before St John the Baptist's Day, and therefore found some definition in comparison with the Minstrels' Court held on the following day, and also in comparison with the Corpus Christi procession – and perhaps the accompanying play – which would probably have continued until the suppression of the feast in 1548 and could even fall on the same day as the Show in certain years. The Show was an amalgam of genres.[47]

---

[45] 'A collection of the maiors who haue gouerned this Cittie of Chester and the tyme when the gouerned the same by Willm Aldersey a Citizin theirof 1594', Chester CRO, Aldersey Family Papers, CR 469/542, f.26v.

[46] Clopper, pp. 71–2.

[47] This account substantially summarises my comments in 'Chester Ceremonial: Re-creation and Recreation in the English "Medieval" Town', *Urban History Yearbook*, 18 (1991), pp. 1-19.

At its centre was the Watch of marching men in armour who were provided by the freemen of the city in fulfilment of their customary duty to defend the city against invasion. The second element was the parade of the companies in their livery with their banners. The third was the carnival element, a number of giant figures paid for by the officers of the city and provided and cared for by the Painters' Company. These included a giant, the mayor's mount, a ship, the elephant and castle, a number of beasts, and a dragon accompanied by costumed 'naked boys'. In addition, each company was required to provide its own 'show', which might consist of one or more characters from its Whitsun play, such as the Cooks' alewife and her devil, or a small boy on horseback with attendants, splendidly dressed. Unlike the Corpus Christi procession, the Show toured the city, starting at the Northgate Bar, where money was distributed to the prisoners in the city gaol, and including the castle, where the prisoners in the earl's gaol likewise received largesse.

Chester could readily have found models for such displays, obviously in London, but also in cities such as Coventry with which it had frequent connection. It is, effectively, Chester's Mayor's Show. Together with the completion of the Pentice, it represents an outburst of civic exuberance and confidence which found a fitting focus in the visit of the prince and the honour bestowed upon the city's mayor. In some respects it could be read as implicitly parodic of the Corpus Christi procession, and certainly developed as a spectacle to attract people to the city and to increase trade. The antiquarian David Rogers tells us that the mayor and council had to choose between the Show and the Whitsun plays each year – the companies were evidently not required to bear the cost of both – and it is possible that the creation of the civic Whitsun plays reflects a purposive alternative to the Show.[48] The interchange between the genres suggests that in the early sixteenth century their civic and economic functions overlapped.

The reference to the play at the Abbey Gate in the 1498/9 annals is also significant, for the *Assumption of Our Lady* is listed in the pre-Reformation lists

---

[48] '[W]hen the whitson playes weare played. then the showe at midsomer wente not. And when the whitson playes weare not played. then the midsomer showe wente onlye', Clopper, p. 252.

and the Banns of the plays as the responsibility of the wives of Chester.[49] Presumably this was a religious guild dedicated to the Virgin Mary, and since the feast of her Assumption is on 15 August, the month of the prince's visit, the performance was appropriate. But the choice of the abbey as venue warrants comment. The abbey had been re-endowed by the earl in 1092 in response to the intended presence in the city of the bishop of Lichfield at the designated cathedral of St John. While St John's flourished in the fifteenth century, the abbey, according to Burne, suffered from weak leadership, financial mismanagement and indiscipline for much of that period.[50] This period of decline seems to have been arrested with the abbacies of Simon Ripley (1485–93) and John Birchenshawe (1493–1524 and 1529–35), which saw the resumption of a major building programme. When the prince saw the play, he also would have seen the newly completed west front of the church. In the sixteenth century, St John's was in decline, while the abbey became the more prestigious, and when the Chester diocese was created in 1541 it was the abbey church that became the cathedral.

As we enter the sixteenth century the *locus* of power has shifted from the south to the north of the city. This shift is signalled by the performance-route of the Whitsun plays, which began at the Abbey Gate, then moved to the Cross in front of the Pentice, and then went into 'every street' – the Watergate, then Bridge Street and finally to Eastgate Street (see Map 2). Set alongside the route of the Corpus Christi procession, which we may assume continued until the suppression of the feast in 1548, this performance-route carried a very different political symbolism, just as the plays had themselves been constructed in a very different way in their transfer to Whitsun. Moreover, embracing the whole city, the plays now fulfilled an inclusive function comparable to that of the Show, making the interchange between the two genres understandable.

---

[49] The wurshipffull Wyffys of this towne
fynd of our Lady th'Assumpcon;
it to bryng forth they be bowne,
and meytene with all theyre might.
    (lines 128–31)

[50] R.V.H. Burne, *The Monks of Chester: The History of St Werburgh's Abbey* (London, 1962), esp. chapter 4.

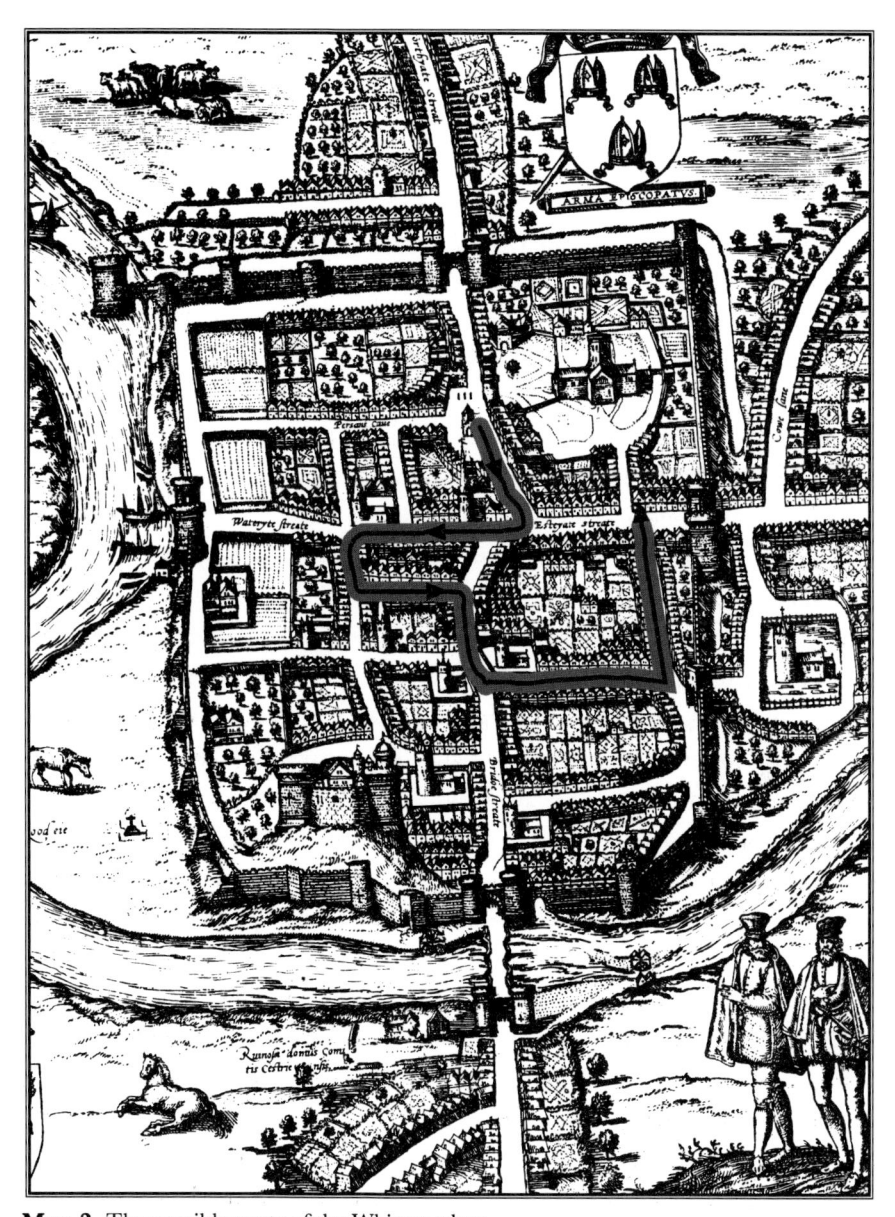

Map 2. The possible route of the Whitsun plays.

We should consider the possibility that the political significance of the route, like that of the performance, might have changed with the changing political circumstances of the time. In the latest version of his *Breviary*, *c.* 1636–7, David Rogers offers us a cosy picture of church/town co-operation in the plays:

> The. firste place where they begane, was. at the Abaye gates, where the monks and Churche mighte haue the firste sight: And then it was drawne. to the highe Crosse before the mayor and Aldermen. and soe from streete to streete.[51]

Significantly, this is a late reading of the route. The gift of a barrel of beer to the players at the 1572 performance noted in the cathedral accounts does suggest some such endorsement.[52] But I find it difficult to read the production outside the abbey – assuming that it was indeed held there – in the years after 1506 when the new privileges conferred on the town by the great charter were being fiercely contested by Birchenshawe, in that way. Rather, it would look more like a proclamation of civic authority within a genre that had previously served to endorse ecclesiastical power and was now paraded in front of the abbey which was fighting to retain its traditional rights. It is against that situation that we need to revalue the much debated authorship-traditions of Chester which, perhaps because of literary priorities, have tended to overshadow the unchanging mayoral connection.

Two authors were proposed. The proclamation of William Newhall, town clerk, in 1531/2, states confidently that the plays were written by Sir Henry Francis, whose name appears in lists of 1377, 1379 and 1382 as a monk of St Werburgh's. A different author, the famous monk-historian Randle Higden, who was at St Werburgh's from 1299 to 1364, is proposed in the late (post-Reformation) Banns.[53] It should be noted that Clopper's citations of references to Higden are misleadingly early, since he lists annalists' entries under the dates of the entry and not under the date of the manuscript in which the annals

---

[51] Clopper, p. 436.
[52] Ibid., p. 96.
[53] Ibid., pp. 27–8; Banns, lines 1–27.

appear; and in dating the early (pre-Reformation) Banns as 1539/40 he does not sufficiently stress that the list that precedes it postdates those Banns and is probably of the late sixteenth century. Setting aside the textual problems here, it is worth noting that the proclamation boldly sets out not only the partnership of town and church but also the plays' Catholic origins, stressing that they were performed by consent of the Pope and carried indulgences for those attending, as the revised version of the proclamation in 1539/40 indicates:

> devised and made by one Sir Henry Frances, somtyme moonck of this monastrey disolved, who obtayning and gat of Clemant, then Bushop of Rome, a 1000 dayes of pardon, and of the bushop of Chester at that tyme 40 dayes of pardon, graunted from thensforth to every person resorting in peaceble maner with good devotion to heare and see the sayd playes from tyme to tyme as oft as the shall be played within the sayd citty.[54]

Given the date of the earliest version of the proclamation and the strong hints in it that the plays are being revived, the performance looks very much like a political statement of Catholic orthodoxy in accordance with declared national policy. Goodman, in 1572, objected that the plays had been written by a monk 200 years before and were part of a popish plot to keep Chester faithful to Catholicism, which suggests that it was the words of Newhall's proclamation that he had in mind.[55] Higden, who is constructed in the late Banns as a proto-Protestant bringing the Gospel to the people in their own tongue, looks like an acceptable scholarly alternative offered by supporters of the plays in the face of

---

[54] BL, MS Harley 2013, f. 1r, quoted from Lumiansky and Mills, *Essays*, p. 215. It may be relevant to note that a proclamation 'Prohibiting Erroneous Books and Bible Translations', issued on 22 June 1530, rejected claims for a vernacular Bible and required that the people 'have the Holy Scripture expounded to them by preachers in their sermons'; *Tudor Royal Proclamations: vol. 1, The Early Tudors*, eds Paul L. Hughes and James F. Larkin (New Haven and London, 1964), no. 129, pp. 193–7. The emphasis upon a clerical translation with papal authority offers a defence.

[55] Clwyd County Record Office (Ruthin), Plas Power MSS DD/PP/839, p. 119: 'Where-as certain plays were devised by a monk about 200 years past in the depth of ignorance, & by the Pope then authorised to be set forth, & by that authority placed in the city of Chester to the intent to retain that place in assured ignorance & superstition according to the Popish policy.'

the kind of objections that Goodman was making. These authorship proposals therefore characterise the different political justifications offered for productions of the plays at moments of religious crisis, and by implication define the nature of the opposition to them.

Although our records of drama and ceremonial in fifteenth-century Chester are sparse, they offer an index of changing power centres and structures in the city. As the city developed its own administrative and economic autonomy, it also developed and elaborated its own ceremonial corpus to signify the former and further the latter. From the earliest reference, the plays were an early means by which the mayor could exert his authority over the growing number of companies. But, still attached to the Corpus Christi procession, the plays served primarily to underline the city's subservience to earl and Church. What we see is a symbolic liberation of the genre such that in subsequent centuries the plays would be regarded as the product and commemoration of the city's administrative independence through association with its first mayor. Small wonder then that the suppression of the plays in 1575 was attended with mixed feelings, even by some of those who disapproved of their 'papist origins'.

2
LOCAL EQUITY JURISDICTIONS IN THE TERRITORIES OF THE ENGLISH CROWN: THE PALATINATE OF CHESTER, 1450–1540

Tim Thornton

Historians have traditionally said that palatine privilege, like that possessed by Cheshire, was irrelevant by the fifteenth century.[1] While the superficial trappings of semi-independence remained, perhaps hindering political and social peace, it is alleged that in reality Cheshire was just another county of England – different perhaps, but only in so far as each English county had its peculiarities.[2] This assumption has been at the heart of studies of Cheshire that have provided the foundations for some of the most important general interpretations of British history in the late medieval and early modern periods.[3] Historians of other palatinates and of similarly privileged

---

[1] Thanks are due to Dorothy Clayton, Diana Dunn, Ralph Griffiths, Philip Morgan, Tony Pollard, and John Watts for their patient comments; the views expressed remain entirely my own.

[2] G. Barraclough, 'The Earldom and County Palatine of Chester', *Transactions of the Historic Society of Lancashire and Cheshire*, 103 (1952 for 1951), pp. 23–57, was seminal; see H.J. Hewitt, *Cheshire under the Three Edwards* (Chester, 1967), esp. p. 11; J.T. Driver, *Cheshire in the Later Middle Ages 1399–1540* (Chester, 1971); J. Beck, *Tudor Cheshire* (Chester, 1969), pp. 1–5; D.J. Clayton, 'The Involvement of the Gentry in the Political, Administrative and Judicial Affairs of the County Palatine of Chester, 1442–85' (unpub. Liverpool Ph.D. thesis, 1980), pp. 81–100; D.J. Clayton, *The Administration of the County Palatine of Chester 1442–1485* (Manchester, Chetham Society, 3rd ser., 35, 1990), pp. 45–67; J.W. Alexander, 'The English Palatinates and Edward I', *Journal of British Studies*, 22, pt. 2 (Spring 1983), pp. 1–22; W.J. Jones, 'Palatine Performance in the Seventeenth Century', in *The English Commonwealth 1547–1640: Essays in Politics and Society Presented to Joel Hurstfield*, ed. P. Clark, A.G.R. Smith and N. Tyacke (Leicester, 1979), pp. 189–204.

[3] M. Bennett, *Community, Class and Careerism: Cheshire and Lancashire Society in the Age of Sir Gawain and the Green Knight* (Cambridge, 1983); E.W. Ives, 'Court and County Palatine in the Reign of Henry

areas have done nothing which might encourage a challenge to the emphasis of such writing on Cheshire.[4] Because they believe that Cheshire's privileges were irrelevant, historians tend to see its gentry community as cemented by ties of class, interest, and patronage. They therefore write Cheshire's history around the fortunes of regional nobles, holding power because of their landed wealth, or around more direct ties, perhaps through lesser men as courtiers, between the gentry community and the court of the English king.[5] These historians misunderstand the reality of power and politics in Cheshire and, by extension, in the complex of territories under the over-all sovereignty of the English king. To a large extent authority and lordship continued to flow along palatine channels, and these were more significant than the influence of noblemen and courtiers.

The most dramatic expression of the importance of the palatinate in the fifteenth century is seen in the field of taxation. In view of the importance of taxation in constitutional, political, and social relationships, it is important to note that in the fifteenth century resources in Cheshire were mobilised for political ends through local palatine mechanisms of consent, allocation of burden, and collection.[6] It is also important to recognise that these were

---

VIII: The Career of William Brereton of Malpas', *Transactions of the Historic Society of Lancashire and Cheshire*, 123 (1971), pp. 1–38; J.S. Morrill, *Cheshire 1630–1660: County Government and Society during the English Revolution* (Oxford, 1974).

[4] C.M. Fraser, 'Prerogative and the Bishop of Durham, 1267–1376', *EHR*, 74 (1959), pp. 467–76; J. Scammell, 'The Origin and Limitations of the Liberty of Durham', *EHR*, 81 (1966), pp. 449–73, esp. pp. 469–73; M. James, *Family, Lineage, and Civil Society: A Study of Society, Politics, and Mentality in the Durham Region, 1500–1640* (Oxford, 1974), pp. 40–1; R.L. Storey, *Thomas Langley and the Bishopric of Durham 1406–1437* (London, 1961), pp. 52–5, 116–34; R.B. Dobson, *Durham Priory 1400–1450* (Cambridge, 1973); A.J. Pollard, *North-Eastern England During the Wars of the Roses: Lay Society, War, and Politics 1450–1500* (Oxford, 1990), pp. 144–50.

[5] M. Bennett, 'A County Community: Social Cohesion among the Cheshire Gentry, 1400–25', *Northern History*, 8 (1973), pp. 24–44; M. Bennett, *Community, Class and Careerism*; M. Bennett, '"Good Lords" and "King-Makers": The Stanleys of Lathom in English Politics 1385–1485', *History Today*, 31 (1981), pp. 12–17; Ives, 'Court and County Palatine in the Reign of Henry VIII'; Morrill, *Cheshire 1630–1660*.

[6] R.S. Schofield, 'Taxation and the Political Limits of the Tudor State', in *Law and Government under the Tudors: Essays presented to Sir Geoffrey Elton*, eds C. Cross, D. Loades and J.J. Scarisbrick (Cambridge, 1988), p. 227. Not everything was fiscalised, however, and taxation is only one indication of the means of mobilising resources.

partially independent of English mechanisms. Cheshire was exempt from English parliamentary taxation. The county voted its own form of taxation, the mise, giving consent through an institution or occasion that was sometimes called a parliament. The process of consent required before the tax could be levied was as real as that operating in the English parliament. This process might mean outright refusal, or partial grants, and could involve redress of grievances. Cheshire tended to pay less in taxation than neighbouring English counties.[7]

Yet the lordship and power represented by the negotiation and grant of taxation was exercised relatively infrequently. There was, for example, no grant of mise by Cheshire between 1441 and 1463. It might be argued that, as a consequence, for twenty years the privileges of the palatinate meant nothing.[8] There were, however, other areas where lordship intervened or was called upon far more frequently. In fifteenth-century Cheshire, this overwhelmingly meant arbitration and, when expressed through sovereign authority, the still-fluid field of equity. The complexities of late medieval law – land law in particular – and the slow pace of proceedings in the courts of common law meant that men and women needed a resort that would substitute for the process of common law courts; a resort that would achieve a settlement reflecting the realities of their disputes, not abstruse legal analysis; and a resort that had the authority to hold both parties to an agreement.

Noble arbitration, and especially that of the Stanleys of Lathom, contrary to the myth propagated by the Stanleys themselves, did not play a dominant role. Even after Bosworth, the Stanleys' holdings of land south of the Mersey were limited, although Sir William Stanley of Holt did hold significant lands in

---

[7] Clayton, *The Administration of Chester*, pp. 45–51; B.E. Harris, 'A Cheshire Parliament', *Cheshire Sheaf*, 5th ser., 1, pp. 1–2; T. Thornton, 'Political Society in Early Tudor Cheshire, 1480–1560' (unpub. Oxford D.Phil. thesis, 1993); Thornton, 'A Defence of the Liberties of Chester, 1451-2', *Historical Research*, 68, pt. 3 (1995), pp. 338–54.

[8] A point made to me by Philip Morgan of Keele University. The absence of a grant of mise does not rule out the continual presence of connected issues in the minds of Cheshire people: during the period in question, the absence of a grant was partially due to their strenuous resistance: H.D. Harrod, 'A Defence of the Liberties of Chester, 1450', *Archaeologia*, 2nd ser., 7 (1900), pp. 71–86; Clayton, *Administration of Chester*, pp. 45–8.

Cheshire before his execution in 1495.[9] Arbitration panels working in Cheshire from 1480 to 1521, when the second earl of Derby died and was succeeded by a minor, included few Stanleys. They might be expected to appear as 'umpires', even if not (as important noblemen) as members of the arbitration panels themselves. Yet the only trace of such activity is in two arbitration panels where George, Lord Strange, acted as 'umpire' should the main group of arbiters fail to come to a decision. After 1495, and up to the death of the second earl in 1521, or indeed until 1560, no Stanley role has been uncovered in any of one hundred or so Cheshire arbitrations examined.[10] This is not to say that the Stanleys never had a role in resolving Cheshire disputes. For example, in or shortly before 1480, James Stanley, archdeacon of Chester, wrote to Sir William Stanley, chamberlain of Chester, and William Venables, the escheator, handing over responsibility for an arbitration because he had to travel to Lancashire. This has been presented as Stanley reallocation of a Stanley arbitration; the truth is not so simple, as the intended recipient of the letter was Venables rather than Sir William Stanley. James Stanley wrote: 'I pray you will labour to the partyes yff they wyll abyde the dome of my broder chamberlayn, Nedam iustice and me or elles any lernetmon yt wold be egall be twene thaym.'[11] The Stanleys were not to arbitrate alone but with the deputy justice of Chester, John Needham. The Stanleys were involved as local office-holders under the palatinate.

This arbitration can only fully be understood in the context of the shadowy body of office-holders and other men who were the king's, prince's, or earl's

---

[9] The best account of the land holdings of the family is J.M. Williams, 'The Stanley Family of Lathom and Knowsley, c. 1450–1504: A Political Study' (unpub. Manchester M.A. thesis, 1979). B. Coward's account in *The Stanleys, Lords Stanley and Earls of Derby, 1385–1672: The Origins, Wealth and Power of a Landowning Family* (Chetham Society, 3rd ser., 30, 1983), pp. 11–13 is over-enthusiastic; see M.M. Condon, 'Ruling Elités in the Reign of Henry VII', in *Patronage, Pedigree and Power in Later Medieval England*, ed. C. Ross (Gloucester, 1979), p. 136, n. 20.

[10] JRULM, Rylands Charters 1679; CCRO, DBA 58 (unnumbered); these and the broader sample are listed in Thornton, 'Political Society in Early Tudor Cheshire', pp. 41–51.

[11] BL, Add. MS 34,815, f. 5; M.K. Jones, 'Sir William Stanley of Holt: Politics and Family Allegiance in the Late Fifteenth Century', *Welsh History Review*, 14 (1988), p. 7 (who ends his quotation with the word 'chamberlayn').

councillors in Cheshire. The earl was potentially the dominant force in the political life of the county palatine of Chester. The pattern of his lordship in land and jurisdiction was so dense that his influence was far stronger than that of a lord elsewhere in England. This potential was fulfilled most completely when the earl was an adult, as under Edward, the Black Prince, or Henry of Monmouth. After the latter's accession to the throne, no adult held the earldom until 1610.[12] Henry VI's son, Edward, received his lands when he was just two but was younger than eight when his father was deposed. Edward, son of Edward IV, was invested with the earldom in 1471 but when he succeeded to the throne he was still just twelve. Richard III's son Edward, born in 1473, died less than a year after he was invested in September 1483. The creation of Arthur Tudor as earl occurred in November 1489, when he was just three years old, and his investiture took place late in February 1490. Arthur came closest of all the earls of this period to achieving his majority, but he died on 2 April 1502. His brother Henry, born in 1491 and created earl in February 1504, was nearly eighteen when he became king but he was never invested with the lands of his earldom.

Yet the lack of an adult earl was not of overwhelming significance. An underage earl might be invested with his estates and provided with a council to govern his household and manage all his lands.[13] Even when princely counsellors and servants were identical with those of the king, the interests of

---

[12] *CP*, 3, pp. 173–6; P. Booth, *The Financial Administration of the Lordship and County of Chester, 1272–1377* (Chetham Society, Manchester, 1981); P. Booth, 'Taxation and Public Order: Cheshire in 1353', *Northern History*, 12 (1976), pp. 16–31; A.E. Curry, 'Cheshire and the Royal Demesne, 1399–1422', *Transactions of the Historic Society of Lancashire and Cheshire*, 128 (1979 for 1978), pp. 113–38.

[13] E.g. Edward son of Henry VI: born 13 Oct. 1453, created earl 15 Mar. 1454, received his lands Nov. 1455 and had a council appointed 28 Jan. 1457: see R.A. Griffiths, *The Reign of King Henry VI: The Exercise of Royal Authority, 1422–1461* (London, 1981), pp. 724, 755, 781. On the council of the prince, see C.A.J. Skeel, *The Council in the Marches of Wales: A Study in Local Government during the Sixteenth and Seventeenth Centuries* (London, 1904), pp. 18–28; P.H. Williams, *The Council in the Marches of Wales under Elizabeth I* (Cardiff, 1958), pp. 3–9; R.A. Griffiths, 'Wales and the Marches', in *Fifteenth-Century England, 1399–1509: Studies in Politics and Society*, eds S.B. Chrimes, C.D. Ross and R.A. Griffiths (Manchester, 1972), pp. 159–65.

their two masters did not necessarily coincide. The two Edwards, sons of Henry VI and of Edward IV, are good examples: through the former, Margaret of Anjou's influence might outweigh that of the king himself, and Anthony, Earl Rivers, used the latter prince's cofferer as his agent, payments being made on warrants under Rivers' seal.[14] Even when there was not even an under-age earl to rule the palatinate, in the late fifteenth century the conditions were in place for autonomous lordship to operate through councillors. This was in spite of the apparent interruptions to the existence of the formally-constituted Marcher Council. The Marcher Council appointed by Edward IV ceased to exist on his death, and did not resume activity until about 1490.[15] Conciliar power in Cheshire has been underestimated because of the lack of formalised institutions and instructions directing councillors' activity. Yet as long as there was a prince or monarch, he had councillors in Chester. This group of councillors lacked institutional structure because it was defined by its purpose and activity, not its membership. Instructions were the product of special occasions: in Cheshire such occasions were absent.[16]

This fluidity and informality were qualified by factors which suggest we should treat the councillors operating in Cheshire as more than part of the broader informal councils of the king of England or prince of Wales. First, the lack of personal attendance of, or direction by, the prince or king suggests that being a councillor in Cheshire was more than simply being a royal minion or

---

[14] Griffiths, *Henry VI*, pp. 776–7; Williams, *Council in the Marches*, pp. 6–9; M.A. Hicks, 'The Changing Role of the Wydevilles in Yorkist Politics to 1483', in *Patronage, Pedigree and Power*, pp. 75–9; D.E. Lowe, 'The Council of the Prince of Wales and the Decline of the Herbert Family during the Second Reign of Edward IV (1471–1483)', *Bulletin of the Board of Celtic Studies*, 27, pt. 2 (1977), pp. 278–97. As John Watts pointed out to me, the lack of an adult earl affected the way that palatine power expressed itself, if not its importance.

[15] R. Horrox, *Richard III: A Study of Service* (Cambridge, 1989), pp. 205–12; Williams, *Council in the Marches*, pp. 9–10; S.B. Chrimes, *Henry VII* (London, 1972), p. 250; P.R. Roberts, 'The "Acts of Union" and the Tudor Settlement of Wales' (unpub. Cambridge Ph.D. thesis, 1966), pp. 1–10. At Arthur's death, however, while the prince's lands remained in the king's hands, a council continued to exercise this function: ibid., pp. 250–1.

[16] M.M. Condon, 'An Anachronism with Intent? Henry VII's Council Ordinance of 1491/2', in *Kings and Nobles in the Later Middle Ages*, eds R.A. Griffiths and J. Sherborne (Gloucester, 1986), pp. 228–53; J.L. Watts, 'The Counsels of King Henry VI', *EHR*, 106 (1991), pp. 279–98.

adviser. Second, being 'of the council' was frequently associated with occupation of certain offices, most obviously those of justice and chamberlain of Chester. Third, the council was perceived as specific to one territory, the earldom of Chester. A belief in the distinctiveness of the earldom and its institutions, including parliament, is expressed in the petition presented by the county palatine in 1450: 'Where the seide comite is and hath ben a comite palatyne als well afore the conquest of Englond as sithen distincte & separate from youre coron of Englond within which comite ye & all youre noble progenitours sith hee came into youre hondes & all erles of the same afore that tyme have had youre heighe courtes parliamentes to holde at youre willes.'[17] The prince's councillors in Chester represented the prince but were not a sub-committee or delegation from a superior council elsewhere. Under the lordship of Edward, prince of Wales, in the 1480s, for example, 'our counsail there', operating in the Chester exchequer, was ordered to arrest Geoffrey Warburton. Geoffrey 'by force of recognissances' made *coram consilio domini Regis*, as the formula ran, in the exchequer of Chester, had been imprisoned there pending action 'by our counsail there'. His release had been inadvertently ordered; he was to be rearrested 'to abide vnto the tyme he be deliuered by our counsail there after the tennor effect and purport of the recognissance'.[18] The councillors were on occasion willing to appeal to the royal council for support but were eager to ensure that punishment was determined by palatine courts.[19]

---

[17] Harrod, 'A Defence of the Liberties of Chester', p. 75.

[18] PRO, Exchequer, Treasury of Receipt, Council and Privy Seal Records, E 28/92 (22 Mar. 1480). For the form of recognizances, see Clayton, *Administration of Chester*, pp. 245–6. This Geoffrey Warburton has not been identified. It cannot be Sir Geoffrey, since he died 1448: see G. Ormerod, *The History of the County Palatine and City of Chester*, second edn, revised and enlarged by T. Helsby (3 vols, London, 1882), 1, p. 574.

[19] PRO, E 28/92 (20 Sept. 1479): the prince's request in this petition that punishment be imposed by the king on the advice of his council was changed to a call for the king's council to make the defendant find surety to appear *in the county palatine of Chester* (my italics). The list of 'Petitions relating to Cheshire, to the Prince of Wales' Council', given in P. Worthington, 'Royal Government in the Counties Palatine, 1460–1509' (unpub. University of Wales, Swansea Ph.D. thesis, 1990), pp. 411–12, should be treated with care; it includes, for example, this petition, which is directed by the prince to the king.

To an extent, the channels through which royal counsel could flow were open to be shaped by the king, but to an extent they were also fixed. Royal counsel may have represented the free flow of royal power, but it was royal power mediated through (and to an extent shaped by) independent agents and flowing within defined spheres peculiar to each of the royal domains. Cheshire was one such element.[20]

Councillors can be seen operating in Cheshire in relation to the first aspect of lordship discussed, namely in commissions negotiating taxation with the representatives of the Cheshire community. The detailed account of the 1436 negotiation shows that the commissioners negotiating for the Crown were considered to be *de consilio dicti domini regis*.[21]

During the fifteenth century until 1497 those responsible for negotiating on behalf of the Crown were, overwhelmingly, local men holding local offices (see appendix).[22] The group usually centred on the chamberlain and justice. The 1463 commission is remarkable in this respect, consisting simply of the Stanley brothers, Chamberlain William and Justice Thomas. Most of the other commissions do include some outside element in the form of the auditors for Chester and North Wales, men like John Geryn (1430), Richard Bedford (1436 and 1441), and John Brown (1441). The character of the commissions begins to

---

[20] This has implications for other 'councils' in this period. The north was another area where royal councillors operated as a body. Only under Richard III did they have a specific commission for causes between individuals: usually none was necessary. Under Henry VII, the earl of Surrey had a commission of array, and the commission of oyer and terminer for Yorkshire included many lawyers. Membership of such commissions was consequent upon, and not the reason for, membership of the Council in the North: R.R. Reid, *The King's Council in the North* (London, 1921), pp. 77–85; F.W. Brooks, *The Council in the North* (Historical Association pamphlet 25, rev. edn., 1966); F.W. Brooks, *York and the Council of the North* (York, St Anthony's Hall Publications, 5, 1954); Condon, 'Ruling Élites', pp. 116–19. See Margaret Beaufort's royal council in the Midlands, settling disputes sometimes at the instance of a royal privy seal writ, sometimes in response to local petition: M.K. Jones and M.G. Underwood, *The King's Mother: Lady Margaret Beaufort, Countess of Richmond and Derby* (Cambridge, 1992), pp. 86–90.

[21] Clayton, *Administration of Chester*, pp. 53–4; Harris, 'A Cheshire Parliament', pp. 1–2.

[22] See the discussion of the councillors involved in tax negotiations between 1436 and 1485 in Clayton, *Administration of Chester*, pp. 53–7, although she still wishes to show that the council was a delegation of the king's council (conventionally defined) or that appointed for the prince.

change in 1474, showing the influence of the newly-extended princely household and council. The 1474 commission was headed by the president of the Council in the Marches, and many – but not all – of the other places were filled by important post-holders in the prince's household, his relatives, or members of his council.[23] This pattern was not continued. Henry VII's early dependence on the Stanleys, seen at its most complete before the battle of Stoke, and also against the 1489 rebels,[24] meant in 1486 and 1491 that local men again predominated. On the former occasion, the first five names on the commission were either Stanleys or Savages. On the latter, the Stanley presence was balanced but hardly overwhelmed by the prince's chancellor, the deputy justice (another prince's man), and Robert Sherborne, secretary to Cardinal Morton.[25] The year 1497 signalled a shift from reliance on local magnates, and the Council in the Marches was the leading force on the commissions. Local men continued to appear, especially the first earl of Derby and his son George, but even they disappear in 1500, and in 1517 the second earl was omitted. Yet this was not to last: in 1547, the commission was led by members of the Council in the Marches, but they were reinforced by a group of local men. Thomas Venables, Henry Delves, John Done and Philip Egerton in fact constituted the majority of those who were actually present when the grant was made. So the evidence provided by records of negotiation over taxation shows the body of councillors in Cheshire was fluid, never subsumed in the Council in the Marches, and its membership depended on the function it was intended to fulfil.

The main purpose of this paper is, however, to explore the second aspect of lordship mentioned above – arbitration and equity. The activity of the earl's councillors sitting in the exchequer at Chester in a quasi-judicial or judicial capacity before the accession of Elizabeth has barely been discussed. Any

---

[23] Clayton, *Administration of Chester*, pp. 54–7; *CPR, 1467–77*, pp. 283, 366. The names should also be compared to those of king's councillors identified by J.R. Lander for Edward IV's reign: see his 'Council, Administration and Councillors, 1461–85', in *Crown and Nobility 1450–1509* (London, 1976), pp. 309–20.

[24] M. Bennett, 'Henry VII and the Northern Rising of 1489', *EHR*, 105 (1990), pp. 34–59, esp. p. 44.

[25] A.B. Emden, *Biographical Register of the University of Oxford to A.D. 1500* (3 vols, Oxford, 1957–9), pp. 1685–7: he acted as king's secretary in taking fines from the West Country rebels.

possibility of such action before the early sixteenth century has been dismissed.[26] Yet the role in financial matters of the chamberlain of Chester sitting in the exchequer has been extensively examined, and it has long been acknowledged that the chamberlain had jurisdiction over cases linked to financial administration.[27] The exchequer was also the place where the county's Domesday Roll and its successors, the Enrolments or Recognizance Rolls, were kept. The chamberlain in the exchequer therefore had jurisdiction over cases involving production of the rolls, farms, the tallies issued by the chamberlain and auditors' certificates, and similar business. For example, in 1481 he dealt with a dispute over the inquisition *post mortem* of Sir Robert Fouleshurst.[28] And crucially the exchequer was home to the seal of the earldom, and the chamberlain was its guardian. It therefore produced the writs that drove the judicial process of the county; and the chamberlain and those associated with him were in a prime position to intervene in that judicial process.

The Westminster Chancery sprang from the action of the king and his council. While other lords' councils had a role in peace-keeping and arbitration, the administrative power of the king's council meant its intervention as arbiter in disputes was especially sought after.[29] Yet equity jurisdiction was still developing at Westminster during the fifteenth century.[30] It is therefore unsurprising to find no developed equity court in Cheshire in the early fifteenth

---

[26] *VCH, Cheshire*, 2, ed. B.E. Harris (Oxford, 1979), p. 21; Worthington, 'Royal Government in the Counties Palatine', pp. 182–3.

[27] R. Stewart Brown, 'The Exchequer of Chester', *EHR*, 57 (1942), pp. 294, 296–7.

[28] PRO, Special Collections, Ancient Petitions, SC 8/344/1262, discussed in Worthington, 'Royal Government in the Counties Palatine', p. 296; Stewart Brown, 'Exchequer of Chester', pp. 294, 296. See the fourteen cases in PRO, CHES 7, Palatinate of Chester, Returns to writs of Certiorari, (inventory in *DKR*, 21, pp. 44–5), which are largely the result of writs of *certiorari* on inquisitions.

[29] C. Rawcliffe, 'Baronial Councils in the Later Middle Ages', in *Patronage, Pedigree and Power*, pp. 87–108; C. Rawcliffe, 'The Great Lord as Peacekeeper: Arbitration by English Noblemen and their Councils in the Later Middle Ages', in *Law and Change in English History*, eds J.A. Guy and H.G. Beale (London, Royal Historical Society, Studies in History ser., 40, 1984), pp. 37–9; J.B. Post, 'Equitable Resorts before 1450', in *Law, Litigants and the Legal Profession*, eds E.W. Ives and A.H. Manchester (London, Royal Historical Society, Studies in History ser., 36, 1983), pp. 68–79.

[30] Action before the council and imprisonment in the Tower could still follow indictment at common law in 1511: see Condon, 'Ruling Élites', p. 141.

century. By 1484–5, however, a formalised equity jurisdiction was developing from the activity of the earl's council.[31] A file connected with William Tatton's farm of the Cheshire advowries – the privilege of giving men protection from the law – includes a petition from John Brigg of Newark, advowryman, to the 'Justice and other of the kynges counsell at Chestre',[32] explaining that 'Where as it hase byn used owte of tyme of mynde that whatsumeuere person that by fortune of the see or otherwise hath lost is godes soo that he by cause of nowne pouerte may not pay his dettes shall be admytte in to the kynges pryvelag of aduocarye of his Erledome of Chestre', he had been arrested by sheriffs Piers Smyth and John Runcorn. Brigg then referred to a judgment 'thoght and determynt' by 'the full honorable lorde Thomas lorde Stanley greyte Constable of England and Justice of Chestre and Sir William Stanley knyght chamberleyn of Chestre and other of the Kynges counseill'. The bill concludes with the words 'and this in way of charite', a formula characteristic of equity bills later in the history of the Chester exchequer.[33] The bill is neatly annotated on the reverse, suggesting some form of procedure had developed by this time for the presentation and admission of such bills. The decision of the 'Kynges counseill', referred to by Brigg, may survive in the form of an annotation to another petition on the same file, from the reign of Richard III[34]:

The Shirrefs [to] take the first xxs. and that they discharge the residue; . . . providet alwey that it be left to the saide Shirrefs if any such persons in the

---

[31] Was the development of the Chester exchequer's equity jurisdiction linked to periods when the Marcher Council was weak? The first clear example of Chester 'exchequer' action dates from Richard III's reign, when the Marcher Council was in eclipse. Another petition to the earl of Derby, from John Cowle of Chester (1491/2), was presented before the full revival of the council under Arthur: PRO, Exchequer, King's Remembrancer, Miscellanea, E 163/9/26, m. 1. (The association of this case with m. 2, *Savage and Coton v. Venables*, is suggestive of the forum in which the latter was presented to its addressee, Prince Arthur.)

[32] JRULM, Tatton of Wythenshawe, 440–4; petition 443.

[33] Jones, 'The Exchequer of Chester', p. 135.

[34] JRULM, Tatton of Wythenshawe, 444. The bill's address to Thomas, Lord Stanley, great constable of England, places it after Nov. 1483 (*CPR, 1476–85*, p. 367), and before 27 Oct. 1485 (Coward, *The Stanleys*, p. 13.)

saide Advowerez will occupe any marchandise or craft w[i]t[h]in the Cite to take of thaym resonable fines by the assent of the maier and his brethern and co[un]cell of the Cite.

T Stan[ley] k W Stanley k.

By the 1520s the Chester exchequer was operating as an equity court in the form familiar to us through our exposure to Westminster Chancery records.[35] A bill presented by David Warburton against Richard Merbury, alleging that the latter had withheld rent, resulted in a writ of *subpoena* on 14 December 1520. Depositions were taken in the exchequer on two occasions, and on 7 August the deputy justice ordered Merbury to pay up, 'unto suche tyme he shewe afore the said Justice a reasonable cause why he ought so to do', a typical qualification of equitable judgments.

The way in which the body of councillors acting in the exchequer might bring a case to a conclusion remained flexible. At Westminster, equity jurisdiction was a specialised role of the chancellor from an early period; in Cheshire, it was still not clear early in the sixteenth century that the chamberlain specifically had assumed this role. In the 1480s, the justice, chamberlain, and possibly others still sat together to decide cases. Of the 196 earliest surviving bills presented to the Chester exchequer, 32 are addressed to the justice and chamberlain together, and 2 are addressed to the justice alone.[36] Nor were procedures rigidly established. The chamberlain and other officers might make a decision on the spot.[37] Or they might call parties to appear and present evidence, as in 1538, when Richard Kardiff was placed under recognizance to 'appere at Chester from Shier to shier to answr to the bylles of Complaynt' of two plaintiffs, 'and performe such ordre as shalbe taken by the

---

[35] JRULM, Arley Charters, 15/37; William Beamont, *Arley Charters: A Calendar of Ancient Family Charters preserved at Arley Hall, Cheshire* (London, 1866), p. 30; an exemplification made during action before the Marcher Council in 1538.

[36] Only one group of Papers in Causes survives from before the accession of Elizabeth, providing evidence for 200 cases, mostly from the late 1530s: PRO, Palatinate of Chester, Exchequer: Pleadings, CHES 15/1; Bills to Justice: CHES 15/1/23, /125. The majority, of course, are to the chamberlain alone: 152 (77.55 per cent).

[37] As in the case concerning land in Vaynoll: see below, pp. 41.

Court her in the sames'.[38] The matter might be put to arbitration under the responsibility of councillors, and the panel might be recorded in the exchequer enrolments. Alternatively, the panel might be semi-official, with ordinary laymen and clerics possibly working alongside officials of the court and palatinate. A case from the last quarter of the fifteenth century concerning township boundaries between Roger Downes and Thomas Tytherington saw the parties 'condescendet and agreyd befor my lorde Prynce Councell in thexchequer [sic] of Chester to stande to and abyde the reporte and Certefycathe' of John Worth of Tytherington and Richard Smith, vicar of Prestbury.[39] Any study of Cheshire arbitrations during this period significantly reveals an absence of lawyers from the metropolis but the frequent inclusion of members of the small Cheshire legal establishment. In the 1480s and 1490s the name of Edmund Bulkeley, for example, continually crops up. Bulkeley had a close relationship with the administration of the county, holding the post of attorney of the earl in Cheshire from 1495 to the early part of Henry VIII's reign.[40] It is impossible for us to decide whether these men officiated in arbitrations in a strictly private or in a public capacity – in Cheshire the two shaded seamlessly into one another. This was all part of the web of princely lordship that found its clearest expression in the exchequer.

The earliest surviving Appearance Rolls from 1512 provide a full day-to-day record of the business of the exchequer as a court and the place of equity within it. The rolls were partly prepared in advance: details of recognizances that were about to expire were entered, followed by a space in which action taken was recorded by the clerk in court. The highest level of business in 1512/13 was at Michaelmas and Easter, or, to be more precise, on the Tuesday after each festival.[41] Some entries clearly relate to equity cases. The issue of a *subpoena* writ

---

[38] PRO, CHES 15/1/24.

[39] CCRO, DDS 5/3. Datable to the years of Prince Edward after Smith's arrival (1478–83) or of Arthur or Henry (1489–1509).

[40] Worthington, 'Royal Government in the Counties Palatine', p. 348.

[41] On 5 Oct. 1512, 62 items were transacted and 115 on 12 Apr. 1513: PRO, Palatinate of Chester, Appearance Rolls, CHES 5/1, roll for 4 Henry VIII. The rolls do not suffer from the partial recording or business characteristic of the more formal record of the Recognizance Rolls or the damaged files of Papers in Causes.

directed to Thomas Huyde on 10 May 1513, returnable on 18 May, appears to be linked to a suit also involving Thomas Warde of Norbury.[42] The roll for 1529/30 shows that the court was handling an increasing burden of equity cases.[43]

In particular, the Appearance Rolls throw further light on the connection between equity and one judicial aspect of the exchequer's activity that has been thoroughly discussed recently, the making of peace bonds. By the fifteenth century, the enrolments of the court were dominated by recognizances to keep the peace. It has been suggested that in some way the justice had acquired powers to summon potential law-breakers to the exchequer and cause them to be bound in sums of money.[44] These ranged from £40 to £1,000, either to keep the peace in general or towards specified individuals. Although these bonds usually coincided with sessions of the county court, their subjects were rarely parties to criminal actions there. The bonds were therefore preventative measures, taken to stop gentry disputes leading to violence. It could be that these bonds were entered voluntarily. Yet, in many cases a bond is entered by only one party to a dispute. Also, bonds came in several varieties, and a case due to disagreement over the right form, involving John Busshell and Thomas Finlow, priest, demonstrates the absence of consensuality in entering into these obligations.[45] Bonds of good behaviour towards all the king's lieges, rather than against specific individuals, were reserved for the most disreputable elements of society. Busshell objected that Finlow's demand for such a bond was 'ayanst all right and Justice your seid orator beyng of gud name and fame and noo browlyng person but dylygent and loborous to opteyn his lying [sic] by his occupacon and mystery'. Busshell had remained in prison for a long time because he could get 'non of his neyburs to be suretyes to so hie and chargeable boundz'. The Appearance Rolls suggest links between the multitude of these bonds that were made in Cheshire in the fifteenth and sixteenth centuries and

---

[42] PRO, CHES 5/1, 4 Henry VIII, m. 5v.

[43] PRO, CHES 5/3, roll for 21 Henry VIII. The extant bills of the 1530s cannot be compared with Chester Appearance Rolls, since none survives for the decade after 1529/30.

[44] Clayton, *Administration of Chester*, pp. 266–7, 277 (n. 107).

[45] PRO, CHES 15/1/23.

the issue of *subpoena* writs out of the exchequer during an equity case. An especially good example of the connection between dispute, bill, *subpoena* and recognizance comes in a case during the chamberlainship of William Brereton between Edward ap Hoell ap Tudor, and Rees ap Benet of Vaynoll (Flintshire) and Thomas his son, concerning land in Vaynoll.[46] On 28 June 1534 William Brereton wrote from Holt to 'my deputie [chamberlain of Chester] Rondall Brereton of Chester' on behalf of 'this berer', the plaintiff. Edward had told him how Rees and Thomas 'wrangfully haue entred in to the premisses with force'. William commanded Randle

> that you direct a sub pena agaynst the said Res and Thomas to appere bifore you in the exchequier of Chester at a shorte day by you lymytted and at their apparaunce to take such order and direccion concernynge the premisses so that this said pore man may peasably haue occupie and enioye the said lands. . . . And also that they be bounden in recognisaunce to obserue and bere the peace for theym self childer tenants seruants and parte takers vnto the said berer his childer tenants and seruants apon payn of xli.

On the reverse of the letter is a note, dated 29 June, of the issuing of a writ of *subpoena* to Rees and Thomas commanding their presence in the exchequer on the following Friday (which was 3 July). Randle appreciated the urgency and wrote on the letter, 'Make this bearer a sub pena retornable apon fryday next commyng for the persons within named. He hath payd me for the same. Make it in contynent &c'. On 6 July Rees and Thomas, along with three others, entered a recognizance in £40.

The Chester exchequer was therefore intervening in the judicial process and acting as an equity court at the end of the fifteenth century. The exchequer's jurisdiction grew rapidly because it offered the many advantages of equity. The decision in the advowry case demonstrates one such attraction of equitable remedies: judgment was not aimed at narrowing the point at issue as much as possible and then awarding an absolute verdict for or against each party, but

---

[46] PRO, CHES 15/1/173. Vaynoll is now Bodelwyddan: *Early Chancery Proceedings*, 9 (PRO, Lists and Indexes, 52, 1933), p. 348.

rather at looking at a problem in the round and producing a balanced, workable solution which did not represent an outright victory for either side. The advowry tenants had their privileges confirmed, but with the pragmatic amendment to the custom of the county that the city sheriffs might regulate their economic activity in Chester.

The two hundred cases from the early Papers in Causes provide evidence of the speed of action of which the exchequer was capable. Some bills petition for attachments and other common law writs returnable at the sessions of the county court, but most request a *subpoena* to compel attendance in the exchequer. In 47 cases the type of writ and date for return are known, and of these, 29 are *subpoenas*, 2 *subpoenas sicut alias*, and 1 a *subpoena sicut pluries*.[47] Of the ordinary *subpoena* writs, the modal number of days between the date of the writ and the date for return is just two. The mean interval is 3.79 days. Even an opponent who resisted the first *subpoena* could be brought rapidly to issue. On 12 June 1538, Fulk Lloyd was the victim of a rescue when he attempted to drive away sheep grazing his land at Rhuddlan. He secured a *subpoena* the following day, but this was unsuccessful and he returned to obtain a *subpoena sicut alias*, and, this also being unsuccessful, a *sicut pluries* on 23 June, returnable on 29 June. Depositions were taken on 4 July, just three weeks after the alleged offence.[48] Such examples may be compared with the time permitted for the return of the common law writs of *destringas* and attachment: in the former case the mean number of days is fourteen and in the latter twenty.[49] The Chester exchequer also compared very well with the speed of action in Westminster equity courts which themselves compared very well with central common law courts. To Bayne and Dunham ten days between offence and injunction appeared extreme haste. In many cases this very speed of action made a plaintiff's choice of the Chester exchequer necessary. Jane Thornton prosecuted Peter Asheton of Acton, carrier, in the exchequer because he was allegedly 'fugitive & nowe sellynge suche godes as he hathe and hathe takyn a house in

---

[47] There are also two *corpus cum causa* writs and one *certiorari*.

[48] PRO, CHES 15/1/100.

[49] C.G. Bayne and W. Huse Dunham, *Select Cases in the Council of Henry VII* (Selden Society, 75, 1958 for 1956), pp. cviii–cx.

nottyngham shire and thither wolbe gonne within these iii or iiii days comyng'.[50]

Other classic advantages of resort to an equitable remedy were evident in Chester exchequer cases. Detinue of deeds was cited by Thomas Aston against John Dutton of Helsby and Ralph Thomason, his chaplain, after the death of Aston's grandmother, Margaret Vernon. When Henry Helsby of Alvanley took Robert Lloyd's oxen to a place unknown, Lloyd was unable to replevy them and had to resort to the exchequer.[51] The impossibility of getting justice at common law because of the activities of a powerful local gentleman led Peter Corker of Arclid, 'a werey pore man', to take a case against his landlord, John Mainwaring of Nantwich, 'a grett gentilman', to the exchequer.[52] Most obviously and controversially, the exchequer could be used against the officials and courts of the city of Chester. Thomas Harper prosecuted Sheriffs William Glasior and Roger Whitehead for false imprisonment, claiming that a bill exhibited against him in the Pentice by Christopher Waren of Coventry was insufficient.[53]

The Chester exchequer's advantages were appreciated by a wide range of suitors, from knights and abbots to poor widows. Sir Edward Fitton brought a suit against eleven people for cutting down trees on his manor of Gawsworth in 1538, and another against Henry Stanway, a tenant of his in Betchton, in the parish of Sandbach.[54] John Harware, abbot of Vale Royal, was a particularly frequent plaintiff, for example, seeking to have an innkeeper from his lordship of Over bound not to receive fugitives, 'vacabunds, comen Carders and disers' in a disorderly alehouse.[55] At the other end of the scale came Margaret Parre, who described herself as 'a pore wydow and dwellyng in a foreyn Countie' in her bill against William Whiksted and others.[56] The only type of case that

---

[50] PRO, CHES 15/1/3, /60, /168.
[51] PRO, CHES 15/1/5, /102.
[52] PRO, CHES 15/1/31.
[53] PRO, CHES 15/1/50.
[54] PRO, CHES 15/1/44–5.
[55] PRO, CHES 15/1/174–6.
[56] PRO, CHES 15/1/124.

appears to be absent is between high status adversaries: a knight or abbot might prosecute a yeoman or husbandman, but would not take on another senior gentleman.

The lordship that provided these solutions to problems in Cheshire still flowed naturally through the medium of the prince's Chester council. If Cheshire's palatinate really was a dinosaur, persisting beyond its time, then the new national courts of equity should have monopolised all potential equity business from Cheshire. Yet they did not. One of the main charges levelled against the palatinates by those who see them as moribund in the fifteenth century is that they were no longer able to innovate; in particular, that they could not respond to new needs with new legal forms. In concluding this section, therefore, it should be noted that Chester was able to adopt and benefit from the most important new writ of the late medieval period, the *subpoena*, from at least 1483/4, and to use it to develop an equity jurisdiction.[57]

The activity of councillors in Chester as an equity court, if in a less developed way than had been achieved by the Westminster Chancery, is not unparalleled in other territories ruled by the English king, where a council of some sort existed and dealt with disputes, arbitrating with the backing of the power of its sovereign lord.[58] In some, this arbitration was already being delegated to the chancellor or his equivalent, and the beginnings of a formalised equity court were apparent. In the palatinate of Lancaster, created in 1351 without any reference to an equity jurisdiction, there had developed the chancery of the duchy, sitting in Lancaster. By 1473/4 this had an equity jurisdiction.[59] In Durham, a closer parallel to Chester in that its palatinate was considered to have existed from time immemorial, the chancery of the bishop was by this time

---

[57] W.M. Ormrod, 'The Origins of the Sub Pena Writ', *Historical Research*, 61 (1988), pp. 11–20.

[58] See R.R. Reid, *The King's Council in the North*, pp. 54–7.

[59] R. Somerville, 'The Palatine Courts in Lancashire', in *Law-Making and Law-Makers in British History: Papers Presented to the Edinburgh Legal History Conference*, ed. A. Harding (Royal Historical Society, Studies in History, 22, 1980); Worthington, 'Royal Government in the Counties Palatine of Lancashire and Cheshire', pp. 179–81. This should be distinguished from the Duchy chamber, which met in the capital.

also taking on an equity role.[60] In Ireland, from the 1490s the chancery began to take over the equity powers previously wielded by the Irish council and parliament.[61] In Man a separate equity court does not seem to have begun to emerge until the 1560s, although the lord's council was determining equity cases from earlier in the century.[62] Cecil Calvert, the absolute lord of Maryland, his powers based on those of the palatine lord of Durham, was from the 1630s able to create the rudiments of such an equity court in his distant lordship.[63]

So Cheshire saw a day-to-day flow of palatine lordship or sovereignty through the equity jurisdiction of the exchequer. But the equity jurisdiction of the exchequer might have been irrelevant, when compared with the equity jurisdiction of Westminster, and therefore the flows of English lordship. In short, did Cheshire people either choose, or have, to use the alternative equity jurisdictions of Westminster? All the evidence is that they did not. This was in spite of the strong motives of self-interest that were present to encourage Cheshire men to go to Westminster to exploit the opportunities for parallel actions or use the courts there to challenge a case already decided in Cheshire.

Cheshire chancery cases calendared in the period up to 1515, using the

---

[60] C. Kitching, 'The Durham Palatinate and the Courts of Westminster under the Tudors', in *The Last Principality: Politics, Religion and Society in the Bishopric of Durham, 1494–1660*, ed. D. Marcombe (University of Nottingham, Department of Adult Education, Studies in Local and Regional History, 1, 1987), pp. 49–70; K. Emsley and C.M. Fraser, *The Courts of the County Palatine of Durham from the Earliest Times to 1971* (Durham County Local History Society, 1984), pp. 72–90, esp. pp. 74–5.

[61] S.G. Ellis, *Tudor Ireland: Crown, Community and the Conflict of Cultures, 1470–1603*, (London, 1985), pp. 163–4. As elsewhere in these territories, it was often hard to distinguish between what might have been seen in England as a private Act of Parliament and the decision of the council: see the 'parliamentary' occasion in Cheshire in 1353 described by Booth, 'Taxation and Public Order', p. 22.

[62] Manx National Trust Museum and Library, Douglas, Isle of Man, Lib. Plit. 1543–69, *sub* 1568, 26 July; J.R. Dickinson, 'Aspects of the Isle of Man in the Seventeenth Century' (unpub. Liverpool Ph.D. thesis, 1991), pp. 10, 30–1, 54–6, 62, 65–6.

[63] B.C. Steiner, 'Maryland's First Courts', *Annual Report of the American Historical Association*, Washington (1902 for 1901), 1, pp. 213–29. See the equity jurisdiction exercised by the warden of the Cinque Ports: K.M.E. Murray, *The Constitutional History of the Cinque Ports* (Manchester, 1935), pp. 102–19, esp. pp. 112–13.

allocations to counties made by the authors of the calendar,[64] can be compared with cases in chancery from the neighbouring counties of Staffordshire and Derbyshire. During Edward IV's reign surviving Cheshire cases were a negligible proportion of those known to have been heard by the chancellor. Three are listed. Two in fact date from the reign of Henry VI.[65] The remaining one is only coincidentally a Cheshire case: that of John de la Pole, duke of Suffolk, was due to his wardship of Francis Lovell, and Cheshire was only one minor element in a case that embraced a complex of lands in Shropshire, Yorkshire, Oxfordshire, Wiltshire, and Northamptonshire.[66] Even if we go beyond cases listed as concerning Cheshire it is difficult to find examples involving Cheshire men.[67] The proportion of Cheshire cases in chancery increased under Henry VII, but still only reached twenty-four, or 0.157 per cent, for the whole period 1485–1515. In each period, Staffordshire cases made up about twenty times as much of the court's recorded business as did Cheshire suits. Even cases regarding Derbyshire are over ten times more frequent in their appearance. Neither Staffordshire nor Derbyshire extant cases include more than a tiny handful in which the decision of the courts of a town or city are challenged, and so the larger number of surviving cases cannot be explained in this way. When Edward IV's reign is compared with that of Henry VII, both Staffordshire and Derbyshire show considerable increases in the frequency of extant cases: the percentage of Staffordshire cases in existence more than

---

[64] This includes cases allocated to several counties. Where a case applies to both Derbyshire and Cheshire, for example, it will appear in the statistics for each county: e.g. PRO, Chancery, Early Chancery Proceedings, C 1/220/68, which relates to lands in Staffordshire, Cheshire and Shropshire, appears twice in the table, in the total for cases from Staffordshire and in the total for Cheshire. All these and subsequent statistics are based on the class C 1; although some cases in the class C 4 have also been examined, calendaring of the documents is so rudimentary that it has not been possible to use these.

[65] Brought by Sir John Gresley: PRO, C 1/39/87–8.

[66] PRO, C 1/40/322.

[67] Twenty-four Cheshire chancery cases are datable to 1485–1515, many brought by non-Cheshiremen or relating to counties other than Cheshire, e.g. that brought by Hugh Champyn, a London shearman, or that concerning estates in Shropshire and Staffordshire as well as Cheshire brought by Richard Patryk and his wife. There are also, however, cases which deal with exclusively Cheshire matters, such as the Ardern dispute over the manors of Alvanley and Harden: PRO, C 1/125/23, /220/68 (see also C 1/257/35, /280/79, /290/58); C 1/83/27.

trebles, and that of Derbyshire cases doubles. Cheshire's rate of increase is of the same order, but the significant fact remains of Cheshire's remarkably low proportion of total extant cases compared to that of the other two counties.

The record of Cheshire activity in chancery is comparable with the experience of the king's council in its judicial capacity, which was to become the court of Star Chamber formalised by Thomas Wolsey.[68] There are just two cases which have been misplaced among the proceedings of the reign of Henry VIII, and transcripts of the proceedings of the council also produce one closely related case.[69] The difficulties encountered by the plaintiffs in one of the Cheshire cases known from Henry VII's reign suggest why. The dispute over the Venables inheritance, a long-running affair,[70] is first seen in Henry's council in 1491, then reappears in 1500. Thomas Venables' obstinate refusal to produce title deeds eventually led to the cancellation of a recognizance for attendance, and the case went back to common law. Venables was adamant: 'all oder londes & tenementes within the seid Countie be & of the tyme wherof the mynd of man is not to the contrarie, have been enpleaded And the title therof triable & tried withyn the seid Countie [of Cheshire] And in non oder place'.

An interesting point emerges from the thirteen suits concerning Cheshire in chancery before 1485. Few of them can be accurately dated, but the six or so cases that can tend to cluster in two periods. The first is the 1430s. Two cases were brought by Sir John Gresley against Ralph Egerton and Richard Delves, and against Sir Geoffrey Mascy, probably in 1434/5;[71] a case between Alice Hogh and Robert Legh of Adlington belongs to 1432/3 or slightly later;[72] and

---

[68] On the court of Star Chamber, see J.A. Guy, *The Cardinal's Court: The Impact of Thomas Wolsey in Star Chamber* (Hassocks, 1977), and J.A. Guy, *The Court of Star Chamber and its Records to the Reign of Elizabeth I* (London, PRO Handbooks, 21, 1985).

[69] Guy, *Star Chamber and its Records*, pp. 67–73: PRO, Court of Star Chamber, Proceedings: Henry VIII, STAC 2/20/177 (*Wykestede v. Manweryng*); /29/188 (*Savage and Cotton v. Venables, Chomley, Grafton et al.* 1500) – the latter is discussed in Bayne and Dunham, *Cases in the Council of Henry VII*, pp. clvii–clviii, and printed ibid., pp. 130–4. Transcripts: *Cotton v. Venables* (1491): Bayne and Dunham, *Cases in the Council of Henry VII*, p. 24 (Huntington Library, California, Ellesmere MS 2654, f. 14).

[70] Ormerod, *Chester*, 3, pp. 193, 199.

[71] PRO, C 1/39/87–8.

[72] PRO, C 1/75/41.

in about 1440, William Sais brought a case against the sheriff, Ranulph Brereton, which also included criticism of the chamberlain, William Troutbeck.[73] The second cluster is around 1450. Then Ralph Holynshed brought a case against Hugh, John and Roger Browdhurst concerning land in Macclesfield hundred;[74] and most significantly William Denny put in a bill against the chamberlain, John Troutbeck.[75] Both groups of cases have a clear political context. That in the 1430s provides the background for the demand by Cheshire representatives in negotiating over the mise of 1441 that no further privy seals should be sent into Cheshire – a demand the Crown granted.[76] And the cases in the period around 1450 are almost certainly linked to the disgrace of the chamberlain of Chester for his obstinate defence of Cheshire's taxation privileges and resistance to resumption voted by the English parliament.[77] The fact that in two of the cases the chamberlain is specifically criticised by the plaintiff, and that Sais attacked Sheriff Brereton with a list of (unspecified) 'orrible offenses . . . to mugh to put in a bill to yore said lordeship for thay wold occupie a hole parchement Skyn and more', underlines the political nature of the cases. Privilege ebbed and flowed with the tides of politics and was never set in stone – it was constantly shaped and reshaped by circumstance.

In the fifteenth century, it seems, Cheshire people neither wanted to use Westminster equity jurisdictions, nor were forced by central government to do so. Even in the early seventeenth century the Chester exchequer was a powerful jurisdiction, its position enshrined by a judgment of the Westminster chancery.[78] Again, comparison with other territories of the English Crown suggests that Cheshire's experience was not unique. In the fifteenth century their equity jurisdictions usually excluded those of the Westminster courts. Very

---

[73] PRO, C 1/73/117.

[74] PRO, C 1/18/164.

[75] PRO, C 1/19/133.

[76] CCRO, Shakerley of Holme MSS, DSS, Vernon MS 3, f. 190; *CPR, 1436–41*, pp. 560–1: discussed in my thesis, 'Political Society in Early Tudor Cheshire', pp. 5–7.

[77] Thornton, 'Defence of the Liberties of Chester', p. 340.

[78] *DKR*, 39, p. 250 (22 Oct. 1619).

few cases came to chancery from these peripheral territories.[79] Before 1485, thirteen cases are attributed to France outside Calais, seven to Durham, thirty to Wales, and four to the Channel Islands. When we come to look in detail at the cases attributed to Ireland, for example, we discover that, of the twenty-one cases listed up to 1518, only nine concern property or actions in Ireland, or between two Irish parties. Two cases listed as concerning Ireland from the reign of Richard III illustrate the point. The action by the merchants and citizens of Waterford to recover their charter is against the heirs of a man who had taken the charter into his safe-keeping in Bristol, where they now detained it. And a case brought by an Irish merchant was against his agent in Bristol, a local merchant who refused to hand over money he had in his keeping.[80] Before 1515 we are left with just seven, of which two are from foreigners who probably did not understand the system and who cannot be seen as typical litigators. 'Great John', a Prussian merchant, complained against his imprisonment in Ireland, and some Luccan merchants objected that they could not use English common law to take action over a bond entered into in Dublin.[81] A similar picture could be painted for the other peripheral territories. Even when a bill was presented concerning one of these peripheral territories, it seems that there was no guarantee that it would be accepted by the Westminster jurisdictions. We know that in many of these cases, palatine or other privilege was objected to by the defendant. It is significant that where chancery action is recorded in one case, concerning lands in Yorkshire, Leicestershire, Nottinghamshire and Durham, the injunction concerned land in the first three counties but was silent concerning Durham.[82]

---

[79] This is calculated from the List and Index Society volumes, the compilers of which allocated cases to these areas with somewhat excessive generosity; see n. 72 above and R.A. Griffiths, 'The King's Realm and Dominions and the King's Subjects in the Later Middle Ages', in *Aspects of Late Medieval Government and Society*, ed. J.G. Rowe (Toronto, 1986), pp. 83–105, who sees greater significance in the existence of evidence for a few suits than its paucity; see also F. Metzger, 'The Last Phase of the Medieval Chancery', in *Law-Making and Law-Makers*, p. 82.
[80] PRO, C 1/65/215, /63/242.
[81] PRO, C 1/69/132, /203/5.
[82] PRO, C 1/402/44.

In conclusion, therefore, Cheshire history in the late medieval period must be written in terms of the palatinate. Lordship and sovereignty flowed overwhelmingly through the earldom of Chester, in the person either of the prince of Wales or of the king. If noblemen had significance, it was as officers of the palatinate. Those who mattered were the princes and their representatives. Westminster and the court mattered far less than we have been led to expect. The same was true in Ireland, Man, the Channel Islands, Durham, and Wales; and the way we see royal authority in all of the territories of the English king should be reassessed. It was less concentrated on the centre, both in terms of Westminster and the person of the king, and more focused at the local level, supportive of local peculiarity.

APPENDIX

COMMISSIONERS TO REQUEST MISES, CHESHIRE, 1430–1547

1430[a] Sir John Stanley; John Fray, baron of the exchequer; William Troutbeck, esquire, chamberlain of Chester; John Geryn, one of auditors of the exchequer.

1436[b] Robert Frampton, baron of the Chester exchequer; William Chauntrell, serjeant at law and deputy justice of Chester (to Humphrey, duke of Gloucester); William Troutbeck, chamberlain of Chester; Richard Bedford, auditor for North Wales jointly with Frampton; *& aliis de consilio dicti domini Regis.*

1441[c] William de la Pole, earl of Suffolk, justice of Chester and North Wales; Sir Thomas Stanley, deputy justice of Chester; John Troutbeck, chamberlain of Chester; Richard Bedford and John Brown, auditors.

1463[d] Thomas, Lord Stanley, justice of Chester; William Stanley, chamberlain of Chester.

---

[a] PRO, Palatinate of Chester, Enrolments, CHES 2/100, m. 4(12); (*DKR*, 37, pp. 134, 670).

[b] PRO, CHES 2/107, m. 6(2); (*DKR*, 37, p. 671). These were the commissioners present when the grant was made.

[c] This is a commission for Flint but that for Chester is likely to have been similar in composition: 23 Oct. 1441, PRO, CHES 2/115, m. 1(4); (*DKR*, 37, p. 592).

[d] PRO, CHES 2/135, m. 2d.(9); (*DKR*, 37, p. 693).

LOCAL EQUITY JURISDICTIONS

1474^e   *John Alcock, bishop of Rochester; John Hales, bishop of Coventry and Lichfield; Richard Redman, bishop of St Asaph; Thomas Grey; *Thomas, Lord Stanley; *Sir William Stanley; Thomas Vaughan, chamberlain of Edward, earl of Chester; *John Nedeham & Thomas Lytilton, justices; *Richard Haute senior and *Thomas Brugges.

1486^f   *Thomas, earl of Derby; *George, Lord Strange; Sir William Stanley; Sir John Savage, senior; Sir John Savage, junior; Thomas Salesbury, senior; *Andrew Dymmoke; *Richard Harper; *John Hawardyne, serjeant at law; *John Luthington, auditor.

1491^g   Thomas, earl of Derby and George Stanley, Lord Strange, joint justices of Chester; Sir William Stanley, chamberlain of Chester; Philip Arundell, the prince's chancellor; Thomas Englefield, 'lieutenant' justice of Chester; Robert Sherborne, clerk.

1497^h   William Smith, bishop of Lincoln, president of the prince's council; John Arundel, bishop of Coventry and Lichfield, chancellor of the prince; Thomas, marquess of Dorset, the prince's uncle; Thomas, earl of Derby, and George, Lord Strange, justices of Chester; Sir Richard Pole, chamberlain of Chester; Sir Richard Croft, seneschal of the prince; Sir Henry Vernon, the prince's treasurer; Sir William Uvedale, controller of the prince; Robert Frost, prince's almoner; Thomas Englefield and Thomas Poyntz, counsellors of the prince.

1500ⁱ   William Smith, bishop of Lincoln, president of the prince's council; Robert Frost, chancellor of the prince; Sir Richard Pole, treasurer; Thomas, abbot of Basingwerk; Sir Thomas Salisbury; John Chaloner, a justice of Chester; William Tatton, baron of the exchequer; Ralph Birkenhead.

* Commissioners present when the grant of mise was made, if this is ascertainable from the source.

^e PRO, CHES 2/146, m. 1(1); (*DKR*, 37, p. 141).

^f PRO, CHES 2/158, m. 3; (*DKR*, 37, p. 201).

^g Abortive warrant: PRO, Palatinate of Chester, Warrants, CHES 1/2/7; (*DKR*, 26, p. 21).

^h PRO, CHES 2/167, m. 5v. (*DKR*, 26, p. 25). The commissioners who actually negotiated the grant were John Challoner, Derby's lieutenant, Robert Chauntrell, *& alii de consilio dicti domini principis* unspecified.

ⁱ *DKR*, 26, p. 25: no enrolment of the grant, and therefore no detail on who actually negotiated the grant, survives.

1517[j]   *Geoffrey Blythe, bishop of Coventry and Lichfield, president of the Council in the Marches of Wales; *Sir William Uvedale; *Sir Gruffydd ap Rhys; Sir Edward Belknap; *Sir Thomas Cornwall; Anthony Fitzherbert, serjeant at law; John Porte; *Peter Newton; *George Bromley; Richard Sutton; Thomas Lynham; *Richard Snede.

1547[k]   Richard [Sampson], bishop of Coventry and Lichfield, president of the Council in the Marches of Wales; Robert [Warton alias Parfew], bishop of St Asaph; Henry, earl of Worcester; Walter Devereux, Lord Ferrers; Edward Grey, Lord Powes; *Robert Townshend; Thomas Bromley; Richard Devereux; Rees Mansell; Edward Carne; John Packington; John Pryce; Adam Mytton, knights; David Broke, serjeant at law; *Richard Hassall; George Willoughby and *Richard Germyn, esquires; *Thomas Venables; *John Donne; *Henry Delves; and *Philip Egerton.

* Commissioners present when the grant of mise was made, if this is ascertainable from the source.
[j] PRO, CHES 2/186, m. 3; (*DKR*, 39, p. 178).
[k] PRO, CHES 2/209, m. 1.

3
ARBITRATION IN GENTRY DISPUTES: THE CASE OF BUCKLOW HUNDRED IN CHESHIRE, 1400–1465

David Tilsley

In terms of the maintenance of law and order in the later middle ages, the self-regulating properties of local communities have increasingly drawn the attention of historians.[1] Nowhere is this more apparent than in the growing corpus of historical research on the subject of arbitration. A consensus has arisen that this method of settling disputes was speedier and certainly cheaper than recourse to the law courts. More importantly, the final award, being the result of debate and reasonable discussion, held greater potential for success. Arbitration afforded the possibility of a compromise solution acceptable to both parties and contrasted with the law courts which could deal only in black and white decisions, winners and losers. Most studies of the process have concentrated primarily on these general principles. What the present paper hopes to add is a detailed study, with a quantitative emphasis, of the operation of arbitration among the gentry of a relatively small geographical area, Bucklow hundred in Cheshire, during a relatively short period, the years from 1400 to 1465. The picture that emerges is of an élite group which made serious attempts to resolve its internal tensions, aided by the institutions and officials of the palatinate of Chester.

---

[1] J.W. Bennett, 'The Mediaeval Loveday', *Speculum*, 33 (1958), pp. 351–70; I. Rowney, 'Arbitration in Gentry Disputes of the Later Middle Ages', *History*, 67 (1982), pp. 367–76; E. Powell, 'Arbitration and Law in England in the Late Middles Ages', *TRHS*, 5th ser., 33 (1983) pp. 49–67; C. Rawcliffe, 'The Great Lord as Peacemaker: Arbitration by English noblemen and their councils in the Later Middles Ages', in *Law and Social Change in British History*, eds J.A. Guy and H.G. Beale (London, 1984); S.J. Payling, 'Law and Arbitration in Nottinghamshire 1399–1461', in *People, Politics and Community in the Later Middle Ages*, eds J. Rosenthal and C. Richmond (Gloucester, 1987), pp. 140–60.

The idea that there was in the later middle ages a cohesive community of gentry in Cheshire is well established. First postulated in modern historiography by Michael Bennett in his seminal article of 1973, the case has been reinforced by the more in-depth researches of Bennett himself and those of Dorothy Clayton.[2] The emergence of the Cheshire gentry as a self-conscious ruling élite rested upon two interlinked factors: the near total dominance of this class in both landholding and local government, and the absence of resident noble influence. As Bennett argued, the durability of the social cohesion generated by this common interest in landed estate and participation in the palatinate administration was dependent to a large degree upon the ability of this oligarchy to resolve its internal conflicts. Gentry disputes, although potentially disruptive in the short-term, provided an opportunity to promote class solidarity through communal attempts to resolve them. In the palatinate of Chester, the mediation of a third party was central to those attempts: the surviving recognizance rolls of the Chester exchequer contain over one hundred arbitration recognizances for the period 1400–65.[3] Other disputes within the palatinate were dealt with privately, the documentary evidence surviving in the numerous family muniment collections.

These collections are particularly rich for the gentry families of Bucklow, the hundred which forms the bulk of northern Cheshire. In Daniel King's *The Vale Royall of England* of 1656, Bucklow's appearance on the map is compared to an isosceles triangle whose two longest sides are formed by the rivers Mersey and Weaver.[4] At the time of Domesday, the Bucklow hundred of the fifteenth

---

[2] M. Bennett, 'A County Community: social cohesion among the Cheshire gentry, 1400–1425', *Northern History*, 8 (1973), pp. 24–44; M.J. Bennett, *Community, Class and Careerism: Cheshire and Lancashire Society in the Age of Sir Gawain and the Green Knight* (Cambridge, 1983); D.J. Clayton, 'Peace Bonds and the Maintenance of Law and Order in Late Medieval England: The Example of Cheshire', *BIHR*, 58 (1985), pp. 133–48; D.J. Clayton, *The Administration of the County Palatine of Chester, 1442–1485*, Chetham Society, 3rd. ser., no. 35 (Manchester, 1990).

[3] *DKR* 36, pp. 116, 120–1, 155, 293–4, 340, 493; *DKR* 37, pp. 17, 47, 58, 73–4, 103, 117, 210, 226–9, 231, 233, 243, 246, 273–4, 296, 299, 323–5, 329–30, 345, 361, 372–4, 377, 411, 430–1, 433, 443, 447, 458, 494–6, 515, 517–8, 594–5, 600–601, 614, 629, 637–8, 642–3, 658, 667, 670–1, 674, 737, 739–40, 742–4, 750, 759–63, 774, 779, 782, 808, 818; PRO, Palatinate of Chester, Enrolments, CHES 2/103.

[4] D. King, *The Vale Royall of England, or The County Palatine of Chester* (London, 1656), p. 93.

century had consisted of two separate hundreds, Bochelau and Tunendon. The first of these had the second annexed to it sometime in the intervening centuries. Like the other six Cheshire hundreds, Bucklow had a distinct place within the framework of county administration. Cheshire's palatinate status meant that it was not included in the national taxation system, and the parliaments which granted subsidies to the Crown did not include any representatives from the county. The palatinate contributed to the royal coffers in the form of a traditional tax, the so-called mise, which was always collected along hundredal lines. The sole surviving assessment list for the fifteenth century dates to 1406 and was drawn up to aid collection of an instalment of the mise granted in 1403. Assessment was by township, and the Bucklow section lists seventy of these, including the boroughs of Altrincham, Knutsford and Halton, these being the main centres of population.[5] The last of these gave its name to the most significant enclave within Bucklow, the barony of Halton, part of the duchy of Lancaster.

The various *ad hoc* commissions, of array for example, were organised in the same way as those to collect the mise. The burden of performing these administrative duties in the hundred, as with those at county level, fell upon the gentry. Bucklow has been described as having more than the average complement of men of that class. Referring to Camden's description of Cheshire as 'the most surprising nursery of ancient gentry', the seventeenth-century antiquarian Sir Peter Leycester termed Bucklow 'the prime border of that nursery'.[6] The gentry of the hundred were certainly well represented in the ranks of those Cheshire gentlemen who resorted to the mediation of a third party in the event of dispute. Arbitration recognizances, which were enrolled at the Chester exchequer, represent the main source of evidence for the operation of the process in the palatinate, and will be discussed in more detail later. For the years 1400–65 they give the names of over five hundred protagonists seeking

---

[5] JRULM, Tatton MS 345. The order in which the townships are listed seems to be in two sections which correspond to the original two hundreds.

[6] W. Camden, *Britannia* (Gibson's edition, London, 1695), p. 663; Sir Peter Leycester, *Historical Antiquaries, in Two Books . . . The second containing particular remarks concerning Cheshire* (London, 1673), p. 192. Camden's *Britannia* was first published in 1586.

arbitration, fifty-two of these coming from Bucklow gentry society.[7] The names of a further twelve Bucklow gentlemen in dispute are given in private deeds.[8] In all, evidence survives of thirty-four separate disputes involving members of Bucklow gentry families during our period. Some two hundred years later, Daniel King in his *Vale Royall* wrote of another Bucklow gentry dispute which involved George Holford, esquire, and his niece Lady Mary Cholmondeley, and which centred on 'those great lands of Holford'. This had recently 'finally and happily composed and ended, to the great joy and contentment of themselves, and of the whole country'.[9] This impression, that Bucklow gentry disputes were the concern of not just the disputants but the wider community, is certainly borne out by the fifteenth-century evidence.

The experience of the Holford family in the seventeenth century is testimony to the fact that landed estate formed the bedrock of gentry society and as such held great potential as a source of conflict. A gentleman's position and, more importantly, the future prospects of his family, rested on his capability to retain the lands he inherited and, if possible, to extend them. Unfortunately, the recognizance rolls seldom give details of the cause of a dispute. In only one of the Bucklow cases is a clear indication given. In April 1431, it was 'the title to the possessions which John son of Randal Minshull lately held in Chircheminshull', which divided Sir Peter Dutton, veteran of the battle of Shrewsbury, on the one side and William Venables, senior along with his daughter Eve, on the other.[10] This hint given by the official sources that it was matters of land tenure which were likely to have divided those gentlemen who turned to arbitration is reinforced by evidence from private deed collections. Matters of territorial boundaries sometimes caused disagreement. In 1446, the two premier knights of the hundred, Sir Geoffrey Warburton and Sir Robert Booth, then sheriff of the county, were in dispute over the border between the

---

[7] *DKR* 36, p. 493; *DKR* 37, pp. 58, 120–1, 226–9, 231, 323–4, 361, 373, 411, 433, 447, 494–5, 517, 637–8, 641–3, 671, 743, 761, 762–3, 808; PRO, CHES 2/103.

[8] JRULM, Mascie of Tatton MS 39; University of Keele, Legh of Booths Charters, nos 332, 335–7; JRULM, EGR 1/1/2/4; JRULM, Arley Charters, box 8, no. 17; Chester CRO, CR 63/2/679; CCRO, DDX 78/4; CCRO, Tabley House Collection, DLT/A12/1.

[9] King, *Vale Royall*, p. 99.

[10] *DKR* 37, p. 228.

manors of Dunham Massey and Warburton. The area in debate was moss land and later evidence suggests that it was rights of turbary in particular which were at issue.[11] Similarly, in 1464 John Daniel and Geoffrey Boydell contended the boundary between three parcels of land in Lymm township.[12] In addition to those arguments which saw neighbours taking issue with one another, disputes centred on land could be wholly family affairs. After the death without issue of Thomas Massey of Tatton on 8 August 1420, Margaret his widow and Geoffrey his brother fell into disagreement over the division of his lands. Alice, the late Thomas's mother, was owed rent out of the estate of her dead son and supported Geoffrey in the dispute. The recently widowed Margaret was no doubt concerned to protect her interests but, unsympathetic to her position, one nineteenth-century observer pointed to the 'perverseness of her sex' in explaining the origins of the dispute![13]

At times, the Bucklow gentry found themselves embroiled in more widespread disputes. These perhaps initially revolved around such clear-cut issues of the type already mentioned but became increasingly intractable in the absence of an immediate settlement. Such an escalation probably led to a widening of the circle of protagonists. In 1441, Sir John and Randal Mainwaring of Over Peover, 'and other diverse of their feysshyip, tenauntes and servantes' were in dispute with a near neighbour John Legh of Booths, his brother Roger and their likewise described followers. Similarly, in 1445 the same John Legh of Booths, William Legh of Timperley and Richard Ashton clashed with five members of the Carrington family. In neither case is a clearly defined reason for the disagreement given. In 1446, two disputing parties headed by Sir Lawrence Fitton of Gawsworth and John Legh of Booths respectively were subject to an arbitration award. Three of the more obscure individuals named had been involved in a fracas, Honkyn Lawrence striking John and Lawrence Asthill. After the assault, John Legh had provided protection for the perpetrator. Why such high-ranking gentlemen should involve

---

[11] JRULM, EGR 1/1/2/4; JRULM, Arley Charters, box 12, no. 24.
[12] CCRO, DDX/78/4.
[13] *DKR* 37, p. 516; JRULM, Mascie of Tatton MS 21. The nineteenth-century commentator was a certain T. Hughes in *The Cheshire Sheaf*, 2, ser. 1 (1883), pp. 42–3.

themselves in such a dispute is not clear, but it is possible that the men named were either their servants or tenants. What is clear is that the disagreements between the two groups were quite complex and that issues concerning land tenure were an ingredient in them. One of the party's subsidiary disputes was between Sir Robert Booth and Robert Fawdon and concerned a parcel of land in Warford. In 1450 there was another display of violence apparently prompted by a struggle over landed estate. A group headed once again by John Legh of Booths was at loggerheads with Thomas Daniel of Tabley senior over the 'ravishment and away taking of Margerie doghter and here to William of Tabley and warde to ye same Thomas Danyell' by Legh and his associates. It is apparent from the terms of the eventual award that a disagreement over the inheritance of Margerie had prompted the abduction.[14]

The prominent position of John Legh of Booths in the foregoing accounts is noteworthy, the details of his confrontations coming down to us in an impressive collection of family deeds. Whether he was typical of his social class and time in terms of the extent to which he involved himself in such disputes we cannot tell. His peers may well have been more reasonable or may simply have been faced with fewer contentious situations. Alternatively, accidents of survival may mean that details of their conflicts are lost to us. To measure accurately gentry conflict and its relative levels would require a complete historical record producing not just crude statistics, but also a faithful picture of individual personalities and potential crisis points. In the absence of this, such an assessment is impossible.

When such crisis points arose, the whole potential for the success of a mediation rested upon a degree of consensus among the disputing parties: they had to agree that the matter dividing them required resolution. Where this initial consensus was present, there was a greater chance of the eventual settlement being a lasting one and, in this, arbitration had a distinct advantage over settlement through the law courts. There must have been a number of different types of pressure which led those in dispute to turn to arbitration. In many cases there would have come a point when continued conflict became obviously detrimental to both parties. Human nature inevitably dictates a wide range of social conflicts but fortunately it also prescribes an appreciation of the

---

[14] University of Keele, Legh of Booths Charters, nos 332, 335–7.

need for compromise, whether borne of self-interest or a concern for the greater good. Competing property claims must have made estate management extremely difficult, particularly in terms of rent collection. Peer pressure must also have been a factor in many decisions to turn to arbitration. An idea of how this may have operated is given in a letter from the Plumpton Correspondence. When Sir William Plumpton and Henry Pierpoint, esquire, found themselves in dispute in the early 1460s, Sir William received a letter from Sir Richard Bingham to whom he was related by marriage. The letter strongly suggested that the two should put their differences to the arbitration of Sir Richard and Sir John Markham. Sir Richard Bingham argued that for them to do so would not only be in their own best interests, but also in those of 'the rest of the country'.[15] The resolution of conflict was, therefore, seen as the concern not simply of those in dispute but also of the wider community: no doubt the gentry of Bucklow heard similar appeals to the greater good. Arbitration probably came to be seen as the natural course of action in the event of a dispute which was not immediately resolved by other means. The regularity with which the gentry of Bucklow hundred resorted to its use certainly suggests that this was the case.

The alternatives to arbitration included recourse to the law courts. In fact, Edward Powell asserts that 'the most striking feature of arbitration in late medieval England is the frequency with which it occurs in conjunction with litigation'.[16] In a number of the Bucklow cases, it is clear that the dispute had resulted in a legal suit prior to coming before the arbiters. Faced with the costly and convoluted legal procedures of the time, it is understandable that gentlemen in dispute chose arbitration. Whether the initial attempts to seek a solution in the law courts were ever intended to be pursued to the end, or were simply used as a means to force the other party to accept arbitration as a means of settlement, is debatable. If the latter was the case, then this perhaps removed the voluntarism upon which the potential for success of the arbitration process to an extent rested, and may explain some of its failures. Alternatively, the decision to turn to arbitration in such circumstances may have been a result of

---

[15] *The Plumpton Correspondence*, ed. T. Stapleton, (Gloucester, 1990) p. 4.
[16] Powell, 'Arbitration and the Law', p. 55.

encouragement offered by the established legal system, rather than a reaction against it. By the fifteenth century a long tradition of law courts promoting 'lovedays' had been established, and the officials and institutions of the palatinate of Chester were certainly geared towards aiding gentlemen in dispute who wished to settle their differences by means of arbitration.[17]

However the decision to follow the course of arbitration came about, the next step was to make out an arbitration bond. These bonds represent the most substantial type of evidence for arbitration. There were two types. Those which were made privately may be found in the numerous family muniment collections. There are only four surviving examples of these for Bucklow hundred.[18] Alternatively there are those which were made in the exchequer at Chester, forty-five of which involved the Bucklow gentry during our period.[19] Even allowing for the higher rate of non-survival among the private bonds, these figures would suggest that the enrolment of a bond at the exchequer was the preferred option. In both types, the parties in dispute recognised a fictitious debt which, in private bonds, is always to the other party. It has been suggested that these were kept by an impartial third party in case of default, to be produced for the benefit of the offended in such an event.[20] In the official bonds the debt is nearly always to the king or earl of Chester, occasionally to the other party, and sometimes, but rarely, to another named individual. It is from these bonds that the arbitration process took its legal force. The actual awards could not be enforced by a court of law, but, in the event of default by either party, the other could take out an action for debt. In both the official bonds from the Chester exchequer and the extant private bonds the parties in dispute promised to abide by the terms of the eventual award. Consequently, the calendarer of the recognizance rolls has termed these entries as recognizances 'to abide the award of . . .'. This though is, in a sense, a misnomer. The final clause of arbitration bonds in Cheshire, both official and private, is always that the

[17] Bennett, 'The Medieval Loveday', pp. 353–7.
[18] JRULM, Arley Charters, box 8, no. 28; Chester CRO, CR 63/2/679; CCRO, DDX 78/3; CCRO, DLT/A12/1.
[19] See n. 3 above.
[20] Powell, 'Arbitration and the Law', p. 57.

acknowledged debt becomes null and void upon the day of the making of the award itself. Presumably, after this, the legal force of the bond was lost. Thus, although the spirit of observance is expressed in the bonds, their real purpose was to ensure the production of an award, the policing of that observance *ad infinitum* being seen as unrealistic.

Many of the surviving early recognizances have the appearance of being real rather than fictitious debts, the recording of these real debts apparently being the original purpose of the recognizance rolls.[21] Quite how the practice evolved of enrolling bonds of obligation at the exchequer in the form of mutually acknowledged fictitious debts is not clear, but it was certainly an established practice by the beginning of the fifteenth century. The fact that there was a facility at the Chester exchequer to take out bonds with the specific purpose of settling a dispute by means of arbitration suggests that the process had become institutionalised. The choice of arbiters and the organisation of the ensuing negotiations may well have been within the remit of the exchequer staff. The fact that the vast majority of the recognizances enrolled at the exchequer acknowledged debts to the earl or king rather than to the other party certainly indicates that the palatinate officials actively encouraged the gentry of the county to resort to arbitration in the event of dispute, with the extent to which palatinate officials acted as arbiters reinforcing this view. The idea gains further weight when arbitration recognizances are considered in the context of the researches of Dorothy Clayton into similarly enrolled recognizances to keep the peace which, along with recognizances to appear, far outnumber arbitration recognizances. Clayton concluded that the high incidence of these, far from indicating a high level of uncontrolled social conflict among the Cheshire gentry, was due to pre-emptive attempts to maintain law and order by the palatinate authorities and the gentry community.[22] Sometimes an arbitration recognizance followed closely after the making of one to keep the peace and, in one of the Bucklow cases, the two types of recognizance were combined. Hence those involved were bound both to keep the peace and to put their differences

---

[21] *VCH Cheshire*, 2, ed. B.E. Harris, (Oxford, 1979) p. 22.
[22] Clayton, 'Peace Bonds', p. 148.

before the arbiters.[23] Arbitration recognizances were probably encouraged as an alternative to peace recognizances in cases where arbitration seemed the appropriate course of action. It is important, therefore, that the participation of the Bucklow gentry in the making of arbitration bonds is set firmly in the wider context of other conditional bonds which were officially enrolled. Given this high level of official involvement, the making of private bonds was perhaps indicative of a concern on the part of the protagonists to retain control over the settlement process, or perhaps to avoid the charges made by the exchequer.

The success of attempts at arbitration necessitated the committed involvement of many more individuals than those in disagreement. The sums involved in the making of initial bonds were not insignificant, ranging from £10 to £2000. In the vast majority of cases, therefore, it was considered necessary for those in dispute to find sureties for the reciprocal debts they recognised. In all but eight of the Bucklow recognizances, sureties were required. The remainder detail the names of well over a hundred individuals who acted in this capacity.[24] It might be thought that the surety system exacerbated the divisions within the local gentry community by encouraging the taking of sides. While an examination of the composition of surety groups emphasises the importance of the familial bonds, there is no evidence of more widely based factions. Indeed, on occasions, the same people acted as sureties for both parties.[25] Arbitration encouraged social cohesion within gentry society, class solidarity being crucial to its operation.

Also critical to the success of the arbitration process in Bucklow hundred was the committed involvement of those who acted as arbiters. Private bonds rarely contain the names of those nominated to this role, while those enrolled at the Chester exchequer and the awards themselves always give these details. The surviving recognizance rolls give the names of 125 individuals who were elected to act as arbiters. Of these, forty-nine were, at some point, nominated to arbitrate in a dispute which involved the Bucklow gentry. In addition, supplementary sources provide the names of fourteen others who acted in the

[23] *DKR* 37, pp. 227, 762.
[24] *DKR* 37, pp. 58, 225–7, 495, 642, 743, 763.
[25] *DKR* 37, p. 493.

same capacity.[26] Thomas Gascoigne wrote of how the 'quarrels and dissensions which arose within a parish or between parishioners' were settled by the 'good handling and advice' of the local clergy.[27] In contrast to this rather idealised view, mediation in gentry disputes was almost wholly secular in the palatinate of Chester, there being no evidence of a churchman acting as arbiter in a Bucklow dispute. Whereas sureties tended to be drawn from the full spectrum of local gentry society, arbiters were more likely to have come from palatinate officialdom. Of forty-five Bucklow recognizances, sixteen name the chamberlain as either the sole arbiter or one of a group. Individuals who played a prominent part in the palatinate administration, such as William Chaunterell, sergeant-at-law, were named in this capacity on twenty-seven occasions.

Arbiters in the Bucklow cases were without exception male. In the wider arena of the palatinate, there is evidence of only one woman being nominated for such a role. This was in a non-Bucklow dispute, and the woman concerned was Joan, wife of Chamberlain William Troutbeck. She was the daughter of William Massey of Rixton in Lancashire, and in 1430 received an annuity of £20 out of the Chester exchequer on account of her overseas service in the company of Katherine of Valois, the king's mother.[28] There is evidence of what might be termed 'great man' arbitration, when a single powerful man acted alone in deciding upon a settlement. His influence had to be such that a unilateral settlement would be taken seriously. By far the most prominent sole arbiter in a Bucklow dispute was William de la Pole, earl of Suffolk. He was granted the office of justice in Chester in February, 1440, but there is no evidence to suggest that he ever visited the palatinate during his justiceship. It is possible that he heard the case between Sir Geoffrey Warburton, Maria widow of William Arrowsmith and a group headed by Sir John Savage, from a distance, but it is more likely that he acted through local representatives, probably his official deputies, Sir Thomas Stanley, William Burghley and Richard Bold.[29] William Troutbeck, appointed chamberlain in 1412, was a

---

[26] For the documents from which these calculations were made see nn. 7 and 8 above.
[27] Cited in *York and Lancaster 1399–1485*, ed. W.G. Jones, (London, 1920) p. 73.
[28] *DKR* 37, p. 518; *CPR, 1429–30*, p. 81.
[29] *DKR* 37, pp. 673, 763.

staunch Lancastrian who became a nationally significant figure, acquiring many grants of offices, lands and honours, mainly in the palatinates of Lancaster and Chester. He acted as sole arbiter in a Bucklow dispute on two occasions.[30] Other individuals who made such unilateral awards and who held prominent positions in the local government of Chester were William Chaunterell, John Dedwood, and James del Holt.[31] All three at some time held the position of vice-justice or vice-chamberlain of the palatinate. Sometimes, individuals who acted alone in this capacity did not hold high office within the palatinate administration. Sir John Stanley, Hamo Massey of Rixton and John Leycester of Tabley fall into this category. The first half of the fifteenth century saw the Stanleys of Lathom grow to be the most powerful family in the north-west of England. Despite being first and foremost a Lancashire family, its members were heavily involved in Cheshire affairs, being well established in the county by the second quarter of the century. Sir John Stanley (d. 1437) is named as sole arbiter in four of the recognizances relating to Bucklow disputes. Hamo Massey was also a Lancastrian from just across the Mersey, and John Leycester of Tabley was the head of a Bucklow gentry family of the middle ranks. Each acted as sole arbiter on one occasion, in disputes which were not referred to them through the exchequer.[32] A broadly based settlement probably stood more chance of lasting success. Arbiters in Bucklow disputes usually acted in groups, with two or more individuals acting together in formulating terms. It was common for two or three arbiters to be elected on behalf of each party. This was desirable in particularly contentious disputes, possibly involving violence, and allowed for negotiations to be conducted by those not directly involved while ensuring that each side was well represented. In cases like this it was no doubt often difficult to arrive at a satisfactory settlement. Consequently, it was usual for an ultimate sole arbiter to be named who was to make an award in the

[30] A full account of Troutbeck's career is given in J. Brownbill, 'The Troutbeck Family', *Journal of the Chester and North Wales Archaeological and Historic Society*, new ser., 28, pt. 2 (1928), pp. 147–79. For his role as sole arbiter in Bucklow disputes, see *DKR* 37, pp. 58, 517.

[31] Both Chaunterell and Holt served as vice-justice: *DKR* 37, p. 671; *DKR* 36, p. 242. Dedwood held the office of vice-chamberlain: *DKR* 36, p. 140; *DKR* 37, p. 197.

[32] *DKR* 37, pp. 229, 447, 641; JRULM, Arley Charters, box 8, no. 17; University of Keele, Legh of Booths Charters, no. 337.

event of a stalemate. In the surviving examples, this is normally either William Troutbeck or Sir John Stanley.[33]

Although they no doubt had some prior knowledge of the details of a particular dispute, the arbiters were obliged to give each party its opportunity to present a case. Quite how this pre-award process worked in detail is not clear, but the awards indicate that each would have had an opportunity to put forward both verbal and written testimony. A small sample of arbitration recognizances indicates that the period between bond and award was normally at least two months. When the dispute revolved around matters of land tenure, one can assume that the presentation of documentary evidence played a significant part in the process. William Paston wisely advised his son Edmund to study law because, as his wife later reiterated, 'whosoever schould dwell at Paston schould have need to con defend himself'.[34] No doubt many Bucklow gentlemen had received similar advice. A legal background would certainly have aided them in putting their cases forward, but they must have relied primarily on the family muniment chest. This was obviously seen as an armoury of written title to be used in the event of any hostile challenge. When, in around 1420, John Legh of Booths raided the family home of his wife, Anne, it should not surprise us that, along with 'a gret newe long mete table', 'vi silver spoons', and 'ii pairs shetes for gentilmen newe', he also took all the 'munimentes, evidences and dedes' that he found. By this confiscation, he severely weakened the family's hold on its estates and, not surprisingly, when Legh agreed to return the stolen property, he also had to swear on the Bible that the deed collection was complete.[35] As part of the settlement to the Massey of Tatton inheritance dispute, Margaret was to deliver to Geoffrey 'all dedes and mumyments yat she has or may gete'. Interestingly, she was also to relate whatever information she had concerning documents in the hands of others which might have a bearing on Geoffrey's inheritance.[36] It was therefore considered important to have not only a strong collection of title deeds, but also

---

[33] e.g., PRO, CHES 2/99.
[34] *The Paston Letters*, ed. N. Davis, (Oxford, 1983) p. 8.
[35] University of Keele, Legh of Booths Charters, no. 3.
[36] JRULM, Mascie of Tatton MS 39.

a good knowledge of relevant deeds held elsewhere. With both in his possession, a gentleman would be well placed in the event of a dispute.

The awards are the most informative documents associated with the arbitration process. Although there was a facility to enrol bonds at the exchequer and there was a heavy involvement on the part of the palatinate officials in the award process, there are no surviving official copies of the eventual awards. The extant awards in Bucklow cases come from family muniment collections and provide details of those in dispute, those chosen to arbitrate, and usually the cause of the disagreement. Most importantly, they give the terms of settlement. In cases where there appears to have been a general breakdown of good relations it was usual for the first clause to be a simple direction for amity between the two parties. The award made by Thomas Weever and Thomas Fitton in such a dispute decreed that the two parties should be 'gode fryndes' and went on to state that the two parties should not pursue any legal actions against each other which related to offences committed before the award date.[37] In this case, therefore, arbitration was being used to call a truce between the two parties, the root cause of the trouble not being addressed in any detail. The lack of a fundamental solution should not be seen as a failure of the process, but rather as an indication of its flexibility. No doubt in many cases a cessation of hostilities was the best that could be hoped for.

In those disputes where the matters at issue were more clearly defined, the terms of the award were more specific. It is upon these terms that the reputation of the arbitration process for common sense largely rests. They display a real concern for achieving a settlement acceptable to both parties. In terms of the Bucklow cases, this spirit of compromise is best seen in the award by James del Holt in the Massey of Tatton inheritance dispute. Its contents are worthy of detailed description.[38] As was explained earlier, the dispute was sparked off by the death of Thomas Massey of Tatton and involved Margaret, his widow, on the one part, and Geoffrey, his brother and heir, along with Alice, his mother, on the other part. Holt decided that Alice should receive the rent arrears owed out of Thomas's estate and that Margaret should retain possession

---

[37] University of Keele, Legh of Booths Charters, no. 332.
[38] JRULM, Massie of Tatton MS 39.

of all lands which she and Thomas had received as jointure. Margaret was also to have £15 worth of land, this presumably being equal to the third of Thomas's lands to which she was legally entitled. The conveyance was to be made only after consultation with Geoffrey's brothers, and was to be overseen by the arbiter. Wider family involvement reduced the possibility of continued disagreement. After Margaret had received what was rightly hers, Geoffrey was to take possession of the remainder of his brother's estate. The award also deals with the implementation of these terms in some detail, and again there is an obvious effort to avoid further conflict. To this end, Holt ensured that Margaret's retreat from the family seat was gradual. She was to be allowed to use the barns at Tatton to shelter her cattle and store corn until March, paying the usual charge for each animal lying out. After this date Margaret was to be allowed the use of the barns outside the gates of the same manor until 3 May. As the award was given on 9 January 1421 these terms meant that Margaret was not forced to make alternative arrangements until the winter had passed.

It was matters of topography rather than family affairs which faced William Massey, esquire, John Needham, and Roger Legh, arbiters in the border dispute between Sir Robert Booth and Sir Geoffrey Warburton. No doubt the troubles surrounding the disputed border had involved trespass by both parties. However, instead of dealing with these symptoms of the problem by apportioning blame, the arbiters arrived at a practical solution aimed at removing the root cause. The eventual award, delivered on 8 August 1446, consisted of an attempt to demarcate more clearly the boundary of the two manors.[39] It was decided that three great stones were to be set at specified places, the border being the imaginary line running through their centres. In 1465 a similar resolution was arrived at in the previously described dispute between John Daniel and Geoffrey Boydell, concerning the boundaries of three parcels of land in the township of Lymm.[40]

Arbitration was well used by the Bucklow gentry. Whether as a disputant, surety, or, more rarely, as an arbiter, a significant proportion of the Bucklow gentry would have had personal experience of the process during their lifetime.

---

[39] Both copies of the indented award survive: JRULM, Arley Charters, box 8, no. 15.
[40] CCRO, DDX 78/4.

The relationships within such a closely knit society would have ensured that those who had no direct involvement would none the less have seen arbitration at close quarters. In terms of identifying those who were considered to be the gentlemen of the hundred at the time, there is one particularly helpful document which, unfortunately, only survives as a manuscript copy made by the nineteenth-century historian of Cheshire, J.P. Earwaker.[41] The original, dated 1445, appears to have been a list of all those in Cheshire who were eligible for jury service. Arranged by hundred, the Bucklow section gives the names of sixty-six individuals. Their inclusion on the list stemmed from the prime indicator of gentility in Cheshire at that time: involvement in the palatinate administration. It does indeed have the appearance of a directory of Bucklow's significant families with a small number of sub-gentry inclusions, this being confirmed by supplementary sources. The most prominent Bucklow families of the period were: Warburton of Warburton, Booth of Dunham Massey, Carrington of Carrington, Aston of Aston, Savage of Rock Savage and Clifton, Massey of Tatton and Dutton of Dutton. These families constituted the knightly class of the hundred and this is well represented in the evidence for arbitration. Indeed, of the sixty-four recorded Bucklow protagonists, thirty-eight came from these six families. In addition, these families often supplied sureties for gentlemen in dispute, the Dutton family of Dutton doing so on seventeen occasions.[42] The over-representation of the greater gentry in the historical record may be due to the fact that they had easier access to the officially sanctioned process through the exchequer. It may also be due to the fact that their more substantial, and often diffuse, estates provided greater scope for disagreement. The middle ranks of the Bucklow gentry, represented by families such as Mainwaring of Over Peover and Legh of Booths, also turned to arbitration in the event of disagreement, and the gentlemen of such families acted as sureties for others. From the lower end of the spectrum of Bucklow gentry society came families such as Millington of Millington, Legh of Timperley and Mere of Mere, who were also participants in the arbitration process on several occasions during our period.

[41] Chester CRO, CR 63/1/7/1.
[42] The figures given have been derived from those documents listed in nn. 7 and 8 above.

Arbitration was central to the resolution of gentry disputes in Bucklow hundred. However, it is difficult to assess exactly how successful the process was in achieving lasting settlements, particularly when the cause of the dispute is obscure. It is true that successive arbitration bonds were often made by disputants, sometimes spanning a number of years. This would suggest that initial attempts at an enduring resolution failed in these cases. It is important to recognise, though, that the protagonists no doubt realised that this might be the case and that the arbitration process allowed for these opening failures. This was made clear in a dispute between Isabella, widow of William del Mere, Matthew del Mere and the families of Leycester of Tabley and Daniers. In the initial bond of 1408, the two parties agreed to abide by the award of Sir Lawrence Fitton, John Legh del Booths, Robert Townley, Sir Peter Dutton, Sir Philip Brereton and Henry Bircheles. The bond also provided for the eventuality that these arbiters might not be able to arrive at a satisfactory award and so named a reserve group of arbiters: Sir George Carrington, John Savage and John Pigot.[43] The document provides a reminder that the arbitration process could fail because those named as arbiters could not agree on a judicious settlement rather than because the protagonists were not keen to compromise. The intricacies and vagaries of medieval land law not only provided scope for argument, but made for difficulties in resolution.

One case which did see a satisfactory resolution was the Massey of Tatton inheritance dispute. This is the best example of successful arbitration in Bucklow hundred. It is also the best documented of all the Bucklow cases, there being twelve pieces of documentary evidence pertaining to the execution of the settlement, the last of these attesting to the delivery by Margaret to Geoffrey Massey of 294 charters relating to his estates.[44] It would be inappropriate, though, to apply the simple measure of 'success' or 'failure' to all the Bucklow cases. The surviving evidence does not allow such an analysis and, in a society where methods of law enforcement were so unsophisticated, such an approach would be crude. The crucial fact is that the gentry of Bucklow, and of Cheshire as a whole, persisted in their resort to arbitration in times of dispute. At best,

[43] CCRO, DLT/A12/1.
[44] JRULM, Mascie of Tatton MS 38–48, 50.

this indicates that the process proved a resounding success; at worst, and perhaps more realistically, it meant that they recognised the intervention of a mediating influence as consistently holding the best chance of a lasting settlement. I have already mentioned the dispute surrounding the border between the manors of Dunham Massey and Warburton which, in the middle of the fifteenth century, divided Sir Robert Booth and Sir Geoffrey Warburton. At that time, these two knights were simply the immediate possessors of a dispute which dated back at least to the beginning of the previous century. As the conflict persisted into the sixteenth century, the award, delivered in August 1446, could be regarded as a failure. Despite this, the inheritors of the dispute continued to place their faith in the arbitration process. When, in 1517, Sir William Booth and John Warburton again placed the matter before the arbiters, they eventually agreed once more to observe the boundary markers decreed by the settlement more than seventy years earlier. These were by then known as the 'old meyn stones'.[45]

---

[45] For the fourteenth-century reference see JRULM, Warburton of Arley Muniments, box 1, folder 1; JRULM, Arley Charters, box 12, no. 5.

4
'I SEE BY SIZT OF EVIDENCE': INFORMATION GATHERING IN LATE MEDIEVAL CHESHIRE

Deborah Marsh

Medieval society depended on the records of the past. By the fifteenth century the expansion of practical literacy and the increasing availability of written material meant more people were becoming accustomed to referring to a book or an archive for information.[1] Deeds were commonly used to support claims to land, legal rights and ancestry. Within Crown administrations, monastic communities, and some noble households, the collection of evidence and its systematic organisation into archives was already advanced.[2] As a consequence these muniments have received considerable attention by latter-day historians. However, there has been a relative neglect of the archival work undertaken by those among the middle strata of society. This paper examines the way in which information relating to property and family rights was gathered and utilised among late medieval Cheshire gentry. It briefly surveys the reasons for collecting information and the likely places of storage. It then focuses on one particular Cheshire gentleman, Humphrey Newton of Newton and Pownall (1466–1536), and investigates his motives for gathering information, the sources upon which he drew, and the methods he employed. Finally, it explores the influence that the research attempted by Humphrey and others had on the growing interest

---

[1] For the increasing importance of written documents from the reign of Edward I, see M.T. Clanchy, *From Memory to Written Record: England 1066–1307* (2nd edn., Oxford, 1993), particularly p. 330.

[2] Ibid, pp. 154–72. For an archive organised by a nobleman, Edward, duke of Buckingham (d. 1521), see C. Rawcliffe, 'The papers of Edward, duke of Buckingham', *Journal of the Society of Archivists*, 5 (1976).

in local history and topography – often called antiquarianism – evident from the fifteenth century onwards.

As land was a source of wealth and prestige, considerable time and effort were put into protecting and extending property. Brute force and bribery played a part in this, but even here justification for action was usually supported by reference to written evidence. Title deeds were the most important, particularly as the law decreed that they rightly belonged to the party with the best claim to a holding. Deeds did not in themselves 'prove' a title to land; it was the decision of the court or of commissioned arbitrators that verified the claims. Yet legal action often hung on the production of deeds. Arbitrators commonly asked to see all deeds and proofs which the disputing parties could provide in support of their case.[3]

A wise landlord did not wait until a legal action raised the question of evidence. In a 'law-minded' age, it was best to be prepared. On entering a new inheritance, or before purchasing land, the basis on which land was held and the possibility of present and future claimants needed to be ascertained. The complications brought about by the increased use of entails – with the rise in the number of relevant deeds – meant careful and lengthy research was required.[4] Those with claims to land were advised to gather pertinent information however small the probability of a claim seemed at the time. Misfortunes could rekindle old claims, accidents elevate obscure men to new heights.[5] Even if the deeds had no obvious use in the collector's lifetime, there was the chance that later generations would be grateful to their careful ancestor as they reaped the rewards of a windfall inheritance.[6] Deeds were equally necessary in defence of a particular right such as a licence for free warren, or the avoidance of certain county duties. Cheshire inhabitants, for example, were required to produce

---

[3] P. Fleming, 'The character and private concerns of the gentry of Kent' (unpub. Ph.D thesis, University of Wales, 1985), p. 346.

[4] P.S. Lewis, 'Sir John Fastolf's lawsuit over Titchwell 1448–55', *The Historical Journal*, 1 (1958), pp. 1–20.

[5] For the chance advancement of John Hopton on account of relatives' deaths and infertility, see C. Richmond, *John Hopton: A Fifteenth-Century Suffolk Gentleman* (Cambridge, 1981), ch. 1.

[6] T. Foulds, 'Medieval cartularies', *Archives*, 17, no. 77 (1987), p. 21, on the collecting of deeds without knowing their immediate use.

INFORMATION GATHERING 73

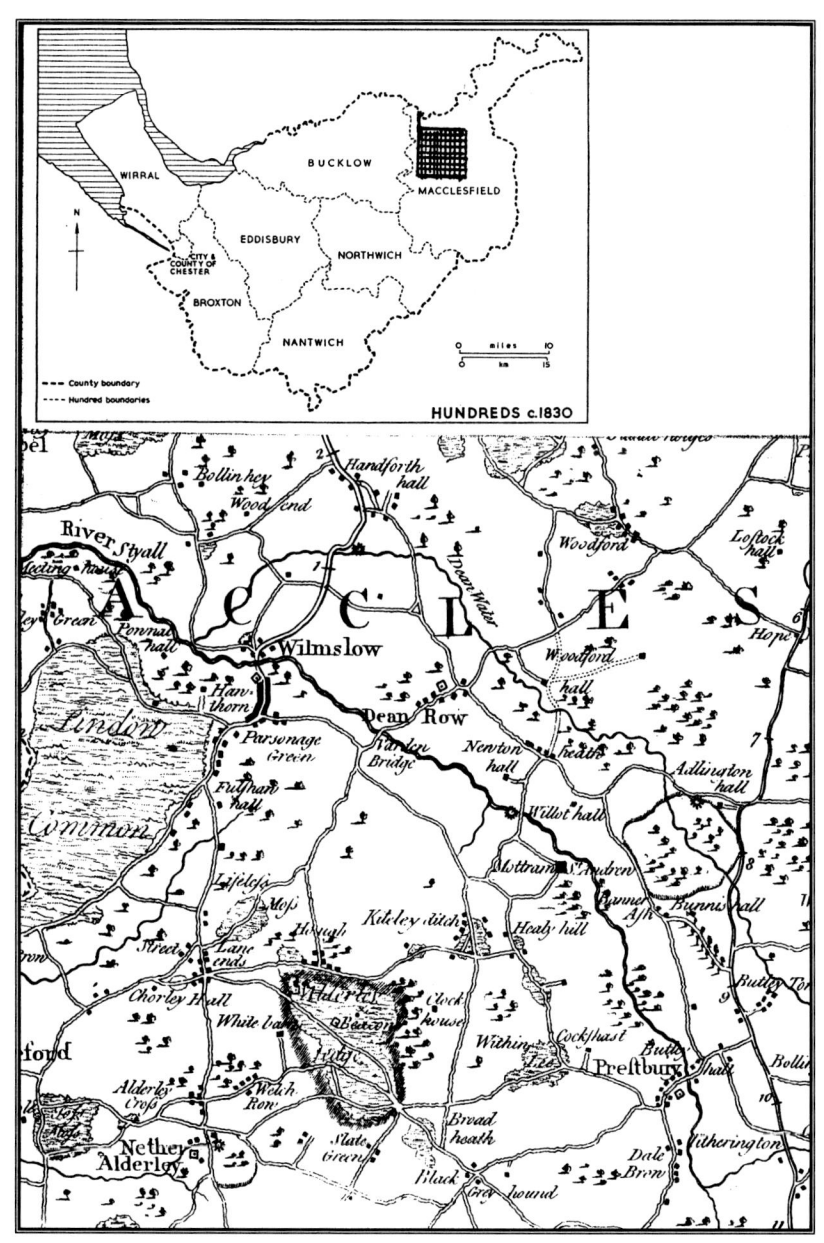

The area of Humphrey Newton's estates in Macclesfield Hundred, Cheshire, from Peter Burdett's map of Cheshire, 1777.

evidence for privileges claimed by charter of the earl of Chester at *quo warranto* proceedings held at Chester in 1499.[7] Attached seals could play a major role in attributing armorial bearings; an example is provided by the famous Scrope/Grosvenor case.[8] Recorded names of grantor, grantee, feoffees and witness lists were of key importance for constructing genealogies which were used to prove an ancient and distinguished pedigree, and had the practical value of identifying heirs and titles to land. And from the sixteenth century heralds placed emphasis on the production of deeds to prove a right to bear arms.

It was therefore essential that a family knew what documentation was available to defend its land, rights and status. Ideally the landholder would be in possession of all deeds relevant to his holdings. By the eleventh century the importance of written evidence had led to its safe-keeping among precious objects such as jewels or within illuminated manuscripts.[9] The substantial growth in documentation in subsequent centuries encouraged the monasteries, and eventually the Crown, to create permanent repositories organised with a view to being used for reference. By the fifteenth century the gentry were also finding themselves the holders of numerous documents. It is clear from the contents of the fifteenth-century cartulary owned by Sir John Byrom of Clayton (south Lancashire), that he had a well organised archive, or treasury, containing over three hundred deeds.[10] Not all families took care of their muniments and too little survives to reconstruct Cheshire family archive organisation. The need to ensure that deeds remained within the family residence is, however, evident in the bequests which mention muniments. In his will Sir Geoffrey Mascy of Tatton (d. 1456), for instance, left his heir, John, all the deeds, muniments and records pertaining to family lands in Audlem and Wrenbury.[11]

---

[7] R. Stewart-Brown, 'The Cheshire writs of *Quo Warranto* in 1499', *EHR*, 49 (1934), p. 680. The petitions are found in the *quo warranto* rolls: PRO, Palatinate of Chester, *Quo Warranto* Rolls, CHES 34.

[8] N.H. Nicolas, *The Scrope and Grosvenor Controversy* (2 vols, London, 1832), *passim*.

[9] Clanchy, *From Memory to Written Record*, p. 154.

[10] Bodl, MS Rawlinson B460.

[11] W.M. Fergusson Irvine, *A Collection of Lancashire and Cheshire Wills* (Record Society of Lancashire and Cheshire, 30, 1896), p. 15. See also the number of medieval documents stored in Cheshire family archives which are now housed in the Cheshire Record Office and the John Rylands University Library, Manchester.

Nevertheless, it was inevitable that certain deeds would be stored away from the family residence either by choice or by force. At times title deeds were kept with the overlord of an estate; at others they were retained by a residing tenant or farmer. Documentation might also be lost or stolen. Court cases provide ample examples of appropriated deeds in late medieval Cheshire. William Davenport of Bramhall, esquire, and his wife, Alice, were accused of burning the evidence which supported the claims of Nicholas Davenport to land in Wilmslow. Sir Edmund Trafford allegedly stole the deeds of John Trafford that concerned Wimbold Trafford, and John Mainwaring of Peover, esquire, was accused of taking deeds and evidences belonging to John Gibbons and documenting lands in Staffordshire and Shropshire.[12] Such cases showed the clear need for a secure repository for deeds; it often led to their placement in trust with a third party. A common location was a monastery in which an archive already existed. A church was another favoured repository.[13] Cheshire parishioners are known to have placed important deeds with clergymen: at the turn of the sixteenth century several gentlemen entrusted a cleric, Robert Tatton, with documents relating to the manor of Ashton, Cheshire.[14]

Dispersed deeds meant that landholders needed to look beyond their own households for appropriate information. There was an expectation that landholders would know the exact whereabouts of their deeds. In an arbitration award of 1421 James del Holt, arbitrator between Geoffrey de Mascy of Tatton and Margaret his mother, required both Mascy's deeds of inheritance and 'also ye foresayd Mergret shall gyf as gode enformacon & knawlege as sho con or may quere & in quos possession any deds bene þt appenten to the forsayd heritage'.[15] The only sure way of identifying all, or at least a majority of, the information on one's landed interests was to search relevant archives. For wealthy landlords, this was accomplished by employing paid researchers, common throughout the later Middle Ages. Undoubtedly the best known is William Worcester, 'Fastolf's

---

[12] PRO, Chancery, Early Chancery Proceedings, C1/499/2–8, C1/595/10, C1/316/96.
[13] Clanchy, *From Memory to Written Record*, p. 156.
[14] PRO, C1/606/37–39.
[15] JRULM, Tatton MS 39 (transcript kindly provided by David Tilsley).

professional record searcher and tracer of pedigrees'.[16] There was also John Rous, who made searches on behalf of the earls of Warwick.[17] The correspondence of the Paston and Plumpton families reveal paid researchers: the lawyers and stewards who searched for information on behalf of their lords.[18]

That, however, was at the top end of society. Professional researchers were beyond the resources of lesser landholders. Several fifteenth-century letters illustrate the expense of a researcher's fee, travel and the money paid to make the searches in the courts: 'The serch and the copy of the wrytts out of the cort to another costeth much money, and the feed of them and great soliciting . . . the premysse maketh my purse light.'[19]

Humphrey Newton, a member of Cheshire's lesser gentry, illustrates one of the options available to those with fewer resources. He made his own journeys to archives and households, and transcribed the necessary deeds by his own research. His information gathering is detailed in two manuscripts he compiled in the late fifteenth and early sixteenth century: a cartulary and a commonplace book. The cartulary now survives in a copy made by his son c. 1565.[20] It is a slim volume consisting of thirty-two leaves which betrays signs of missing folios. To all appearances it was probably compiled in relation to a rather ambitious case Humphrey was formulating against his more powerful neighbour, Robert Pigot of Butley (d. 1536).[21] The larger and more important manuscript is the commonplace book, a work of 129 leaves, predominantly paper, written in

[16] K.B. McFarlane, 'William Worcester: a preliminary survey', in *England in the Fifteenth Century: Collected Essays* (London, 1981), p. 207. Fastolf was also aided by many other researchers: see Lewis, 'Sir John Fastolf's lawsuit', pp. 9–15.

[17] T.D. Kendrick, *British Antiquity* (London, 1950), pp. 19–29; A. Gransden, *Historical Writing in England, II: c. 1307 to the Early Sixteenth Century* (London, 1982), p. 311; *The Rous Roll* (Gloucester, 1980), particularly the introduction by C. Ross, pp. v–xviii.

[18] *The Paston Letters, 1422–1509*, ed. J. Gairdner (London, 1904, repr. Gloucester, 1986), e.g. nos 10, 355 and 370; *The Plumpton Correspondence*, ed. T. Stapleton (Gloucester, 1990), nos xv, lxiii; and cxiii; A. Gransden, 'Antiquarian studies in fifteenth-century England', *Antiquaries Journal*, 60 (1980), pp. 84–9; N. Ramsey, 'Retained legal counsel, c. 1275–c. 1475', *TRHS*, 5th ser., 35 (1985), pp. 101–2.

[19] *The Plumpton Correspondence*, p. 91.

[20] BL, Add. MS 42134A; a reasonable though not always reliable transcription by J.P. Earwaker is provided as BL, Add. MS 42134B.

[21] Briefly, this was an attempt to elevate Newton, a hamlet of the township of Butley, into a township in its own right: see PRO, Court of Star Chamber, Proceedings: Henry VIII, STAC 2/30/86.

English, Latin and some law French.[22] It was begun in 1497 and is an important witness to the interests and work of a member of the lesser gentry. Among its varied contents are household accounts, medical recipes, literary extracts and poetry. Both manuscripts contain copies of deeds and corresponding local information pertinent to Humphrey's estates, collected during c. 1497–1525. What makes these manuscripts particularly relevant to the subject of information gathering is Humphrey's method of citation: almost every deed includes an indication of the archive whence it came.

Humphrey Newton became head of the Newton family in 1497.[23] His inheritance was small, comprising the single holding of Newton (a farmhouse with no manorial tenure and held mostly in demesne) and a scattering of lands and tenements in western Cheshire. It was augmented with land acquired through Humphrey's marriage in 1490 to a local co-heiress, Ellen Fitton of Pownall: he secured the manor of Pownall (comprising 8 messuages and 360 acres of land, pasture wood and waste) and lands in Minshull Vernon and Eardswick. In addition to managing lands and property, Humphrey was an active steward of a number of manors in Cheshire and was a small-time lawyer acting for friends and neighbours. He was not a particularly litigious man, yet he suffered a fair number of disputes and instigated a few of his own. Newton lay in an area where land was becoming scarce and pressure was mounting on remaining commonland. Setting aside a drastic upset in landownership, the only hope for expansion was in the extending of borders. Consequently, it was important to possess some knowledge of neighbouring boundaries. Humphrey was careful to exploit this route; on a deed describing the boundaries of Newton he wrote: 'the meers of this deed must be taken for the most advantage of the heirs of Newton'.[24] From his knowledge of early deeds and of the boundaries

---

[22] Bodl, MS Lat. misc. c. 66.

[23] The following information on Humphrey Newton and his estates is derived from my Ph.D. thesis 'Humphrey Newton of Newton and Pownall (1466–1536): a gentleman of Cheshire and his commonplace book' (unpub. Keele Ph.D. thesis, 1995). For printed material, see J.P. Earwaker, *East Cheshire* (2 vols, London, 1877, 1880), 1, pp. 120–4; 2, pp. 264–7; R.H. Robbins, 'The poems of Humphrey Newton esquire, 1460–1536', *Publications of the Modern Language Association of America*, 65 (1950), pp. 249–81.

[24] BL, Add. MS 42134A, f. 14r.

detailed therein, Humphrey made claims to fields adjacent to west Newton, and to heathland on the east of Newton. At the same time, problems of defence at the newly acquired manor of Pownall centred on the claims of a co-heiress, Margaret Fitton, who maintained – and rightly so – that she had been disinherited of a large portion of the Fitton inheritance. Humphrey faced a number of attacks from Margaret and her husbands which included the production of forged documentation.[25]

Although propounding claims to land and defending current holdings, the Newtons were not blessed with an extensive archive. This in part was due to Newton's relatively uneventful history, coupled with its lack of manorial tenure and few tenants. It was also because the deeds which did exist were scattered among several landholders. This was the case with documentation relating to holdings in west Cheshire which had come to the Newtons following the division of the Milton inheritance between three co-heiresses. The deed referring to the division was stored at the home of the Mascy family, as Humphrey recorded: 'this deed remayneth with the heirs of Massey of Grafton to keepe of truste for the heirs of Newton and Brome'.[26] Deeds relevant to Pownall were kept with the overlords, the Booths of Dunham Massey and the Traffords of Trafford (Lancashire). Deeds pertaining to Humphrey's land in Mottram St Andrew were kept in the hands of the long established tenants of the area, the Mottersheads.

On inheriting Newton, Humphrey began visiting official archives, neighbouring homesteads and manors with the intention of drawing together and transcribing available documentation for his estate. Not all gentry could have attempted this task. Although the majority could read, this was mainly in the vernacular at a period when most deeds were in Latin. There was also the hurdle of handwriting. Growing numbers of scribes, who needed to write faster to keep up with demand, ensured that late medieval writing was far less uniform and neat than in earlier times.[27] Humphrey, however, was suitably qualified

---

[25] PRO, Palatinate of Chester, Miscellanea, CHES 38/26/8.

[26] BL, Add. MS 42134A, f. 4r.

[27] H.J. Graff, *The Legacies of Literacy* (Indiana, 1987), pp. 95, 101–2, 105; K. Thomas, 'Literacy in early modern England', in *The Written Word: Literacy in Transition*, ed. G. Baumann (Oxford, 1986), pp. 98–101.

through his work as a lawyer and steward which had taught him the skills of reading diverse hands and documents. These qualifications may also have helped him gain access to information recorded on official records. Entries in the commonplace book and cartulary show that on three occasions Humphrey undertook research in the administrative records of Cheshire. While in the exchequer at Chester he gleaned information from the deputy escheator, Richard Leftwich, relating to land in Handley. He traced the descent of the families of Fitton and Venables in records belonging to the justice of eyre; and he noted the marriages of Sir Edmund Trafford and Sir Robert Booth 'after the warranto in the eires at Chester made for the claims that John Scot gave'.[28]

More interesting is the information gathered from Humphrey's travels to several Cheshire households. One main research project concerned the lordship of Bollin which covered a large area of the parish of Wilmslow. Several deeds belonging to William Fitton of Fernleigh, esquire (d. 1523), were transcribed with the intention of establishing Fitton's title to lands in the lordship of Bollin (then held by the Booths of Dunham Massey). Humphrey's motive is clearly stated alongside the deeds: in accordance with an agreement between the men, if Fitton secured Bollin then Humphrey would be given certain lands he claimed in the area. All deeds were annotated with a statement of their relevance to the case Humphrey was formulating. None of the deeds was fully transcribed and they often appear as some form of index system:

> item. Also I see another dede in the kepyng of the sd William wch beg. Omnibus present etc. Johes de Scocia . . . et dedisse Rob Fitton etc. . . which dede is of many liberties in Bolyn whereof the copie is her aftr in the boke which most be writen her and was in the days of Henry iij$d$.[29]

Further information connected with the case was established from deeds belonging to yeomen Thomas and Oliver Wittonstall and a certain Thomas Curbishley of Wilmslow. Other searches drew on deeds from the yeomen family

---

[28] Bodl, MS Lat. misc. c. 66, ff. 51r, 57r and 63r. For *quo warranto* proceedings, see n. 7 above. 'John the Scot' was the last Anglo-Norman earl of Chester (d. 1237).

[29] Bodl, MS Lat. misc. c. 66, f. 18v.

of Mottershead to tenancies in Mottram St Andrew; and a deed relating to an exchange of land in 1329 was copied from the household of John Redditch of Dewysnape.[30]

Larger gentry archives were available. The Leghs of Adlington were one of the Newtons' more important and most influential neighbouring families. Potentially Humphrey could have inspected much at Adlington: the Leghs appear as appropriators of the documents of at least three families.[31] Humphrey took interest in deeds originally belonging to the Willots of Foxtwist, a yeomen family who lived on land Humphrey intended to procure. More significantly the Leghs also held a thirteenth-century title deed of the Newton holding; it is not clear whether that too had been purloined, or if the Newtons had entrusted it to the more secure archive of powerful neighbours. A second Newton title deed, kept at the nearby manor of Handforth, was certainly likely to have been entrusted for safe-keeping.[32] In addition, deeds at the manor of Poynton furnished Humphrey with an unusually detailed genealogy of the Warrens of Poynton, then headed by Sir John Warren (d. 1518). Most information drawn from that archive related to Woodford, a neighbouring manor of Newton, and held during Humphrey's majority by Nicholas Davenport (d. 1521) who had persistently attempted to expand his territory into Newton. Here is an illustration of the virtue of obtaining deeds relating to neighbouring estates. Humphrey defended Newton against Davenport by analysing Newton's title deeds and by ordering a servant to measure the perimeter of Newton. Yet at Poynton, Humphrey had obtained a copy of the 'original deed of Woodford', which set out the bounds of the manor and clearly (to Humphrey's mind) supported his claims regarding the position of its boundaries.[33]

---

[30] Bodl, MS Lat. misc. c. 66, ff. 11v, 15v–17r, 18v, 19v, 54r.

[31] From the Verdons of Fulshaw (PRO, C1/368/52); from the Leghs of Altrincham and Prestbury (PRO, C1/633/64); and from the Willots of Foxtwist (BL, Add. MS 42134A, f. 14r).

[32] BL, Add. MS 42134A, ff. 14r and 21r–v; JRULM, Bromley Davenport Collection, 'Newton by Mottram' 3/100/9. The Handforths of Handforth had long been close associates of the Newton family. William Handforth (d. 1513), for example, acted as a feoffee for Humphrey: PRO, Palatinate of Chester, Plea Rolls, CHES 29/211, m. 7.

[33] Bodl, MS Lat. misc. c. 66, f. 54v.

More significant were the deeds collected for the Pownall estate. As noted above, the majority were in the hands of the Booths of Dunham Massey and the Traffords of Trafford. They had become overlords in the early fifteenth century as a result of the marriages of Sir Edmund Trafford of Trafford (d. 1457) and Sir Robert Booth of Barton (d. 1460) to the two co-heiresses of William Venables, Lord of Bollin. On securing Pownall, Humphrey made thorough searches in the archives of the overlords. Of the two, Humphrey's most fruitful researches were at Dunham Massey.[34] In particular his information was drawn from a work called on two occasions 'the boke of sir Robt Both', and on a third 'a book of remembrances' – again of Sir Robert Booth.[35] Humphrey was mainly interested in the book's genealogical data, particularly that relating to the Fittons of Gawsworth and the Venables family. The inconvenience which the lack of a complete and organised archive at Newton could incur was greatly reduced by Humphrey's transcriptions; these furnished the family with workable copies and facilitated access to the original deeds. Not only was the source of the deeds noted, but it appears that a theoretical order was imposed on the documentation. The title deeds, for example, were numbered in chronological order: Humphrey referred to one deed as the *tercia carta originalis de Neuton*.[36] The Newton archive, therefore, came together and existed simply, but effectively, in book form.

Access to family deeds and papers stored in private collections depended on the permission of the holders. Although Humphrey's manuscripts only include successful research, it does appear that he met with a large degree of cooperation in his information gathering. Both lesser families and wealthy neighbours provided Humphrey with the necessary records to defend and extend his land base. Access was not unusual elsewhere in England; it is well expressed in the opening lines of the Hylle cartulary: 'If any cause shall arise in

---

[34] Only one instance is recorded of Humphrey's searches for deeds 'at Trafford' in a feoffment relating to lands in Wittonstall: Bodl, MS Lat. misc. c. 66, f. 70r. Their Fitton charters remained within the Trafford family archive which is now in the Lancashire Record Office, call number DDTr.

[35] Bodl, MS Lat. misc. c. 66, ff. 51r, 70v.

[36] BL, Add. MS 42134A, f. 15r.

the future concerning questions of doubt or debate in any of the manors, lands or tenements, the services of the same or any part of them, anyone can go to the said treasury and there make scrutiny of the muniments, for informations and evidences which may be necessary in the case of.'[37] This notwithstanding, access was not always permitted: successful gentry needed some advantage over the opposition.[38] What could occur is summed up in the last line of Humphrey's recording of the deed of Thomas Wittonstall: '. . . so wold have the kepyng of it that no man shuld knowe of it and so he promised'.[39] Humphrey himself was placed at a disadvantage when William Minshull used 'deeds, charters, decrees and muniments' concerning the Pownall inheritance to convey premises to himself, his wife and others. Humphrey was forced to petition Chancery to compel Minshull to reveal the documents.[40] Such secrecy was in itself a reason to copy deeds when opportunity presented itself. The reasons behind the granting of admission appear complex. The cooperation given to Humphrey by a few landholders is perhaps surprising. This is the case with the Leghs of Adlington who supplied information to Humphrey and the Newtons during a period when relations between the two families were strained at best.[41] Moreover, although the Leghs were involved in a protracted land dispute with the Willot family, they allowed Humphrey access to their Willot deeds in order to pursue a claim which could affect their own interests.[42] Likewise the Booths of Dunham Massey provided Humphrey with information even while the latter was trying to undermine the Booths' rights to Bollin in favour of William Fitton. There were no doubt many risks in allowing an 'open house' on deeds.

[37] *The Hylle Cartulary*, ed. R.W. Dunning (Somerset Record Society, 68, 1968), p. 3. Sir John Byrom also appears to have had access to the deeds of his neighbours, Bodl, MS Rawlinson B460, ff. 1v, 5, 85v.

[38] See the prefaces to several monastic cartularies where the monks are warned to be careful to whom they show their manuscripts: see Foulds, 'Medieval cartularies', pp. 23–5.

[39] Bodl, MS Lat. misc. c. 66, f. 44v.

[40] PRO, C1/548/81.

[41] For disagreements between Humphrey and Thomas Legh of Adlington (d. 1519), see Bodl, MS Lat. misc. c. 66, f. 60; BL, Add. MS 42134A, ff. 1–2.

[42] After examining the Willot deeds, Humphrey called the Leghs' title to the lands 'surmised', BL, Add. MS 42134A, f. 14.

Arrangements such as the *quid pro quo* agreement between Fitton and Humphrey may have helped open up some collections. Others may have perceived additional benefits. Offering admittance would have presented an opportunity to display a fine archive and advertise the evidence which supported an ancient lineage and boast a secure title to land.

The manipulation of written evidence partly ensured that researchers continued to resort to oral information. Methods of enquiry into court cases depended to a great degree on the memories of older parishioners.[43] Elders were consulted on local customs and family details. The inquisitive Worcester and Leland exercised the memories of a number of locals during their itineraries.[44] Polydore Vergil recognised the importance of eye-witness accounts for near contemporary events: 'when on approaching our own times I could find no such annals . . . I betook myself to every man of age'.[45] Likewise Humphrey relied on a number of old men for local information. One proficient source was Richard Clerk of Prestbury, aged eighty in 1498. He had gathered the tithe corn for Prestbury church during his youth and therefore knew the area covered by the tithe. He was consequently an important witness to the traditional boundary of Prestbury parish and provided details on the origins of the spittle house lying near Prestbury: 'Richard Clerk of Prestbury of the age of [eighty] years seid and deposed that sir John Duncalfe vicar of Prestbury telled him for trouth that the spetyll hous was geven by Erle Rundulph to the fynding of a lazar or lazars barn within the same parish and if non war to the relevyng of a prest to syng afor our lady for hym & alle the parish.'[46]

In the main Humphrey's use of oral evidence was for genealogical purposes.

---

[43] The ages of the witnesses were usually recorded; the eldest witness was often listed first.

[44] *William Worcestre Itineraries*, ed. J.H. Harvey (Oxford, 1969), *passim*; McFarlane, 'William Worcester', p. 200; *The Itinerary of John Leland in or about the Years 1535–1543*, ed. L.T. Smith (5 vols, London, 1964). Another member of the Fastolf circle questioned around twelve witnesses for their recollections of one Sir John Paveley; a list of seventeen questions was prepared and the answers of each witness diligently recorded: BL, Add. MS 39220 ff. 3–7v. My thanks to Colin Richmond for providing me with his notes on the manuscript.

[45] M. McKisack, *Medieval History in the Tudor Age* (Oxford, 1971), p. 100.

[46] Bodl, MS Lat. misc. c. 66, f. 14r. Earl 'Rundulph' was Earl Ranulf III; John Duncalf was vicar of Prestbury (1416–48).

From the recollections of friends and acquaintances Humphrey was able to compile brief genealogies of several neighbouring families – Pigot of Butley, Crowther, Mottershead, Duncalf of Foxtwist, the Davenport families of Henbury and Woodford, the Legh families of Adlington, Booth and Baguley – and record information on important individuals. His sources offered far different pedigrees to those recorded by the heralds and later family historians. Since the Middle Ages, for example, the family of Legh has displayed a distinguished pedigree. Conversely, Humphrey's informant in the commonplace book – one Richard Legh – described the Legh families of Baguley, Booth and Adlington as descending from the three bastard sons of a vicar of Rostherne. Furthermore, the Adlington estate had come to the Leghs following their abduction of, and the forcible marriage of one of their number to, the heiress of that estate.[47] John Davenport of Henbury (d. 1390) appears in genealogies as the natural younger son of Thomas Davenport of Welltrough; but Humphrey's informant told an alternative story: that John was a bastard, the product of his father's rape of the wife of a man named Longshaw. A final example is detailed by the octogenarians Mottershead and Sumpter who recounted a seedy story from the early history of the manor of Mottram St Andrew. A 'lady' of Mottram had instructed her bailiff to give the widow of one Sherd, lord of Mottram, thirty acres of the best land she held in Mottram. On reaching the widow, however, 'the bailey desired to have layn with her and she denyd and then he gaf her xxx of the worst lande in alle Mottram'.[48]

No evidence survives to verify these stories, although what remains tends to undermine the assertions of Humphrey's informants. For the present discussion, however, the truth of the tales is irrelevant. What matters is that they were believed and were circulated in the locality. The origins and ancient lineage of a gentry family were proclaimed through genealogies; local power was generally proportional to the length of time a family had lived in an area. How attractive therefore were those versions which declared that supposedly ancient households had less than auspicious beginnings? The origin of the Newton family was also being debated among Humphrey's neighbours. Humphrey drew

[47] Bodl, MS Lat. misc. c. 66 ff. 14r–15v.
[48] Ibid. f. 15r.

attention to a contemporary belief that the Newtons were a branch of the Davenport family who had changed their name in the late thirteenth century. Humphrey refuted that notion with a series of deeds; in his cartulary, however, he admitted the limitation of the documents. Yet equivocal evidence could be advantageous, as Humphrey realised: though he presently denied the Davenport connection, 'howbeit if there were any advantage it might be said there name was changed'.[49]

Conflicting stories, therefore, abounded in oral and written accounts to the frustration of diligent researchers.[50] Sources had to be compared with one another, oral information helped to interpret written material. Genealogies often required considerable probing. In Humphrey's record of the descent of the Fitton family one branch was incorrect and had been crossed out. At the side Humphrey noted that it was to be 'mendit' with a Fitton pedigree kept at Dunham Massey.[51] One of the clearest combinations of oral and written sources was Humphrey's brief history of Newton. Based on deeds and old stories, it concentrated on the tenants and land use of the area from the time of Henry III to that of Humphrey himself. This is how the history accounts for the loss of tenements in the fourteenth century: '. . . and after there fell the pestilence and was a deth of people and then these tenementes deccessed which was called the great deth aftr whos decesses the landes of Neuton wer in decay and parte of theym was lest out to enter comyn to the seid wey and parte of theym was taken from theym by the lords of Bolyn.'[52] Whether Humphrey had firm evidence for the effects of plague, or whether it was informed guesswork, is unclear. As ever, people chose the story best suited to their own purposes. Evidence was always to be manipulated; the aim was to know all the possibilities of the case.

In compiling manuscripts of deeds and family information Humphrey was not unusual: the activity may be traced in other Cheshire gentry families. Although surviving examples are few, a careful examination of seventeenth- and eighteenth-century writings reveal earlier manuscripts which have since

---

[49] BL, Add. MS 42134A, f. 18v.
[50] Lewis, 'Sir John Fastolf', p. 13.
[51] Bodl, MS Lat. misc. c. 66, f. 50r.
[52] Ibid., f. 20r.

disappeared. The evidence indicates that several of Newton's neighbouring gentry (most of whom Humphrey visited for documents) also gathered together books or rolls of deeds. It is possible that they were available to Humphrey or acted as stimuli for his own collecting. At present only one of those deed collections is known to have been read by Humphrey: the remembrance book(s) compiled by Sir Robert Booth of Dunham Massey (d. 1460). Remembrance books were usually notebooks of memoranda and could contain any amount and variety of information. Booth's interest in collecting was perhaps influenced by his father who compiled a cartulary of the lands of the Booths of Barton c. 1403–4.[53] Although none of Booth's manuscripts appears to have survived, the works of later antiquarians hint at the extent of his collection. In the early seventeenth century Randle Holmes II and his son referred to the books, deeds and rolls in the Booth archive. Most interesting is the 'parchment book in quarto, very faire and anciently written with a table of the deeds'.[54] The book detailed the lands Sir Robert Booth had obtained from Randolph Barton. A book scoured by Roger Dodsworth (1585–1654) was a source containing information on the towns in Richmondshire held by Robert Booth and Edmund Trafford; it also included a number of Fitton deeds.[55] Furthermore, in the 1630s Peter Shakerley used entries from an 'ancient' book of Robert Booth; it is that information which is closest to the book entries which Humphrey used a century earlier: Shakerley's copy of the Venables genealogy and a number of Fitton deeds also appear in Humphrey's commonplace book.[56]

During the fourteenth century the Leghs of Booth drew together thirteenth- and fourteenth-century deeds in a parchment roll.[57] Similarly a *rotulo pargamento* belonging to the Davenports of Henbury was probably compiled during the Middle Ages.[58] In the early seventeenth century antiquarians made use of the

---

[53] A part transcription is found in Bodl, Dodsworth MS 149, ff. 150–165.
[54] BL, Harley MS 2131, f. 34r.
[55] Bodl, Dodsworth MS 61, f. 98.
[56] CCRO, DSS Box 22/3, ff. 173, 178; Bodl, MS Lat. misc. c. 66, ff. 51r, 57r, 70v.
[57] Keele University Library, Legh of Booth Charters 326.
[58] CCRO, DLT /B1 (Peter Leycester's *Liber A*), f. 144. Leycester's notes regarding the roll omit a likely date of compilation, but the deeds it contained date mainly from the reigns of the first three Edwards.

so-called 'Black Book of Trafford', an ancient book containing numerous deeds and other 'evidences' which appears medieval in origin.[59] A Harley manuscript contains fragments of genealogical information gathered by the Leghs of Adlington c. 1477.[60] Other books are indicated by the heralds who occasionally lifted complete genealogies and arms from old books. For the 1580 visitation the Fitton arms, for example, were 'taken out of an old Book at Goseworth wherein they were limmed long ago'.[61] It was perhaps the same book as the 'old parchment work' later transcribed by Peter Shakerley.[62] Similarly the 1580 heralds took the pedigree of the Warrens of Poynton out of 'an old writing in latine'.[63] These works suggest that accumulating and organising material relating to lands and family was a well-used method by north-east Cheshire landholders of the Middle Ages. How they were compiled remains obscure. It is possible that they were assembled in the form of cartularies, which suggests that cartularies belonging to secular owners were not as rare as surviving numbers imply.[64] Their appeal to the Cheshire gentry lay beyond their aid in land disputes. Cartularies were regarded as a means to display gentility.[65] In compiling them the gentry were glorifying the wealth and longevity of their families. Both manuscripts of Humphrey Newton show his family to their best advantage. Offering one's cartulary or like manuscript to interested friends and neighbours was one method of publicising family and landed success.

Whatever the original intentions of the compilers, it may be argued that the

---

[59] BL, Harley MS 2077, f. 292. Note that John Byrom's cartulary was called 'the Black Book of Clayton'.

[60] BL, Harley MS 2059, particularly ff. 4–5 where deeds are used to construct a family tree.

[61] *The Visitation of Cheshire, 1580*, ed. J.P. Rylands (Harleian Soc., 18, 1882), p. 99.

[62] CCRO, DSS Box 22/3, f. 140. The Fittons also possessed a family psalter which was kept at Gawsworth church. The book contained obits of the Fitton family dating to the 1490s and early sixteenth century: Bodl, Barlow MS 1.

[63] *The Visitation of Cheshire, 1580*, p. 240.

[64] See G.R.C. Davies' list in *Medieval Cartularies of Great Britain* (London, 1958). Although slightly flawed by both omissions and the inclusion of some 'registers' in the list, the ratio reflects the imbalance between known religious and lay cartularies: 1185 to 169. S.J. O'Connor believes few lay landlords thought a cartulary worth the effort: *A Calendar of the Cartularies of John Pyel and Adam Fraunceys* (Camden Soc., 5th ser., 2, 1993), pp. 75–6.

[65] O'Connor, *A Calendar of the Cartularies*, pp. 76–9.

manuscripts came to have a wider significance: that those manuscripts, and Humphrey's researches in particular, are related to the emergence of antiquarian studies during the fifteenth century and their rapid expansion in the sixteenth century. 'Antiquarianism' describes the enthusiasm for historical research, undertaken by an individual to satisfy his own curiosity of his country's past. Its practitioners were gentlemen or clergy; their 'antiquarianism' combined local history with the antiquities of the British Isles. Despite K.B. McFarlane's and Antonia Gransden's stress on the contribution of fifteenth-century laymen to historical study,[66] those seeking examples of secular antiquarians are usually only able to evidence John Rous, William Worcester and, to a lesser extent, John Hardyng. The origins of secular antiquarianism have never been fully explained or contextualised; consequently Worcester and Rous appear as highly unusual and individual in their preoccupation with investigating the past. Likewise the industrious Cheshire historians of the Elizabethan era onwards are assumed to have exhibited a new-found enthusiasm and spirit of enquiry.[67] A closer look at Humphrey's work must lead to a revision of these assumptions.

Certain conditions in fifteenth-century England facilitated historical research by laymen. As noted, the country contained numerous researchers sifting through family papers and records of the central and local government administrations. There were the manuscripts which created family histories by detailing lands acquired and marriage alliances made. None of these can be described as antiquarian. The researchers who only undertook paid work and the manuscripts which only contained specific family deeds were not part of this movement. It is possible, nonetheless, to see in the manuscripts the compiler's interests moving beyond the specific work of deed transcription.[68] In addition those collections provided useful material for sixteenth- and seventeenth-century antiquarians and to some extent directed the enquiries of those later researchers. William Worcester's record-searching famously encouraged and

---

[66] K.B. McFarlane, 'William Worcester'; A. Gransden, 'Antiquarian studies'.

[67] For the latest survey of Cheshire's antiquarians, see A.T. Thacker, 'Cheshire', in *English County Histories: A Guide*, eds C.R.J. Currie and C.P. Lewis (Stroud, 1994), pp. 71–84.

[68] See Foulds, 'Medieval Cartularies', p. 3.

advanced his interest in antiquarian studies. Humphrey Newton, as entries in the commonplace book intimate, was another whose interests went farther than those of the majority of researchers. First and foremost comes the genealogical information of his neighbours; although used for practical purposes, it also presented a general and social history of the region. Humphrey paid attention to the different spellings of local place-names: he noted alternatives to Adlington (Ordishilton and Adhilton) and to Henbury (Heith ber and heethyn bury). He also explained the etymology of some field names: 'Werewhynestred' field and 'Harper's Croft' field, for example, were named after thirteenth-century occupants.[69]

The commonplace book contains various entries which illustrate Humphrey's own diverse interests in historical matters. There are snippets of information relating to the destruction wrought by fourteenth-century plagues, lists of kings from the Conquest, of fifteenth-century battles, and English towns, parish churches and knight fees.[70] Humphrey had an interest in his county's early history. Three lists of the earls of Chester are transcribed; they prefigure the typical comital genealogies which appear in later antiquarian manuscripts. His inquisitiveness led him to copy down a prayer to the Virgin he came across in a chained book in the parish church at Newark, Nottinghamshire.[71] Moreover, like Worcester and Leland, Humphrey made the trip to Glastonbury. His notes display that interest in British history which has often been regarded as a stimulus to antiquarian research;[72] he noted at Glastonbury a number of relics relating to the Arthurian legend: the crystal cross of Arthur, the stirrups of Arthur and the ribs of Sir Bors. Like Leland he also transcribed the inscription on the black marble tomb which purportedly contained the remains of Arthur and Gwynefar.[73]

Humphrey's antiquarian work was limited compared with that of the

---

[69] Bodl, MS Lat. misc. c. 66, f. 20.

[70] Ibid. Prophecy and astrology also feature prominently and provide interesting interpretations of past events and readings of the future.

[71] Bodl, MS Lat. misc. c. 66, f. 18r.

[72] Gransden, 'Antiquarian studies', p. 309.

[73] Bodl, MS Lat. misc. c. 66, f. 3v; *The Itinerary of John Leland*, part 3, p. 288.

more famous collectors of his time: he produced no works of similar quality, and did not undertake their extensive journeys and researches. He is, however, important for the later antiquarian movement. His parochial interests and attention to genealogy have much more in common with the later Cheshire antiquarians, a group which has been described as 'from the local gentry, and their interests primarily genealogical'.[74] The mass of material produced by Cheshire antiquarians, like the Randle Holmes manuscripts in the British Library, appears to owe its existence to the early work of men like Humphrey Newton rather than to the better-known activities of Worcester or Leland.

Antiquarians were, therefore, not new to Cheshire in the later sixteenth century, nor did the Elizabethan practitioners rely entirely on their own research and transcriptions. It is true that they referenced deeds and charters which they examined in family collections. Nevertheless, much of the cited work was attributed to books of collected document transcripts in someone's possession. This was not surprising at a time when family papers remained in private hands. Owners of the records believed it safer to offer a book of copies, and the antiquarian no doubt found it less time-consuming to look through a ready-made book of deeds. Antiquarians in general relied on the works of their predecessors. It is already recognised that the works of two of Cheshire's earliest known antiquarians, Laurence Bostock (writing *c.* 1560) and John Booth of Twemlow (1584–1659), were used heavily by later researchers.[75] It is not so well noted that Bostock and Booth were themselves copying from earlier compilations such as those brought together for the families of Booth, Fitton and Trafford mentioned above. Rather than initiating the process of information gathering, the Elizabethan antiquarians were often merely synthesizing the work of late medieval collectors. Humphrey's commonplace book was itself recognised as a useful source for local information. John Booth of Twemlow borrowed the book in the first decade of the seventeenth century. He kept the manuscript over a long period and did not treat it particularly well; Humphrey's descendants took the manuscript away from Booth because of this

---

[74] Thacker, 'Cheshire', p. 73.

[75] Ibid., pp. 72–3.

rough handling.[76] Other antiquarians were not so anxious – or were perhaps unable – to look at the original. J.P. Earwaker (1847–95) transcribed the Newton genealogy from a copy made by Christopher Townley (1604–74), which the latter had taken from notes of the commonplace book made by William Vernon (c. 1585–1667): a good illustration of antiquarians relying on second-hand transcriptions.[77]

The late medieval gentry landholder relied heavily on written material to support his or her interests. None expected to possess all the records relevant to his or her cause, but all believed that they should know what could be obtained. It was a question of discerning the gaps in the evidence and how these could be filled; or, equally significant, who was likely to be able to provide the missing evidence and its interpretation. Not every landlord would bother; some waited until problems occurred and then relied on lawyers or local custom. Our example, Humphrey Newton, in his bid to expand his estates and deflect opponents, set about establishing what was known and retrievable about his landholdings. Unable to finance researchers and possessing the requisite skills, Humphrey chose to travel around north-east Cheshire to ascertain the history of his neighbourhood and the claims to his estate. Although his books only show his successes, they nevertheless reveal a degree of openness among the families of the area. How that information was regulated (if it was), what was made public, and what was destroyed we cannot know.

That the late medieval gentry had a keen interest in compiling and advertising their own lineages is well known. For many years this information had been exhibited in stained-glass windows and monuments in parish churches; but the gentry had also become aware that written evidence was crucial for social advancement. Documents could betray family secrets; they could also be manipulated to reinforce landed and aristocratic pretensions. Oral testimony remained an alternative source, although it was gradually becoming discredited. The gentry, heralds and antiquarians ensured that the diverging tales circulating in Humphrey's days were replaced by one accepted version based on written evidence. In his own manuscripts Humphrey attempted to

---

[76] Bodl, MS Lat. misc. c. 66, f. 1.
[77] Chester CRO, CR 63/1/93/8

reduce divergence in the interests of a consistent narrative. His interpretations were influenced by entirely personal and familial reasons. Humphrey did not intend his notes to be an extended general work on the history of Cheshire. Nor did he write a book to instruct interested parties on antiquities. He was neither a monk engaged on a detailed historical narrative, nor a university-educated researcher who devoted free time to the pursuit of knowledge. He was not what has been long regarded as the typical medieval antiquarian. He nevertheless employed methods and research from which antiquarianism was to evolve. Humphrey adds to our understanding of how necessary skills, interests and opportunities arose to produce so many historians in the sixteenth century.

5
MEDIEVAL CORONERS' ROLLS: LEGAL FICTION OR HISTORICAL FACT?

Carrie Smith

Over the past twenty years or so economic and social historians have been putting to use the legal records generated by the medieval English judicial system to try to generate a better understanding of life and society among the peasantry. It is only natural that those seeking to contribute to our knowledge of the lives of medieval peasants should turn for information to the few sources in which such people appear. Details of the individual lives of the great mass of the population below the ranks of the nobility are hard to come by, and manorial and central legal records, including the rolls of medieval coroners, form the majority of these sources.

The most active among these historians has been Dr Barbara Hanawalt, whose published work includes two books and a number of articles based on legal records, in particular records of gaol delivery sessions and the rolls of medieval coroners.[1] Focusing in particular on crime in the fourteenth century, she has published studies of violent death, crime and conflict in English communities, and economic influences on the pattern of crime. In 1986 she published *The Ties that Bound*, a book in which she used accidental death verdicts contained in late-medieval coroners' rolls from six counties to establish patterns of daily activities and lifestyles among peasant families. Her work, however, has attracted much criticism. Two of her most vocal critics have been Dr R.F.

---

[1] For example: *The Ties that Bound – Peasant Families in Medieval England*, (Oxford, 1986); *Crime and Conflict in English Communities 1300–1348*, (Harvard, 1979); 'Violent death in fourteenth- and early fifteenth-century England', *Comparative Studies in Society and History*, 18 (1976), pp. 297–320; 'Economic influences on the pattern of crime in England 1300–1348', *American Journal of Legal History*, 18 (1974), pp. 281–97.

Hunnisett,[2] whose own special area of research has been for many years the office of the medieval coroner, and Dr John Post.[3] Both of these critics are legal and judicial historians who argue – Dr Hunnisett in particular – that the unreliability of medieval legal records is so great that they are simply unsuitable as sources upon which to base such broad studies. The published opinions of such critics have tended to discredit not merely the work of Dr Hanawalt, but the sources on which it was based. I believe that the time has come to separate the two and to attempt to rehabilitate medieval legal records as valid historical sources, but to do so within a framework of critical criteria which must be applied by any researcher seeking to use them. This paper explores some of the criticisms made by Dr Hunnisett in particular, with special reference to the surviving coroners' rolls for Wiltshire. First, it considers how representative of their activities the coroners' rolls really are; then it addresses some of the criticisms of the way in which Dr Hanawalt used coroners' rolls, arising out of the methods by which those documents were generated; and finally it explores some of the problems connected with verdicts recorded in the rolls, and how far they may reflect historical truth. A brief explanation is needed of the functions of the medieval coroner, and how the surviving documents came into existence.[4]

---

[2] R.F. Hunnisett's published works include *The Medieval Coroner* (Cambridge, 1961); 'The reliability of inquisitions as historical evidence', *The Study of Medieval Records; Essays in Honour of Kathleen Major*, eds D.A. Bullough and R.L. Storey (Oxford, 1971), pp. 206–35; 'Pleas of the crown and the coroner', *BIHR*, 32 (1959), pp. 117–37; 'The medieval coroners' rolls', *American Journal of Legal History*, 3 (1959), pp. 95–124, 205–21, 324–59; *Sussex Coroners' Inquests 1484–1558* (Sussex Record Society, 74, 1985).

[3] Among John Post's works with specific reference to this enquiry are; 'Crime in later-medieval England; some historiographical limitations', *Continuity and Change*, 2 (1987), pp. 211–24; 'Criminals and the law in the reign of Richard II, with particular reference to Hampshire' (unpub. Oxford D.Phil. thesis, 1976); 'The evidential value of approvers' appeals: the case of William Rose, 1389', *Law and History Review*, 3, no. 1 (1985), pp. 91–100; 'Legal record and historical reality', *Proceedings of the Eighth British Legal History Conference*, ed. T.G. Watkin (London, 1987), pp. 1–7; 'Jury lists and juries in the late fourteenth century', *Twelve Good Men and True*, eds J.S. Cockburn and Thomas A. Green (Princeton, 1988), pp. 65–77.

[4] The passages describing coroners' duties are summarised from Hunnisett, *The Medieval Coroner*, *passim*.

The office of coroner was established in 1194. Shrieval corruption had long been a problem to the Crown, depriving it of much potential revenue, and royal finances were in a particularly parlous state at this time because of the enormous ransom which had been demanded for the release of Richard I, who was captured while on crusade. The establishment of the office of coroner was intended to act as a check on the activities of sheriffs and to ensure that judicial revenue, such an important part of the king's income, reached his coffers. Coroners' records were to be regarded as the official rolls of record, so that sheriffs could no longer enjoy the almost unlimited potential for extortion which accompanied their previously unchallenged positions of power in the counties. The coroner was expected to undertake a variety of duties. Anyone bringing a private suit of felony – the medieval equivalent of a private prosecution – had to approach the coroner, who recorded the details. Suspects or criminals seeking sanctuary in a church had up to forty days in which to ask for the coroner: when they did so, the coroner recorded their confessions and assigned them a port from which to abjure the realm. He had to assemble a jury to assess the value of the abjuror's possessions, these being forfeit to the Crown. The coroner was summoned to prisons to record the evidence of anyone awaiting trial who turned approver (which would today be called Queen's evidence). County coroners were supposed to attend all county court and gaol delivery sessions and keep careful records of the complicated procedure of exigent by which individuals were outlawed. They had to attend gaol delivery sessions, bringing copies of any relevant homicide inquests. All future legal process concerning any of these matters depended upon examination of, or reference to, the written record of the coroner concerned. In addition, coroners were sometimes required to step in and undertake the duties of the sheriff if his competence or honesty was suspect, and the men who served as coroners were often called on to act as tax-collectors, keepers of the peace and so on. But most coroners' records which survive are concerned primarily with the holding of inquests into sudden or unnatural deaths, and it is with this body of evidence that this paper is most concerned.

In theory, a representative of the local community should have summoned a coroner to attend whenever a death was suspected of occurring as a result of violence or accident. In most cases, this meant sending for one of the county coroners, of which there were usually between two and four. Some towns – Salisbury and Wilton, for example – were entitled to their own borough coroners. On arrival, the coroner had to inspect the body for marks and injuries and assemble a jury of twelve free men, as well as representatives of the four nearest townships or tithings. These two latter terms are used synonymously on the rolls, but actually refer to the tithing, which functioned in theory as a kind of community self-policing agency. Every unfree male over twelve years of age, unless a member of the clergy, had to belong to his local tithing, which was under the authority of two chief pledges or tithingmen. Twice a year records of membership were updated before the sheriff. Tithings were expected to produce to any court which required them members suspected of infringing the law, and to respond rapidly to the hue and cry raised when a crime was discovered, arresting any suspects if possible. Failure to comply with these obligations brought fines on the whole tithing. At least one of the tithingmen from each of the four nearest tithings had to attend at a death inquest.

What happened next is unclear. The two groups of men (free jurors and tithingmen) may have assembled separately and reached two separate verdicts which were then conflated into one, or they may have consulted together. In any case, they were expected to inform themselves on how the death had occurred and to report their findings to the coroner. In this respect medieval juries were significantly different from the modern, supposedly impartial and uninformed juries to which we are accustomed today. The details they gave were probably jotted down initially in rough versions on scraps of parchment, which are termed files.

Theoretically these notes should have been written up on a formal roll at the earliest opportunity, but human nature being what it is, this seems rarely to have been the case. Although a coroner who had conducted a homicide inquest had to bring the record of that inquest before gaol delivery justices if the suspect was tried, or send a copy into King's Bench if the case was removed to that court, the formal roll of all his inquests was never required until the royal justices arrived in the county. As this was, in the fourteenth century, a most infrequent occurrence, the files were often neglected for years, even decades. Only when the sheriff received notification that a judicial visitation was imminent did a great flurry of activity occur as this transference of information to a formal roll, which is termed engrossment, took place. Signs of great haste – scrawled, often almost illegible handwriting, for example – are often apparent. Many years might elapse between a coroner's term of office and the next visit by the justices. Despite the fact that the heirs of coroners were held responsible for producing the records of coroners who had died, and fined if they were unable to do so, one can see at once what implications such time-lags might have for the completeness of surviving records. William de Whyteclyve, for example, served as a Wiltshire coroner between 1341 and 1349: in 1350 the writ for his replacement stated that he was dead: yet thirty-four years passed before his roll was required by the justices.[5] His is not an isolated case. There can be no way of knowing how many inquest files have been lost between the inquest itself and the time when engrossment took place.

The first ground on which critics have questioned the use of coroners' rolls therefore relates to the use of statistics drawn from the numbers of inquests engrossed on those rolls. Dr Hanawalt's figures appear to suggest that fights ending in the death of one of the participants were more frequent between March and August, when social contacts during communal cultivation were frequent but food stocks low, and took place in the fields. She concluded that these disputes must be concerned with tensions over food production.[6] Such a conclusion may be tempting to draw, but major factors have been left out of account. First, the numbers of inquests which have survived can only represent a tiny proportion of the numbers actually held (and these, for various reasons, are probably much smaller than the numbers which should have been held). Only twelve rolls survive for Wiltshire from the reigns of Edward III and Richard II, a period of over seventy years. But the names of at least forty-seven other coroners who held office during that time can be found on close roll writs ordering their replacement, while there are still others whose activities are recorded in various legal records, but for whom no writ exists: and the records

---

[5] Whyteclyve's roll is PRO, Justices Itinerant, Coroners' Rolls and Files, JUST 2/194; *CCR, 1349–1354*, p. 261. All the extant Wiltshire rolls were collected at the visit of King's Bench, 7 Richard II: see PRO, Court of King's Bench, *Coram Rege* Rolls, KB 27/492, fines and forfeitures, rots 2–6 dorse.

[6] Hanawalt, *Violent Death*.

of all of them have been lost.[7] Second, even when a coroners' roll is a large and impressive document containing large numbers of inquests – and five of the Wiltshire rolls fall into this category – one cannot be sure that it contains records of all that coroner's inquests.[8] Homicide cases were sometimes called into King's Bench, and when this occurred writs instructed the coroner who had held the inquest to forward a copy to that court. Some coroners might therefore feel it unnecessary to include such cases on their engrossed rolls since they had already been dealt with, although the Wiltshire coroners (or those who were responsible for compiling their records) in general do seem to have incorporated them. Gaol delivery records have also been found in which the coroner's inquest is referred to, yet cannot be traced on the relevant roll, probably for the same reason.[9]

In addition to these deliberate omissions, which were probably small in number given the inefficiency of the machinery for catching and keeping safely confined until trial those suspected of homicide, unknown large-scale losses can be detected even from one fairly cursory survey. John Everard acted as one of the Wiltshire county coroners from 1341 to 1355.[10] He appears to have held no inquests at all in the first six months of 1344. There is a gap between October 1351 and March 1352, and another from June until December 1353, when one inquest is recorded. After that there is none until June of the following year. John Everard, like other coroners, was periodically entrusted with other duties by the Crown, but none seems to coincide with these periods that might explain his apparent lack of activity during these months.[11] Although William de

---

[7] *CCR* various volumes. John Gybone, coroner, was fined 20s for various extortions at the visit by King's Bench, yet no writ or other record of his activities survives; similarly, Nicholas de Rolveston is named as coroner on gaol delivery records of the 1330s, but neither writ nor his records remain: PRO, Justices Itinerant, Gaol Delivery Rolls, JUST 3/121, rot. 2 dorse; 130, rot. 12 dorse.

[8] PRO, JUST 2/193, 194, 195, 200 and 203.

[9] See Dr Post's analysis of Hampshire inquests in *Criminals and the law*, pp. 163–71. Analysis of Wiltshire gaol delivery records, however, suggests that those Wiltshire coroners whose rolls survive did generally incorporate into them cases already dealt with at gaol delivery.

[10] Everard's roll is at PRO, JUST 2/195.

[11] Records of such commissions are usually found either in *CPR* or *CFR*. All the volumes covering the fourteenth century have been checked.

Whyteclyve, the other county coroner, was operating in an area which overlapped with Everard's until 1349, his roll shows no corresponding rise in the numbers of inquests in Everard's empty months, as one would expect had he been standing in for his colleague. While illness is not impossible, Everard went on to serve as sheriff and escheator, neither of them jobs suitable for a man whose health was poor. There seem to be four alternative explanations. Either there were no suspicious deaths at all throughout his franchise during these months, or such deaths were going unreported, or Everard was failing to respond to such reports, or some of his inquest records were lost before engrossment. Persistent failure to hold inquests when required was likely to lead to complaints resulting in the issue of an amoval writ: since Everard continued to serve unobstructed, it seems probable that he carried out his duties adequately. Of the remaining possibilities, and given the high mortality levels of the fourteenth century, the first may be safely dismissed. More will be said about under-reporting shortly, but it is most unlikely that no one at all reported a suspicious death in the whole of Everard's populous franchise during these periods. It may be concluded that in all probability unknown numbers of Everard's inquests were lost before engrossment.

There is no doubt that there was substantial under-reporting of all types of death, which provides the third factor requiring discussion in the context of statistics bearing on seasonality and homicide. Coroners were unpaid, and, as Dr Hunnisett has demonstrated, fined if they were found to have taken payment or bribes for performing their duties (or, in some cases, omitting to perform them).[12] At Salisbury in 1384 King's Bench justices fined six serving or recently serving coroners sums of between one mark and 40s for extortion.[13] They were removed from office if they held insufficient property to maintain their expenses without resorting to extortion. But the job involved much time and trouble, a great deal of travelling, and often, no doubt, considerable inconvenience. Corruption was inevitable, and it is likely that coroners against whom no complaints of extortion were apparently made were not as innocent as they appear – that they were wise enough to settle for a sum which local

---

[12] Hunnisett, *The Medievel Coroner*, passim.
[13] PRO, KB 27/492, fines and forfeitures, rot. 1.

communities were willing to accept as reasonable compensation for their time and trouble. In most cases, therefore, the unfortunate residents of a locality where a person had died under suspicious circumstances faced the expense not only of the coroner's (unofficial) fee, but of food and accommodation for himself, his servant or servants, his clerk if he had one, and their horses, for at least one night and often more. Jurors and tithingmen summoned from neighbouring communities also required hospitality, while being themselves inconvenienced by having temporarily to abandon their livelihoods. The bereaved family no doubt also exerted pressure on the rest of the community not to inform the coroner unless homicide was suspected. The law required that the body be left unburied where it was found until after the coroner's examination, and he might take several days to arrive. Burial was desirable not only to relieve the distress of the grieving family, but to prevent the unpleasantnesses consequent on the increasingly intrusive presence of a decomposing corpse which might be in the middle of the public highway, or in a stream from which villagers drew their water, or on the floor of someone's house.

To these perpetual disincentives to summon the coroner were added, in the autumn and winter, the greater difficulties of travelling – muddy roads, swollen rivers and shorter hours of daylight. Simultaneously, such conditions decreased the likelihood of a chance word reaching the coroner that a death had occurred about which he had not been informed. And if he did find out, he might be both less willing to turn out and more prepared to turn a blind eye if the weather was particularly bad. When a homicide occurred as a result of a sudden argument, as was frequently the case, other factors contributed to a desire for concealment in which even the family of the victim might collude. There was no differentiation between murder and manslaughter. The penalty was death. When death had occurred from the infection of a minor wound during a scuffle, or where provocation had been great, or where the victim was generally disliked, or the perpetrator generally liked, no doubt reluctance was felt to subject the accused to the consequences of a homicide verdict. Factors such as these are unquantifiable, but they surely influenced decisions taken by the local community when the death occurred. So, if we return to Dr Hanawalt's theory on the apparent seasonality of homicides, it seems that under-reporting of deaths is as good an explanation as any. And as for motivation, certainly the Wiltshire rolls only rarely give any indication of this apart from robberies, when, of course, it is self-evident. The justices did not require to know why or how an argument had begun, so there was no need to report it. Even in the most detailed blow-by-blow accounts of fights given in some of the Salisbury inquests,[14] the reason for the dispute is not mentioned. If Dr Hanawalt drew her conclusions from the slender evidence of doubtful statistics alone, she was treading on treacherous ground indeed.

A second major criticism of using coroners' rolls for sociological or criminological purposes arises out of the way in which inquest details were transferred from the files at engrossment. Dr Hunnisett alleged that many details were altered or lost during this process.[15] He argued that the use of precedent books and formularies dictated the presentation of information in such a stereotyped manner that the enrolled versions bear little resemblance to actual events; that clerks falsified dates in order to make coroners appear more efficient than they were; and that carelessness in copying the names of individuals and places is evidence of the scant importance attached by all to getting the details right. This last point can be dismissed straightaway. There is no evidence of any expectation, in the Middle Ages, of consistency in, or standard spelling of, personal or place-names. A version which was phonetically recognisable seems to have been all that was required. Nor have the other allegations been found to be sustainable. Only one example of a precedent book has been traced, and that in any case dates from the last quarter of the fourteenth century and would not have been available to clerks in the reign of Edward III.[16] No other such document has so far been located, which seems odd if they were indeed in common use. The examples in that surviving manuscript bear very little resemblance to the way in which the Wiltshire rolls have been engrossed, and actually omit certain items of information which

---

[14] The Salisbury coroners' rolls are PRO, JUST 2/199 and 204.

[15] Hunnisett, 'The reliability of inquisitions'.

[16] BL, Lansdowne MS 560, ff. 34–5. This document and its author are discussed by H.G. Richardson in 'Business training in medieval Oxford', *American Historical Review*, 46 (1941), pp. 259–81.

should always have been given, such as the names of the neighbouring townships and those of the neighbours nearest to the place of death. Dr Hunnisett has suggested that perhaps extant rolls and files were used as precedents. But there are difficulties with this scenario. If files were, as he has said, just rough notes, then they would provide little in the way of a formula to follow. On the other hand, if it is true that most rolls were not engrossed until required by the justices, whose clerks then took them away to finish estreating them, there would never be any locally kept rolls which could have been used as exemplars. In any case, although many inquest narratives are frustratingly brief and lacking in any but the barest essential details, this is not necessarily a result of the need to present information according to prescribed formulae. Parchment was expensive. From the record the justices only needed to be able to ascertain the identities of the deceased, of any suspects, and the values of any property due to the Crown arising out of the death. County coroners covering large rural areas, holding many inquests and with little personal knowledge of those with whom they came into contact, were probably uninterested in recording more than the essential details. The following, an inquest from 1343 on Whyteclyve's roll, serves as a typical example. After the opening preamble, the narrative runs: 'At Westbury on Saturday after St Matthew apostle [27 September] Roger son of Matilda Coleman of Mourton struck Simon le Cock in the back with a knife and killed him. He lived for four days and had the last rites. Roger's chattels are valued at 2s.'[17] This was quite sufficient for judicial purposes, frustrating though it may be for the modern researcher.

However, the formulaic method of presentation allowed ample opportunity for including detailed information if the coroner so chose. In the Salisbury rolls, for example, many of the inquests are much fuller and provide an entertaining and sometimes exciting narrative.[18] This is not surprising. Borough coroners, although drawn from the urban aristocracy, lived as integral members of a compact, crowded community, whose physical proximity and daily activities ensured that the life of each individual was closely involved with the lives of many others. Even personal opinions may be found in their inquests, as when Peter atte Watere died

[17] PRO, JUST 2/194, rot. 5, no. 4.
[18] PRO, JUST 2/199, 204.

in 1370. The narrative states that as Peter, the bishop of Salisbury's miller, came along St Martin's street opposite John Peny's house, there stood in the street John Hulon's empty cart with no horses attached to it. Peter took the bishop's horses from the mill and foolishly coupled them to the empty cart but without putting a horse under the shaft to support it. And so, stupidly, Peter drove the horses and carried the shaft of the cart himself as far as the open gate of Richard Berewyk's tenement. The horses entered and Peter was crushed between the gatepost and the cart, from which he died almost at once, having had the last rites. Only the body of the cart moved to his death, value 20*d*.[19] We do not know Peter's motivation for pursuing this ill-advised course of action, but we have a pretty good idea of the opinions of those at the inquest concerning the intelligence he displayed in doing so, although it was information quite unnecessary for any judicial purpose. (The jurors may have been under pressure from the bishop. Having lost his miller, he would hardly welcome having to pay the value of the horses as a deodand, as would have been the case had the inquest not exculpated them.)

Another narrative from the same roll, this time concerning a homicide in 1373, demonstrates the fullness of which formulaic presentation was capable:

On Wednesday in Easter week [20 April] at about firelighting time a dispute arose in John le Cooke's house between Richard Clere and Margaret his wife on one side, and William Polemond on the other, so that in arguing Richard threatened William that he would meet with him and assault him the next day. And because Richard had a terrible name for homicide and was reputed to be dangerous, William was in great fear of him and his threat. Richard left the house with his wife and lay in wait for William. When at last William came out of the house, he did not notice that Richard was so close. One of William's neighbours shouted out in a loud voice that William should guard himself from Richard. So Richard, to stop William getting away, threw his cloak over William's arm. William, from terror and fear at Richard's assault, struck Richard on the arm with a sword, price 6*d*. Richard languished until the day of this inquest [1 May] on which he died, having had the last rites.[20]

[19] PRO, JUST 2/199, m. 3 dorse, no. 2.
[20] PRO, JUST 2/199, m. 5 dorse, no. 3.

These are not isolated examples, and while the numbers of borough coroners' records may be fewer than those of their county colleagues, they do refute Dr Hunnisett's allegation that formulaic presentation precluded the incorporation of highly specific information about individuals.

What about the accusation that the clerks who engrossed the rolls tampered with inquest dates in order to make coroners appear more efficient than they actually were? While it would be rash to suggest that this never took place, there are good grounds for arguing that it was not a general practice. In the first place, local juries had to keep their own records of matters of interest to the justices, including forfeitures arising from accidental deaths as well as suicides and homicides. Their presentments were compared with those on the coroners' rolls, which had been placed beforehand into sealed bags. Any discrepancies, which the justices were only too eager to find, resulted in fines. Elaborate collusion would have been necessary between coroners and juries to ensure that their accounts tallied, particularly since most rolls were prepared so long after the actual event. Second, Dr Hunnisett believes that in most counties coroners' rolls were engrossed by teams of clerks acting as a scribal agency.[21] The evidence from the Wiltshire rolls does suggest that some of the rolls there were written up by common hands. This practice made sense. Every town had resident scribes and clerks competent to undertake such a task. Although coroners should have employed a clerk between them if not individually, the expense was hardly justified in view of the extremely sporadic nature of judicial visitations. It was cheaper to wait until a visitation was announced and then have all the documentation completed at once in return for a one-off payment – especially since it might never be required at all. Professional clerks working in a writing office and not in the personal employ of an individual coroner can have had little interest in enhancing his image for reasons of loyalty or job security. And finally, as long as a coroner was not so persistently negligent that complaints were made to them, the justices seem to have had little interest in whether a coroner took two or twenty days to hold an inquest, only in the fact that he had carried out his duty to hold one. In sum, it appears as if there were few incentives for the falsification of dates.

---

[21] Hunnisett, *The medieval coroners' rolls*.

Indeed, a survey of the Wiltshire rolls offers little evidence that clerks tampered with dates. Occasionally the phraseology of the inquests is ambiguous and it is impossible to be certain whether death occurred on the day of the fatal incident or some days or even weeks later. One may reckon that a week between death and inquest was a reasonable interval to allow for a message to reach the coroner, who might be away from home attending to duties some distance away, and for him to travel to the inquest location and assemble jurors and township representatives. But over ten per cent of the 475 death inquests so far examined are stated to have taken place more than a week after death apparently occurred or the body was discovered. Sometimes – as when death occurred in an isolated place, or from drowning in running water which might carry the body away – delay in finding the corpse may account for long intervals. Walter Wodewyk, for example, fell into the River Avon at Avoncliff, but the inquest was not held until thirty-four days later at Winsley; the inquest into Robert Gregory's death was held at Melksham, where his body was stated to be, seven weeks after his boat overturned between Beanacre and Woodrow.[22]

Deliberate concealment of homicide victims sometimes caused delays. One man tried to hide his victim's body under a collapsed wall, another was caught attempting to hide his in a heap of straw, and John le Taillour was said to have killed his houseguest with an axe, robbed him, and buried his body in the courtyard.[23] No doubt that explains the delay of sixty-eight days before the inquest into the latter's death was held. Leaving aside cases such as these, there still remain many occasions on which inexplicable delays occurred. One may here cite a few examples. John Wybern fell out with his travelling companions, who then attacked him with staves and knives. He survived for ten days – plenty of time to identify the killers and, presumably, for it to become apparent that he would not recover – but his inquest was not held until twelve days after his death. Henry Cole was crushed by a fallen oak tree which rolled onto him while he was cutting the branches off. He lived for six days, and another eight elapsed before the inquest. John de Coubrigge was said to have died at once when struck on the head by an axe, but forty-four days were to pass before his

---

[22] PRO, JUST 2/194, rot. 3 dorse, no. 4; 200, rot. 7, no. 5.
[23] PRO, JUST 2/195, rot. 10, no. 6; 194, rot. 9, nos 3 and 4.

inquest. Finally, Christina, wife of Michael le Ropere, was said to have fallen onto her unsheathed weaving knife while drunk. She was probably found quite quickly since she lived in a small town, but her inquest did not take place for twenty-one days.[24]

It is difficult to account for most of these lengthy intervals. In one case there are two delayed inquests concerning the same incident, and here the explanation is straightforward. On 29 March 1347 an armed gang descended on Beamish manor, where Marjory, the widow of Nicholas de la Beche, was living. They killed Michael de Ponynges, knight, and another man, kidnapped some of Marjory's servants, and made off with goods worth £12. At the first inquest, twelve days later, the leader of the gang was named as John Dalton, knight, of Lancashire. Further information must have come to light later, since eight weeks after the first inquest another was held. There another two suspects were named. Since a coroner's inquest was probably a necessary preliminary to the issuing of a writ of arrest for a homicide suspect, the second inquest served both to present further information and as a means of beginning legal process against the other suspects.[25] But for the most part there is no discernible pattern. One might feel that delayed inquests were perhaps more acceptable in accidental deaths, since apart from the assessment of deodand values no further action was required, whereas in homicide cases there were suspects to be identified so that legal process against them could begin. However, this consideration seems to have prompted no particular sense of urgency; delayed inquests into homicides outnumbered those into deaths by misadventure.

Whatever the reasons for these delays, the fact that so many of them are recorded is surely irrefutable evidence that engrossing clerks in Wiltshire were certainly not attempting to tamper with dates. And, as has already been

---

[24] PRO, JUST 2/194, rot. 12, no. 5; rot. 3, no. 3; 193, rot. 3, no. 1; rot. 1, no. 6.

[25] PRO, JUST 2/195, rot. 8, no. 5; rot. 8 dorse, no. 4. The case provides an appropriate example of the difficulties of bringing those indicted for homicide to justice. Matilda, widow of Thomas le Clerke, brought an appeal before King's Bench for the death of her husband: PRO, KB 27/357, rex 34. The case dragged on for years: some fourteen years later one of the individuals she accused finally appeared with a pardon, and obtained reversal of his outlawry on the grounds that at the time it was executed against him he had been at the siege of Calais: PRO, KB 27/402, rex 24 dorse.

mentioned, it can often be difficult to establish how long after the fatal incident an individual died, especially if he or she is said to have received the last rites. While some clerks carefully indicated for how many hours, days or even weeks the unfortunate lingered (if at all), others only recorded the incident date. If, in such cases, the subject of the inquest in fact survived beyond the date on which the fatal injury was received, then ironically some inquest records may give the impression that a coroner was less, not more, efficient than was actually the case. If one is willing to accept that engrossing clerks were subject to the usual margins of error arising out of haste and simple copying mistakes, and not generally guilty of deliberate falsification, one must then consider whether the narratives and verdicts they recorded were truthful in the first place. The need for a cautious approach cannot be too strongly emphasised. Medical knowledge was poor; forensic science unknown; and the process of decomposition doubtless concealed, conveniently for some, signs that a death had occurred in a manner other than that in which the jurors believed (or said that they believed. These two may not be the same thing at all.)

Let us begin with suicide verdicts. Because suicide was a felony, any property belonging to the suicide was forfeit to the Crown unless evidence of insanity was brought. If a father committed suicide this would be hard on his family; and as well as facing material loss, his family was subjected to the trauma and social embarrassment of burial rituals which were both physically brutal and spiritually comfortless. It is only too probable that the families and friends of suicides sought, where possible, to disguise the true nature of death either as an accident or perhaps even a killing by one of the ubiquitous 'unknown strangers' who appear from nowhere, commit a homicide, and disappear as mysteriously as they arrived. The sympathy of the whole community, and an understandable desire by that community not of necessity to become responsible for the support of a destitute family, might also extend to the jurors and tithingmen responsible for presenting the information relevant to the death at the inquest. Conversely, it is quite conceivable that a killer might conceal his crime under the guise of suicide. One of the male suicides in the Wiltshire records seems to contain some highly suspicious elements. The inquest states that Nicholas Workeman, a guest in the house of Thomas Houpere, got out of bed in the middle of the night and went to the mill-pond, where he drowned himself. He is said to have had no belongings.[26] Attention has already been drawn to one instance where a host is said to have killed his guest with robbery as the motive, and it is not the only such case. Perhaps here we have a killing of the same kind, in which luck was on the side of the killer. The inquest was not held until eight days later, by which time any physical marks caused by asphyxiation or a blow on the head were probably undetectable.

As regards the concealment of suicides, perhaps we should look for these in some types – or rather a particular type – of misadventure verdict. In 1970 Paul Hair suggested that suicide by drowning was, to Tudor women, the equivalent of the drug overdose or inhalation of exhaust fumes to their modern counterparts.[27] He even advanced a statistical formula on which a calculation might be made of the real numbers of female suicides thus concealed. It is certainly true that in the fourteenth century also female drownings are extraordinarily numerous compared with those of men, and remain so even when allowance is made for the fact that the fetching of water for household needs was predominantly a female responsibility, made hazardous by slippery plank bridges, muddy river or stream banks, the lack of protective fences or walls around wells, pits and ponds, and the absence of artificial lighting. While these dangers made women more vulnerable to death by drowning, it is highly likely that among apparently accidental deaths there are some suicides which were either genuinely believed to be accidents or were claimed to be so for the reasons already suggested.

Non-accidental deaths may also lie behind some misadventure verdicts: those concerning the deaths of children should perhaps be treated with special caution. Despite the social and legal structures of the twentieth century designed to protect this vulnerable group – a paid police force, vigilant teachers, social workers, telephone helplines, and media awareness – scarcely a week passes which does not bring to light cases in which parents or other responsible adults have tortured or abused the children in their care. The Wiltshire

---

[26] PRO, JUST 2/202, rot. 2, no. 2.

[27] P. Hair, 'A note on the incidence of Tudor suicides', *Local Population Studies*, 5 (1970), pp. 36–43; 'Death from violence in Britain: a tentative secular survey', *Population Studies*, 25 (1971), pp. 5–24. I am grateful to Dr Post for further helpful discussions on this topic.

coroners' rolls contain literally dozens of infant deaths from burning or scalding. The layout of a peasant house, with its central unguarded hearth over which a trivet supported a cooking pot full of hot liquid or food, but which was the warmest place to nurse a child, leave a cradle or for toddlers to play, was a hazardous environment for small children. Dr Hanawalt found cases where inquests blamed hens or pigs for starting fires as they wandered in through open doorways and scattered burning embers, or knocked over cooking pots and scalded small children.[28] In one case from Wiltshire, it was said that a five-year-old boy, John Cok, had been left minding his one-year-old brother William, who was lying in a cradle beside the fire. The cradle caught fire because John was not paying enough attention, and William died.[29] But abuse inflicted on children today often takes the form of deliberate scalding or burning. There is no reason to suppose that some adults in the fourteenth century did not injure the children in their care, the difference being that those responsible were more likely to escape discovery. Despite the harsher discipline to which minors were subjected, infanticide was far from being tolerated.[30] Fear of retribution is always a strong motive for concealment of the truth. The fairly detailed and often highly plausible accounts of how various small children pulled cooking pots on top of themselves or fell into pans of boiling water may in most instances be true. On the other hand, they bear uncomfortably close resemblance to the elaborate explanations concocted today by guilty adults to explain away their childrens' injuries.[31] Although there is no evidence that medieval parents were sadistic villains who routinely tortured their children, neither should medieval family life be seen through the roseate glow of nostalgia

---

[28] Hanawalt, *The Ties that Bound*, pp. 31–65, provides a useful survey of peasant housing structures based on archaeological evidence. The chapter on 'Childhood', pp. 171–88 is also helpful. Unfortunately, her document references are rarely so specific as to enable quick checking of her inquest information.

[29] PRO, JUST 2/200, rot. 2, no. 8.

[30] So far I have only found one case where a parent is accused of killing his or her own child. In this instance the mother is said to have stabbed her newborn child with a knife, thrown it into a river and fled. Since the mother is named with reference to her own mother and not to a husband, she was possibly young and unmarried: PRO, JUST 2/194, rot. 5 dorse, no. 4.

[31] For examples, see PRO, JUST 2/203, rot. 1, no.1; 194, rot. 2, rot. 5.

for 'family values'. Human nature is fairly constant: if a proportion of today's adult population inflicts violence on children, then a similar proportion of the medieval adult population probably did so as well.

When one bears in mind that it is impossible to establish, in most cases, whether there were any witnesses to the fatal incidents discribed in coroners' inquests, it becomes clear that all types of verdict must be scrutinised extremely carefully. Homicide accounts should perhaps be subjected to more stringent criticism than any other type of inquest. The naming of an individual as a suspect should not invite the assumption of guilt.[32] Medieval legal records abound with inquisitions held at the behest of individuals claiming to have been maliciously accused of all types of crime, including homicide. These enquiries frequently found in the complainants' favour. Most homicide cases were never tried before a court because most of those accused fled – but the flight of a suspect should not necessarily predispose us to consider that suspect as a convicted killer. The prospects for any arrested individual, innocent or guilty, were not hopeful. First, an unknown period of time might elapse before trial, if trial was ever undergone. Although gaol delivery justices regularly cleared the gaols at Old Sarum and Salisbury, for example, there are no surviving records of them ever visiting any of the other Wiltshire towns known to have gaols, and prisoners from other gaols do not seem to have been transferred to either of the two they did visit. While in gaol a prisoner depended on his or her own resources for sustenance. The drain on the family might thus be considerable. Conditions in medieval prisons were appalling. Their bad reputation is borne out by the roll of John Everard, who conducted numerous inquests in Old Sarum gaol into the deaths of prisoners who apparently died from unspecified illnesses. He held six such inquests between the end of November 1344 and the end of the following February alone – a rough average of one a fortnight, presumably the result of some kind of epidemic. Another inquest there found that one prisoner had simply died of weakness as he was brought back to the gaol after the justices had failed to hear his case that day.[33] An innocent suspect

---

[32] Hanawalt is prone to make the assumption of guilt on the basis of accusation alone.
[33] PRO, JUST 2/195, rot. 12 dorse, no. 4.

might survive until trial, but the trial brought equal hazards. Those accused of capital offences were allowed no defence counsel unless to raise points of law and only permitted to speak in response to questioning by the justices. The speed with which trials were conducted allowed little opportunity for the presentation of evidence or argument. If a guilty verdict was found, execution followed rapidly upon sentencing – there was no appeal procedure. The prospects of both survival and acquittal for anyone accused of homicide, whether innocent or guilty, made flight the preferable alternative.

Another problem in homicide cases arises from the paradoxes inherent in the law, which made no distinction between premeditated killing and what we would term manslaughter. Anyone guilty of a homicide should in theory have been hanged. On the other hand, those convicted of killing by accident or in self-defence could sue for pardon (provided of course they could afford the fee).[34] It is important to remember that the lack of medical expertise meant that many who received fairly minor injuries died from blood-poisoning or gangrene, often after a lengthy interval. Scuffles in which knives were used – and since everyone carried a knife if only to cut up food, such incidents were frequent – very often led to such fatalities. The death penalty seemed an unnecessarily harsh one for those who had merely lost their tempers, perhaps under severe provocation, and not even inflicted much damage on their opponents. Thus there were considerable incentives to describe the events leading up to such deaths in terms which would allow pardons to be applied for, whatever the true sequence of events might be, and communities cannot have been uninfluenced by factors such as the popularity and character of the individuals. Local status doubtless had its effect also. An inquest held in November 1345 describes how John Flour, acting for the Prior of St Nicholas, refused to allow William Walkyn, the tithingman of Winterslow, and his deputy

---

[34] Comprehensive treatment of pardons is found in Naomi Hurnard, *The King's Pardon for Homicide* (Oxford, 1969). Much of the discussion which follows is based on her book. Bernard Knight, *Forensic Pathology* (London, 1991), has been used as the source for the difficulties of post-mortem diagnosis up to and including the present day, and the author himself refers to the frequency of fatal infections after minor traumas before the development of antibiotics. Particularly relevant to the subjects raised in this paper are pp. 51–69, 125–36, 213–16 and 326–68.

Richard Godchild, to collect an ox in payment of the prior's tax arrears. The argument developed into a fight in which, according to the jurors, John assaulted the tax-collectors, so that in self-defence Richard hit John over the head with a staff, an injury which caused his death five days later.[35]

This narrative sounds plausible enough on first reading. But the more one examines cases where self-defence is claimed, the more apparent becomes the stereotypical account of events. The dead person is conveniently blamed for starting the fight. (This helped to slant the balance of evidence and made it easier to sue for pardon.) The two men meet.[36] One attacks the other, who turns and flees, only to find his escape blocked by an obstacle such as a wall or hedge. He turns and faces his attacker, sometimes (not always) drawing his knife but without striking out with it. By this time his attacker, who has been continuously threatening to kill him, is apparently so demented with blood lust that he hurls himself upon his intended victim and is promptly impaled by that victim's knife, either held innocently in the hand or even more innocuously tucked into a belt. It is all his own fault. There are no grey areas here: inquest jurors, confused by what was necessary if a pardon was to be obtained, and concerned to ensure that the suspect received a favourable verdict, brought in every element possible to demonstrate not only self-defence but a certain degree of accident as well. Occasionally jurors even denied that a homicide had taken place. In a Salisbury inquest of 1345, the jurors described how Henry and William Devenays set about their brother John with swords in the Canons' Close, wanting to kill him. John's son John arrived, saw his father on the ground and in danger of death, and came and stood near his father, begging his uncles to stop. The uncles then turned on their nephew and wounded him, whereupon he stabbed his uncle William in the stomach with a knife in self-defence. They then stated that no-one was guilty of the death.[37] Now this was patently untrue in law, but it does reflect community opinion that William got what he had coming to him – and

---

[35] PRO, JUST 2/195, rot. 10 dorse, no. 5.

[36] In the only case of this kind I have so far found where a woman successfully pleaded self-defence, at a gaol delivery session at Old Sarum in 1365, the jurors said that she was defending herself against rape: PRO, JUST 3/153, rot. 3.

[37] PRO, JUST 2/199, m. 5 dorse, no. 2.

since Henry was apparently not wounded and presumably fit to give his opinion at the inquest, he either agreed or was coerced into submission. There is no evidence of his bringing a private appeal for his brother's death, although a marginal note reveals that William (prudently perhaps) secured a pardon for himself.

These few points make it clear that inquest verdicts of all types must not simply be taken at face value or accepted as representations of historical fact. Many factors, all of them unquantifiable, influenced the reaching of a verdict, and one must be aware of them in order to avoid jumping to unwarranted conclusions which do not stand up to critical scrutiny. Our sources of information about everyday life among ordinary people in the middle ages are so few that it is all too easy to succumb to the lure of narratives which are often lively and frequently touch us with pathos, humour, excitement, pity, or simply fascination. The graphic narratives of fights may remind us of Errol Flynn buckling his swash, but we must remember that just as his swordplay was carefully rehearsed, so were many of the accounts given to coroners – the difference being that to those present at a homicide inquest the blood-shed had been real, and the life of whoever had spilt it was also at stake. However, provided that one retains a firm grip on one's critical faculties, it is possible to assess which verdicts are likely to be more accurate than others, and there are enough of these to redeem coroners' inquests from the charge of total unreliability. For instance, in 1344 an inquest was told that John son of Christine le Neetes was leading a horse to pasture by a rope tied to his right hand: the horse was startled and bolted, dragging John behind it for some distance so that he died.[38] Stories such as these are not untypical. People are crushed as they dig in quarries or fell trees or demolish old houses; they fall off horses, carts, haystacks, roofs or ladders. Winches break as women draw up water so that they fall into wells. Horses or cows kick or gore those tending them. Both men and women get drunk and fall off bridges or drive their carts into ditches. Sometimes more unusual incidents occur, but ones which still have the ring of reality, like the attack by a wild boar on John le Bailiff as he worked in a coppice in the royal park at Clarendon. Although he and his companions

---

[38] PRO, JUST 2/194, rot. 6, no. 5.

caught and killed the boar, he had been gored in the leg and died four days later.[39] Urban accidents were occasionally bizarre, such as that which caused the death of William Pap. As he walked through the bell tower of St Martin's church in Salisbury one evening a beam of the tower fell on him and crushed him to death.[40]

Finally, there is the story of Robert Cotiller's bear. Dr Hanawalt referred to it in *The Ties that Bound*, but since it took place in Salisbury it may be quoted here for those unfamiliar with her book. At about midnight on 11 May 1368 the bear, which had been chained up in a room in Thomas Stoke's inn, broke its chain and smashed the partition wall of the room where it had been confined. It then climbed up to a high chamber, where another wall collapsed (presumably from the bear's weight), and where a seven-year-old girl called Emma was lying in bed. The bear killed her. Thomas Stoke, the innkeeper, was first on the scene and raised the hue. But (unsurprisingly) no one was willing to chase and arrest the bear when they heard what it had done because, the jurors said, of its malice and uncertain temper. Some method of capturing it must eventually have been found because we are next told that the bear is in the custody of the bishop of Salisbury's bailiff, and that the bishop will answer to the king for its value, which is 2s.[41] There is no reason to disbelieve any element of this story, although one would dearly love to know how the bailiff managed to catch the bear, whether anybody helped him, and what became of it afterwards.

The arguments presented here demonstrate that medieval coroners' rolls are not complete legal fictions. While there were losses of unknown numbers of inquests arising out of the time-lag between inquests and subsequent engrossment, and while human errors inevitably led to equally unquantifiable copying mistakes, there are good reasons to believe – based on the Wiltshire rolls at least – that the narratives record fairly truthfully what was said at the inquest, albeit often condensed to the barest minimum. The one area where the charge cannot be refuted is that of the actual verdicts reached; those present at inquests wittingly or in ignorance sometimes brought in verdicts which were not

---

[39] PRO, JUST 2/195, rot. 14, no. 4.
[40] PRO, JUST 2/199, m. 1, no. 2.
[41] Ibid., m. 6, no. 2.

in accordance with the reality of events. Occasionally jurors and tithingmen may have been the dupes of unscrupulous killers; sometimes they no doubt created retrospective explanations for deaths which had gone unwitnessed; sometimes they connived at distortions of the truth, or at downright deceit, in order to protect members of their communities from punishments commonly perceived to be disproportionately harsh; sometimes they were simply mistaken.

But that the inquests record what the jurors *said* had happened, there is no doubt. Thus much of their value may lie in what they tell us about community solidarity and the astuteness of community responses to royal officials, and to the inflexibilities and inefficiencies of a legal system which contemporaries bewailed and historians have criticised ever since. If approached with care, they can be used as a historical source. Most medievalists would agree that this is as much as can be said for any form of document generated almost six hundred years ago. In point of fact, since coroners' inquests were held in local communities, dealing with individuals known to people whose memories of events were still fresh, it may be that in their own way they are more reliable than the records, for example, of court hearings such as those before the remote figures of King's Bench justices, whose cases frequently concerned events which had happened several years earlier to individuals with whom few present in the court had any familiarity: and they are certainly more informative than the majority of accounts of cases heard before gaol delivery justices. We do well to look to whatever sources are available to reconstruct the realities of life (and death) in medieval society provided that we understand the purposes for which those records which we use were originally intended, the methods by which they were generated and the factors which influenced the information (or misinformation) incorporated in them. Let us be realistic in the questions we ask of our records, and stringent in the critical criteria we apply to them. No farmer would dream of allowing his corn to rot in the fields because it is unusable unless the worthless chaff is first winnowed out. Neither should we.

6
RELATIONSHIPS BETWEEN LONDON'S COURTS AND THE WESTMINSTER COURTS IN THE REIGN OF EDWARD IV

Penny Tucker

Late medieval London, like a number of other towns, had long enjoyed considerable privileges.[1] One of the most advantageous, in terms of protecting its jurisdiction, was the concession that 'no freeman of the city [was] to implead another elsewhere if he could recover in the Sheriffs' or Mayor's Court', the penalty being loss of the freedom, imprisonment and fine, unless he could satisfy the court of aldermen that city officers had 'failed to do right' in his case.[2] Another advantage was that, while the city's courts were common law courts, they dealt with civil actions according to 'the common law and the custom of the city', as well as 'according to law merchant' and 'according to conscience' (equitably). This gave their procedures a flexibility that the fifteenth-century Westminster common law courts lacked. So long as the city's governors were alert to infringements, they could keep within their jurisdiction any civil case to which they could sensibly assert a claim.[3]

---

[1] *Borough Customs*, ed. M. Bateson, Selden Society (2 vols, 1904 and 1906), 1, p. xiv. Examples of boroughs granted the same 'custom, law and liberty' as London are Oxford and Norwich: *Calendar of the Early Mayor's Court Rolls of the City of London, A.D. 1298–1307*, ed. A.H. Thomas (Cambridge, 1924), p. xi; and *Minutes of the Norwich Court of Mayoralty 1630–1631*, ed. W.L. Sachse, Norfolk Record Society, 15 (1942), p. 12.

[2] *Liber Albus: the White Book of the City of London*, ed. and tr. H.T. Riley (London, 1861), pp. 133 and 360.

[3] Thus actions in debt and account arising from commercial arrangements entered into outside the city could be brought in the city's courts if the payment was due to take place there: *Liber Albus*, pp. 190–1. Actions involving London property could be claimed, even if the owner lived elsewhere and was, almost certainly, not a citizen: e.g. CLRO, Husting Roll, Pleas of Land 165, mm. 1 and 1v.

Whether these advantages were sufficient to protect the city's courts from poaching by the central courts, either deliberate or accidental, is another question. Beyond the city's boundaries, the traditional picture of many of the older common law courts during the late middle ages is one of decline – towards extinction, in some cases. This decline affected both the main Westminster courts, the combined profits of king's bench and the common pleas from one, probably indicative, source of revenue falling from more than £500 a year at the start of the century to less than half that at its end.[4] The second half of the fifteenth century saw the beginning of a sudden flowering of newer equity courts such as chancery and the star chamber, a flowering which has been viewed as threatening not merely the income of the old central courts, but even the common law itself. Not until well into the next century did king's bench, followed at some distance by the common pleas, manage to recover its former supremacy. How were London's courts affected by the early stages of this period of change and challenge? Were they in competition with the central courts and, if so, how did this manifest itself? How well did they manage to retain and protect their jurisdiction during Edward IV's reign? Above all, what benefits did the continuing existence and potency of a city system of law offer to London and its government?

The city courts of law were the sheriffs' court (or 'courts', since cases were initiated at a particular sheriff's counter and heard before that sheriff alone), the ancient court of husting and the mayor's court. In addition, there were the wardmotes. Complaints made before an alderman, in or out of the wardmote, evidently played a fairly important part in the maintenance of civic law and order. It may well be that a good deal of lesser business was dealt with by the alderman in an administrative or quasi-judicial fashion: offenders may simply have been ordered to amend their property or their ways. Others were remanded to the sheriffs' court, while those who had offended against civic ordinances, 'the correction of which pertains to the city', found themselves the object of the attention of the mayor's court.[5] Although wardmotes were clearly a

---

[4] M. Blatcher, *The Court of King's Bench 1450–1550: A Study in Self-Help* (London, 1978), pp. 17–21.

[5] Chancery petitions very frequently complain that the petitioner has been imprisoned by the sheriffs at an alderman's instance, awaiting an appearance in court: e.g. PRO, Chancery, Early Chancery Proceedings, C1/32, mm. 53, 79, 371, 377, 413, 433 and 434; *Liber Albus*, p. 33.

part of the overall judicial system, they had no power to determine cases, and they were mainly concerned with the enforcement of civic regulations, such as ordinances against property nuisances, regulating prices, or preventing immoral or anti-social behaviour. It is on the relationships between the three higher courts of the city and of the central, Westminster courts that this paper concentrates.[6] Moreover, because evidence for the exercise of London's criminal jurisdiction is scant, most of the evidence of the relationship between the city courts and the Westminster courts is to be found in the surviving records of civil actions. The focus here is therefore on the city's jurisdiction in civil litigation.

Moving upwards from the wardmotes, next in the hierarchy of city courts was the sheriffs' court, the court of first resort for most individuals and most kinds of civil and criminal actions, although it did not proceed beyond the presentment stage with serious crimes. Theoretically, it was also unable to handle civil cases involving rights to and in land.[7] Otherwise, its competence was wide, and it dealt with a range of common law personal actions such as debt, detinue and trespass.

In the absence of any contemporary sheriffs' court rolls (the last surviving medieval roll is for 1318–20), it is impossible to do more than estimate the activity level of this court during the late fifteenth century. The best evidence comes from a series of chancery writ files, many of which mention actions dealt with by the London courts. These show that the equity side of chancery rarely entertained fewer than 100 or more than 200 petitions relating to cases in the sheriffs' court in any one year, the annual average being 116. These figures, therefore, represent the absolute minimum for the numbers of actions brought before the sheriffs. It is highly likely that only a fraction of the actions brought in the sheriffs' court resulted in petitions to chancery. At one point in the 1450s, the mayor's court was receiving at least 374 bills a year, whereas the number of surviving chancery writs relating to mayor's court actions during Edward IV's

---

[6] *Calendar of the Plea and Memoranda Rolls of the City of London, 1413–37*, ed. A.H. Thomas (Cambridge, 1943), pp. xxviii–xxix.

[7] In fact it did hear such actions, because it could entertain offences which were 'trespasses and contempts against the king', i.e., offences against statute; and among these were included offences against the late fourteenth- and early fifteenth-century statutes against forcible entry (5 Richard II to 8 Henry VI).

reign averaged 14.5 a year. Unless there was a dramatic reduction in the business handled by the mayor's court after 1460, therefore, probably less than 4 per cent of its cases ended up in chancery. If the same ratio applied to the Edwardian sheriffs' court, it would have been entertaining on average around 3,000 civil actions a year. Even if one assumes that sheriffs' court cases were more likely than mayor's court ones to be the subject of a chancery petition (and it is a debatable assumption, given that the London mayor and aldermen seem to have been very willing to intervene forcefully in cases of default by the lower court or its officers), it seems improbable that more than 10 per cent of all civil actions initiated in the sheriffs' court were brought to the attention of chancery. On this more conservative basis, the Edwardian sheriffs' court would have been handling at least 1,000 civil actions a year, in addition to its criminal presentments and other law-and-order cases. This was about as many as the court had been entertaining in the early fourteenth century.[8] It would equate to between a quarter and a sixth of the number of civil cases recorded on the rolls of the court of common pleas, and would mean that the civil business of the sheriffs' court roughly equalled the entire workload of king's bench.[9] Although London is incomparable, evidence from elsewhere suggests that the more conservative figure could well under-estimate the workload of the sheriffs' court. Nottingham's borough court between 1422 and 1457 seems to have been entertaining at least 850 personal actions a year, and possibly as many as 1,000.[10] Between the late fifteenth and the early sixteenth century, when Shrewsbury's population may have been only a twentieth of London's, about 450–500 actions a year were being brought in its *curia parva* alone.[11] The probability is that only about half of the sheriffs' court actions would have got as

---

[8] In the Michaelmas term 1320, up to 476 pleas were entered on the court's rolls (though not all terms may have been as busy as this): CLRO, Sheriffs' Court Roll 1318–20, mm. 1, 5v, 8, 9, 10–10v, 14, 17, 18–18v, 22, 25v (intervening membranes record associated process).

[9] Based on M. Hastings, *The Court of Common Pleas* (Ithaca, New York, 1947), p. 27, fn. 47, and Blatcher, *The Court of King's Bench*, p. 21.

[10] T. Foulds, Jill Hughes and M. Jones, 'The Nottingham Borough Court Rolls: The Reign of Henry VI (1422–57)', *Transactions of the Thoroton Society of Nottinghamshire*, 97 (1993), p. 76 and n. 7.

[11] W. Champion, 'Litigation in the Boroughs', *Journal of Legal History*, 15 (1994), pp. 202–4. This court heard real, mixed and personal actions, combining some of the functions of the London husting and the sheriffs' court.

far as a determination in court; as many as 60 per cent of cases may have been abandoned or compromised. Certainly this was true of the sheriffs' court in the first quarter of the fourteenth century.[12] Low prosecution rates seem to have been a characteristic of most medieval courts; of all the recorded actions begun in Nottingham's borough court between 1422 and 1457, for example, fewer than 20 per cent definitely went as far as a jury or wager of law.[13]

As far as types of action are concerned, the chancery writ files indicate that, while there were marked short-term fluctuations, on average about 52 per cent of cases involved actions of debt and about 33 per cent were of trespass. The ratios found in the writ files are similar to those obtainable from surviving fifteenth-century city records (none, unfortunately, contemporary).[14] This is in line with the evidence from the 1320s: then, over 50 per cent of the actions were for debt and just under 35 per cent were for trespass.[15] It therefore looks as though the number of cases entertained by the court, on the 'civil' side at least, suffered no decline between the early fourteenth and the late fifteenth century. It may even have risen substantially. The proportion of debt and trespass cases seems to have held steady over the same period.

Of course, not all cases concerned personalty. In theory, anyone who wanted to bring a real action, one involving the title to or possession of land, had to turn to the court of husting. Husting was divided into two sides. One, the husting of pleas of land, concerned itself almost entirely with the rightful ownership of land. The other, the husting of common pleas, dealt with a range of rights arising out of

---

[12] For example, on 1 July 1320 there were (excluding obvious duplications) 39 new pleas. In 47 cases which were already under way, there were 10 wagers of law, 6 jury verdicts, and 3 judgments rendered (40.5 per cent); in addition, 9 lovedays and 5 licences to concord were granted (29.75 per cent), and 14 individuals were amerced for failure to prosecute (29.75 per cent): CLRO, Sheriffs' Court Roll 1318–20, mm. 1–5.

[13] Foulds, Hughes and Jones, 'Nottingham Borough Court Rolls', pp. 74–87, especially p. 76.

[14] CLRO, Sheriffs' Rolls, box 1 (early fifteenth century), and Sheriffs' Register of Writs 1458–9, ff. 1–18. Unfortunately, the (no doubt substantial) section in the Register recording chancery *corpus cum causa* and *certiorari* writs, summoning either the case or a record of it into chancery, is missing, leaving only a relatively modest number of equivalent king's bench, exchequer and common pleas writs (*habeas corpus* and *recordari*), together with some chancery writs *capias/attachias*, ordering the arrest or attachment of defendants for appearance on the common law side of the court.

[15] CLRO, Sheriffs' Court Roll 1318–20, mm. 1, 5v, 8, 10–10v, 14, 17, 18–18v, 22, 25v and 26v. The calculation excludes eight entries in which the nature of the action is uncertain.

possession or temporary occupation of land (for example, dower and rents). By the late fifteenth century, the court dealt entirely with actions brought by (royal) writ.

In the first thirteen years for which an apparently complete fifteenth-century record of sessions on both sides of husting survives (1448–61), there were on average about 12.5 sessions a year on both sides of the court. From 1461 onwards, and particularly from 1465 on, the total number of sessions increased markedly. Between then and the end of the reign, the annual average was just under nineteen; around sixteen a year between 1461 and 1471, and twenty-one a year thereafter. Only in one year, 1479, did it drop back towards the earlier average; and two years later there were thirty sessions. This suggests that something had occurred which revivified the ancient court.

Table 1

TYPES OF ACTION BROUGHT IN HUSTING, 1448–81

Type of Action[a]	1448–61	1461–71	1471–81
Right	25	44	66
Error	15	11	3
Waste	4	4	–
Dower	6	9	8
Gavelet	4	6	2
Partition	1	–	–
Replevin/'Naam'	14	14	21
TOTAL	69	88	100
Lovedays granted	–	1	8[b]

[a] Types of action:

[1] Waste: brought by heir against guardian or doweress, etc. who has allegedly reduced the value of lands held during minority.

[2] Gavelet: brought for restitution of services or rents, or recovery of property for non-performance.

[3] Partition: brought by one parcener (co-heir) against another.

[4] Replevin/'naam' ('vee de naam' or 'withernam'): brought to recover allegedly wrongly-distrained property.

[b] Fifty-six lovedays granted, but relating to only eight cases.

The main reason for the increase in business, apart from a rise in replevin cases (brought for the recovery of distrained property) in the final decade of Edward IV's reign, was that the writ of right, an old-fashioned action with distinct procedural drawbacks, took on a new lease of life in the mid-1450s. The first example of this 'new' writ-of-right action to be recorded in both the hustings book and the formal pleadings roll is a case from May 1454, brought again in May 1460, between the under-sheriff of London, Rigby and others, against Thomas Pinchon.[16] Thereafter there was a steady trickle of such actions: between one and four a year, plus a few others which were repeats. A good number of them are paralleled by deeds enrolled in the husting. The first recorded example from Edward IV's reign of this dual approach occurred in 1462, when Thomas Pinchon's heir, Baptist Pinchon, quitclaimed to Rigby and his associates the five messuages over which a further writ-of-right action had recently been brought in the husting.[17] As the repeated appearance of the same properties indicates, these actions were not genuinely contested ones. The Pinchons were using the tenements to raise loans or pay off existing debts, and got them back again once they had paid their creditors. It is possible that the increase in writ-of-right actions alone accounted for the increased number of sessions, since in the three periods the latter increase follows a broadly similar profile to that of the writ-of-right actions. By this means, the husting's level of activity was enhanced. The court had long been of value to citizens as a place of public record. The fictitious actions begun by writs of right seem to have been used for similar purposes from the mid-1450s onwards. Nonetheless, the development of the writ-of-right action is in itself evidence of a more general and negative trend. As a public forum in which to witness and prove important events, agreements or documents, the husting held its ground between the 1450s and the 1480s, but as an active court of law, it was almost moribund.[18] It was increasingly becoming a kind of register office, its sessions confined to

---

[16] CLRO, Husting Roll, Pleas of Land 167, m. 1; Hustings Book, f. 27 and Husting Roll, Pleas of Land 167, m. 11.

[17] CLRO, MS Calendar of Husting Wills and Deeds, p. 28 (item 192/4).

[18] If the collusive writ-of-right actions are ignored, the two courts were entertaining some 44 actions per decade, or fewer than 4.5 new cases a year, between 1448 and 1481.

monthly or fortnightly meetings, at a number of which, until they got bored with doing so, the clerks recorded 'no pleas'.

The picture is different again when one turns to the mayor's court. This, unlike the husting, was a relatively new court. It developed a distinct identity towards the end of the thirteenth century, having taken over from the husting such matters as the enforcement of civic ordinances. Possibly it was also viewed as being somewhat superior, but this is doubtful, since the judges in both courts were the same. The mayor's court had both a formal and an informal aspect, or, more accurately, a public and an *in camera* aspect. When it sat *in camera* (*iudicaliter sedentes*, as the city's administrative records put it), its clerks did not always trouble to distinguish legal business from administrative affairs.

How much civil business the mayor's court as a whole was handling is impossible to determine accurately, although it was almost certainly much less occupied with this type of action than the sheriffs' court. A good deal of evidence relating to the activities of the mayor's court in Edward IV's reign has undoubtedly vanished entirely. Although many documents from a class of records known as the plea and memoranda rolls have survived from this period, the number of recorded actions in them is quite low. This is not because very few cases were brought in the mayor's court. Some idea of what has disappeared can be obtained by comparing the memoranda roll entries of the mid-1450s with a file of bills from the same period. This file, consisting mainly of cases arising in 1456/7, contains 264 bills, and the contemporary numeration reaches as high as 374.[19] The memoranda roll records the affirmation of just one bill. It does not of course follow that the court in

---

[19] CLRO, Files of Original Bills, MC1/3A. These bills give the date of the alleged offence and sometimes, where process ensued, dates when this occurred; e.g. on 4 August, a defendant denied and sought jury; 1 July, another defendant acknowledged a debt; 1 August, a third defendant said that she owed nothing and asked to wage her law: MC1/3A, mm. 3, 9 and 12. Most were brought in the mayor's court proper, although it was possible to bring an original bill in the inner chamber; in the absence of other evidence, the fact that the case is simply described as an 'action', not an action of debt etc., indicates that the venue was probably the inner chamber: PRO, Corpus Cum Causa Writ Files, C244/118, m. 68.

session was handling between 300 and 400 civil actions each year, as well as its other work. Fewer than a third of the 264 bills record process of any kind; fewer than a tenth record determination (recovery, delivery or non-prosecution). Even so, there is clearly a considerable discrepancy between the number of actions heard before the court and the number recorded in the memoranda rolls.

As has already been mentioned, mayor's court cases were sometimes referred to in chancery petitions. The number of such references fluctuated greatly throughout Edward IV's reign, from a low of five in 1464/5 (mayoral year, November to October) to a high of forty-one in 1473/4. Allowing for variable losses in the evidence itself, these fluctuations seem to align themselves with periods known to have been quiet or turbulent, and there is certainly no downward trend. Indeed, it is possible that the trend was upwards. The only years in which the total number of references to civil actions brought in the mayor's court in all known sources exceeded forty, apart from the civil war years of 1470–2, were four years in the final decade of Edward IV's reign (1473/4, 1475/6, 1479/80 and 1480/81).

The chancery writ files appear to provide evidence of a change in the distribution of personal actions between the three main categories of debt, trespass and 'other'. This shifted gradually but quite substantially during Edward IV's reign. Debt formed a much smaller element in mayor's court cases between March 1461 and October 1471 (55 per cent, similar to the proportion found in the sheriffs' court) than it did between November 1471 and October 1481 (76.5 per cent). Indeed, in 1481/2 it stood at over 90 per cent. Another peak year was 1474/5, when the proportion of debt cases shot up to just under 80 per cent. This, however, may very well reflect the economic dislocation created by the French expedition of 1475, as creditors called in debts in order to pay the enormous sums granted to the king in taxes and gifts.

Leaving aside the special case of 1474/5, it seems that there were changes in the type of actions begun in the mayor's court which were not attributable simply to transient political or economic factors. Debt seems to have come to dominate its workload, and this was not because, in a declining market, debt simply maintained its position. The only reason to doubt that there was a genuine long-term shift in the relative importance of the main types of action is the fact that the 1450s' file of original bills is also dominated by debt, at over 90 per cent. However, given that no more than 70 per cent of the original bills survive on this file, and that it is not clear whether some principle or simple chance determined the survival of the extant bills, this evidence merely adjusts the balance somewhat. A cautious conclusion would be that debt, which had dominated the court's workload before Edward IV's usurpation, lost ground thereafter, but re-asserted itself towards the end of his lifetime.

With the exception of the court of husting, the city's courts appear to have been maintaining their levels of activity during Edward IV's reign. They may even have been entertaining more actions in this reign than they had done previously. It is, however, possible that the threat to their continuing vitality lay, not in the poaching of existing city court business by any of the Westminster courts, but in some shift in legal fashions which created new types of work elsewhere, and would eventually cause the types of case being brought in the London courts to wither on the vine. Just as it was probably the waning in popularity of writ-initiated real actions which reduced the husting to a shadow of its former self, so some analogous change in legal fashions could have already been at work, preparing to undermine the London courts. If this was indeed the case, one would expect to see some evidence in the records of the central courts, where the nature and proportion of the London cases might be expected to change even if, for other reasons, their total number did not rise.[20] It might also show up as an increasing specialisation by the late fifteenth-century London courts in particular forms of action, and in different patterns of business in the city and central courts.

The city did have an Achilles heel which could render it vulnerable to external interference. There were a number of limitations on its jurisdiction, some formal, some informal and some temporary, depending upon the political climate or pressures from other courts. In particular, the fact that city jurisdiction was still basically local jurisdiction had its consequences, as when a debtor 'withdrew' from London to avoid litigation, or when individuals challenged the right of city courts to hear cases where the matter allegedly arose

---

[20] For example, because the central court concerned was itself losing business to chancery: E.W. Ives, 'The Common Lawyers of Pre-Reformation England', *TRHS*, 98 (1968), pp. 165–70.

elsewhere in England or abroad.[21] The rules governing the removal of cases to the central common law courts were, however, quite restrictive. The city could and did resist any abuse of established procedure. In 1454 the city despatched the common serjeant to persuade the justices of common pleas not to allow London citizens to sue out writs of privilege from that court when they should have prosecuted their action in the city's courts. In this, it was successful.[22] In 1469 it scored what was evidently regarded by London's administrators as an even more significant victory over a chancery clerk who was also a London citizen, Peter or Piers Peckham, who had attempted to exploit the common law privilege of that court in order to avoid having to answer in one of the city's courts.[23]

What may have posed a more serious threat to London's own courts were certain less controlled developments in the Westminster common law courts. For instance, it was possible for plaintiffs to sue by bill in king's bench if either the offence had occurred in Middlesex or the defendant was already a prisoner of the court. At some stage, plaintiffs found a means of getting individuals who neither had committed an offence in Middlesex nor were king's bench prisoners into the nominal custody of the marshal of the prison; thereafter, they were able to use the less complex and expensive, and sometimes more successful, bill procedure against their opponent. It was during the late fifteenth century that the seeds of this device, known as 'the bill of Middlesex', seem first to have germinated.[24]

Other Westminster courts offered bill procedures for use by and against officers and against prisoners of the court. The exchequer also possessed a writ

---

[21] For example, CLRO, Journal of the Common Council 7, f. 14v; PRO, C1/46, mm. 407 and 181 (where it was objected that neither party to an action brought in the sheriffs' court lived in London); PRO, C1/44, m. 253; C1/45, m. 2 and C1/46, m. 323.

[22] *Calendar of the Plea and Memoranda Rolls of London 1437–57*, ed. P.E. Jones (Cambridge, 1954), p. 136. The city's case in this instance was probably strong, since the plaintiff seems to have been trying to abuse the privilege of court by raising a counter-suit in common pleas to his opponent's action in the London mayor's court (the fact that the case was 'pending' gives the game away).

[23] *A Calendar of the Letterbook L of the City of London*, ed. R.R. Sharpe (London, 1912), pp. 89–90; the victory was also recorded in a near-contemporary London custumal, known as Liber Dunthorn: CLRO, Ancient Custumal Liber Dunthorn, p. 409. For details of the confrontation: CLRO, Journal of the Common Council 7, ff. 202v, 203, 204v and 205.

[24] Blatcher, *The Court of King's Bench*, p. 121.

of privilege, which could be used by individuals who were not exchequer officers to sue in that court on the assertion that they were 'the less able' to repay the king because their own debtors would not pay them. In common pleas, it is true, use of the bill of privilege to offer a speedier process to non-officer plaintiffs was not permitted.[25] The fact that this court's activities were so much discussed may of itself have prevented the kind of undercover developments that occurred in king's bench, or it could be that the 1454 protest against the abuse of privilege by a London citizen was the decisive factor.[26] In any event, there were other ways in which common pleas could make itself more accessible to would-be litigants. Professor Baker suggested that the extension of the action of *assumpsit* allowed the common law 'to escape the procedural shackles of debt and covenant' sometime between 1450 and 1500.[27] Once freed from the constraints of the older actions, the common pleas could offer one great advantage over courts which operated according to merchant law and local custom: the ability to reach defendants in almost all parts of the country.

In all these cases, evidence of sensitivity to encroachment by one or other of the central courts would give reason to suspect that such encroachment posed a genuine threat. There are certainly examples to be found of city resistance to outside interference. The 1454 protest against the abuse of the common pleas writ of privilege is one among many.[28] The way in which the court of aldermen behaved over the Middlesex undershrievalty suggests that they might have been particularly concerned about possible poaching by king's bench. This office was 'filled by a succession of king's bench clerks and filacers', who normally changed annually by arrangement with the sheriffs.[29] However, on a number of occasions

---

[25] Hastings, *The Court of Common Pleas*, p. 26.

[26] The first prothonotary (chief clerk) and other officials there were ordered strictly 'not to make, or to allow to be made, any such writs, upon pain etc.'. *Calendar of the Plea and Memoranda Rolls of London 1437–57*, p. 136.

[27] J.H. Baker, *The Legal Profession and the Common Law* (London, 1986), pp. 348–9 and 353–4.

[28] Examples from 1466 alone are: CLRO, Journal of the Common Council 7, ff. 108 and 114v (common pleas); ibid., ff. 107v, 135v and 136 (king's bench).

[29] Blatcher, *The Court of King's Bench*, pp. 42–3; and see p. 35, where this is described as 'invariably' so.

in Edward IV's reign the Middlesex undersheriffs were chosen by the city.[30] In 1482 an ordinance was issued in the common council which had the aim of limiting tenure to men of substance and resident in the county, 'in order to avoid the extortions and scandals arising from the nomination of undersheriffs'.[31] Moreover, on one occasion when the mayor and aldermen decided to appoint John Stocker undersheriff of Middlesex, they made it clear that they were referring to the city's common huntsman.[32] One possible explanation for these interventions is that the 'bill of Middlesex' was already beginning to attract business into king's bench which should not, strictly speaking, have been there. As a result, perhaps, the mayor and aldermen were becoming increasingly sensitive to the Middlesex side of king's bench business, and increasingly concerned to have 'one of them' as the clerk responsible for the receipt of Middlesex writs and bills.

Finally, there is evidence that a good many litigants did not work their way through the city law system before appealing to chancery for assistance. In a scandalous case in which John Weatherley, a prisoner, accused Sheriff Simon Smith of extortion, the plaintiff seems to have begun by appealing to the chancellor. Weatherley's action was remitted to the mayor's court; when the court had reached its initial judgment, Smith promptly complained to the chancellor.[33] It seems that both men saw chancery as a first resort, and resorted to it without evident complaint from the city.

The evidence does not suggest that the Westminster common law courts, at least, were poaching substantial amounts of business which properly belonged in the London courts of law. Certainly the number of cases with the marginal note 'London' on the record of plea (civil) side of king's bench was never large. A sampling of files at approximately five-yearly intervals from 1462 reveals a

---

[30] Stocker probably held office on five or six occasions, and another man, Henry Morland, a king's bench clerk but one selected by the city, on three: for Stocker, see CLRO, Journal of the Common Council 7, ff. 129v, 155v, 192v; PRO, Court of King's Bench, Ancient Indictments, KB9/334, m. 2, KB9/335, m. 2v; KB9/347, mm. 10 and 49, and KB9/362, m. 40; for Morland, see CLRO, Journal of the Common Council 7, f. 40v; PRO, KB9/321, m. 131 and KB9/338, m. 32.

[31] CLRO, Journal of the Common Council 8, f. 287v.

[32] CLRO, Journal of the Common Council 7, f. 129v.

[33] Ibid., ff. 187–7v and 191–1v; PRO, C1/45/376.

rise in the number of London cases during the 1470s, but it tails off towards the end. Throughout, the majority, some 80–90 per cent, are writ-initiated actions of trespass.[34] There is nothing to suggest a significant increase in king's bench business at the expense of the London courts. Certainly there is very little sign of any manipulation of process, of the type associated with the 'bill of Middlesex'.[35]

Undoubtedly the common pleas entertained far more 'London' cases than did king's bench. Even so, there is little reason to suppose that this activity occurred at the expense of the London courts. Most of the actions recorded were brought by London citizens either for the recovery of what appear to be straightforward loans to, or trade debts owed by, various gentlemen and esquires, or advances to clothworkers, chapmen, dyers and the like, made in the course of

---

[34] The remainder were almost entirely actions of debt, detinue and account. The numbers of London cases in Michaelmas 1462, 1467, 1472, 1477 and 1482 were 33, 40, 59, 55 and 41 respectively. Michaelmas 1467 was an unusual term, in that only 61 per cent of the actions were trespasses. In the other years, trespasses constituted at least 80 per cent, and on two occasions, 90 per cent or more, of the actions: PRO, Court of King's Bench, *Coram Rege* Rolls, KB27, mm. 806, 826, 845, 865 and 882. (It is possible that, because bills were not enrolled until they reached a certain stage in the process, the king's bench *panella* files, which are in a poor state, contain more bills and a different ratio of trespass to other cases; see, for example, the decision of the common pleas that a plaintiff should have a reattachment after the flight of Edward IV in 1470 'notwithstanding that there had been no process in the original because it was by bill, etc., because otherwise the plaintiff would lose the advantage of the earlier pleading and his costs': *Year Books of Edward IV, 10 Edward IV to 49 Henry VI (AD 1470)*, ed. N. Neilson, Selden Society (1931), p. 115. However, on the basis of a cursory inspection of the only surviving complete (?) files for the Michaelmas terms, for 1463 and 1474, it looks as though trespass dominated here, too: PRO, Court of King's Bench, KB146/7/3, m. 3 and KB146/7/14, m. 3.

[35] 'London' bills numbered 1, 18, 5, 7 and 4 respectively in the five years already mentioned (but note the caveat in n. 34, above, concerning the possibility that some bills were never enrolled). Middlesex bills involving Londoners seem in fact to have declined during the period, down from six in 1462 to none in 1477. The only suspicious case is one in which a king's bench clerk appeared as the attorney of a party who sued a man who, as a result of the clerk's original bill, was now 'in custody': PRO, KB27/872, mm. 36v and 42v. The clerk/attorney concerned was William Porter, underclerk of the prothonotary, Reginald Sonde, and the object of both his and his client's actions was William Letters, scrivener – quite possibly the chamber of London rent-collector of that name.

business.[36] Generally, these defendants lived outside London, and since many of the outworkers at least were presumably of modest means, they are unlikely to have travelled to London to acquire or to settle their debts. Therefore, the actions in which they were concerned probably involved agreements entered into and payment due in some other part of the country. London's own courts had never had jurisdiction over such cases. Moreover, even defendants who were Londoners are almost invariably described as 'formerly of London'. Fewer than 2.5 per cent of entries involve a defendant who is stated to be a citizen of London; the proportion was in fact higher in 1462 than at any time subsequently.[37] Therefore, while it is true to say that the common pleas rolls are full of commercial actions brought by London tradesmen and merchants, it does not necessarily follow that the court of common pleas was absorbing much business that rightly belonged to the city's courts. It might, however, be the case that some other mechanism (changing commercial practices, perhaps) enabled an increasing number of 'London' cases to be brought, quite properly, in common pleas. There is certainly a growth in the number of 'London' entries in the common pleas rolls during the course of Edward IV's reign, an increase which at least matches the physical growth of the rolls themselves, including a near-doubling between Michaelmas 1462 and Michaelmas 1472 (up from 333 to 715). However, although the 1462 figure was lower than all the rest, thereafter the number of entries fluctuated between 400 and 550, and was at its highest, apart from 1472, in 1467. The high 1472 figure may have been the result of a backlog, caused by disruption of the court's programme during three years of

---

[36] The common pleas samples are from the same Michaelmas terms as the king's bench ones: PRO, Court of Common Pleas, Plea Rolls, CP40/806, /825, /844, /852, /864 and /882. Taking, for example, Michaelmas 1477: Will. Parker, tailor, was suing Lady Latimer for £20, Maurice Berkeley esquire, ex-Stoke Gifford, for £6, and a Northumbrian gentleman, Thos. Manash, for just over £3; Alderman Basset was suing an Essex mariner, two Gloucestershire glovers, an ex-London haberdasher, a clerk and a prior; and the goldsmith and future London chamberlain Miles Adys was pursuing a Buckinghamshire gentleman for £5: CP40/864, mm. 29v; 172v; 173; 179v.

[37] Had these cases resulted in the issue of a *latitat* to the London sheriffs (alleging that the defendant 'lurked' there), the suspicion would be that the 'formerly' was mere window-dressing, masking the fact that the defendant in fact had been in London thoughout and so could have been summoned in a city court. Very few did, so it seems that most of these defendants had genuinely put themselves beyond the reach of the city courts.

intermittent civil war. Moreover, the action of *assumpsit* is chiefly remarkable for its absence; debt dominated throughout the period.

The exchequer evidence also gives no grounds for supposing that this court poached any significant amount of business which properly belonged to London courts. Although the surviving writs, particularly from the early 1480s, include one or two cases which appear to be straightforward actions between citizens, this probably reflects a failure of the writ adequately to explain the justification for bringing the action – for instance, that the defendant was already in custody.[38] Certainly a sampling of the plea rolls produces relatively modest numbers of 'London' cases, none which definitely looks suspicious, and nothing to suggest a significant upwards variation between 1461 and 1483.[39] Throughout, the great majority of cases involved either exchequer officials or exchequer accountants.[40] Indeed, the most interesting 'London' cases are two from 1472, in which plaintiffs tried in vain to bring the sheriffs, who were of course exchequer accountants, to book for alleged misconduct.[41] If these cases are anything to go by, the plaintiffs would have done better to enlist the aid of the mayor's court or, failing that, of chancery.

---

[38] For example, PRO, Exchequer of Pleas Writ File E5/562, writ and attornments in an action of debt for £8 between Thomas Witham, brewer and citizen of London, and William Rede, goldsmith and citizen of London. In other cases from the same term, *Paris v. Denys*, *Hunt v. Eborall*, *Caniziani v. Malvery* and *Sharp v. Malvery*, either the defendants were said to be 'present in Court in the custody of the Fleet', or one of the parties was stated to be an exchequer accountant (e.g. Philip Cook, answering as son and heir of Sir Thomas Cook, formerly one of the collectors of customs and subsidies in Southampton). The only example in this file which might involve some manipulation of the writ of privilege is an action brought jointly by William Nottingham, chief baron of the exchequer, and John Collins, mercer and citizen of London, against William Birkhead of London, gentleman. However, it could very well be a genuine joint action.

[39] The only slightly suspicious case is an action of trespass brought jointly by Brian Roucliff, an exchequer baron, and London Undersheriff Rigby against John Sharp, citizen and currier, for allegedly stopping up their right of access into and out of a property in St Sepulchre's parish onto Field's Alley. Again, however, this is likely enough to be a genuinely joint ownership or mortgagorship: PRO, Exchequer of Pleas, Plea Roll E13/162/2.

[40] The rolls sampled are for 1461, 1472, 1477 and 1482 (PRO, E13/148, /158, /162, /167).

[41] In both cases, no outcome is recorded, either because the defendants' successors as sheriffs persistently failed to return the writ or because of repeated jury defaults: PRO, E13/158, mm. 54–54v and 56v; ibid., mm. 65v and 66–66v.

The most accessible evidence about the relationship between chancery and the city is contained in the files of surviving chancery petitions, which have been calendared by the List and Index Society. The majority of Edwardian petitions relating to the conduct of courts or officials are contained in one of four bundles.[42] From these it appears that there may have been a particularly marked rise in petitions against London sheriffs in the period between Chancellor Nevill's enforced resignation in 1467 and the resignation of Chancellor Stillington in 1473, possibly reflecting some change in the receptiveness of chancery to petitions against London's governors and administrators. However, it is clear from a comparison between the total numbers of 'anti-official' petitions and of the writs that the survival rate of petitions was low.[43] The evidence of the writ files indicates that the apparent rise in petitions complaining about the conduct of officials or their courts during Robert Stillington's chancellorship is an illusion. On the other hand, what the writ files do indicate is that mayor's court cases were proportionately more likely to feature in chancery petitions between 1468 and the mid-, or possibly the late, 1470s than at other times. Before that, mayor's court cases are mentioned in well under 10 per cent of all 'anti-official' complaints. Thereafter, the average is just under 16 per cent, the only low years being (with the possible exception of 1470) after 1478. Numerically, too, references increased between 1468 and 1476, exceeding twenty on four occasions, and forty in 1474. The only other year when the number was as high was 1480.

---

[42] PRO, C1/31, /32, /46 and /67. Very occasionally, petitions brought against individuals and contained in other files mention that an action was levied in the sheriffs' court, e.g. Richard Kneesworth's petition against Thomas Woodhull and Henry Etwell, which refers to a 'plea of debt in the Counter of London': C1/40, m. 250.

[43] The four Edwardian 'anti-official' files contain *c.* 450 petitions against officials; if one allows (generously) *c.* 10 per cent for references in other files, the total is *c.* 500. By contrast, the writ files contain references to nearly 3,000 separate actions. Because plaintiffs often sued the same defendant on two or more counts, and chancery petitions probably encompassed all proceedings brought by any one plaintiff, the difference is not as great as this suggests; but, even if one assumes that every writ equated to no more than one petition, which is unlikely, writs would still outnumber petitions by approximately three to one. An additional problem with the petitions is that the dates assigned by the List and Index Society editors are inexact, and may sometimes be misleading, although this is unlikely to have much impact on the figures overall.

It is also possible that chancery was attracting to itself (or creating for itself) business which would otherwise have contributed to a substantial rise in the levels of activity of all London's courts. Between 1460 and the mid-1470s chancery petitions in general (that is, those directed against individuals as well as 'anti-official' ones) almost doubled, then doubled again in the following decade, before settling down to a more gradual increase over the next thirty years. During the same period, both the number and the proportion of 'London' cases in the surviving petitions also grew sharply, up from some 20 per annum in the first four years, to around 90 per annum between 1465 and 1472, to some 180 per annum thereafter. In percentage terms, the increase was from 14 per cent to over 30 per cent.

It has to be admitted that there are severe difficulties in relation to attempts to use chancery petitions to identify changes in patterns of litigation. The writ files show that the surviving petitions certainly do not include all complaints made against officials, and it is very probable that considerable numbers of complaints against private individuals have also been lost. In addition, not only were an unknown number of petitions presented orally, as Dr Guy has pointed out, but the London evidence gives reason to suppose that there could have been a shift from oral plaint to written bill during this period.[44] By swelling the written records with cases which formerly would have left little or no trace, this would create a 'rise' out of nothing. Even so, it would not explain the greater proportion of London petitions, unless Londoners were disproportionately, and increasingly so, inclined to present written petitions. Therefore there could well have been an increase – perhaps as much as a doubling – in the number of city petitioners over the whole period. Bearing in mind the possibility, mentioned earlier, that signs of specialisation in city courts might provide evidence that cases were being litigated elsewhere using new methods, it is of interest that the mayor's court (but not the sheriffs') does seem to have become increasingly

---

[44] J.A. Guy, 'The Development of Equitable Jurisdictions, 1450–1550', in *Law, Litigants and the Legal Profession*, eds E.W. Ives and A.H. Manchester, Royal Historical Society (1983), pp. 82–3. Between 1437 and 1481, the proportion of plaint-initiated cases recorded in London's Plea and Memoranda rolls reduced from 66.75 per cent of all cases in 1437–45, to 17.5 per cent in 1445–57, to 13.75 per cent in 1457–71, to 2 per cent in 1471–81.

concerned with actions of debt in the 1470s. However, the small amount of evidence available for 1481/2 suggests that this phenomenon was somewhat less marked at that period, which would not support the proposition that the mayor's court was becoming steadily more specialised because chancery was attracting away an ever-increasing amount of other types of cases.

The early to mid-1470s also saw an apparent change in chancery practice relating to 'inner chamber' cases. At this point, the city seems for the first time to have sent copies of all the documents relating to these cases with the return made to chancery, a practice which ceased after a couple of years.[45] It is possible that this is an illusion. There are very few references to 'inner chamber' cases in the chancery files, and it may be that a couple of important or difficult cases happened to occur in the 1470s, and the records happen to survive. On the other hand, taken together with the numerical and proportionate rise in mayor's court cases at the same period (disregarding 1468, which was an unusually troubled year for the city), it could be evidence of increasing chancery intervention in the city's exercise of equitable jurisdiction during the early 1470s. It was around this time (November 1475) that the court of aldermen passed an ordinance controlling the exercise of the mayor's equitable jurisdiction. It may well be significant that they were concerned above all with the possibility that the mayor might be 'insulted' (a strong word to use) by having a case removed from him. Moreover, twice in 1477, and again in 1479, the mayor and aldermen agreed to requests by the chancellor and the master of the rolls that chancery clerks should have the next vacancies for attorneys in the sheriffs' court.[46] It was a shortlived but nonetheless noteworthy phenomenon, which may have coincided with a downturn in the number of petitions concerning mayor's court cases.

The effect and extent of any threat to civic jurisdiction should not be exaggerated. In general, it may well be that the most accurate picture of the

---

[45] *Penn and Bolley v. Wade*, 1474, and *Newchurch v. Doys (Deux)*, 1475: PRO, C244/119, mm. 28 and 70; *Derikson v. Caniziani and Caniziani/Stockton* and *Spincars v. Caniziani and Caniziani/Stockton*, 1476: PRO, C244/123, m. 33.

[46] The chancery clerks concerned were Thomas Chaplin, Richard Elliot and John Chamberlain: CLRO, Journal of the Common Council 8, ff. 146, 146v and 205.

normal relationships between the city's courts and the central courts comes from an item incidentally recorded in the journals: the list of costs presented by Reyner Lomner, 'lawn merchant of Cambrai', at the end of his long suit against John Cooper.[47] Lomner started by presenting a bill in the mayor's court; obtained two writs (one to restart process in the mayor's court) out of chancery; appeared in the court of common pleas; returned to the mayor's court twice; thence he went to king's bench; back to the mayor's court for a third time; before finally achieving his ends in king's bench. It looks as though he was forced to resort to the latter court because the defendant absconded from the city's jurisdiction: he sued out four *latitatias* (*sic*). Bringing this particular defendant to book evidently took skill as well as money, and the impression given is of the courts and their officers being brought to cooperate rather like sheepdogs, to herd and then pen an evasive defendant. The mayor's court certainly made no difficulty over accepting that Lomner should recover the £10 8s 10d he had expended in various courts during his lengthy pursuit.

In general, London's governors appear to have been successful in their attempts to protect its system of law. The Edwardian city courts seem neither to have lost existing business to the Westminster common law courts, nor to have been undermined by the creation of new types of legal work there. The only exception is chancery. The equitable side of this court does seem to have increased its activity substantially during Edward IV's reign, and an increasing proportion of this work involved cases brought by Londoners against other private individuals. These cases probably could have been heard in the city courts. Assuming that they could not be determined justly at common law, they could have been removed into the mayor's court. If this did not happen, it was important because a prestigious part of the mayor's court function may have been usurped in consequence. There is nonetheless the possibility that many petitioners were not seeking a resolution in chancery, but were doing what John Weatherley and Sheriff Smith did: putting a warning shot across the city's bows.

---

[47] I can find no mention of this case in king's bench or common pleas rolls; there are, however, various references to Reginald Lomner, 'lawndeman de Cambrey', who was suing William Sewster and his attorney Henry Middleton for £62 14s 9d in 1471: PRO, C244/112, mm. 133, 216 and 219.

Unfortunately, it is not normally possible to tell from the surviving records what the outcome of the petition was.[48]

Even if the majority of these cases were in fact determined in chancery, it would probably be wrong to imagine that the city was in a state of constant defensiveness against that court. The position may have been worse in the mid- to late 1470s than it had been previously, and it is possible that it improved somewhat just before Edward IV's death. In any event, the picture that emerges is not of a jurisdiction under perpetual siege, struggling frantically to hang on to its privileges, but of one which was both protective of its liberties and almost as conscious of the possibility of abuse of its own powers as it was of the possibility that the powers of other jurisdictions might be abused.

---

[48] *Weatherley v. Smith* was remitted to the mayor's court, as was a case involving the imprisonment of a London common council man, Will Capell, for insulting an alderman, and another case, described as a *querela super causa mercatoria*: CLRO, Journal of the Common Council 7, ff. 191–1v (1468); CLRO, Journal of the Common Council 8, ff. 191 (1478) and 140 (1476).

7
THE EDUCATION AND TRAINING OF GIRLS IN FIFTEENTH-CENTURY LONDON

Caroline M. Barron

T he Parliament of 1406 was concerned, as many Parliaments had been since the Black Death of 1348–9, to ensure that there was an adequate supply of labourers to work the land. The Commons observed that there had been a drift away from the comparative unfreedom and poverty of agricultural labour, to the freedom and prosperity of work in the towns. In order to reverse this 'undesirable' trend, the Commons promoted a statute which laid down that no one was to apprentice his son or daughter unless he had lands or rent to the value of twenty shillings (i.e. formal apprenticeship was not for the poor, but for the substantial, countryman). The statute went on, however, to qualify the restriction; it was not to infringe the right 'of every man or woman, of whatever estate or condition he be, to set their son or daughter to take learning at any manner of school that pleaseth them'.[1]

The purpose of those who drafted this statute was not to describe the training opportunities available to boys and girls at the beginning of the fifteenth century but, rather, to introduce a further measure to control the freedom of labour. But it is precisely because the statute is *not* about education that its information is so valuable: what it tells us is incidental to its main purpose. The statute makes clear, first, that sons and daughters, boys and girls, were being apprenticed in English towns (presumably), to men and to women; and second, that men and women, fathers and mothers, were sending their sons and daughters to schools 'to take learning' (the wording of the statute is *d'apprendre lettereure a quelconq.escole que leur plest deinz le Roialme*). Perhaps it is reasonable to infer that such practices,

---

[1] 7 Henry IV c. XVII, *Statutes of the Realm* (1816), 2, pp. 157–8.

if not universal, were sufficiently widespread for those who drafted the statute to take cognisance of them. The apprenticing of girls and their 'taking of learning' at schools must have been sufficiently common to be restricted in one case and protected in the other. Those who framed this statute believed that men and women with annual incomes of less than twenty shillings were placing their sons and daughters as apprentices and/or sending them to school. We may presume that they knew what they were talking about and were not legislating about an imaginary state of affairs. This paper attempts to draw together some scattered evidence about the training and teaching of girls in London in the period between the Black Death and the population rise of the late fifteenth century.

It has been customary to take a rather pessimistic view of female learning in the later medieval period. This may be the result of placing too much emphasis upon Latin scholarship. In 1922 Eileen Power produced her magisterial study, *Medieval English Nunneries, c. 1275–1535*. In chapter six, on education, she is critical, indeed censorious, of the low level of Latin learning: she notes, in passing, that the nuns were to be taught 'in song and reading' (i.e. the Latin song of the liturgy, and the reading of English books) but she laments that 'the majority of nuns during these two centuries would seem to have understood neither French nor Latin'.[2] Doubtless that was largely true – we have only to remember the pretentious prioress among Chaucer's pilgrims who knew the French of 'Stratford atte Bowe' – but all learning is not Latin learning. We know of some women who did know Latin, like Jane Fisher, a nun of Dartford who, in 1431, was taught in grammar and the Latin tongue, or Dame Eleanor Hull (d. 1460), who translated French and Latin works into English.[3] But Eileen Power is right: such women were the exceptions. Power's preoccupation however with Latin led her to overlook the flourishing vernacular learning and culture of the nunneries (for example, Syon), with their wide reading in English

---

[2] Eileen Power, *Medieval English Nunneries, c. 1275–1535* (Cambridge, 1922), p. 247.

[3] Ibid., p. 247, n. 2; A. Barratt, 'Dame Eleanor Hull: A Fifteenth-Century Translator', in *The Medieval Translator: The Theory and Practice of Translation in the Middle Ages*, ed. R. Ellis (Cambridge, 1989), pp. 87–101; *Women's Writing in Middle English*, ed. A. Barratt (London, 1992), pp. 219–31. See also Felicity Riddy, '"Women talking about the things of God": a late medieval sub-culture', in *Women and Literature in Britain, 1150–1500*, ed. Carol M. Meale (Cambridge, 1993), pp. 104–27.

and in the English mystics.[4] What we know of the contents of the libraries of medieval nunneries in England suggests that the nuns certainly had access to spiritual works written in French and, more particularly, in English. The Minoresses at Aldgate owned copies of 'Pore Caitiff', 'The doctrine of the heart', and the works of Walter Hilton.[5]

Historians of medieval education have tended to focus on grammar schools, largely because we can sometimes glimpse them in the ecclesiastical records, but then only by chance. They did not have to be licensed, although in London there were three 'old' schools (St Paul's, St Martin le Grand, St Mary le Bow) and the bishop protected their monopoly not out of concern for the content of the curriculum, as would later be the case in the sixteenth century, but to preserve the economic advantages of a monopoly.[6] In these medieval schools, the main subject was Latin and for this reason girls rarely, if ever, attended grammar schools since their purpose was to prepare boys for 'clerical' careers, usually as priests, or as 'civil servants' or as lawyers or physicians.

Although it is unlikely that girls attended grammar schools in England, or indeed that women were conducting such schools, it may be interesting to look across the channel at this point, in particular to Paris. In 1380 the chancellor of the university licensed *rectores quam rectrices scolarum grammaticalium*. He noted that forty-one *magistri* and twenty-one *rectrices* took the oath. The forty-one men and twenty-one women are recorded by name. They were noted as discreet and honourable people fit to teach *scolas in arte grammatica* in Paris and its suburbs.[7] Charles Jourdain in his *Memoire sur l'éducation des femmes au moyen âge* prints a licence from the chancellor dated 6 May 1384 to Perrette la Couppenoire, *docendi et instruendi puellas in bonis moribus*,

---

[4] J.T. Rhodes, 'Syon Abbey and its Religious Publications in the Sixteenth Century', *Journal of Ecclesiastical History*, 44 (1993), pp. 11–25; Christopher de Hamel, *Syon Abbey: the Library of the Bridgettine Nuns* (Roxburgh Club, 1991).

[5] N.R. Ker, *Medieval Libraries of Great Britain: A List of Surviving Books* (London, 1964), p. 123.

[6] Caroline M. Barron, 'The Expansion of Education in Fifteenth-Century London', in *The Cloister and the World: Essays in Honour of Barbara Harvey*, eds J. Blair and B. Golding (Oxford, 1996), pp. 219–45, esp. pp. 225–7.

[7] *Chartularium Universitatis Parisiensis*, eds H. Denifle and E. Chatelain (Paris, 1894), 3, pp. 289–90.

litteris grammaticalibus ac aliis licitis et honestis.[8] In fact such licensing by the chancellor goes back at least to the 1350s when it was ordained that masters and mistresses were to be sworn to keep respectable schools and not to teach children of the opposite sex.[9] So, in Paris, in the second half of the fourteenth century, women were keeping schools, apparently grammar schools, and for every two grammar school masters, there was a grammar school mistress. We know about this only because they had to be licensed by the university. It is unlikely that there was a comparable number of grammar mistresses in London, but their presence in Paris makes the possibility of their existence in London a little more likely.

This period – the later fourteenth century – is also the period when English 'triumphed'. Probably English was much more widely used in written form in the earlier fourteenth century than we realise, but it is largely hidden from us. The survival of written English versions of the Lord's Prayer and the Creed from the late thirteenth century, and the existence of English craft and fraternity oaths and ordinances in London from the mid-fourteenth century, suggest that written English was becoming more common outside official government circles.[10] The later fourteenth century was a period of prosperity for the wage labourer; lay men and lay women were able to take time to learn to read their native tongue and, no doubt, to cast sums, to oversee accounts, and even, to some extent, to write. It was the broadening of the written culture to include English, which gave lay men and lay women a chance to participate in this new, non-clerical form of literacy. How did boys and girls learn to read (and write) English in the late fourteenth century? There must have been small, informal, temporary, household schools, dependent upon individual teachers.

---

[8] Charles Jourdain, *Excursions Historiques et Philosophiques à Travers le Moyen Age* (Paris, 1888), pp. 465–509, esp. p. 504.

[9] *Chartularium Universitatis*, eds Denifle and Chatelain, pp. 51–2.

[10] *Councils and Synods, with other documents relating to the English Church*, eds F.M. Powicke and C.R. Cheney (Oxford, 1964), pp. 134, 172, 465, 1076; Vincent Gillespie, 'Vernacular Books of Religion', in *Book Production and Publishing in Britain, 1375–1475*, eds J. Griffiths and D. Pearsall (Cambridge, 1989), pp. 317–44; Caroline M. Barron and Laura Wright, 'The London Middle English Guild Certificates of 1388–9', *Nottingham Medieval Studies*, 39 (1995), pp. 108–45, esp. pp. 113–14.

The existence of such schools has been noted in the context of late fourteenth-century Lollardy. What were the Lollard schools? Perhaps they were more likely to be occasions than institutions, when one or two gathered together to read and teach. Margaret Aston has argued that although many Lollards (both men and women) denied that they could read, yet from other evidence it is clear that they could in fact do so but deemed it dangerous to admit to such skills.[11] Most recently Shannon McSheffrey has argued that there was a significant gender gap between Lollards who could read and those who could not: whereas one in five Lollard men could read, only one in thirty-three Lollard women could do so. She writes that 'outside the Lollard community, opportunities for women to acquire literacy were virtually non-existent'.[12] The chronicler Henry Knighton, however, observed that John Wyclif translated the Bible into English for the laity and for women who knew how to read. Perhaps Knighton was aware of the existence of such women in Leicester?[13]

Although the ability of both men and women to read may have been less widespread than some optimists have thought, there is no doubt that the society of the late fourteenth century was increasingly 'text-based'. English was used for letter-writing, proclamations, wills, accounts, court ordinances, fraternity rules, religious instruction; and, in this predominantly lay environment, women must, to some extent, have been drawn into this written vernacular culture. A quiet – and perhaps slow – revolution was at work in English society and if no women anywhere in England were going to school, why would the 1406 statute so specifically have referred to the phenomenon? It is quite likely that London was exceptional (as it often is) but there is some interesting evidence for the education of women – taking education in its broadest terms. This paper will consider the practice of female apprenticeship, the 'schooling' of girls in

---

[11] Margaret Aston, 'William White's Lollard Followers', *Catholic History Review*, 48 (1982), pp. 469–97.

[12] Shannon McSheffrey, 'Literacy and the Gender Gap in the Late Middle Ages: Women and Reading in Lollard Communities', in *Women, the Book and the Godly*, ed. Lesley Smith and Jane H.M. Taylor (Cambridge, 1995), pp. 157–70, esp. p. 169.

[13] *Knighton's Chronicle, 1337–1396*, ed. and trans. G.H. Martin (Oxford, 1995), pp. 242–5: *et mulieribus legere scientibus*.

London, and finally some evidence for the literacy of women in fifteenth-century London.

The existence of women trading as *femmes soles*, and of girls being formally trained as apprentices in London in the late medieval period, has recently been dismissed as 'anecdotal' and insignificant.[14] Although Judith Bennett is clearly right to emphasise that there were not as many girl apprentices as there were boys, and that the range of skills which they learnt as apprentices was more limited (they were not apprenticed in overseas trade such as mercers and drapers, although they later took part in these trades as widows), yet a London apprenticeship did offer to 'middle-class' girls a formal training, the opportunity to acquire a marketable skill, economic independence and a chance to live – and marry – away from home.

The custom of London stated that 'married women who use certain crafts in the city by themselves without their husbands, may take women as their apprentices to serve them and to learn their crafts, and such apprentices shall be bound by their indentures of apprenticeship to the man and his wife to learn the mistery of the women, and such indentures shall be enrolled, whether for women or for men'.[15] In fact, the practice was even wider than the stated custom allowed; for it is clear that unmarried (as well as married) women took on boys, as well as girls, as apprentices. John Kemesyngg, a goldsmith, in his will of 1341, left 40*s* for his daughter Alice to be apprenticed to a trade.[16] Five years later John Spicer from Oxfordshire left 100*s* for his daughter Agnes 'for teaching her some craft'.[17] In 1374 a fishmonger, Robert de Rameseye, left 20*s* for his daughter Elizabeth which was to be used 'for her marriage and for putting her to a trade'.[18] Apprenticeships had to be bought. The master or mistress was paid a premium in return for sharing the secrets, or skills, of the

---

[14] Caroline M. Barron, 'The "Golden Age" of Women in Medieval London', *Reading Medieval Studies*, 15 (1989), pp. 35–58; Judith M. Bennett, 'Medieval Women, Modern Women: Across the Great Divide', in *Culture and History, 1350–1600: Essays on English Communities, Identities and Writing*, ed. David Aers (London, 1992), pp. 147–75.

[15] Barron, 'Golden Age', p. 52, n. 21.

[16] *Calendar of Wills in the Court of Husting, London, 1258–1688*, ed. R.R. Sharpe (London, 1889), 1, p. 445.

[17] Ibid., 1, p. 498.

[18] Ibid., 2, pp. 157–8.

craft with the young apprentice. Sometimes the existence of female apprentices is noted in wills. In 1412, for example, Peter Smert, a draper, had only two apprentices and they were both women.[19]

The records of the mayor's court in London note the pursuit (and sometimes the settlement) of disputes about broken apprentice contracts and many of these refer to girl apprentices and to mistresses.[20] Moreover, several of the surviving ordinances of city craft fraternities record the existence of girl apprentices. In 1388 the Brewers provided for the mutual good treatment of apprentices who were the sons and daughters of members and ten years later the leathersellers enjoined that 'no one shall set any man, child [no sex specified] or woman to work in the same trade unless such a person was first bound as an apprentice and enrolled in the craft'.[21]

The City of London's own regulations about apprenticeship are instructive. In 1300 it was simply ordained that all apprentices were to be enrolled at the Guildhall within the first year of the term.[22] But by 1393 when the ordinance was reissued, the wording had changed: no man or woman was to take a male or female apprentice unless such an apprentice was enrolled during the first year of his or her term.[23] The expanded wording suggests an expanded range of apprentices. When, in the early fifteenth century, the City embarked upon the expensive business of rebuilding the Guildhall, all the enrolment fees were increased to pay for the work. The list of new charges specified that 'every

---

[19] Guildhall Library, Archdeaconry Court Wills, MS 9051/1, f. 276v. The two apprentices were Johanna Sexteyn and Johanna Wiche. Smert left their uncompleted terms to his wife Margaret. When she drew up her will two years later, Johanna Wiche (Wynche) was still her apprentice, Johanna Sexteyn had left, or completed her term, and Margaret had taken on Robert Legge as her apprentice. Ibid., f. 320v.

[20] *Calendar of Plea and Memoranda Rolls, 1364–81*, ed. A.H. Thomas (Cambridge, 1943), pp. 12, 42–3, 53–4, 146–7, 229.

[21] PRO, Chancery, Miscellanea, C47/42/206: return of the fraternity dedicated to the Blessed Virgin Mary and All Saints in the parish of All Hallows, London Wall, which was, in effect, the craft fraternity of the Brewers; *Memorials of London and London Life in the XIIIth, XIVth and XVth Centuries*, ed. H.T. Riley (London, 1868), p. 547.

[22] *Calendar of Letter Book C*, ed. R.R. Sharpe (London, 1901), p. 78.

[23] *Calendar of Letter Book H*, ed. R.R. Sharpe (London, 1907), p. 391; *Calendar of Letter Book I*, ed. R.R. Sharpe (London, 1909), p. 134.

apprentice, male or female, shall pay on entrance, towards the support of the New Work, over and above the old fee, 2s 6d.[24] It is clear that whereas female apprentices were not specifically recognised (and probably were quite rare) at the beginning of the fourteenth century, by the end of the century they were sufficiently ubiquitous to be noticed in civic legislation.

The evidence of the city's regulations is corroborated by the survival of a small number of original indentures in which girls were bound, in terms almost identical with those of boys, to mistresses in London. Four surviving indentures range in date from 1378 to 1454.[25] Two women bind themselves, one is bound by her brother and another by her father. One was to learn the skills of a tent (canopy) maker, the other three were to become silk throwsters or silkwomen. They came from Sussex, Norfolk, and Lincolnshire. The survival of apprentice indentures, unlike deeds, is very haphazard since they had no value once the contract had ended and there are only a dozen or so original apprentice indentures altogether surviving from the medieval period in England. That four of these indentures relate to girls suggests that their formal training as apprentices in London was not uncommon.

Some apprentice indentures – although none of these four involving girl apprentices which have been considered – specified that the apprentice should be taught to read and write during the apprenticeship. In an indenture drawn up in June 1458 William Poklyngton, a London haberdasher, agreed that his apprentice, William Kyme from Norfolk, should be taught to read and write: *legere et scribere*.[26] Earlier, in 1415, John Holand from Walsoken in Norfolk complained to the mayor of London that the barber to whom he had been apprenticed was so poor that he could not feed and clothe him properly, nor keep him at school till he could read and write, as had been agreed in his indentures.[27] There is evidence that both the skinners and the goldsmiths – and

---

[24] *Memorials*, ed. Riley, pp. 589–91.

[25] Westminster Abbey Muniments, 5966: indenture of Margaret, daughter of Richard Sleaford of Lewes, 1378; CLRO, Misc. MS 1863: indenture of Katherine Nougle, 1392; Norfolk Record Office, Hare MS 2091: indenture of Eleanor Fincham of Norfolk, 1447; PRO, Exchequer, Ancient Deeds, Series D, E210/1176: indenture of Elizabeth Eland from Lincolnshire, 1454.

[26] Westminster Abbey Muniments, 5962.

[27] *Calendar of Plea and Memoranda Rolls, 1413–1437*, ed. A.H. Thomas (Cambridge, 1943), p. 41.

doubtless other companies also – wanted their apprentices to be able to read and write before embarking on apprenticeships.[28]

Where did boys – and girls – learn to read and write English in London? Not in the few formal grammar schools where Latin was taught (and where an ability to read and write English was a prerequisite for entry). Boys had the opportunity to attend song schools and there were several attached to London parish churches and religious houses, but it is very unlikely that girls would have attended these.[29] Most boys and girls would have gone to the small informal schools, later known as 'dame' schools, of which we occasionally catch glimpses in the records. But they were of no interest to the ecclesiastical authorities, nor to the mayor and aldermen; their proprietors did not form a craft guild, and so they have left only brief traces in the records. Some schools were run by chantry priests, others by scriveners. Eight-year-old Elizabeth Garrard attended a school in London run by William Barbour, a priest. Here she learnt the Paternoster, Ave and Credo, 'with further learning'.[30] A twelve-year-old boy who had attended the school run by the scrivener William Kingsmill in the early fifteenth century was able to 'write, endite and count' and also to speak some French.[31]

Not all of these 'informal' schools were run by men. In 1406 William Cresewyk, a London grocer, left 20*s* to 'E scholemaysteresse' and the Bede roll of the fraternity of parish clerks of London, dedicated to St Nicholas, drawn up before 1440, records the name of Agnes, *doctrix puellarum*.[32] There survive two late fourteenth-century accounts rendered by the guardians of city orphans: one for the maintenance of Thomas atte Boure, the son of a London mercer, and the other for Alice Reigner, the illegitimate orphan daughter of a London

---

[28] *The Early History of the Goldsmiths' Company, 1327–1509*, eds T.F. Reddaway and Lorna Walker (London, 1975), pp. 261–2; S.L. Thrupp, *The Merchant Class of Medieval London* (Ann Arbor, Michegan, 1962), p. 158.

[29] Barron, 'Expansion of Education', pp. 224–5.

[30] Dorothy Gardiner, *English Girlhood at School: a Study of Women's Education through Twelve Centuries* (Oxford, 1929), p. 77.

[31] Thrupp, *Merchant Class*, p. 159.

[32] Guildhall Library, Commissary Wills, MS 9171/2, f. 88: will of William Cresewyk; Guildhall Library, MS 4889, f. 3: Bede Roll of the fraternity of St Nicholas. I am grateful to Norman James for kindly providing me with this reference. See also the example of Maria Mareflete, recorded as *magistra scolarum* in the roll of the Corpus Christi guild at Boston, *VCH Lincolnshire*, 2, p. 451.

corndealer. The cost of teaching Thomas was 2 marks (26s 8d) a year; the cost of teaching Alice was 1 mark (13s 4d) a year.[33] But Alice *was* taught, even if less expensively than a boy. William Rous, a mercer who died in 1486, left nine children, four sons and five daughters. Each of his children, boys and girls, was left the same amount, £22. The three eldest children, two sons and a daughter, were entrusted to William Mylburne, a painter, 'to find them to scole honestly for four years next after my decease'.[34] So his daughter was to go to 'scole' as her brothers did.

It is extremely difficult to find more than incidental references to the existence of schoolmistresses in fifteenth-century London, or to the education of girls. We know rather more about the sixteenth century, not because there was a sudden surge in educational provision (there may have been some increase, but there was a fourfold rise in population), but because there was a far greater measure of ecclesiastical control: licensing of schoolmasters and schoolmistresses was instigated, not, as in the fifteenth century, to preserve a lucrative monopoly, but to control the content of lessons and ensure the teaching of a Protestant 'national curriculum'.

In Elizabethan England, provided that a woman (or man) taught basic subjects to no more than six boys and girls in addition to family members, did not teach boys older than ten, and did not use pupils in the formal operation of the school (that is, to teach as ushers), then no licence from the bishop was required. No licence means no evidence of existence. In some cases the archdeacon did licence a schoolmistress who wished to teach more children or older boys. The archdeacon of Colchester in 1594 charged Audrey Parker of Terling 5s for a licence to teach reading, writing and the rudiments of grammar. Sometimes wives assisted their husbands: Mrs Rose Kinnersley, of Chipping Barnet in Hertfordshire, taught boys and girls their ABCs, catechism, primer and other 'children's books' while her husband taught writing. Women like these were licensed, and there may have been half a dozen or so in the diocese of London in the Elizabethan period. But Professor Anglin has also located the names of forty-seven schoolmistresses who taught in twenty-eight parishes in the

---

[33] *Memorials*, ed. Riley, pp. 378–9, 446–7.
[34] Guildhall Library, Commissary Wills, MS 9171/7, f. 62.

diocese of London between 1560 and 1603. In most cases these women were mentioned incidentally in the ecclesiastical records and so represent a mere fraction of those women actually teaching basic elementary subjects to local youths.[35]

The nature of these records, and the growing anxiety in the Tudor period to control the teaching of young people, brings the existence of women teachers a little more into the limelight but, as Anglin says, 'the ecclesiastical authorities deemed the labours of most Tudor schoolmistresses to fall under the scope of informal education'.[36] But the work of these women, at the bottom of the educational ladder, must have played a crucial role in expanding literacy and there is no reason to believe that what was true in the later sixteenth century had not also been true a hundred years earlier.[37]

It is true that it is difficult to find 'hard' evidence for girls at school in late medieval London; but then it is hard to find much hard evidence about children at all, and the presence of boys at 'ABC' schools is equally hard to prove. The informality and non-clerical nature of such schools make them particularly invisible. There is however some evidence to suggest that some London women could read – and write – in the fifteenth century.

Elizabeth Stonor, the daughter of a London skinner, could certainly read the letters from her husband, Sir William Stonor, and may well have been able to write also.[38] John Paston III intended to conduct a courtship correspondence with the daughter of a London mercer and for this reason he was glad that she could read English since this would help to ensure the privacy of their courtship.[39] Or, if we look once more at Paris, we can see that the Goodman of Paris who wrote a book of instruction for his young wife, assumed that she, and other young bourgeois women, would certainly be able to read, although not always to write. The Goodman was anxious to explain that the properly

---

[35] Jay P. Anglin, *The Third University: A Survey of Schools and Schoolmasters in the Elizabethan Diocese of London* (Norwood, Penn., 1985), pp. 75–90.

[36] Ibid., p. 86.

[37] See J.W. Adamson, 'The Extent of Literacy in England in the Fifteenth and Sixteenth Centuries: Notes and Conjectures', *The Library*, 10 (1929), pp. 163–93.

[38] *The Stonor Letters and Papers*, ed. C.L. Kingsford (Camden Society, 3rd ser., 2 vols, 1919), *passim*.

[39] *Paston Letters and Papers of the Fifteenth Century*, ed. Norman Davies (Oxford, 1971), 1, p. 591.

brought-up young woman knew not to read any letters privately except those from her husband.[40] He had in mind just the sort of situation that the amorous young John Paston was hoping to create.

Moreover, some women certainly knew how to write. In 1420 Alice and Mathilda, the orphan daughters of John Shawe, a London vintner, were apprenticed to Master Peter Churche, a notary public, presumably to acquire skills in writing.[41] Mathilda Penne in her will of 1392 left a small piece of silver to Petronilla, 'scriweyner'.[42] It has been suggested that with the advent of printing women are to be found, in the sixteenth century, occasionally acting as printers; women like Elizabeth Pickering who in 1540 and 1541 printed fourteen books using her maiden name. She was the widow of Robert Redman, a Fleet Street printer. In the first half of the sixteenth century, there are many instances of women carrying on a printing business after the death of their husbands.[43] It is difficult to imagine how an illiterate woman would have been able to run a printing shop – or indeed any substantial business. There is moreover a considerable body of evidence to show that widows in fifteenth-century London were active in business. Silkwomen sold their wares on a large scale to the royal Wardrobe, and female bell founders entered into contracts to make and repair bells.[44] Women like these must have acquired some basic literacy skills if they were able to run workshops and keep control of their accounts.

Doubtless much of the 'literacy' of women in medieval London was somewhat basic and pragmatic. Few women would have spent much time receiving and reading, or indeed writing, the love letters which the Goodman of Paris so greatly feared. But there is, on the other hand, an assumption that women would form part of the book-using community. In 1441 Robert

---

[40] Eileen Power trans., *The Goodman of Paris (Le Ménagier de Paris)* (London, 1928), p. 106.

[41] *Letter Book I*, ed. Sharpe, p. 238.

[42] Elspeth Veale, 'Mathilda Penne, Skinner', in *Medieval London Widows, 1300–1500*, eds Caroline M. Barron and Anne F. Sutton (London, 1994), p. 49.

[43] I am grateful to Professor Paul Christianson for kindly supplying me with information about women in the London book trade, 1500–1560. He will be publishing this interesting material himself.

[44] *Medieval London Widows*, eds Barron and Sutton, p. xxix.

Holland, a draper, commissioned a copy of Walter Hilton's works 'for a comyn profit'. The owners of the book were to pray for Holland and the book was 'to be delivered and committed from person to person, man or woman, as long as it endureth'. Women as well as men were to form part of the chain of commemorative prayer.[45]

Books are rarely referred to in London wills, whether those of men or of women, for all sorts of reasons already well known. Most books listed in wills tend to be liturgical ones: Joan Buckland (d. 1462), who was the daughter of a London fishmonger, possessed seven liturgical books, including a collection of Latin theological texts which she bequeathed to Syon abbey in return for prayers.[46] Beatrice Milreth, who died in 1448, the widow of a London mercer, left her missal and portable breviary to her son John and to Agnes Burgh, her sister, a book 'merce and gramerce' written with gold lettering, together with a roll of the passion of our lord Jesus Christ, the gospel of Nichodemus in French, an unspecified French and Latin book, a French primer, and a roll of fifteen *gaudes beate Marie*.[47]

Agnes Burgh is by no means unique as a woman in finding herself the recipient of books bequeathed in a will. William Palmer (d. 1400) left his copy of *Piers Plowman* to an otherwise unknown woman, Agnes Eggesfield.[48] William Cresewyk, who bequeathed 20s to 'E scholemistress', also left a copy of his *Legend of Saints* to his wife and at her death it was to pass to Holy Trinity Priory.[49] Beatrice and Margaret, the daughters of William Lynne, a London grocer, and his wife Alice, a vowess, were both book owners. Beatrice wrote her

---

[45] See Wendy Scase, 'Reginald Peacock, John Carpenter and John Colop's "Common Profit" books: aspects of book ownership and circulation in fifteenth-century London', *Medium Aevum*, 61 (1992), pp. 261–74.

[46] Jenny Stratford, 'Joan Buckland d. 1462', in *Medieval London Widows*, eds Barron and Sutton, pp. 113–28, esp. p. 126.

[47] Susan H. Cavanaugh, 'A Study of Books Privately Owned in England 1300–1450' (unpub. Ph.D. thesis, University of Pennsylvania, 1980), pp. 585–6; Carol M. Meale, 'Laywomen and their Books in Late Medieval England', in *Women and Literature*, ed. Meale, pp. 128–58, esp. p. 132.

[48] R.A. Wood, 'A Fourteenth-Century London Owner of *Piers Plowman*', *Medium Aevum*, 53 (1984), pp. 83–90.

[49] Guildhall Library, Commissary Wills, MS 9171/2, f. 88.

name in a psalter which she gave to the Minoresses house at Aldgate and both their names are inscribed in a manuscript containing the poetry of Hoccleve and Lydgate. Margaret was married to the scribe, John Shirley.[50] Eleanor Purdelay, a London widow who died in 1433, left 'The story of Joseph', 'Patrick's Purgatory' and a 'sermon of Alcuin' to Johanna, her servant. All these books were in English.[51]

These women of the merchant class who read the poetry of Hoccleve and Lydgate were, clearly, literate and at a level of sophistication above that of the female apprentices whose indentures were noted earlier. What did these literate artisan women read? Pious works perhaps, which they might not have been able to own, but to which they could have had access in the small libraries attached to parish churches. There is evidence, from wills and inventories and from inscriptions in surviving manuscripts, that several London churches in the fifteenth century had small chained libraries of books of devotional instruction.[52] Women parishioners could easily have had access to these books. There also emerged a new type of didactic poetry to be found in London collections or commonplace books. Professor Riddy has discussed the audience for two Middle English texts written in the fourteenth and fifteenth centuries: 'How the good wife taught her daughter' and 'The good wife wold a pylgremage'. She has suggested that these were used by girls leaving home to become servants or apprentices in towns, and also by women who found themselves running households, away from their mothers, and needing help in the bringing up of their own daughters as well as their female servants and apprentices. These two poems were used therefore by 'displaced' women, *arrivistes* seeking advice and reassurance about the training of girls. The context of these poems is, clearly, urban and their audience was probably female.[53] It was in part, therefore, through *reading* that urban women could learn how to

---

[50] Mary C. Erler 'Three Fifteenth-Century Vowesses', in *Medieval London Widows*, eds Barron and Sutton, pp. 165–83, esp. pp. 170–1.

[51] Cavanaugh, 'Books Privately Owned', p. 673.

[52] Barron, 'Expansion of Education', p. 240.

[53] Felicity Riddy, 'Mother Knows Best: Reading Social Change in a Courtesy Text', *Speculum*, 71 (1996), pp. 66–86.

conduct themselves and instruct the female members of their modest, hardworking, respectable households, some way removed from the prosperous mercantile households which nudged them into the world of the gentry.

Those who know Sylvia Thrupp's *Merchant Class of Medieval London* (1948) may well wonder whether much has been added to her few crisp, suggestive and information-packed pages on 'the woman's role'.[54] Thrupp indeed observed that girls in London would have attended elementary schools since illiteracy would have hampered a woman's efficiency in business matters. The attempt here has been to put more flesh on the bones of her argument. There are several ways forward from this point and some sources of information (albeit, and inevitably, tangential) which have not yet been fully explored and exploited. London has thousands – literally – of wills enrolled between 1390 and the early sixteenth century which, if read systematically, might well yield a great deal of information about women, as testators, executors, recipients of bequests, or apprentices. Further, the London church court material from the 1470s onwards can be explored for what it may reveal of the economic and social roles played by women in London, and not simply their educational opportunities. It is time to stop being surprised when we find fifteenth-century women in towns reading and writing; after all, the increase in painted images of the Virgin surprised while reading by the angel Gabriel, and the popularity of statues of St Anne teaching the Virgin to read, suggest that reading women (albeit saints) formed part of the *mentalité* of fifteenth-century men and women.[55] Likewise, those who framed the statute of 1406 took it for granted that men and women might wish to send their daughters, as well as their sons, to school. The teaching of vernacular 'literacy' may have been informal and haphazard, but its imprint may surely be traced in the records of fifteenth-century London.

---

[54] Thrupp, *Merchant Class*, pp. 169–74.

[55] See *Interpreting Cultural Symbols: Saint Anne in Late Medieval Society*, eds Kathleen Ashley and Pamela Sheingorn (Athens, Georgia, 1900).

8
THE ORDER OF THE GARTER, 1348–1461: CHIVALRY AND POLITICS IN LATER MEDIEVAL ENGLAND

Hugh Collins

In recent years a number of important studies of the royal affinity in later medieval England have appeared. These have focused particular attention on the household and its officers, the knights of the chamber, the knights and esquires of the body, and on the royal practice of retaining peers and King's knights by annuity. It seems somewhat surprising, therefore, that the order of the Garter, when seen in this context, has attracted so little attention, especially when one considers the way in which studies of comparable orders such as the Croissant and the Golden Fleece have demonstrated the value of such institutions in bringing together an élite body of loyal servants committed to the interests of their sovereign.[1] Although the Garter has been a popular subject for scholarly examination ever since the publication of Elias Ashmole's encyclopaedic work in the late seventeenth century,[2] few studies have attempted to place the fraternity in its historical perspective, analysing the various political and social objectives that underlay its foundation, and the role it served not only in the English monarch's relations with, and policy towards, his nobility, but also in its overall contribution to the development of aristocratic culture in later medieval England.[3] While it

---

[1] The political value of these two orders to their respective superiors, the kings of Naples and Sicily and the dukes of Burgundy, are discussed by Malcolm Vale in *War and Chivalry: Warfare and Aristocratic Culture in England, France, and Burgundy at the End of the Middle Ages* (London, 1981), pp. 33–62.

[2] E. Ashmole, *The Institution, Laws, and Ceremonies of the Most Noble Order of the Garter* (London, 1672).

[3] The most recent works that attempt at least in part to examine the Garter's practical utility are: J.D. Milner, 'The Order of the Garter in the Reign of Henry VI, 1422–1461' (unpub.

would be ambitious to suggest that this imbalance could be redressed within the space of one paper, we can at least seek to identify the salient characteristics of the order's practical utility in English politics, as manifested through the distribution of the garter insignia, and the criteria that governed eligibility for election.

If the emotional inspiration for the emergence and proliferation of the secular fraternity in later medieval Europe can be found in the growing secularisation of the chivalric ethos, and the fascination of the knightly classes with the romance literature of the twelfth and thirteenth centuries, then the momentum that allowed such projects to be put into effect was essentially political.[4] The concurrent growth in the forces of statehood and nationality during the fourteenth century, which led to the rise of the powerful centralised monarchies of western Christendom, created a context in which these chivalric foundations found a practical role. The princes and monarchs who were to become the patrons and supporters of these knightly brotherhoods perceived their value both as a buttress to royal power, and as a means of controlling the individualism of the chivalric vocation.[5]

In essence, chivalry and statehood were antithetical – the one encouraging the devolution of judicial autonomy and other prerogatives to the knight, the other advocating the centralisation of all authority in the person of the king. If their alignment was a 'marriage of convenience',[6] occurring as both forces concurrently reached their prime in the fourteenth century, then the 'baby' of this liaison, if the metaphor is pursued, was the curial order of the later medieval period. Instead of prohibiting chivalric activity, these institutions made it possible for the prince to assimilate the ideals of knighthood for his own political and dynastic ends. The noble companions, enticed by the prestige

---

Manchester M.A. thesis, 1972); J. Vale, *Edward III and Chivalry: Chivalric Society and its Context, 1270–1350* (Woodbridge, 1982); D. Schneider, 'Der englische Hosanborden: Beiträge zur Enstehung und Entwicklung des "The Most Noble Order of the Garter" (1348–1702), mit einem Ausblick bis 1983' (4 vols, unpub. Bonn Ph.D. thesis, issued 1988, but completed 1983); D'A.J.D. Boulton, *The Knights of the Crown: The Monarchical Orders of Knighthood in Later Medieval Europe, 1325–1520* (Woodbridge, 1987).

[4] M.H. Keen, *Chivalry* (Newhaven and London, 1984), p. 190.

[5] R.W. Kaeuper, *War, Justice and Public Order: England and France in the Later Middle Ages* (Oxford, 1988), pp. 194–7.

[6] Ibid., p. 194.

ensuant upon such honorific recognition, were thus drawn into a close alliance with the interests of their sovereign, one in which the oaths of allegiance and the statutory emphasis on loyalty acted as an additional counter to the weakening bonds of feudal society.[7] While the purely chivalric inclinations of the princely founders should not be underestimated, they pursued in their foundations, whether consciously or not, an undeniably political agenda.

The order of the Garter was certainly no exception to this rule. Founded in 1348 by Edward III, it was one of the earliest curial orders to appear, being preceded only by the Hungarian fraternal society of St George (1326), the Castilian order of the Band (1330), and Duke John of Normandy's chivalric initiative, later to become the order of the Star (1344). Conceived in the aftermath of Edward III's glorious victory at Crécy, the fraternity was intended as a celebration of the highest aspirations of English chivalry. Primarily military in character, with a strong institutional emphasis on the ethics of knightly endeavour and loyalty to the superior of the order, the king of England, the whole organisational structure, the livery, the ceremonial life, was designed to one end: to exalt the pursuit of martial prowess. Admission was restricted solely to those of knightly status, with eligibility for selection governed by chivalric stature and diligence in arms. With its fellowship comprising the most socially-distinguished and martially-renowned knights of the realm, including the king and often his heir, elevation to the Garter's ranks represented the pinnacle of the English aristocracy's *cursus honorum*.

Although the size of the Garter was modest in comparison with its lavish prototype, the Round Table society of 1344, the provisions made for it were nevertheless comprehensive and generous.[8] The fellowship was to number twenty-six knights, new companions only being admitted on the creation of a vacancy in the order's ranks. The Garter brethren were to be supported in the fulfilment of their institutional obligations by a number of officers who

---

[7] M. Vale, *War and Chivalry*, pp. 35–6.

[8] The Round Table society was to number three hundred knights in total. The project was accompanied by extravagant plans for the building of a large circular hall within the precincts of Windsor castle; this was intended to house a great wooden table for the assembled brethren to sit around. Although the exact reasons for the cancellation of this project are unknown, it is likely that the escalating costs of the French war forced Edward III initially to suspend the project, and later to cancel it altogether.

officiated at ceremonies, and also a collegiate establishment designed to provide for the spiritual welfare of the companionship. Placed under the triple patronage of the Blessed Virgin Mary, St Edmund the Confessor, and St George the Martyr, the main corporate activity of the brotherhood centred on the annual celebrations of the feast day of St George (23 April) in the royal castle at Windsor. Other than the occasional electoral assembly, this three-day festival represented the only opportunity for the Garter brethren to meet during the course of the year.

Unlike the later Burgundian order of the Golden Fleece, founded along similar constitutional lines to those of the Garter in January 1430, the English fraternity possessed no formal judicial or legislative powers. While the two institutions shared many common characteristics, not least the comparable size of the fellowship and the centrality of elaborate liturgical observances in the corporate life of each order, the Garter was not as overtly political in its conception as its Burgundian counterpart.[9] Although political aims were undoubtedly served in its existence, the Garter's authority was restricted solely to matters that touched directly upon its institutional coherence, such as unexcused absence from the annual festivities or infractions of the code requiring the constant wearing of the order's insignia. Despite the close association in contemporary eyes between the Garter, *l'ordre et enseigne des Anglois*,[10] and the king of England, the garter emblem was nevertheless independent of the monarch's own retaining badge.[11]

---

[9] M. Vale, *War and Chivalry*, pp. 46–51. The constitution of the Golden Fleece provided it with the facility to examine and correct the conduct of its members. Initially under Philip the Good, this function had not extended to investigating the moral behaviour of the companion-knights; this was to change with the accession of Charles the Bold, however, who sought to control any alleged lubricity among the companionship. In this respect, the Golden Fleece offered the prince a more direct means to extend his authority over his nobility than did the Garter; in matters touching the loyalty of the order's fellowship, this prerogative developed a distinctly judicial function.

[10] Jean Froissart, *Chroniques*, ed. Kervyn de Lettenhove (25 vols in 26, Brussels, 1867–77), 15, pp. 279–80.

[11] Olivier de la Marche, *Mémoires d'Olivier de la Marche*, eds H. Beaune and J. d'Arbaumont (4 vols, Paris, 1883–88), 4, pp. 161–2; M. Vale, *War and Chivalry*, p. 40. La Marche argues that the kings of England could distribute either the emblem of the Garter or a private livery badge such as the Lancastrian SS collar. The insignia of the Golden Fleece was more unusual in that it incorporated the sovereign's personal livery collar, the flint and fire-steel striking sparks, into the device of the order. This badge had been the emblem of the ducal house since the capture of John of Nevers by the Turks in 1396.

If the political benefits gained by the English Crown from the Garter were evidenced in a rather more subtle fashion than those of the Golden Fleece, they were, however, still present. Indeed, practical objectives had been integral to the order since its foundation. Edward III's primary motive in creating the fraternity was to galvanise aristocratic support behind the war in France, presenting it, in the words of Maurice Keen, 'in light of a great adventure pursued by a noble and valiant company of knights against an adversary who was unjustly withholding from their sovereign his rightful inheritance'.[12] The imagery and symbolism associated with the order, not least the adoption of St George, formerly the patron saint of all Christian knighthood, reinforced this underlying agenda. While Edward III may have been partially influenced in his selection by the Hungarian fraternal society of St George, it is far more probable that the warrior-saint was expropriated from the planned order of the Star.[13] This would appear to be supported not only by the strong organisational similarities between the two institutions, but also by King John of France's decision to select a new guardian for his chivalric project following the appearance of the Garter fraternity in 1348. The connection between Edward's foundation and the Plantagenet ambitions to the French throne is further strengthened by the use of blue and gold, the royal colours of France, in the livery and insignia of the order, and by the preference for a French motto as opposed to the more usual choice of English.[14] In this context, the words of the motto, *Honi soit qui mal y pense*, or 'Shamed be he who thinks ill of it', read more as a defiant retort to those doubting the legitimacy of Edward's claim than as a result of an irrational, albeit chivalric gesture in defence of a lady's honour.[15]

---

[12] Keen, *Chivalry*, p. 184.

[13] Renouard, 'L'ordre de la Jarretière et l'ordre de l'Etoile: Etude sur la genèse des ordres laïcs de chevalerie et sur le développement de leur caractère national', *Le Moyen Age*, 55 (1949), p. 290.

[14] J. Vale, *Edward III and Chivalry*, p. 81.

[15] The traditional version of the Garter's foundation tells how Edward III, to defend the honour of a lady of the court whose garter had fallen to the ground, retrieved it before the mockery of the assembled company. He then defiantly attached it to his own leg with the words that were later to be inscribed on the insignia, claiming that he would forthwith institute an order of knights to bear the device. This erotic motif, though hinted at in Mondonus Belvaleti's treatise of 1463, *Tractatus ordinis serenissimi*, is presented in its most complete form in Polydore Vergil's *Anglica Historia*,

The structure of the order displayed an equally political purpose. The pageantry and ceremonial organisation were designed intentionally to promote the authority and prestige of the sovereign. Whether during the religious observances in the chapel of St George or in the assemblies in the chapter house, the monarch occupied a central role. This was apparent even in the more irregular ceremonial obligations of the fraternity; thus in 1429, during the coronation of Henry VI at Westminster, the Garter fellowship was given the unprecedented honour of holding a cloth of state over the head of the king after the acclamation and during the anointing ceremony.[16] The statutes of the order reflected this same monarchical orientation. Although generally moderate in the obligations they placed upon the companion-knight, they nevertheless stressed the loyalty and service owed to the sovereign: article 19, in allowing for the admission of strangers, required only that the companions in question should not hold themselves against the interests of the superior of the order; the same ordinance further emphasised the underlying political function of the fraternity by stating that the knight-elect should be chosen from among the most *prouffitables à la couronne et au royaume*; while article 30 made explicit the sovereign's authority over the companion-knight's right to leave the kingdom, requiring that permission be sought first.[17] The clearest demonstration of the monarch's status within the brotherhood, however, was his possession of a final veto in the election of new brethren. Although the companionship was encouraged to participate in the electoral process by nominating candidates, the final word belonged to the superior who selected either the most popular choice, or the individual he deemed the most worthy.[18]

---

published in 1534. The earliest account of the tale, however, is found in the romance, *Tirant lo Blanc*, written around 1460 by the Valencian writer, Juan Martorell. Martorell must have heard the story for the first time during his visit to the English court in 1438–9.

[16] BL, MS Nero C ix, f. 173 v.

[17] I have taken as my model for the statutes the earliest surviving redaction of the ordinances contained in the document, College of Arms, MS Arundel 48, and printed in its entirety in the appendix of Lisa Jefferson's article, 'MS Arundel 48 and the Earliest Statutes of the Order of the Garter', *EHR* (April, 1994), pp. 356–85.

[18] College of Arms, MS Arundel 48, article 19 d. The votes in the scrutiny were presented to the superior or his deputy, *lequel eslira celui des nommez qui aura plus de voix et que lui semblera plus honnourable audit ordre, ou prouffitable a la couronne et royaume.*

The key to the order's efficacy as an instrument of political patronage, and thus as a buttress to the power of the monarch, lay in the appeal of membership to all levels of English knightly society. Provisions were made in the statutes to ensure that representation was given in the nomination process to the different categories of the second estate. When a stall fell vacant, the companionship were required to put forward nine names in total: three candidates of comital rank or above, three barons or bannerets, and three bachelor-knights.[19] To have done otherwise would have been counter-productive to the order's sense of spiritual solidarity, assiduously developed through its corporate existence, its ceremonial activities and religious rites. In this respect, the Garter was remarkably non-hierarchical; as Jonathan Boulton stresses, as an institution, it gave little advantage to those of high social status either in terms of livery or ceremonial precedence.[20] The use of garter devices on the mantle as a means to differentiate rank fell out of usage in the early fifteenth century, and seating in the chapel of St George was governed by longevity of membership rather than elevation of birth.[21] Equally the sliding scale of obligations stipulated by the statutes, whether for the size of entry fee which a companion should pay or for the number of masses he should provide on the death of a companion, meant that membership of the fraternity was most burdensome for those best suited to pay.

Despite the emphasis on social parity in the order's internal organisation, the criteria for admission were at times far from egalitarian. Although the prevailing ethos of the Garter was martial, chivalric qualifications were often compromised in the election of new companions by social and political considerations. This in turn led to marked differences in the career structures and ages of election of the respective categories of knight-elect, most notably between those situated at opposing ends of the social spectrum. At the lower end of the social scale, military experience was an almost uniform requirement.

---

[19] College of Arms, MS Arundel 48, article 19 b.

[20] Boulton, *Knights of the Crown*, pp. 141–2.

[21] College of Arms, MS Arundel 48, article 22: *Item, est accordé que s'aucun des contes meurge, baneret, ou bacheler, celui qui vendra en son lieu, soit il conte, baneret, ou bacheler, il tendra la mesme estalle que son predecesseur tenoit, et ne changera point.*

The majority of knights-bachelor admitted before 1461 were career-soldiers who had risen to prominence in royal service, either through the pursuit of arms or, in some cases, through diplomatic activity. Election usually occurred in the middle years of their lives while they were still militarily active yet of sufficient age to have established a martial reputation. This pattern seems to have been consistent throughout each reign: Alan Buxhill and John Burley, both bachelors of Edward III, were in their forties at the time of their installation; the chamber knights of Richard II, Simon Burley and Philip La Vache, were respectively forty-five and fifty when they achieved election; while Henry IV's household men, Thomas Erpingham, Thomas Rempston, and John Stanley were honoured with the garter in their late forties to early fifties.[22] Admission to the ranks of the brotherhood was intended not only to recognise past service, but also to encourage future diligence. Despite long years of service in Wales and Ireland, the nominations during the minority of Henry VI of the veteran knights Sir John Fastolf, Sir John Radcliffe, and Sir John Grey were intended if anything to signal increased expectations of service in defence of the dual monarchy.[23] Service to the Crown certainly remained the key factor; indeed, the majority of bachelors elected in this period had been retained by the monarch on the basis of their martial reputations as king's knights, or knights of the chamber. Richard Pembridge, installed in 1369, was made a knight of the king's household in 1353 before promotion to the chamber seven years later.[24]

---

[22] The dates of their elections are as follows: Alan Buxhill (Aug. 1372); John Burley (June 1377); Simon Burley (May 1381); Philip La Vache (Feb. 1399); Thomas Erpingham (April 1401); Thomas Rempston (May 1400); John Stanley (Dec. 1404). It should be stressed that the dominant criterion in the admission of bachelor-knights was not age but military experience; thus, although only twenty years of age at the time of his election in 1388, Henry Hotspur enjoyed a precocious reputation for martial diligence following his early initiation to arms on the Scottish Marches.

[23] Fastolf was elected in 1426, Radcliffe in 1429, and Grey in 1436. At the time of his nomination, John Radcliffe was preparing to serve for a further period in France with a retinue of a hundred men-at-arms and two hundred archers: PRO, Exchequer, King's Remembrancer, Various Accounts, E101/71/3, f. 871; PRO, Exchequer, Exchequer of Receipt, Warrants for Issue, E404/45/140.

[24] PRO, E101/394/16, f. 9; PRO, E101/396/2, f. 56; PRO, E101/396/11, f. 17; PRO, E101/397/5, ff. 43, 45. Pembridge was dismissed from his privileged position as a chamber knight in 1372 when he refused the appointment as lieutenant of Ireland.

Similarly, the household retainers of the Black Prince, Simon Burley and Nicholas Sarnesfield, were to graduate into the service of Richard II as chamber knights following the death of their former patron. Although proximity to the monarch was more especially relevant in the bachelor elections of the fourteenth century, before the political and military imperatives of the Lancastrian dual monarchy led to a greater diversification in the role of royal servants, household connections remained significant throughout the following century. It is not coincidental that the only bachelor to be honoured with the garter between 1450 and the 'Yorkist' assembly of September 1460, Sir Edward Hull, was an esquire of the body, and a knight of the king's chamber.[25]

These sorts of generalisations are best applied to the extreme ends of the social spectrum. The baronial class offered too many variations in lineage, wealth, and political influence, to apply absolutes to their career structures. Indeed, in the case of bannerets, the distinctions in status compared with the more prominent bachelors were often thinly marked. Movement between the social categories only served to obscure the differences further, with Boulton's calculations suggesting that up to a third of the ordinary knights elected before 1461 were elevated to the peerage after installation.[26] With this in mind, it is not surprising that the careers and election criteria of a significant percentage of the baronage, many of whom were indeed professional soldiers, should share common characteristics with those of their bachelor counterparts. This is reflected particularly in the ages at election, which ranged widely from the late twenties to the late fifties/early sixties – this representing in the majority of cases the actual span of activity in arms. Any variations that occurred in this pattern were occasioned by social rank, with those elected in the early years of royal service belonging either to the more favoured members of the baronial class (and thus often enjoying a degree of intimacy with the monarch and a

---

[25] PRO, E101/409/11, f. 38; *CPR, 1436-41*, pp. 232, 234; M.G.A. Vale, *English Gascony, 1399-1453* (Oxford, 1970), p. 118. Hull had become an esquire of the hall and chamber by Christmas, 1442-3. He was also closely connected to Margaret of Anjou, receiving an annuity of forty marks per annum from her as one of the queen's carvers at the time of his election.

[26] Boulton, *Knights of the Crown*, p. 132, table 4.1. A total of fifty-six Garter knights were elected from the foundation of the order until the end of the reign of Henry VI, of whom thirty-six were still bachelors at the time of their death.

tradition of family service to the Crown), or those whose political influence made them a prudent choice for admission. Despite negligible experience in arms, Thomas, Lord Despenser was honoured with admission to the order in 1388 on the basis of his lineage as the son of the distinguished commander and companion of the Black Prince, Edward, Lord Despenser KG.[27] Likewise William, Lord Willoughby and Hugh, Lord Stafford were to benefit from their fathers' service to the house of Lancaster when they were invested as companion-knights in 1416 and 1418.

Such non-martial priorities naturally increase in significance in the nomination of the greater magnates, those companions admitted as viscounts, earls, marquesses and dukes. That, of course, is not to deny the military contribution of the upper nobility who continued to remain essentially a martial cadre during the period. As a small social élite, however, whose number rarely exceeded twenty at any one time, they enjoyed a position of political preeminence in the realm, wielding considerable influence in the localities through large-scale landholdings, amassed wealth and offices, and extensive family connections through intermarriage. In view of the dangers in excluding them from the order's privileged ranks, a degree of pragmatism was unavoidable in the nomination process. Although not a peer himself, Sir Thomas Ufford was installed as a companion-knight in 1360 on an exclusively social and political rationale – although totally lacking in military experience, he was the youngest son of one of the kingdom's most powerful magnates.[28] For the majority of great peers, election appears to have occurred within five to six years of their receiving livery of their lands and titles. This pattern remained in force until the second half of Henry VI's reign when the span between receipt of livery and admission to the Garter lengthened. Perhaps reflecting Henry's less circumspect use of patronage, or alternatively a less obvious appreciation of the Garter's

---

[27] J.L.Gillespie, 'Richard II's Knights: Chivalry and Patronage', *Journal of Medieval History*, 13 (1987), p. 156; J.L. Leland, 'Richard II and the Counter-Appellants' (unpub. Yale Ph.D. thesis, 1979), p. 21. Despenser's resentment of Robert de Vere and the court clique ensured his admission to the order under the auspices of the Appellant regime. Ironically, Despenser was later to join the court faction in the 1390s, receiving investiture as earl of Gloucester from Richard II in 1397.

[28] G.F. Beltz, *Memorials of the Order of the Garter* (London 1841), pp. 100–1, 127–8. Thomas was the youngest son of the distinguished knight and Garter companion, Robert Ufford, first earl of Suffolk.

value in monarchical relations with the peerage, elections such as those of John Talbot, earl of Shrewsbury, and James Butler, earl of Ormond, were based more upon curial or partisan associations than on an awareness of the nobility's role as the king's natural counsellors.[29]

At the far end of the social scale was the royal family. The association between the ruling dynasty and the Garter, in common with other great curial orders, was an essential component in the order's social and political function. The presence of the sovereign, as well as other members of the immediate royal family, implied an immediate dynastic objective in the distribution of membership. The inclusion of princes of royal blood, while advantageous to the monarch in the consolidation of his authority, also served to increase the appeal of membership for the nobility who were attracted to its enhanced social exclusivity. Regardless of the degree of wealth or lineage a companion-knight enjoyed, the Garter offered him a unique relationship with both the present monarch and often the future one too. In actively fostering this spirit of fraternal unity, the monarch, motivated by both chivalric concern and political necessity, sought to emphasise the spirit of alliance and friendship between the king and his peerage embodied in the order's foundation. The admission of the sovereign's male relatives broadened this emphasis on loyalty from allegiance to the monarch alone, to allegiance to the entire dynasty. This, as we shall see, was of particular relevance during the troubled years following the Lancastrian usurpation.

The ties between the Garter and the royal family developed rapidly after 1348: in 1361, Edward III elected his three sons, Lionel of Antwerp, John of Gaunt, and Edmund of Langley; five years later, the first of Edward's sons-in-law, Enguerrand de Couci, was admitted – Couci having married the king's second daughter, Isabel, in the previous year. He was to be joined in the ranks of the fraternity in 1371 by another of Edward's sons-in-law, John Hastings, earl of Pembroke.[30] By 1377, with the nominations of Richard of Bordeaux and Henry Bolingbroke, the relationship between the Garter and the royal family had extended to include grandchildren. The trend for electing companions of

---

[29] Shrewsbury was elected *c.* 1456–7, while Ormond was installed around 1457–8.

[30] *The Dictionary of National Biography (DNB)*, eds Leslie Stephen and Sir Sidney Lee (London, 1900), 9, pp. 131–2. John Hastings married Edward III's fourth daughter, Margaret.

more elevated lineage at a younger age reached its apogee in the admission of those knights of royal blood. The founder's three sons elected in 1361, Lionel, John, and Edmund, were respectively twenty-two, twenty, and eighteen. Edward's youngest son, Thomas of Woodstock, was admitted to the fraternity in 1380 at the age of twenty-five. Richard of Bordeaux, the future Richard II, and his nemesis Henry Bolingbroke, were simultaneously elected at the tender ages of nine and ten, while Richard's cousin, Edward Plantagenet, was similarly honoured, aged only thirteen. Little was to change following the Lancastrian revolution with, the admission in 1399 of Bolingbroke's sons, Henry, Thomas, John, and Humphrey at the respective ages of twelve, eleven, ten, and nine. As Boulton comments, by the end of the fifteenth century, of all Edward III's agnatic descendants who had reached manhood, only Edmund of Langley's younger son, Richard of Conisburgh, and Henry and Edmund Beaufort, great-great grandsons of Edward III through Gaunt's liaison with Katherine Swynford, died not having been installed as companion-knights.[31]

The dynastic objectives implicit in the association between the royal family and the Garter allowed the election process to be used at times as a symbol of political intent. This is certainly apparent in the admission of the future Richard II which occurred at a time when suspicions of Gaunt's ambitions to the throne were running high among the Commons. To calm the situation, Richard was rapidly installed as prince of Wales, ironically with the support of Gaunt who wished to allay such fears; soon after, he was also elected to the Garter stall left vacant by the death of his father, to sit opposite Edward III as heir to his grandfather's position as superior of the order, and thus also of the kingdom itself.[32] Henry Bolingbroke was similarly to use the symbolic potency of the Garter following his usurpation in 1399. Having already worn the device on his leg during his coronation ceremony,[33] he secured the election of all four

---

[31] Boulton, *Knights of the Crown*, p. 133. Henry (d. 1464) and Edmund (d. 1471) were sons of Edmund Beaufort, 2nd duke of Somerset, who had himself been admitted to the ranks of the order in 1436.

[32] *The Brut*, ed. F.W. Brie (EETS, 136, London, 1908; repr. 1971), 2, p. 331. In addition to his investiture as prince of Wales, Richard was also made duke of Cornwall and earl of Chester.

[33] Froissart, *Chroniques*, 16, p. 203.

of his sons in the autumn of the same year – a significant escalation in the relationship between the monarchy and the fraternity. Highly conscious of the weakness of his constitutional argument for seizing the throne, and the dangers in making force a precedent, Henry sought in his use of ceremony to underline the legitimacy of his accession. Thus, he preserved the traditional form of the coronation to the word, imitating the same symbolism used by his predecessor, as well as further enhancing the sanctity of his kingship through the use of unction. The simultaneous elections of his immediate male offspring soon afterwards evoked strong memories of the example set by Edward III in 1361, emphasising the dynastic continuity of Henry's reign as grandson of the order's founder.

The presence of the heir to the throne within the ranks of the society served one crucial political function: to underline the security of the royal succession, and thus the stability of the ruling house. It is for this reason that Bolingbroke was particularly keen to secure the installation of his eldest son, Henry of Monmouth, in 1399. The same rationale was also evident in Margaret of Anjou's decision to hold open a Garter stall in 1459 until her son, Prince Edward, came of age, and could thus be admitted to the fraternity as heir to his father, Henry VI.[34] Bearing in mind the child elections of Richard II and Henry IV, however, Margaret's decision to wait for Edward to reach his majority before securing his election is somewhat surprising.

Although social and political considerations undoubtedly affected the rigour of the application of the martial yardstick in the selection of new companion-knights, military service remained the pre-eminent qualification for candidature. There is little evidence to suggest that there was either a significant decline in the military quality of companions admitted, or a noticeable debasement of the order's chivalric ethos between 1348 and 1461. Edward III, in his foundation of the Garter fraternity, had chosen the original fellowship largely on the basis of military experience acquired in his service during the campaigns of 1346–7.[35] These founder knights set the standards by which

---

[34] J. Anstis, *Register of the Most Noble Order of the Garter* (London, 1724), 2, p. 163.
[35] J. Vale, *Edward III and Chivalry*, pp. 87–8.

subsequent companions of the order were judged, not only during the remaining years of Edward's reign but throughout the medieval period. With the accession of the young Richard II, the martial character of the order was to be consolidated through the introduction of such distinguished knights as John Burley and Lewis Clifford, former retainers of the Black Prince who had entered into the service of his son and heir. Even with the increasing number of courtier elections towards the close of the century, as the Garter was increasingly assimilated into the ceremonial life of the *curia regis*, diligence in arms, displayed either on the field of battle or in the lists, remained the key qualification for admission. Although they were members of the dominant court clique of the 1390s, William le Scrope, Thomas Holland, earl of Kent, and John Montagu, earl of Salisbury could qualify their obvious political credentials with long years of campaigning in England's continental wars.[36]

Following the accession of Henry IV in 1399, military service in France was subordinated to more domestic imperatives arising out of the political circumstances of the Lancastrian accession. The large number of stalls vacated as a result of the failed uprisings and political challenges in the early years of the reign offered Henry a unique opportunity to reconstitute the order on Lancastrian lines; the pattern of admissions that emerged reflected not only the factors that governed Bolingbroke's selection of new companions, but also his scale of political priorities in the early and unstable years of the regime.[37] Certainly in the immediate aftermath of the revolution, the main criteria for election rested on the degree and duration of loyalty and service to the house of

---

[36] *The Controversy between Sir Richard Scrope and Sir Robert Grosvenor in the Court of Chivalry*, ed. N.H. Nicolas (London, 1832), 2, p. 40; *DNB*, 17, pp. 1086-7; M.H. Keen, 'Chaucer's Knight, the English Aristocracy and the Crusade', in *English Court Culture in the Latter Middle Ages*, eds V.J. Scattergood and J.W. Sherborne (London, 1983), p. 55; K.B. McFarlane, *Lancastrian Kings and Lollard Knights* (Oxford, 1972), p. 178. William le Scrope had enjoyed an extensive career in arms, accompanying the Teutonic order on a *reise* in 1362, and later campaigning with Gaunt in his expeditions of 1369 and 1373. Montagu and Holland had similarly gained crusading experience in Prussia, the former having also served with Cambridge in 1369 and distinguishing himself at Bourdeille.

[37] The failure of the Earls' Rising in January 1400, combined with the collapse of the successive Percy rebellions culminating in the defeats at Shrewsbury and Shipton Moor, and a series of natural vacancies, placed nine stalls at the disposal of Henry IV by 1405.

Lancaster, those installed all being men who enjoyed the king's trust, either through consanguinity or as members of his *familia*.[38] Beyond that, the criteria seem to have broadened with specific emphasis being placed upon individual considerations such as the speed with which the knights in question joined Henry following his landing at Ravenspur or, alternatively, the extent of their service in areas of instability such as Wales or the Percy-dominated north. The key to Lancastrian policy in these problematic regions was to retain a strong baronial affinity, the nucleus of which Bolingbroke had inherited from the affinity of his father, John of Gaunt. Thus from 1404 onwards, we see garter insignia being used to reward those northern barons who had been most active in the suppression of the Percy revolts, namely Lords Roos, FitzHugh, and Scrope of Masham. After 1406, the same honour went to the Welsh Marcher Lords, Hugh Burnell, Edward Charlton of Powys, and Gilbert Talbot, for their services in quelling Glyndŵr's uprising.[39] By the end of the reign, Henry's policies had created a far more homogeneous institution, with election being used to validate not only the martial credentials of a companion, but also his political and dynastic reliability. This framework was to provide the Garter with a stable base well into the reign of Henry VI.

With the reopening of the conflict in France, and the increase in domestic harmony, the fraternity was able to return to its more traditional role in support of the continental ambitions of the house of Plantagenet. The focus on France as the leading field of chivalric endeavour remained emphatic, both under Henry V and during the minority of his son and heir. The majority of companions elected by Henry V were soldiers of proven military experience whose careers predated the Agincourt campaign of 1415; of the thirteen Garter knights elected below the rank of earl, nine had been retained solely on the basis of martial reputations, gained largely through campaigning on the Celtic

---

[38] In addition to his four sons, Henry IV was to elect during the course of 1400 his cousin, Thomas Fitzalan, earl of Arundel and his half-brother, Sir Thomas Beaufort. They were to be joined in the ranks of the order by loyal members of the Lancastrian affinity such as William, Lord Willoughby (also elected in 1400), and long-serving household retainers such as Sir Thomas Erpingham (el. April 1401) and Sir Thomas Rempston (el. May 1401).

[39] Burnell was installed in 1406, and Charlton of Powys and Talbot in 1408.

'peripheries' of Wales and Ireland.[40] In this respect, Henry V's distribution of garter insignia appears to represent not merely an abstract recognition of individual feats of arms, but the culmination of a long-term policy to cultivate a body of tried and trusted soldiers who were to be the mainstay of his military ambitions, the apotheosis of this being the war in France.

The same considerations were to remain in force after the death of Henry V under the aegis of his royal brothers and custodians of the Lancastrian legacy, John, duke of Bedford, and Humphrey, duke of Gloucester. More than ever, Garter election was used to reward and recognise the services of the nobility in extending England's continental conquests.[41] Even in cases where social and political factors appeared to outweigh chivalric ones, a degree of martial experience, however minimal, was expected. As Henry V had required military service to qualify the loyalty of those heirs of families dispossessed in the early days of the dynasty, so it was expected that Richard, duke of York, despite his social pre-eminence as heir to the greatest inheritance in the land, should participate in the coronation expedition of 1430 before election was granted in the following year. France also continued to be the preferred area for knightly endeavour, a fact particularly highlighted in the elections of John, Lord Talbot, Sir John Fastolf, and Sir John Radcliffe. Despite lengthy and diverse campaign experience in Ireland and, in the case of Talbot, Wales, Garter admission followed only after a concentrated period of service in France under the leadership of the regent, Bedford.[42] It was only after Henry VI had reached

---

[40] As prince of Wales, Henry developed associations with a number of knights who were subsequently to be invested as companions of the order. Thomas, Lord Camoys (el. Sept. 1414), William Harrington (el. Aug. 1415), William, Lord Zouche (el. Oct. 1415), John Blount (el. Feb. 1417), John Grey (el. Oct. 1419), and Louis Robessart (el. May 1421) had all been active to varying degrees in the suppression of Glyndŵr's revolt.

[41] Eight of the ten companions elected during the fourteen years of Henry VI's minority were chosen in recognition of their services in France. They were: John, Lord Talbot (el. May 1424), Thomas, Lord Scales (el. April 1425), John Fastolf (el. April 1426), John Radcliffe (el. April 1429), John Fitzalan, earl of Arundel (el. April 1432), Edmund Beaufort, count of Mortain (el. April 1436), John Grey of Ruthin (el. April 1436), Richard Neville, earl of Salisbury (el. c. 1437–8).

[42] John Talbot is a particularly good example of this. Despite years of campaigning against Glyndŵr in Wales (for which service his brother, Gilbert, was rewarded with Garter election) and then against insurgents in Ireland, election to the Garter had to wait until 1424 – and then only

adulthood in 1437 that household connections began to feature more prominently in the criteria for nomination. Initially, during the period of Suffolk's ascendancy in the 1440s, the decline in chivalric standards was negligible: although the majority of subject-knights admitted were partisans of the king's chamberlain, most had some soldiering experience. A small number, including Sir Thomas Hoo and Richard Wydeville, Lord Rivers, were indeed highly accomplished in arms.[43] With the rise to power of Margaret of Anjou in the later 1450s, however, as the curialist group fought for political ascendancy with the Yorkist lords, factionalism became more commonplace in the admission process. If the Garter was to lose a degree of its military stature during this period, the damage was far from irreparable: as late as 1461, Henry VI's act of attainder could describe the 'prowesse of knyghthode' of William, Lord Bonville, and Sir Thomas Kyriell in the context of their membership of the order.[44]

The potential of the Garter in the monarch's relations with the nobility was not solely restricted to the recruitment and consolidation of aristocratic support for the king's wars. The speed with which the fraternity had been assimilated into aristocratic society as a symbol of social and chivalric precedence meant that it was able to fulfil a more general purpose in the monarch's relations with his peerage. If we consider again the apparent variations in the criteria for admission according to social status, it becomes evident that at the heart of this seeming compromise of the order's chivalric ethos lay the political imperative of

---

after a period of service under the deputy of the order, Gloucester, at the siege of Crotoy: A.J. Pollard, *John Talbot and the War in France* (London and New Jersey, 1983), p. 9; *CPR, 1413–16*, p. 164.

[43] The career of Thomas Hoo, if not marked by brilliance, was certainly noted for its energy, with participation in the expeditions of 1433, 1434 and 1436, and service as lieutenant of the *vicomté* of the Cotentin by 1437. In 1444, he received an annuity of £40 for his services in France. At the time of his installation, Hoo was serving as chancellor of Normandy: *CCR, 1441–47*, p. 172; E.M. Burney, 'English Rule in Normandy, 1435–1450', (unpub. Oxford B.Litt. thesis, 1958), p. 139n; *Appendices to the Report on Rymer's Foedera B, C, D* (London, 1869), pp. 432–3. Richard Wydeville was equally experienced in arms, a fact recognised in his appointments as lieutenant of Calais in 1436 and seneschal of Guyenne in 1450, the year of his election: PRO, Chancery, Enrolments, Gascon Rolls, C 61/138, m. 14; M. Vale, *English Gascony*, appendix ii, p. 245.

[44] *RP*, 5, p. 477.

not excluding those of wealth and influence from access to the sovereign. Induction into the order was a clear indication of royal favour; as such, it could be used by the monarch as an instrument of honorific patronage in the building and consolidation of his associations with the aristocracy. Of particular value during periods of political instability, the number of comital elections to the order rose sharply when the foundations of royal government were at their weakest. This is seen clearly in the closing years of the reign of Edward III when a series of royal mortalities, combined with the demands of the war in France, led the king to re-evaluate his relationship with the peerage. Up to that point, Edward had pursued a patronal policy of family aggrandisement, often to the detriment of aristocratic interests. In the early 1370s, however, Edward began to change this, with the result that from 1373 onwards the Garter began to open its ranks to the younger generation of the upper magnates.[45] Although possessing the necessary qualifications in terms of lineage and territorial inheritance, these peers were either too young to have yet distinguished themselves in war to the same degree, or were denied the same opportunities for the acquisition of chivalric merit.

A similar concern appears to have motivated the elections of Humphrey, earl of Stafford and Richard, duke of York during the minority of Henry VI. The royal council, aware of the dangers in denying these important magnates membership of the socially élite order during the king's minority, honoured both knights with the garter insignia in 1429 and 1433 respectively. In the case of York, his position as heir to three vast inheritances, being the son and heir of Richard, earl of Cambridge (and thus heir of York), and nephew and heir of Edmund, earl of March and Ulster, made this imperative. The royal council could ill afford to alienate the most senior peer in England by descent, and the wealthiest landowner in the realm. In this respect, Garter election was

---

[45] W.M. Ormrod, *The Reign of Edward III: Crown and Political Society in England, 1327–1377* (Newhaven and London, 1990), p. 116. Thomas Beauchamp, earl of Warwick, and William Ufford, earl of Suffolk, were installed as Garter companions in 1373 and July 1375 respectively, largely on the basis of their recent succession to important inheritances in November 1369. They were to be joined by Hugh Stafford, earl of Stafford, in November 1375, and Thomas Holland, earl of Kent, in September 1376. Although more experienced in arms than Warwick and Suffolk, it was their comital rank that was the most significant factor in their elections at those particular times.

consistent with government policy that since 1422 had accorded to York every honour due to his rank and status: not only was he the heir general of Edward III, and heir to the lines of York and Mortimer, but also probably heir presumptive should Gloucester and Bedford have died childless before the king had begotten a son.[46] Even in the last years of Henry VI's reign, garter insignia were being used to reinforce political ties between the nobility and the ruling house. Certainly it is likely that the elections of both Henry, Viscount Bourgchier and John Mowbray, duke of Norfolk in 1450 and 1451 were intended by the court party to help neutralise any potential sympathy either lord may have felt for the duke of York.[47]

In the majority of politically-motivated elections, proximity to the monarch was an important factor, with chamber knights and courtier peers prominent among those elected. The young Richard II did not hesitate to secure the nominations in the early 1380s of his two childhood companions, Thomas Mowbray, earl of Nottingham and Robert de Vere, earl of Oxford, at a time when he was beginning to assert his role increasingly in the affairs of government.[48] Even as a mature adult, Richard was keen to promote the interests of his courtier friends, with Garter election featuring as one of a series of honours bestowed during the 1390s upon such staunch supporters as John, Lord Beaumont, William le Scrope, and John Montagu, earl of Salisbury.[49]

---

[46] Milner, 'Order of the Garter', p. 113.

[47] The political affiliations of both peers were ambiguous at the time of their respective elections, certainly there is no evidence to suggest that they were directly opposed to York at that time. Not only had Bourgchier married the duke's sister in 1426, he also enjoyed friendly relations with Sir John Fastolf, one of York's former counsellors. In the case of Mowbray, he had more recently demonstrated a degree of political sympathy with the duke by joining him in the sacking of Somerset's Ludgate home in November 1450.

[48] Mowbray and de Vere were invested as Garter companions in October 1383 and July 1384 respectively.

[49] Many of Richard II's courtier friends were to be recognised with Garter investiture during the 1390s. The first to be admitted was the staunch of royalist, John, Lord Beaumont, in 1393. He was followed in 1394 by William le Scrope, and in the following year by the chamber knight, William Arundel. Thomas Holland, earl of Kent, John Montagu, earl of Salisbury, and the royal standard bearer, Simon Felbrigg, were invested in 1397. The last Ricardian election was that of the courtier knight and life retainer of the king, Philip La Vache, in 1399.

Although not as susceptible to the influence of curial factions, Henry IV was nevertheless circumspect in his distribution of the Garter at the beginning of his reign, preferring only to patronise those who enjoyed his complete trust. Thus, the early elections (his own sons apart) were dominated either by royal relatives such as Thomas Fitzalan, earl of Arundel and Sir Thomas Beaufort, or by members of the king's *familia* such as the Lancastrian retainers, Sir Thomas Erpingham and Sir Thomas Rempston. The preference for household men was to reach a high point in the middle years of the fifteenth century as the duke of Suffolk and then the royal consort, Margaret of Anjou, assumed control of the king's patronage.

Given the order's prestigious position, and its undeniable attraction as a source of chivalric recognition and social prestige, manipulation of the nomination process was unavoidable, particularly during periods of weak kingship. If the sovereign's powers of self-determination were compromised for whatever reason, whether because he was a child-monarch, as seen during the minority of Richard II, or senile, as witnessed in the later years of Edward III's reign, or merely weak-willed and vulnerable to the influence of court favourites – a character fault most clearly demonstrated in the adult Henry VI – the admission of new companions was often operated with direct benefit to the monarch. The precedent for this can be found as early as the reign of Edward III when, during the closing years of the king's life, a court clique surrounding the chamberlain of the household, William, Lord Latimer, and the king's mistress, Alice Perrers, rose to power. Between 1369 and 1377, three leading associates of this clique, Sir Richard Pembridge, John, Lord Neville, and Sir Alan Buxhill, were invested as Garter companions. The minority of Edward's heir, Richard II, was to witness a similar predominance of courtier elections, largely under the influence of the king's chamberlain, Simon Burley. It was, however, the ascendancy of William de la Pole, duke of Suffolk, during the 1440s that saw the clearest demonstration of factional interest influencing the pattern of elections. Between 1440 and 1450, admission to the fraternity was restricted almost exclusively to members of the king's household, with Ralph Botiller, Lord Sudeley, chief butler of the household, and the courtier-knight, John, Viscount Beaumont, elected in 1440 and 1441, and the king's carver, Sir John Beauchamp, installed in 1445.

If the influence of prominent courtiers could secure the installation of friends and associates, equally it could ensure that certain less-favoured individuals were excluded from the order's élite ranks. The complete absence of Ralph, Lord Cromwell from the electoral scrutinies between 1445 and 1450, despite a long career in arms, and a prominent position in court and governmental circles, was most probably arranged through the machinations of his powerful enemy, the duke of Suffolk.[50] Exclusion, however, was not the only indication of disfavour for the upper echelons of the peerage: delayed admission, or supercession in the order of election, was equally pointed. As the youngest son of Edward III, Thomas of Woodstock could rightly have expected almost immediate admission to the fraternity on the achievement of his majority. The priority given to the election of his ten-year-old nephew, Henry Bolingbroke, three years before his own investiture, must therefore have been a source of some discontent for the irascible duke.[51] It represented a further snub to Woodstock by Gaunt, who had already forced his younger sibling to share the considerable de Bohun inheritance by securing the marriage of Bolingbroke to the remaining co-heiress of the late earl of Hereford.[52] In this vein, it is equally likely that the premature elevation of Richard II's favourite, Robert de Vere, in 1382, increased the bitterness of Richard, earl of Arundel who, despite his experience as a commander in France, was forced to wait a further three to four years for his own nomination.[53]

The statutes of the Garter, although vague in their definition of the general role of the fraternity, were specific in stipulating the qualities desired in new companions. In addition to the emphasis placed upon membership of the knightly classes, to be a *gentil homme de sang*, it was also demanded that the

---

[50] Cromwell served as the king's chamberlain from 1422 to 1432, and treasurer between 1433 and 1443.

[51] A. Tuck, *Richard II and the English Nobility* (London, 1973), p. 9.

[52] *The Westminster Chronicle, 1381–1394*, eds L.C. Hector and B. Harvey, (Oxford, 1982), pp. 192–3n., 520–1n.; K.B. McFarlane, *Lancastrian Kings and Lollard Knights* (Oxford, 1972), p. 16. Woodstock had married Humphrey de Bohun's eldest daughter, Eleanor, sometime between 1374 and 1376.

[53] Gillespie, 'Richard II's Knights', p. 155.

knight-elect should be in reputation, *sans reprouche*.[54] Certainly honour and reputation had featured significantly in the composition of the original fellowship. Juliet Vale argues convincingly that the earls of Huntingdon and Arundel, two of Edward III's leading commanders, were in fact excluded from the fraternity in 1348 on the basis of their involvement in the constitutional crisis of 1340.[55] This emphasis on reputation, which we see reiterated in 1426 in John Radcliffe's 'presentment' (certificate of recommendation) commending him for his long years of 'unreproched' service to the Crown,[56] was to facilitate the Garter's use as a symbol of political conciliation. It may well be that Richard of York's admission in 1431 was motivated by a desire to alleviate any sense of political marginalisation that he may have felt under the ruling dynasty as the son and heir of the earl of Cambridge, who had been executed for his role in the conspiracy of 1415. If so, it was a conscious reversal of government policy towards the heir of Mortimer,[57] contrasting sharply with Henry V's earlier treatment of the earl of March. Despite official forgiveness for his role in the Cambridge plot, and subsequent years of military service in France, March was consistently denied membership of the fraternity.

The precedents for this usage predate the reign of Henry VI. Indeed, it is possible to identify, albeit tentatively, a conciliatory policy in Bolingbroke's nomination of Edmund Holland in 1404, and that of Henry, Lord Scrope in 1409, the former after the execution of his brother, Thomas, earl of Kent after the failure of the Earls' Rising in 1400, and the latter following the death of his uncle, Archbishop Scrope, in the aftermath of the abortive rebellion of 1405. Following the example set by his father, Henry V was to pursue a similar policy

[54] College of Arms, MS Arundel 48, article 3.
[55] J. Vale, *Edward III and Chivalry*, pp. 89–91.
[56] Ashmole, *Institution*, pp. 269–70.
[57] T.B. Pugh, *Henry V and the Southampton Plot of 1415* (Gloucester, 1988), pp. 69–71. Apart from Roger II, earl of March, elected as one of the founding companions, the Mortimers were in fact markedly absent from the Garter before their direct line became extinct in 1425. The proximity of Earl Roger III to the throne through his mother, Philippa (he was even rumoured by some contemporaries to have been declared heir to the childless Richard II in 1385), guaranteed his exclusion from the fraternity, as well as that of his successor, Earl Edmund, during the reigns of Richard and his usurper, Henry IV.

with the remaining heirs of those Ricardian families alienated by the Lancastrian usurpation. Consequently, between 1414 and 1421, he secured the elections of five peers who, if not all heirs of fathers attainted for treason, were nevertheless all needful of some confirmation of their status under the new regime.[58] Thomas Montagu, earl of Salisbury, was elected in 1414; in the following year, he was joined by John Holland, later earl of Huntingdon, and Richard de Vere, earl of Oxford; and in 1421, John Mowbray, earl Marshal, and William de la Pole, earl of Suffolk were similarly installed as companion-knights. Although Henry V had already made moves towards the restoration of their estates and titles prior to election, admission to the ranks of the Garter was to acknowledge without equivocation the purity of their respective reputations. The emphasis in the statutes on the possession of an unblemished reputation extended as much to the family's honour as to the individual's actions. Elevation to the Garter's ranks therefore removed the final stigma attached to their family name. Jean de Foix, earl of Kendal was to view this requirement with sufficient gravity that in the electoral assembly of 1460 he failed to nominate any candidates on the basis that he knew of none in the realm of sufficient character to be invested with the honour.[59]

Needless to say, it was not always possible to reconcile those who had been politically alienated. Although Henry, Lord Scrope of Masham had enjoyed the trust and intimacy of Henry IV during the early years of the Lancastrian regime, a position evidenced by his appointment as treasurer, his seat on the king's council, and his admission to the Garter fraternity in 1409, he was nevertheless implicated in the Cambridge plot of 1415. As the foremost chivalric achievement for the nobility of later medieval England, membership of the fraternity (whether the result of merit or influence) carried with it a number of obligations and expectations, both as a knight and as a fraternal companion

---

[58] The fathers of Thomas Montagu and John Holland had both died in the failed Earls' Rising of 1400. John Mowbray was the son of Bolingbroke's former enemy, Thomas, earl of Nottingham, while Richard de Vere and William de la Pole were the heirs of families who had enjoyed considerable favour under Richard II.

[59] Anstis, *Register*, 1, p. 166; N.H. Nicolas, *History of the Orders of Knighthood of the British Empire* (4 vols, London, 1842), 1, p. 88.

of the king. The breaking of the bonds of trust encapsulated in the Garter oath was therefore an extreme act of treason. Thus in the parliamentary affirmation of the judgments given in 1415 against the Southampton conspirators, specific emphasis is placed upon the extent of Lord Scrope's treachery in the context of his membership of the fraternity. As one passage states: 'being in the same Order, [on account of] his dereliction should justly be regarded as infamous'. The document is careful to add, however, that despite his crime, no dishonour should reflect upon the fraternity itself.[60] In cases where a companion had contravened his oath of obedience to the statutes, the order was careful to dissociate itself formally from the individual knight by expelling him from its ranks. The first known degradation was that of Robert de Vere, earl of Oxford following his appeal of treason in the Merciless Parliament of 1388. He was to be followed in 1397 by the Appellant lord, Thomas Beauchamp, earl of Warwick, no doubt as a retaliatory gesture for the latter's role in the events of 1388. Degradation from the Garter continued to be used by the ruling power as a penalty for political opposition throughout the fifteenth century. Thus, Henry Percy, earl of Northumberland was expelled in 1406/7 after the failure of his attempt to overthrow Bolingbroke's fledgling regime, while the staunch Lancastrian, Jasper Tudor, earl of Pembroke was similarly removed following the deposition of Henry VI in 1461.[61]

Membership of the order was not without its advantages in difficult moments, however. Indeed, as a validation of knightly honour and chivalric repute, it could often be used as a form of defence. Both Simon Burley, during his trial proceedings in the Merciless Parliament of 1388, and William de la Pole, duke of Suffolk in his impeachment defence in 1450, re-emphasised their position as Garter knights to mitigate the consequences of the prosecution. In the case of the former, as the monk of Westminster informs us, the actual sentence was reduced from hanging, drawing, and quartering to simple beheading in consideration of a series of reasons, not least *quil fuist chivalier del gartour*.[62] In the trial of Suffolk, the reference was more specific, recalling not merely his election

---

[60] *RP*, 4, pp. 64–7.

[61] A complete list of the degradations during the period is printed in *CP*, 2, p. 581.

[62] *Westminster Chronicle*, p. 292.

but also the longevity of his membership having been 'of the felisship of the Garter xxx' years'.[63]

It has been necessary in this paper, in considering only the practical functions of the Garter as an instrument of royal policy, to present a somewhat one-sided image of the institution, to subordinate its significance in purely chivalric terms and seemingly to disregard the value of its intangible goals. This has not been intentional. Although martial factors may occasionally have been relegated in favour of more practical considerations – particularly in the installation of foreign princes or politically significant magnates – the majority of knight-companions elected during the period were soldiers of renown. Even during the last two decades of the reign of Henry VI, when influence at court or favour with the king or the queen appeared to be the main yardstick for elevation to the ranks of the fraternity, martial prowess was never completely disregarded.[64] While it is likely that, as the complexion of the order changed under the aegis of a pacific monarch, the electoral emphasis shifted away from the strictly chivalric qualifications of the mid-fourteenth century to more consciously political ones by the mid-fifteenth century, the fundamental character of the Garter remained unchanged.

Indeed, it was the careful balance maintained between practical and idealistic objectives that was the key to the success of Edward III's foundation. The Garter provided the English monarch with an instrument of political patronage that could function only within a chivalric framework: if denied the prestige accrued through the admission of prominent warriors and military commanders, the fraternity would no longer be desirable as a source of honorific distinction, and would thus be of little use politically. Formal definitions of the Garter's role, other than as an orthodox celebration of traditional chivalric values, were inappropriate: although the statutes alluded

---

[63] *RP*, 5, p. 176. Pole was in fact elected to the Garter in May 1421 rather than 1420, as this claim would suggest.

[64] In the election scrutiny of Edward Hull in 1453, the names of other prominent courtier knights were put forward, including those of Thomas Stanley and Edmund Hungerford. Although high in royal favour, Hull was selected over his rivals most probably on the basis of his considerable martial experience, having distinguished himself on campaign in France in the previous year: Anstis, *Register*, 1, pp. 143, 150.

briefly to the order's practical potential, any more overt delineations in the election criteria would have served only to damage the Garter's cohesion by weakening the institutional emphasis upon the common bond of knighthood. Had the order been allowed to degenerate fully into an instrument of patronage, then it is probable that it would have died out by the end of the fifteenth century in common with its short-lived sister establishment, the ladies of the fraternity of St George.[65] The Garter's longevity as an institution was based upon the enduring appeal of the ideals and virtues celebrated in the chivalric life; while a political function could operate within this context, the order would be lost without it.

---

[65] The patronal functions of the order were to be augmented by the evolution of a complementary female institution known as the ladies of the fraternity of St George. Originating out of the practice in the later years of Edward III's reign of distributing livery to certain favoured court ladies for the St George's day festivities, the association was gradually to grow in size and ceremonial importance under Richard II, before dying out in the middle years of the following century. With no formal or statutory connection to the order, the female associates were free of the martial obligations, fixed membership, and electoral requirements that regulated the nomination process for knightly companions. Responsibility for the disbursement of livery was soley dependent upon monarchical prerogative; as such, the sorority's function was more implicitly political, if less directly effective, than that of the actual fraternity, with the issue of robes to womenfolk being used as an additional means to solicit the support of aristocratic families: J.L. Gillespie, 'Ladies of the Fraternity of Saint George and of the Society of the Garter', *Albion*, 17 (1985), pp. 259–78; Nicolas, *History of the Orders of Knighthood*, 2, pp. lxxvii–lxxxi.

9

ON THE DIFFERENCE BETWEEN VIRTUE AND WEISS: HUMANIST TEXTS IN ENGLAND DURING THE FIFTEENTH CENTURY*

David Rundle

In Italy, it was the *quattrocento* and the Renaissance. In England, it was the fifteenth century, the autumn of the Middle Ages. The same hundred years was, it might seem, both the best of times and the worst of times. Conventionally, the history of Europe in the fifteenth century has been written as a tale of two cultures: the traditional, outdated, but still influential impression has been of two contrasting world views, as different as, say, light and darkness or maturity and childishness. Relatively little research has been done on the intellectual interaction between these supposedly opposed outlooks – little, that is, except for the work of Roberto Weiss.

It is over forty years since the publication of Weiss' thesis on humanism in England in the fifteenth century, but 'with all its faults, [it] is still the best general guide' to its subject.[1] As I am necessarily going to dwell on those faults, it is best for me to express my debt at the outset. I may appear more than a little like the man who, complaining to Emperor Sigismund that there was no liberty, was reminded that his ability to say such things was the paramount mark of his

---

* I would like to thank Dr G. Garnett, Dr C.S.L. Davies and Miss K. Kennedy for their support and advice in the writing of this paper.

[1] R. Weiss, *Humanism in England during the Fifteenth Century* (Oxford, 1941); Weiss' thesis appeared in two later editions (1957 and 1967), with addenda, but the main body of the text remains unaltered and page numbers are unaffected. The quotation is from J.B. Trapp, 'From Guarino of Verona to John Colet' in *Italy and the English Renaissance*, eds S. Rossi and D. Savoia (Milan, 1989), p. 45.

freedom.[2] Likewise, I am aware that I would not be at liberty to write the following pages if it were not for the ground-breaking researches of Weiss himself.

If, as Weiss once remarked, the Renaissance was created by nineteenth-century historians, the concept was nurtured by their twentieth-century inheritors.[3] Weiss' writings did not so much undermine the prevailing perspective as develop it. For him, humanism was the intellectual movement of the Renaissance, an emphasis on classical studies which brought with it a new and modernising vision of the world. Contemporary England, however, failed to take advantage of the complete transformation of cultural values this movement offered.[4] Indeed, on Weiss' interpretation, it could be said, humanism in fifteenth-century England was like a secular equivalent to the word of God: it was a light that shineth in the darkness and the darkness (or medieval England) comprehended it not. In the 1410s and '20s, 'English intellectuals were too immature to derive any real profit from their . . . contacts with Italian humanism.'[5] Fifteenth-century England, for Weiss (like the whole of late medieval northern Europe for Huizinga), seems to have been inhabited by outsized children, to whom the humanists could find no fitter reaction than condescension. And (we are told) when Englishmen did come to read texts by these Italians, they somehow contrived to digest only the most 'medieval' of the humanists' works, such as Bruni's translations of Aristotle.[6]

Historians are not as self-assured, or perhaps it is as clear-sighted, as they were in Weiss' generation.[7] Grand claims for 'humanism' have been replaced by

---

[2] Poggio Bracciolini, *Facezie*, ed. M. Ciccuto (Milan, 1994), no. 28, pp. 148–9.

[3] R.Weiss, *The Spread of Italian Humanism* (London, 1964), p. 11.

[4] For the arguments and phrasing of these sentences, see R. Weiss, 'Learning and Education in Western Europe from 1470 to 1520' in G.R. Potter, *New Cambridge Modern History, Vol. 1: The Renaissance* (Cambridge, 1957), p. 95; Weiss, *Spread*, pp. 12–13; Weiss, *Humanism*, p. 17.

[5] Weiss, *Spread*, p. 90.

[6] R.Weiss, 'Leonardo Bruni Aretino and Early English Humanism', *Modern Language Review*, 36 (1941), pp. 443–8. See also N. Mann, 'Petrarch's Role in Humanism', *Apollo*, 94 (1971), pp. 176–83.

[7] For more recent thinking on humanism in England, see, for example, D. Hay, 'England and the Humanities in the Fifteenth Century' in his *Renaissance Essays* (London, 1988), pp. 169–231; D. Gray, 'Humanism and Humanisms in the Literature of Late Medieval England' in *Italy and the English Renaissance*, eds Rossi and Savoia, pp. 25–44.

narrow definitions – it is now equated with the educational programme which contemporary Italian scholars came to call *studia humanitatis*.[8] There is also now some confusion about how to describe the transmission of Italian culture to other countries. Weiss' favoured metaphor was 'spread'; more fashionable is the concept of 'reception'. Both terms, however, suggest a passive acceptance by a culture acted upon by a potent movement – all England had to do was lie back and think of progress as it was infused with Renaissance *virtù*.[9] Intellectual intercourse is rarely such an unequal relationship.

In this paper, I intend to suggest some of the ways in which we might want to revise our interpretation of the *fortuna* of humanist texts in England. I will concentrate on three formative moments from the early history of humanists' contacts with the country, but my comments, I hope, will have wider implications. There will be some reflections on the humanists' attitude to England, but that is not my main concern.[10] My interest is the English circulation of, and responses to, humanist writings, in particular works which include political thinking. My basic argument is probably already apparent: Weiss and the traditional interpretation too often dismiss the English as backward or, at best, passive recipients of humanism. Instead, on my submission, there is much more intelligent English activity than is usually credited. I would argue that the traditional interpretation not only underrates the English; it also misconstrues the humanists. A series of Italian scholars in the fifteenth century spent a part of their careers in English service – an experience, it is often suggested, that few of the humanists relished. However, I would argue that the usual impression of intellectuals enduring this barbaric land like some wise man's burden is too ingenuous a reading: it takes the available sources – the letters the humanists themselves

---

[8] P.O. Kristeller, 'Humanism' in *The Cambridge History of Renaissance Philosophy*, eds C.B. Schmitt and Q. Skinner (Cambridge, 1988), pp. 113–37; B.G. Kohl, 'The Changing Concept of the *Studia Humanitatis* in the Early Renaissance', *Renaissance Studies*, 6 (1992), pp. 185–209.

[9] P. Burke, 'The Spread of Italian Humanism' in *The Impact of Humanism on Western Europe*, eds A. Goodman and A. MacKay (London, 1990), pp. 1–22 and P. Burke, 'The Uses of Italy' in *The Renaissance in National Context*, eds R. Porter and M. Teich (Cambridge, 1992), pp. 6–20.

[10] See Susanne Saygin's forthcoming Oxford D.Phil. thesis, 'The Transmission of Italian Humanism to England circa 1420–1450'.

wrote – at face value. The pre-eminent example of this is the 'British exile' of Poggio Bracciolini.[11]

Depending on one's interests, Poggio is remembered as the inventor of humanist script, as a retriever of lost classical texts, as an early author of humanist dialogues or as a man of Boccaccian wit (with a lifestyle to match).[12] In 1418, however, he had a glittering future ahead of him. It was not yet apparent that he would become 'one of the greatest humanists of his time.'[13] Certainly, he was known within a scholarly circle for his calligraphical skills and his discoveries of manuscripts; but, even though he was in his late thirties, he had not begun to build his wider reputation as a writer. So, when, at Mantua in November 1418, Henry V's wealthy uncle, Cardinal Beaufort, offered him a place in his entourage, Poggio probably felt honoured to accept, rather than feeling that he was honouring the household with his presence. Poggio was in England for nearly four years, from 1419 to early 1423. His stay in the country has particular significance since it can claim to be the first visit of a humanist to those shores. Accordingly, Weiss' discussion of 'Poggio in England' sets the tone for much of his interpretation. And, on his reading, Poggio's time in England was a case-study in disappointment. The Italian 'failed to stimulate his English [hosts] . . . [because] his studies were far too advanced to find appreciation' among them. What is worse, the English failed to stimulate their illustrious guest: deprived of classical texts, 'he was reduced' to perusing the Church Fathers.[14] Poggio's time in England is also important because, on the basis of his reports, many severe comments have been passed on English learning in the early fifteenth century; Poggio, it is said, made a thorough survey of English libraries and (in the words of Professor Trapp) 'returned home notoriously dissatisfied with the lean harvest of classical texts he had gathered.'[15]

It is not my brief to defend English learned culture against a charge of

---

[11] The phrase is Ernst Walser's in his *Poggius Florentinus* (Leipzig, 1914), p. 74.

[12] The main biography of Poggio is still Walser, *Poggius*; this heavily influences the article in *Dizionario Biografico degli Italiani*, 13 (Rome, 1971), *sub nomine*.

[13] Weiss, *Spread*, p. 90.

[14] Weiss, *Humanism*, pp. 21, 13.

[15] J.B. Trapp, *Erasmus, Colet and More* (London, 1991), p. 8. For what Poggio did find in England, see A.C. de la Mare, *The Handwriting of Italian Humanists*, I (Oxford, 1973), p. 66.

intellectual impoverishment. It is simply my concern to explain that, in any such accusation, the 'proof' of Poggio's sojourn in England is not permissible evidence. The major source we have for Poggio's time in the country is an incomplete series of letters sent by him to his Florentine friend, Niccolò Niccoli. This self-appointed humanist *arbiter elegantiarum* is a shadowy figure; it is typical of him that none of his letters to Poggio survives. However, we can piece together the tenor of his epistles from Poggio's responses; it appears that Niccoli repeatedly wrote to Poggio with eager enquiries about the libraries of England. On the traditional interpretation, Poggio responds with equal interest but with minimal success: his frequent investigations of libraries and catalogues leave him with little more than bitter disappointment. However, this account fails to read both what is on and what is between the lines of Poggio's letters.

If historians have believed Poggio was conscientious in searching libraries, some of his contemporaries did not share this view. Simone de Teramo was the papal collector in England (1420–4); Poggio described him to Niccoli as *vir doctissimus et mei amantissimus* – a judgement he might have wished to revise after the autumn of 1421.[16] For Teramo returned to Italy during that summer and met Niccoli face to face. We can reconstruct Teramo's part of their conversation from a letter of Poggio's written in November 1421. In it, Poggio is on the defensive: '*Nam quod ait Collector esse in hac insula monasteria antiquissima, me nihil vidisse et libros esse infinitos et te propterea te nonnihil suspicari de sirenis, risi mehercule ut illius ostentationem et tuam totiens a me reprehensam credulitatem*'.[17] So, according to Teramo, Poggio was more interested in eyeing up women (*sirenae*) than looking out books. 'Loudmouthed' Teramo could never be judged a sympathetic figure, but his allegations deserve more attention than the polite silence they usually receive.[18] They are certainly scurrilous and also excessive – Poggio did visit some monastic libraries – but they might not be completely inaccurate.[19] It may

---

[16] Poggio Bracciolini, *Lettere*, ed. H. Harth (Florence, 1983), 1, ep. 12 (ll. 30–1; p. 41).
[17] Poggio, *Lettere*, 1, ep. 8 (ll. 121–4; p. 26).
[18] Walser, *Poggius*, p. 82.
[19] Poggio's penchant for pretty women is well-attested; in this same letter, he comments that he is not averse to feminine charms – *homo enim sum*, *Lettere*, 1, ep. 8 (ll. 109–112; p. 25); see also *Lettere*, 2, ep. VIII/2 (ll. 17–8; p. 308).

well be that, in his English letters, Poggio's self-portrait as the diligent library-investigator is a literary construct intended to delight his correspondent rather than an accurate résumé of his activities in England. Poggio does admit in one letter that *paulo tepidior factus sum in hac cura perquirendi novos libros* and there may be another reason – one less flattering to a man than an overactive libido – for this cooling off.[20] The relevant passage appears in a letter which, not surprisingly, did not make it into Poggio's published collection: '*Investigationi librorum vacare non possum prout per litteras pollicebar. Quartus est mensis, ex quo laboro hemoroidibus, que me summe affligunt . . .*'.[21] Poggio was clearly a humanist who well knew about the indignity of man. Small wonder, therefore, if he was not overcome with eagerness to ride off in all directions hunting down monasteries.

Piles effectively incapacitated Poggio soon after his arrival in England. Early in 1420, though, an English friend provided him with library catalogues which he perused; that summer, the plague forced him out of London and he visited Salisbury cathedral, where he failed to find the volumes of Origen that Chrysoloras had seen a decade before.[22] A year later, he travelled with Beaufort to *antiquius monasterium omnibus aliis, que sunt in insula, et magnificentius* – this has tentatively been identified as Glastonbury.[23] Yet, by this time, Poggio had already suggested to Niccoli that he had become less interested in searching for books; he explained in the same letter that he was now occupying his time with study of the Church Fathers. In particular, Chrysostom seems to have been his favourite author while in England.[24] Now, Poggio's interest in patristic literature did reflect the availability of texts, but it was a change that he found congenial. Historians might judge theological tracts inappropriate reading for 'humanists', but these scholars rarely confined themselves merely

---

[20] *Lettere*, 1, ep. 10 (ll. 33–4; p. 35).

[21] *Lettere*, 1, app. ii (ll. 67–9; p. 224).

[22] *Lettere*, 1, ep. 3 (ll. 9–12; p. 8); ep. 7 (ll. 21–5; pp. 19–20); the elusive Origen is probably identifiable with Salisbury: Salisbury Cathedral, MSS 109, 159.

[23] *Lettere*, 1, ep. 13 (ll. 54–5; p. 44); P.W. Goodhart Gordan, *Two Renaissance Book Hunters* (New York, 1974), p. 252.

[24] *Lettere*, 1, ep. 10 (ll. 33–60; pp. 35–6); ep. 3 (ll. 13–23; p. 21); ep. 5 (ll. 23–36; p. 16).

to the *studia humanitatis*.[25] Poggio was not alone in his interest in Chrysostom; Niccoli's letters would appear to have contained eager enquiries about the English manuscripts of this author.[26] And at about the same time, another of Niccoli's coterie, Ambrogio Traversari, was beginning to re-translate Chrysostom.[27] So, this Church Father was a core text not only for the 'medieval' culture of England but also for the Christian humanism of Florence.

After the summer of 1421 and his trip to Glastonbury, Poggio's letters mention book-searches only once more, and that is in the context of defending himself against Teramo's slanders. So, his English epistles include few specific references to having actually visited libraries (as opposed to vague claims or grand promises); there is much more evidence of his other preoccupations – both intellectual and fleshly. There are reasons, then, for doubting Poggio's self-image as a meticulous investigator for manuscripts in English libraries, to which we can add a final quandary: if he did scour the monasteries and catalogues as thoroughly as he claims, why did he find so little? This question occurred to Weiss, who observed: 'the monasteries visited by Poggio cannot have included those at Canterbury, St Albans, Peterborough, Lanthony or other important ones, since he would have found in them several classical manuscripts.'[28] Ironically, though, he confined this comment to a footnote; the text of *Humanism in England*, in contrast, accepts Poggio's eloquent claims that he was an enthusiastic book-hunter. So, historians have proved to be as gullible as Poggio hoped Niccoli would be.

My intention here has not been to bring Poggio into disrepute – only a simpleton or a saint could throw the first stone at such a scholar. Instead, I hope I have sketched an interpretation that recognises Poggio's humanity as well as his humanism. The wider significance of this example is to suggest the circumspection which is necessary when reading humanist epistles. Their

---

[25] *Lettere*, 1, ep. 10 (ll. 53–66); see also Salutati's comment on the connection between *studia humanitatis* and *studia divinitatis*, quoted by Kohl, 'The Changing Concept', p. 192. For criticism of Weiss' exclusively pagan definition of humanism, see M. Harvey, *England, Rome and the Papacy, 1417–64* (Manchester, 1993), pp. 39–41.

[26] Poggio, *Lettere*, I, ep. 7 (ll. 66–70; p. 21).

[27] C.L. Stinger, *Humanism and the Church Fathers: Ambrogio Traversari and Christian Antiquity in the Italian Renaissance* (Albany, New York, 1977).

[28] Weiss, *Humanism*, p. 15.

eloquence might be persuasive but it might also deceive; we need to become more adept at appreciating how meaning is refracted through the humanists' rhetoric. To give another example, humanist letters written in England are often garnished with expressions of pride for the author's home city-state. But it would be naive to take this patriotism as a humanist's driving force. Poggio, on leaving England, went not to his native Florence but to where he could find work: Rome and the papal curia. From there, early in 1423, he wrote to Niccoli: '*Quid acturus sim nescio quoad veniat episcopus Wintoniensis [Beaufort] . . . Coniciam cito conducatne mihi manere in curia, an redire ad Britannos*'.[29] Hardly the words of a man haunted by dire memories of England. But Poggio was certainly not alone in putting his pocket before his *patria*.

Money was, naturally, a perennial concern for those freelance secretaries we call 'the humanists.' However, though patronage was of great importance in arousing a humanist's interest in England, this search for an income has, it seems to me, often been misrepresented. It is usually suggested that, apart from the papal officials sent here on business, the humanists who turned up on the doorstep were rarely more than failures. Denys Hay, talking about the end of the fifteenth century, characterises Carmeliano and the rest of Henry VII's *grex poetarum* as 'somewhat fly-blown foreigners who had failed to make a career at home or sometimes . . . anywhere'.[30] So, England is where bad humanists go to earn. It is admittedly difficult to deny that some of the visiting scholars strike one as rather less than the Renaissance equivalent of young upwardly mobile professionals. A case in point might be that of Tito Livio Frulovisi, who was in England in 1437 and 1438. He is best known for his *Vita Henrici Quinti*, but he also has an unenviable reputation for the dire quality of his poetry.[31] After

[29] *Lettere*, 1, ep. 21(ll. 8–10; p. 62).

[30] Hay, 'England and the Humanities', p. 224.

[31] Two poems by Frulovisi survive: an encomium to Bishop Stafford which its editor says reveals the author's 'incapacity to write tolerable hexameters' (Tito Livio Frulovisi, *Opera hactenus inedita*, ed. C.W. Previté-Orton (Cambridge, 1932), pp. 390–2 and p. xxxv) and the *Humfroidos*. On this, see R. Weiss, 'Humphrey Duke of Gloucester and Tito Livio Frulovisi' in *Fritz Saxl: Memorial Essays*, ed. D.J. Gordon (London, 1957), pp. 218–27. To Weiss' comments can be added the observation that the marginalia in the one extant MS of the *Humfroidos* (Seville: Biblioteca Colombina, MS 7/2/23 ff. 64–86) suggests that the codex was written after Frulovisi's return to Italy. Clearly, the poem's author was untalented enough not to realise his work's poor quality and arranged for other copies of it to be made besides the now lost dedication copy.

repeatedly unsuccessful stints in Ferrara, in England and in Milan, it seems that Frulovisi, 'at last disillusioned of the career of humanism and patron-hunting' (as Previté-Orton puts it), gave up on that vocation and turned medical consultant.[32] But Frulovisi's failure should not be taken as symptomatic of all the humanists who had contacts with England: it is simply not the case that England served as the undiscriminating repository for Italy's cast-offs. Rather, those humanists who travelled to England in search of patronage were part of a wider pattern – in both a geographical and a social sense.

Weiss felt able to divide humanists into some sort of league-table, classing them as first-, second- or even third-rate; he also declared that, with only two exceptions, 'no first-rate humanist went to teach outside Italy or served at a foreign court'.[33] It may be doubtful whether contemporaries had the perceptiveness – or perspective – to rank their peers so definitely. That aside, it is obviously likely that Italians would prefer to travel no further than their peninsula in search of employment and that those who did wander further afield were pushed out by the competitiveness of the market. The consequent humanist diaspora was Europe-wide; England was only one among many countries that played host to job-seeking scholars.[34] At the same time, those humanists who left the Italian peninsula on a patron-hunt are in many ways a subset of those scholars who sought foreign incomes. This is what I mean by the wider social pattern.

The majority of Italians who aspired to English patronage – men like Bruni, Decembrio, Lapo da Castiglionchio (to mention a few from the first half of the fifteenth century) – never visited England: all their dealings were carried out through correspondence. Nor (once again) did such men confine themselves to contacts with the English. For example, Poggio – whose interest in England as a market for his writings followed twenty years after his visit – also attempted to

---

[32] Frulovisi, *Opera*, pp. xv–xvi.

[33] R. Weiss, 'Italian Humanism in Western Europe' in *Italian Renaissance Studies: a Tribute to the Late Cecilia M. Ady*, ed. E.F. Jacob (London, 1960), pp. 69–93 at p. 70. Weiss seems to be referring only to the second half of the fifteenth century; otherwise, his omission of both Poggio and Pier Paolo Vergerio would be surprising.

[34] For a sense of the variety of countries that paid host to humanists, see the highly selective list in Burke, 'The Spread', p. 20.

find patrons in countries as far apart as Hungary and Portugal.[35] Again, to shift the perspective from the dedicators to the dedicatees, Alfonso V of Aragon and (later) Naples was a favourite recipient of humanist epistles even before he arrived in Italy in 1432, and he was certainly not seen as the only potential Spanish patron.[36] Examples could be multiplied from across Europe to reinforce the point: in terms of patronage for the humanists, the Italian Renaissance was an international event. Italians – be they from Milan or Florence, Venice or Rome – might think of other nations as barbarian, but a sense of their own superiority proved no bar to accepting charity from foreigners. Seeking alien patronage was not a shameful but a usual practice. An Italian scholar did not approach (metaphorically or physically) a trans-Alpine court burdened down with a sense of his own inadequacy but with the lightness of step of one in pursuit of wealth.

So, England fits into a European framework of humanist patronage. What is more, even though *penitus toto divisos orbe Britannos*, a comparatively high number of humanists hoped, in the first half of the fifteenth century, to earn from English patrons. The reason for this humanist interest is often thought to be a single English figure; but if we are to search for its origins in the reputation of one individual, we might be better advised turning, in the first instance, not to Henry VI's uncle Humphrey but to his dead father. Though Henry V was no great patron of learning himself, his life and exploits not only raised England's international standing, they also fascinated several Italian humanists.[37] The

---

[35] Martin Davies suggests that Poggio might have hoped to become Emperor Sigismund's biographer – see his 'Poggio Bracciolini as Rhetorician and Historian: Unpublished Pieces', *Rinascimento*, 2nd ser., 22 (1982), pp. 153–82 at p. 167. For Poggio's letter to Henry the Navigator, see *Lettere*, 3, ep. 3/6 (pp. 88–90).

[36] J. Lawrance, 'Humanism in the Iberian Peninsula' in *The Impact of Humanism*, eds Goodman and MacKay, pp. 220–58.

[37] Poggio, for example, discusses Henry V (whom he briefly met) in both a letter of June 1424 (*Lettere*, 2, ep. 1/2 (pp. 5–10) and a late fragment of a history: M. Davies, 'Poggio as Rhetorician and Historian', pp.180–1. P.C. Decembrio translated Frulovisi's life of Henry into Italian: see J. Wylie, 'Decembri's version of the *Vita Henrici Quinti* by Tito Livio', *EHR*, 24 (1909), pp. 84–9 and Weiss, *Humanism* (3rd edn., 1967), addenda, *sub* p. 42, n. 5. Both Bruni and Decembrio (who disagreed on so much else) addressed Humphrey as *frater serenissimi & invictissimi Henrici Regis Angliae et Franciae*: see A. Sammut, *Unfredo Duca di Gloucester e gli umanisti italiani* (Padua, 1980), pp. 148, 180.

impetus, though, for increased cultural contact came ten years after the death of the *inclitus rex*. The diplomacy surrounding the councils of Basel and Florence brought a series of ecclesiastical officials to this politically important kingdom; in the young monarch's uncle, Humphrey, duke of Gloucester, these Italians believed they had found a convenient royal patron. Yet, the humanist cult of Humphrey needs to be handled with care. As I will argue later, the claims for the duke's appreciation of humanist writings are fragile; he was also only one of several potential English patrons. Though Humphrey's connections with the humanists are the best attested, we can catch glimpses of some other lines of communication. For example, John Stafford, chancellor and archbishop of Canterbury, received the attentions of both Frulovisi and Poggio; at the same time, the young Henry VI was perceived as a worthy recipient of humanist begging-letters even before he was an adult.[38] Yet, after the *decennium mirabile*, humanist interest in England declined. This was partly the result of internal factors – Humphrey's political influence was declining and, anyway, he had proved parsimonious, preferring to receive than to hand out gifts; his nephew, meanwhile, failed to grow up to be the philosopher-king of whom the humanists dreamt.[39] At the same time, the diplomatic activity created by the councils declined and Italian patron-hunters found in Alfonso the Magnanimous a king who was now both close to hand and ready to put his hand in his pocket.[40]

The relative decline in humanist interest was not matched by a similar wilting of English appreciation. A core of humanist works had already been collected in English libraries (in particular, of course, by Humphrey's donations to Oxford) and this was increased by those Englishmen, like Gray and Tiptoft, who studied

---

[38] On Stafford, Frulovisi appears to have sent him a copy of his *Vita Henrici Quinti* and appended to it the encomium addressed to Stafford: BL, MS Cotton Claudius E. III, ff. 334–55 seems to be a copy of this MS; on the encomium, see above n. 31; Poggio's letter to him, written in 1446, is *Lettere*, 3, ep. 1/3 (pp. 15–16). On Henry VI, see, for example, R. Weiss, 'Antonio Luxorta e Enrico VI', *Rinascimento*, 4 (1953), pp. 63–5; Leonardo Dati and Porcellio both addressed poems to Henry in the early 1440s.

[39] On Humphrey's parsimony, see, for example, Beccaria's poem in Sammut, *Unfredo*, p. 165.

[40] A. Ryder, *Alfonso the Magnanimous: King of Aragon, Naples and Sicily, 1396–1458* (Oxford, 1990), esp. ch. 8.

or worked in Italy and returned with fashionable manuscripts.[41] These were copied and re-read; at the same time, some Englishmen began to write the new Roman script and a few attempted to learn Greek.[42] This level of activity, however, was transformed late in the century by two factors. First, Henry VII saw as part of his 'new monarchy' a renewed patronage of humanists; cultural magnificence was intended to bolster political fortune. This court patronage of humanists, though, was mediated through Burgundian influence.[43] On the other hand, the invention of print allowed English scholars easier, direct access to humanist works and sources. So, for example, More and his collaborator Erasmus could translate Lucianic dialogues in 1506 because they had before them the Aldine edition of the Greek text.[44] The first information technology revolution quickened the pace of English Renaissance learning.

I would suggest, then, that there was a continuity in the English reading of humanist texts through the fifteenth century. Yet, on the traditional interpretation, it would be objected that those works circulating in England, even if they were written by 'humanists', were in the main essentially 'medieval'. For example, Weiss pointed to the English interest in Bruni as a translator of Greek into Latin and concluded that this 'discloses the various difficulties which had to be overcome before the spirit of the Renaissance could be understood in this country'.[45] This is a claim which deserves further attention.

In 1417–18, Leonardo Bruni retranslated Aristotle's *Ethics*; this text seems to have reached England without assistance from its author. The *terminus ante quem* for its arrival in the country is a letter which Humphrey, duke of Gloucester (or

---

[41] On Gray, see *Catalogue of the Manuscripts of Balliol College, Oxford*, ed. R.A.B. Mynors (Oxford, 1963), pp. xxiv–xlv. On Tiptoft, see R. Weiss, 'The Library of John Tiptoft', *Bodleian Quarterly Record*, 8 (1935–8), pp. 157–64; R.J. Mitchell, 'A Renaissance Library: the Collection of John Tiptoft', *The Library*, (1937–8), pp. 67–83.

[42] *Duke Humfrey and English Humanism in the Fifteenth Century*, Bodleian Library exhibition catalogue (Oxford, 1970).

[43] Hay, 'England and the Humanities', pp. 218–24; G. Kipling, 'Henry VII and the Origins of Tudor Patronage' in *Patronage in the Renaissance*, ed. G. Lytle and S. Orgel (Princeton, 1981), pp. 117–64; Trapp, *Erasmus, Colet and More*, pp. 9–10.

[44] Thomas More, *Translations of Lucian*, ed. C. Thompson, The Yale Edition of the Complete Works of St Thomas More, 3/i (London, 1974).

[45] Weiss, 'Bruni', p. 448.

rather one of his secretaries) wrote to Bruni by the end of 1432.[46] In it, he praises this translation and also suggests that Bruni translate Aristotle's *Politics*. Bruni wrote back announcing that he would accept the duke's advice – and any patronage that was on offer; he included with this letter a list of his other translations and promised to send copies of any which Humphrey desired. This was a promise that, it seems, was taken up and fulfilled: the codex which Bruni sent has recently been identified. It includes renditions of Plutarch, Xenophon and St Basil, along with Bruni's *Cicero Novus*, a piece which is effectively a creative compilation of classical quotations.[47] In this episode, then, Bruni does not mention his other, more original, writings – he projects an image of himself as primarily a translator. This may well be a reaction to Humphrey's praise of his *Ethics*, but he does nothing to challenge, and much to foster, a reputation focused on his renderings of Greek into Latin. So, Bruni is implicated in the creation of his English reputation – unlike modern historians, he had no qualms about centring his renown on translations. At the same time, though, a fairly wide range of Bruni's original pieces did circulate in fifteenth-century England. These included not only his compendium of moral philosophy, the *Isagogicon*, mentioned by John Fortescue, and his speech *Contra hypocritas* (both of which Humphrey seems to have owned), but also some of his speeches and histories.[48] The emphasis, then, needs to be changed: the survival of relatively

---

[46] Humphrey's letter does not survive but its contents can be surmised from Bruni's reply which is printed in Sammut, *Unfredo*, pp. 146–8. The date of neither letter is certain, though Bruni's epistle is now tentatively dated to 12 March 1433: see L. Gualdo Rosa, 'Una nuova lettera del Bruni sulla sua traduzione della "Politica" di Aristotele', *Rinascimento*, 2nd ser., 23 (1983), pp. 113–27 at p. 117. The role of go-between in this exchange has been assigned to various people – Sammut suggests Gerardo Landriani; if so, the re-dating of Bruni's letter would mean that it must have been on his first trip to England that he suggested that Humphrey write to the Florentine chancellor.

[47] The codex is BL, MS Harl. 3426. Its provenance was discerned by Prof. A.C. de la Mare; see her comments in *Duke Humfrey's Library and the Divinity School, 1488–1988*, Bodleian Library exhibition catalogue (Oxford, 1988), p. 43. To this may be added the observation that an early annotator of the MS was Frulovisi: see, for example, the contents list at f. 77v. On the *Cicero Novus*, see E.B. Fryde, 'The Beginning of Italian Humanist Historiography: the "New Cicero" of Leonardo Bruni', *EHR*, 95 (1980), pp. 533–52.

[48] Humphrey gave the *Isagogicon* to Oxford in 1444 – see Sammut, *Unfredo*, p. 81, no. 243. Fortescue mentions this work in *De Laudibus*, ed. S.B. Chrimes (Cambridge, 1942), p. 10. For some suggestion of the range of Bruni's texts in England, see Martin Davies' catalogue in L. Gualdo Rosa, *Censimento dei Codici dell'Epistolario di Leonardo Bruni* (Rome, 1993), pp. 135–68, nos 8, 9, 21, 22, 23, 32, 33.

few English copies of Bruni's original works is not the significant point. Rather, what is important is the determination of some English readers to study Bruni more widely than his self-publicised translations. To slip into the old-fashioned terminology, the 'humanist' might have promoted his 'medieval' works, but the English sought out his 'modern' *opera* as well.

The example of Bruni's *Politics* brings us, once more, to that politician and patron, Humphrey, duke of Gloucester. Modern verdicts on Humphrey's contribution to governing fifteenth-century England have rarely been flattering. Conventionally, though, even if the duke has not scored highly for political acumen, he has taken away a consolation prize as the father of English humanism.[49] It seems churlish, when his political reputation stands so low, to disqualify him from this title as well, but some revision is patently necessary. Weiss himself sounded a warning note about overestimating Humphrey's talents: 'perhaps he was not as interested in [his library's] contents as one would think at first. . . . Possibly . . . he preferred to look at rather than read his books.' This was a judgement that mellowed – or, rather, softened – with its author's advancing years, but we would do well to return to this early scepticism.[50] Undeniably, Humphrey was the pre-eminent – though, as I have suggested, by no means the only – patron of humanist texts and their authors in the 1430s and '40s. However, while scholars might dedicate their writings to this *illustrissimus princeps*, he rarely returned the compliment and dedicated his attention to them. Indeed, some of the humanists who knew Humphrey well gravely doubted their patron's desire or ability to appreciate their works. The most striking example of this is the curious case of *De Vitiorum inter se Differencia et*

---

[49] '[It is] in the realm of ideas [that] . . . he did the good work he failed to do in the realm of action': K. Vickers, *Humphrey, Duke of Gloucester* (London, 1907), p. 339. Humphrey's political reputation has received no favours by the recent concentration on his life-long rival – see G.L. Harriss, *Cardinal Beaufort* (Oxford, 1988), and the same author's 'Good Duke Humphrey', *Bodleian Library Record*, 15 (1995), pp. 119–23.

[50] Weiss, *Humanism*, p. 68; see also Weiss, 'Portrait of a Bibliophile xi: Humfrey, Duke of Gloucester, d. 1447', *The Book Collector*, 13 (1964), pp. 161–70, esp. pp. 168–9. In *Humanism*, p.68, Weiss also mooted the idea that Humphrey felt more at home with French rather than Latin texts. I must emphasise that what follows is concerned solely with the humanist minority of Humphrey's manuscripts and with the image of him as humanist patron.

Comparatione, a dialogue written in 1438 by Pietro del Monte, then papal collector in England.[51]

Del Monte was a canonist who saw his brief in England as putting Eugenius IV's case against the council of Basel.[52] Diplomatically, then, it was expedient for him to ingratiate himself with Humphrey; it also suited his personal ambition to cultivate his relationship with this prince. He projected himself as an *arbiter elegantiarum* and set out to prove himself a literary as well as a legal scholar. So, del Monte presented the duke with a tract which, though undeserving, has had the honour of being called 'the first humanistic treatise written in this country'.[53] Undeserving because *De Vitiorum Differencia* is, to say the least, less than wholly original. The tract's preface overflows with effusive praise of Humphrey: the duke is a prince who spends his leisure hours in study, reading widely and remembering everything he reads. Yet these florid compliments sit uneasily with the text that follows. For *De Vitiorum Differencia* is by and large identical to an earlier dialogue – *De Avaritia* written in the late 1420s by none other than Poggio Bracciolini. Certainly, the *dramatis personae* are changed and certain passages are added, but the bulk of del Monte's tract is simply lifted from *De Avaritia*.[54] *Quattrocento* humanists might have been less obsessively concerned than modern authors about intellectual property rights, but this reproduction of page after page of Poggio's work surely goes far beyond any theory of legitimate *imitatio*. The only suitable word to describe it is, perhaps, plagiarism.[55]

---

[51] For a possible parallel case involving Humphrey's secretary, Beccaria, see V.R. Guistiniani, 'Traduzione latini delle Vite di Plutarcho nel Quattrocento', *Rinascimento*, 2nd ser., 1 (1961), p. 17.

[52] On del Monte, see *Dizionario Biografico degli Italiani*, 37 (Rome, 1990), *sub nomine*, and D. Quaglioni, *Pietro del Monte a Roma* (Rome, 1984). An incomplete edition of his letters from England appears in J. Haller, *Piero da Monte. Ein Gelherter und päpstlicher Beamter des 15. Jahrhunderts* (Rome, 1941).

[53] Weiss, *Humanism*, p. 25.

[54] Of *De Vitiorum inter se Differencia*, the only part published is the preface, for which, see Sammut, *Unfredo*, pp. 151–3. Poggio's *De Avaritia* is available in his *Opera Omnia*, ed. R. Fubini (3 vols, Turin, 1964), 1, pp. 1–31, but this is a copy of the first recension – del Monte was working from the second official but less popular recension, which only exists in manuscripts. A start on editing the two recensions has been made by H. Harth, 'Niccolò Niccoli als literarischer Zensor', *Rinascimento*, 2nd ser., 7, (1967), pp. 29–53.

[55] On Renaissance concepts of plagiarism, see H.O. White, *Plagiarism and Imitation during the English Renaissance* (Cambridge, MA, 1935), ch. 1; G.W. Pigman III, 'Versions of Imitation in the Renaissance', *Renaissance Quarterly*, 23 (1980), pp. 1–32. There are, of course, famous cases of large-

That del Monte dedicates this cribbed text to Humphrey was certainly disrespectful; that he presents 'his' work at about the time a copy of Poggio's original dialogue was circulating in the duke's circle makes it downright audacious.[56] For Humphrey would have been able to read both texts and, if (as del Monte's preface claimed) he did have both voracious reading habits and a photographic memory, he would surely not have taken long to spot the papal collector's sleight of hand. With that, any pretensions on del Monte's part to being an original humanist writer – and constructing such a reputation was, after all, the purpose of presenting this manuscript – would necessarily be undermined. So, that the humanist was willing to take the risk of his cribbing being noticed suggests that he thought the chance of being caught rather low. In other words, it would seem that, after three years of observing Humphrey's mannerisms and tastes at close range, del Monte had concluded that the good duke was a book-lover but not a book-worm. And that he got away with his plagiarism in 1438 (and for five and a half centuries since) suggests his judgement was well-founded. It also reveals, once again, the circumspection with which one has to treat humanist letters; del Monte constructed his preface to *De Vitiorum Differencia* around the concept of an aristocratic literary aficionado, but he must have hoped – or, rather, been confident – that Humphrey would fail to live up to that ideal.

Del Monte seems to have quite enjoyed the irony of writing 'his' tract; it was not only in the preface that he allowed himself a private joke. In one of the few original passages of *De Vitiorum Differencia*, he asks a rhetorical question: '*Tolle a libris lectionem ac studium in quibus eorum est usus, quid, queso, cuiquam proderit*

---

scale copying in other Renaissance texts but this example – with its near-complete reproduction of a dialogue by a living author – is, I would suggest, highly unusual.

[56] Richard Petworth, a former colleague of Poggio's in Beaufort's household, had access to a copy of *De Avaritia* by 1439 at the latest; see Poggio's letter to him of 24 May 1440: Harth, *Lettere*, 2, ep. IX/18, (pp. 378–9). For Petworth's connections with Humphrey, see a later letter from Poggio, dated 30 July 1442 edited, from a German MS copy, by Walser, *Poggius Florentinus*, p. 454 – the best surviving copy is in Oxford: Bodl, MS Bod. 915, f. 99; on Petworth in general, see *Biographical Register of the University of Oxford*, ed. A.B. Emden (Oxford, 1957), *sub* Petteworthe. Perhaps Petworth was using the manuscript of *De Avaritia*, first recension, which was in Humphrey's library and which made its way to King's College, Cambridge after the duke's death – see Sammut, *Unfredo*, p. 93, no.147.

innumerabilium voluminum bibliotheca?'[57] The answer, of course, is that even unread books can be a status symbol. A well-stocked library was a sign, not of its owner's wisdom, but of his recognition of the importance of wisdom; it was a symbol of his magnificence; it was also testimony to the honour in which others held him. For many of the books in Humphrey's collection were gifts, not purchases.[58] Indeed, as a high proportion was presented or donated to him, the duke's library bears witness to the tastes not of one man but of a whole circle.[59] It was certainly not accidental that Humphrey received so many manuscripts: from an early stage he had associated his political fortunes with scholarship.[60] However, it suited the humanists to develop this reputation of Humphrey the intellectual, portraying him as an *avant-garde* literary patron. For them, Humphrey served the purpose of a hat-stand on which they could hang their preoccupations and aspirations. The image they created, then, tells us more perhaps about those around Humphrey than it does about the duke himself.

Lest this interpretation seem overly iconoclastic, let me emphasise that on one

[57] Bodl, MS Auct. F.5.26, p. 22, *recte* p. 21.

[58] If we take the 40 surviving manuscripts from Humphrey's library (that is 38 from Sammut's list of 40 from *Unfredo*, pp. 98–126, excluding his no. 2 and 4, which were not in the duke's library, but taking his no. 27 as two codices and adding the recently identified BL, Harley MS 3426, the list includes 10 which were presented to him by their authors, 11 which were definitely given to him, as is proved by the *ex libris*, and 6 more which were most likely gifts but are not explicitly recorded as such. Of the rest, 1 (Sammut, no. 17) was bought and 3 probably commissioned from Pier Candido Decembrio. There is no clear evidence of how the other 9 entered Humphrey's library. Even if all those which were probably given were left aside, those presented or donated constitute over half of this sample. Again, if we take merely the humanist manuscripts, including the 'pre-humanists', Petrarch and Salutati, but not the French Boccaccio (Sammut, no. 33), of 14 in all, 7 were presented, 3 given, 3 commissioned and 1 is of indeterminate origin.

[59] Note in particular, for our purpose, Nicholas Bildeston's gift in the late 1430s of a Petrarch MS to Humphrey (Sammut, no. 31); Bildeston's interest in Petrarch is also attested in one of Poggio's letters – Harth, *Lettere*, 1, ep. 48, p. 140 (20 November 1424 – not 1425 as usually dated). See also Andrew Holes' gift of Salutati's *De Laboribus Herculis* (Sammut, no. 38); on Holes' books, see M. Harvey, 'An Englishman at the Roman Curia during the Council of Basle: Andrew Holes, his Sermon of 1433 and his Books', *Journal of Ecclesiastical History*, 42 (1991), pp. 19–38.

[60] At the very start of Henry VI's reign, Humphrey referred to, first, civil law and, then, historical examples, in the debate over his tutorship of the infant king; see S.B. Chrimes, 'The Pretensions of the Duke of Gloucester in 1422', *EHR*, 45 (1930), pp. 101–3; P. and F. Strong, 'The Last Will and Codicils of Henry V', *EHR*, 96 (1981), pp. 79–102. I hope to discuss this issue elsewhere.

point it concurs with the traditional image: in the history of humanism in England, Humphrey is exceptional. If he were not, the archetypal English 'humanist' would be one who collected rather than read manuscripts and a man whose interest in the new scholarship had more to do with his persona than with him personally. On the contrary, English readers in general are more attentive and much more active than that. A duke like Humphrey might be able to wait for codices to be presented to him, but others had to search for or copy works themselves. A duke like Humphrey might be content to admire shelves full of books, but others preferred to read the texts. This is what a close study of the extant manuscripts makes clear.

Manuscripts are an unplumbed well of information. It is not only that collating a text can reveal links (or disconnections) between different copies; nor is it just that a palaeographical study can provide invaluable information about the scribe. The make-up of a manuscript – its appearance and its combination of contents – can give some idea of how the scribe perceived a text. For, unlike with earlier codices, there seems often to be some rationale to the selecting of contents for a humanist manuscript – the scribes do not just copy, they also construct. Once again, marginalia can suggest a number of readers' interests. There is, naturally, a difficulty here: annotations only record the responses of readers when they are being 'active'. Reading is, as it were, a 'silent' process – the reader only speaks to the historian when he becomes a writer. Marginalia may not, then, tell us the full range of responses to a text, but they can at least suggest some of the reactions.

I hope that an example, using works that have already been mentioned, can give some intimation of manuscripts' potential as sources. Poggio's *De Avaritia* and del Monte's *De Vitiorum Differencia* both enjoyed something of a vogue in the second half of the fifteenth century. In neither case does Humphrey's manuscript survive, but, even with this loss, five other (partial or complete) English copies of each text survive.[61] Moreover, in each copy four or five readers

---

[61] *De Avaritia*: Cambridge University Library, MS Ff.v.12; Oxford: Balliol College, MS 127; Bodl, MS Bod. 915; Oxford: Corpus Christi College, MS 88; Oxford: Merton MS E.3.35 (iii–v), fragments. *De Vitiorum inter se Differencia*: Cambridge: Corpus Christi College, MS 472; Cambridge University Library, MS Ll.i.7; London: Lambeth Palace Library, MS 341; London: Lambeth Palace Library, MS 354; Bodl, MS Auct. F.5.26. As well as Humphrey's lost copy of *De Vitiorum Differencia* – Sammut, p. 84, no. 273 – John Whethamstede was sent a copy which does not seem to have survived; see R. Weiss, 'Piero del Monte, John Whethamstede and the Library of St Albans Abbey,' *EHR*, 60 (1945), pp. 399–406.

have written marginalia: clearly, each manuscript is being used and reused. Yet, even with this fairly wide circulation of both Poggio's dialogue and the derivative *De Vitiorum Differencia*, none of the scribes or readers noticed del Monte's plagiarism from *De Avaritia*. This, though, does not reflect on English readers' power of observation as much as on their ability to see both works. The early circulation histories of the two dialogues are quite discrete; each work served different circles of humanist readers.

Del Monte's tract was part of Humphrey's 1444 donation to Oxford University and it was disseminated from there. One, perhaps two, of the surviving copies were made in Oxford; the other three, which are closely related and can be called the 'Virtue and Vice' group (after their shared mistake of titling del Monte's tract *De Virtutum et Vitiorum Differencia*), derive from a lost manuscript which was copied from Humphrey's gift.[62] The 'Virtue and Vice' group, though, circulated outside the university town and was probably copied in Canterbury.[63] By contrast, in the early *fortuna* of Poggio's dialogue, Oxford does not play so central a role. By the quirk of Humphrey's death, his copy of *De Avaritia* ended up in King's College, Cambridge and we can only be certain that the work arrived in Oxford by the end of the fifteenth century when two copies were presented to college libraries. One of these manuscripts had been copied in 1450 for Richard Bole by the Dutch scribe, Theoderic Werken, who perhaps wrote it in London.[64] Yet the circulation seems to have been even more complicated than this suggests. Most of the extant manuscripts are not directly connected: they derive from different copies, all of which are now lost. In other

---

[62] The two manuscripts not in the 'Virtue and Vice' group are the Corpus Christi, Cambridge, MS 472 and Lambeth MS 354. Collation of the 'Virtue and Vice' group suggests that Bodl, MS Auct. F.5.26 and Lambeth MS 341 are independent copies of the *exemplum*, while Cambridge University Library, MS Ll.i.7 was probably copied from the Bodl MS. On these three MSS, see *Duke Humfrey's Library*, pp. 92–3.

[63] Lambeth MS 341 is in a contemporary Canterbury binding and some of its headings are written by a scribe who was for a time active there (he also wrote Bodl, MS Auct.F.5.26), see *Duke Humfrey's Library*, p. 106. The possibility remains, however, that it was copied in Oxford and transported to Canterbury.

[64] Balliol College MS 127. On Werken, see R.A.B. Mynors, 'Theoderic Werken', *Cambridge Bibliographical Society Transactions*, 1 (1949–53), pp. 97–104 at pp. 100–1; *Duke Humfrey and English Humanism*, p. 25.

words, *De Avaritia* enjoyed a wider circulation than merely counting extant codices would suggest.

If the texts had separate circulations, the construction of these codices suggests that the scribes also viewed the works differently. In the case of *De Vitiorum Differencia*, it was most often copied with other humanist works (including Bruni's translations of Xenophon and Basil) which could be found in Humphrey's collection donated to Oxford University. In the manuscripts of the 'Virtue and Vice' group, the texts are also followed by a glossary of difficult words, suggesting a desire to learn humanist vocabulary.[65] None of these copies retains the fashionable beauty of Humphrey's *de luxe* manuscripts; they are written in current gothic hands with rarely more illumination than simple red and blue intials. These, then, are not presentation editions but working copies; their intention seems to be to make accessible to a wider circle the new works and translations which had recently arrived in Oxford.

In both the Werken copy of the Poggio, which Bole bequeathed to Balliol, and the copy Richard Fox gave to his foundation, Corpus Christi, *De Avaritia* is paired with another Poggio work, his *De Nobilitate*, as well as Petrarch's *Secretum*.[66] All three works share a common distinction: they are leading examples of the modern revival of the dialogue form.[67] So, the compilers of these manuscripts have a common rationale – they were interested in the works' structure.[68] They also, incidentally, paid Poggio a compliment by judging him

---

[65] The glossary is at its most extensive in the Lambeth MS 341, ff. 202–210vb.

[66] The manuscripts are Balliol MS 127 and Corpus Christi, Oxford, MS 88. Collation of the preface to *De Avaritia* demonstrates that, *pace* Prof. N. Mann, 'Petrarch Manuscripts in the British Isles', *Italia Medioevale e Umanistica*, 18 (1975) pp. 139–527 at p. 473n.; neither of these manuscripts could be descended from the other.

[67] D.Marsh, *The Quattrocento Dialogue* (London, 1980).

[68] In the Balliol MS, the three works mentioned are accompanied by texts by Cicero, including two dialogues; in the Corpus MS, the Petrarch was written by a different scribe from the other two texts but they were clearly placed together at an early date, as they survive in one fifteenth-century binding. A similar compilation occurs in Cambridge University Library, MS Ff.v.12, where fifteenth-century copies of *De Nobilitate* and *De Avaritia* are paired with a twelfth-century copy of Cicero's *De Officiis*; here, though, it is perhaps the discussion of moral issues rather than structure which is the unifying principle.

worthy to be read alongside that lionised figure, Petrarch. In other copies of *De Avaritia*, however, Poggio stands on his own. These are the work of the prolific scribe, Thomas Candour, whom Poggio himself called *vir ornatissimus mihique summa familiaritate coniunctus*; he seems to have been eager to promote his Italian friend's reputation in England.[69] Candour produced lavish manuscripts on good quality parchment, written in a fine humanist hand and with white vine-stem initials painted by Candour in the best Florentine style. In the one manuscript which survives complete, Candour includes the corpus of Poggio's works until the early 1440s (adding supplementary material which demonstrates Poggio's links with England). Here are Poggio's works which deserve to be read not for their novelty but because of who wrote them.

The irony in the different scribal reactions to the works is, of course, that the text was substantially the same. Both works are dialogues, divided into three speeches, the first attacking avarice, the second defending it and the final oration re-emphasising the censure of greed by particular reference to Chrysostom. (Poggio here finds a way to profit from his English reading.) So, though two works were copied, effectively one text was read. However, the marginalia in the various copies of this text reflect a variety of responses.[70] It is sometimes suggested that 'medieval' reading was fragmentary, skimming the text in search of notable quotations.[71] Certainly, the most frequent annotations in both fifteenth- and sixteenth-century hands mark references to certain classical (and, less often, patristic) authors and *exempla*. The classical quotation which is most repeatedly noted is Virgil's description of the Harpies which Poggio's first speaker interprets as an allegory for avarice. It is ironic that this should be so approvingly annotated by English readers for, when Poggio revised his dialogue, he added to the second speech a criticism of just this sort of

---

[69] Poggio, *Lettere*, 3, ep. 1/3 (ll. 22–3; pp. 15–16); on Candour's work as a scribe, see Prof. de la Mare's comments in *Manuscripts in Oxford: R.W. Hunt Memorial Exhibition*, Bodleian Library exhibition catalogue (Oxford, 1980), pp. 95–6.

[70] For the detailed references for the following sentences, see my forthcoming Oxford D.Phil. thesis, 'Of Republics and Tyrants'.

[71] P.-Y. Badel, *Le Roman de la Rose au XIVe siècle: étude de la réception de l'œuvre* (Geneva, 1980), esp. pp. 499–502; J. Dagenais, *The Ethics of Reading in Manuscript Culture: Glossing the 'Libro de buen amor'* (Princeton, 1994), esp. pp. 168–9.

allegorisation. Though this passage did not appear in the recension of *De Avaritia* which circulated in England, it is a section which (like so much else) was repeated word-for-word in del Monte's *De Vitiorum Differencia*. Yet it evoked little response from its English readers: in this particular instance, it would seem that some readers ignored the humanist censure of traditional literature. Here, then, is (depending on your preferred turn of phrase) an 'appropriation' of the text or a 'failure' to read the work. However, it would be misguided to assume that all readers who selected particular *exempla* or *sententiae* were doing so at the exclusion of digesting the whole text. On the flyleaves of one manuscript, in a mid-sixteenth-century hand, there is a series of notes extracting rhetorical passages and classical anecdotes from *De Vitiorum Differencia* – but the sections copied are not merely eloquent, they are also relevant to the central arguments of the dialogue. For this reader, at least, the dialogue's classical references and its meaning are inseparable.

There were certainly readers earlier than this Tudor annotator who employed the text as something other than a thesaurus of *exempla*. A small group appear most interested in tracing a particular theme, like eloquence or the political impact of avarice; they mark passages on the topic through the text. A larger number marked the text as an *aide-mémoire*, so as to help them follow the structure and argument of the work. These readers seem able to appreciate the novelty of the work – its use of the Ciceronian dialogue form and, especially, the inclusion of a speech in favour of avarice. Indeed, for some readers, the oration defending the vice (the least 'medieval' section of the dialogue) was, to judge by their marginalia, the most fascinating part of the work.

Yet, in the end, this ability to appreciate a humanist text is not altogether surprising. Weiss dismissed all political tracts before Machiavelli as 'medieval in outlook and only humanistic in presentation'.[72] This rather underestimates the originality of *quattrocento* political discourse. For example, some humanist texts are said to contain a conflict between 'civic humanists' in the pay of republics and those scholars who receive princely patronage.[73] The anti-monarchism of

---

[72] Weiss, 'Italian Humanism', p. 74.

[73] This is argued most famously in H. Baron, *The Crisis of the Early Florentine Renaissance* (Princeton, 1955).

the civic humanist texts fascinated that early sixteenth-century circle of humanists around More and Erasmus who recovered this context and realised its explosive potential for their own, monarchical societies.[74] Earlier English readers may not have been so preoccupied with this element, though some at least appreciated the humanist claim that the city-state was a locus of political virtue.[75] Yet, despite novel features in their political thinking, humanist 'modernness' should not be overestimated. For example, some critics, reading *De Avaritia*, have suggested that its meaning lies in the second speech and that Poggio's intention is, in effect, to defend avarice; so the dialogue is made to read like a libertarian polemic *avant la lettre*. But this is a misreading.[76] Instead, Poggio (and, after him, del Monte) is employing his classical rhetoric to reinforce the traditional censure of avarice. So, when English readers came to peruse either *De Avaritia* or *De Vitiorum Differencia*, they were faced, not with the literary equivalent of the first fermentation from a New World vineyard, but with old wine in new bottles. Neither the unoriginal sentiment nor the novel rhetoric of these dialogues was beyond the comprehension of an English reader. On issues which are political and ethical, like avarice, there is little difference between the fifteenth-century English and their Italian counterparts: both are on the side of virtue; there is no support for vice.

---

[74] On this, see my essays, 'A New Golden Age? More, Skelton and the Accession Verses of 1509', *Renaissance Studies*, 9 (1995), pp. 58–76 and '"Not so much Praise as Precept": the Panegyric and the Renaissance Art of Teaching Princes' in *Pedagogy and Power*, eds N. Livingstone and Y.L. Too (Cambridge, forthcoming).

[75] This is how I would read Thomas Chaundler's use of Bruni's *Laudatio* in his *Libellus de laudibus duarum civitatum*; see S. Bridges, 'Thomas Chaundler' (unpub. Oxford B.Litt. thesis, 1949), 1, pp. 135–8.

[76] J. Oppel, 'Poggio, San Bernardino of Siena and the Dialogue "On Avarice"', *Renaissance Quarterly*, 30 (1977), pp. 564–87; H.M. Goldbrunner, 'Poggios Dialog über die Habsucht, *Quellen und Forschungen aus italienischen Archiven und Bibliotheken*, 59 (1979), pp. 436–52.

10
THE PIETY OF ISABEAU OF BAVARIA, QUEEN OF FRANCE, 1385–1422[1]

Rachel Gibbons

The aim of this paper is to attempt what might be considered impossible at first sight – to discover and explain the private beliefs and religious practices of a woman living six centuries ago who has left no real record of her faith. Any historical analysis of this kind poses fundamental difficulties, the most daunting of which Swanson has identified as the need to penetrate the mind.[2] Additionally, one may argue that the modern trend towards secularism could prevent the historian from truly empathising with the medieval religious experience. It is certainly necessary to consider the wider context of late medieval religion, essential elements of which were the veneration of relics, pilgrimages, Marian devotions and meditations on the Passion.[3] There has sometimes been a tendency to undervalue these demonstrative, often public elements of late medieval Christianity: Johan Huizinga considered this mushrooming of devotional practice as demonstrating evidence of 'extreme saturation of the religious atmosphere', while Wood-Legh

---

[1] The study of popular piety in the Later Middle Ages has been extensive, from Jacques Toussaert, *Le sentiment religieux en Flandre à la fin du moyen âge* (Plon, Paris, 1960) to M. Aston, *Faith and Fire: Popular and Unpopular Religion, 1350–1600* (London, 1993). Far less has been written on royal and aristocratic piety; work has been concentrated especially on fifteenth-century England: see C.A.J. Armstrong's article of 1942, reprinted as 'The Piety of Cecily, Duchess of York: a Study in Late Medieval Culture' in *England, France and Burgundy in the Fifteenth Century* (London, 1983), pp. 135–56 and Anne Crawford, 'The Piety of Late Medieval English Queens' in *The Church in Pre-Reformation Society: Essays in Honour of F.R.H. du Boulay*, eds C. Barron and C. Harper-Bill (Woodbridge, 1985), pp. 48–57. To date there has been less historical interest in the subject in France.

[2] R.N. Swanson, *Catholic England: Faith, Religion and Observance before the Reformation* (Manchester, 1993), p. 1.

[3] Richard Kieckhefer, 'Major Currents in Late Medieval Devotion' in *Christian Spirituality: High Middle Ages and Reformation*, ed. J. Raitt (New York, 1988), p. 75.

described as 'arithmetical piety' the desire for repeated anniversary masses that appears to give almost 'a magical value to mere repetition of formulae'.[4] An analysis of personal belief raises other inherent problems. The character of any single person from the Middle Ages is likely to be shadowy and difficult to flesh out into three dimensions as individuals rarely provide us with evidence which reveals their innermost feelings. However, there is what Swanson defined as 'forensic analysis'[5] which, in Isabeau's case, means mainly the documentary evidence of treasury and household accounts. The historian must become a detective, sifting and rearranging fragments of information, like pieces of a jigsaw, to attempt to reconstruct a personality. By examining book-purchase, commissions of translations, choice of chapel decoration, destinations of pilgrimages, recipients of charity, and even the names of her children, it is possible to suggest elements of the nature of the queen's spirituality.

The peculiar situation of living within the mores of the highest political, economic and social rank may have dictated a great deal about how this spirituality was expressed in its outward form, and one could hope that Isabeau's example might provide some enlightenment into the general expectations and practices of queenly piety. But this is perhaps dangerous ground; without more research into piety across national boundaries and generations, it might be considered presumptuous to conclude that the devotional practices of one person had a wider significance than their own personal preferences, or choices made from, or in opposition to, the religious fashions of their day and social circle.[6] In fact, it is possible that any attempt to generalise on matters of personal piety could create more anomalies than it seeks to correct: the search to identify constants in medieval devotion through

---

[4] Johan Huizinga, *The Waning of the Middle Ages: A Study in the Forms of Life, Thought and Art in France and the Netherlands in the Fourteenth and Fifteenth Centuries* (Harmondsworth, 1955), p. 147; K.L. Wood-Legh, *Perpetual Chantries in Britain* (Cambridge, 1965), p. 312.

[5] Swanson, *Catholic England*, p. 40.

[6] Christine Carpenter, 'The Religion of the Gentry of Fifteenth-Century England' in *England in the Fifteenth Century. Proceedings of the 1986 Harlaxton Symposium*, ed. Daniel Williams (Woodbridge, 1987), p. 64, asserts that 'lay piety had been moving towards a more informed and personally responsible religion since at least the Fourth Lateran Council of 1215'.

the practices of one individual must take into account the fact that he or she is an individual and, with that, the personal nature of much of medieval devotion.

Isabeau of Bavaria led her religious life with an amount of fervour which rather contradicts traditional stereotyped imagery of her as an incestuous, immoral monster, seeking only pleasure and temporal glory.[7] Her three major biographers all devoted a proportion of their work to the queen's pious practices, although possibly with neither the thoroughness nor the sensitivity that the subject merits. Writing a largely sympathetic account at the beginning of the twentieth century, Marcel Thibault described the queen as: *Excessivement pieuse, puisque, dans cette Cour où les exercises religieux étaient en très grand honneur, elle semble se distinguer par ses pratiques assidués et singulières*. He chooses to put down these 'oddities' to the fact that she was not French, explaining that *elle était dévotieuse à la mode de la Bavière, et même, l'ostentation de ses œuvres piés et l'affection de son zèle pour certains autels privilegiés font penser aux superstitieuses coutumes de la pompeuse Italie*.[8] Midway through the nineteenth century, Auguste Vallet de Viriville had summarised Isabeau's devotional practices as *composée d'une superstition étroite et futile*,[9] while a recent biographer, Jean Verdon, concludes that: *Isabeau était pieuse, mais d'une piété qui, nous l'avons vu, semblait s'apparenter à la superstition*.[10]

Isabeau of Bavaria became queen of France on 17 July 1385 when she married Charles VI in Amiens and, were it not for the tragedy of her husband's

---

[7] She has been the subject of numerous selective vignettes of variable quality, including Gustave Demoulin, *Les françaises illustres* (Paris, 1889), pp. 75–83; Catherine Bearne, *Pictures of the Old French Court* (London, 1900), pp. 107–298; and Juliette Benzoni, *Dans les lits des reines* (Paris, 1985), pp. 77–92.

[8] Marcel Thibault, *Isabeau de Bavière: la Jeunesse* (Paris, 1901), pp. 106–7; see also, Bernd Moeller, 'Piety in Germany around 1500' in *The Reformation in Medieval Perspective*, ed. Steven Ozment (Chicago, 1971), pp. 50–75, on the desire for tangible devotionalism in pre-Reformation Germany.

[9] Auguste Vallet de Viriville, *Isabeau de Bavière* (Paris, 1859), p. 36.

[10] Jean Verdon, *Isabeau de Bavière* (Paris, 1981), p. 231. As Yann Grandeau, the author of several articles on Isabeau, died prematurely, only an abstract of his researches on her piety could be published as 'L'exercise de la piéte à la cour de France: les dévotions d'Isabeau de Bavière' in *Actes du 104e congrès national des sociétés savantes, Orléans 1979: section philologie et d'histoire médievale – 'Jeanne d'Arc, une époque, un royonnement'* (Paris, 1982), pp. 150–2. The fourth major biography – Jean Markale, *Isabeau de Bavière* (Paris, 1982) – only covers the years 1417–22 and makes no mention of the queen's religious practices, so has not been used for this particular essay.

madness, she might well have lived out her life in comfortable obscurity like the majority of medieval queens. In 1393, on recovering from the first attack of what proved to be a lifelong illness, Charles ensured that if, as was clearly feared, he died from this mysterious ailment, Isabeau would have a major role in government as principal guardian of the infant dauphin and as a member of the council. However, the struggle for power between the dukes of Burgundy and Orleans, which escalated from discord into downright aggression by the turn of the century, prompted the real entry onto the diplomatic stage of Isabeau in the role of arbiter. Her success in mobilising the other royal dukes with her as negotiators led the king to entrust her with full powers of mediation in 1402, and later with authority to deal with any other major matters of government business in the king's 'absences'. In 1403 these powers were clarified: she was made *présidente* of a new regency council which included all the royal dukes, the constable, chancellor and others of the king's regular councillors, who would rule by majority vote in Charles' name until he was capable of doing so himself. The assassination of Louis of Orleans in 1407 led to outright civil war, and the need of both sides to control the queen and dauphin made it inevitable that Isabeau would become associated with factional instability, as she agreed to defensive alliances with whichever prince seemed the least threatening. When the death of her ninth child, John, in March 1417 meant that her last son Charles became dauphin and, for the first time, the Orleanist/Armagnac camp had possession of the heir, as well as control of Paris and the king, Isabeau's position became untenable. On the count of Armagnac's orders, she was deprived of her finances, her servants and her liberty, being held captive at Tours for six months before being released by Burgundy. From then on, there was no real deviation in her actions: maintained and protected by the Burgundians, her name was united with theirs in all government decisions, up to and including the surrender of France to the English under the terms of the treaty of Troyes signed in 1420.[11]

---

[11] Apart from her biographies, the most useful works on Isabeau's involvement in French politics are Jacques d'Avout, *La querelle des Armagnacs et des Bourguignons* (Paris, 1943); P. Bonenfant, *Du meurtre à Montereau au traité de Troyes* (Brussels, 1958); M. Nordberg, *Les ducs et la royauté. Etudes sur la rivalité des ducs d'Orléans et de Bourgogne, 1392–1407* (Stockholm, 1964); and R.C. Famiglietti, *Royal Intrigue at the Court of Charles VI* (New York, 1986).

The prominent role played by Isabeau of Bavaria in the politics of her adopted country did not conform with contemporary expectations of normal behaviour for a medieval queen. The accepted duties of a king's wife did not include involvement in the tortuous wranglings of a civil war, but a queen might be expected to exert power in other, perhaps subtler, ways. The importance of the royal consort has tended to be overlooked by historians, but contemporaries were acutely aware of the potential of their queen's influence and, consequently, would have agreed strongly with Anne Crawford that the choice of his wife was 'the single most important decision ever made by a medieval king'.[12] Apart from her most urgent responsibility to become the mother of the king's children, a queen was expected to perform many roles for his people – to be a just, yet sympathetic arbiter, a cultural ambassador and the leader of domestic society, whose character and interests set the tone for the whole nation. For the purposes of this paper, the most important element of the queen's public image was as the kingdom's most prominent example of female piety: how she chose to perform or neglect her pious and charitable duties had an effect on the perception of a queen's worth and character at the time, and still does affect historical opinion on her life. The pious practices of Isabeau of Bavaria will be examined in three broad categories: first, daily activities, such as the use and maintenance of her chapel, distribution of alms and purchase of ordinary devotional items; second, activities that would have been deemed conventional, but perhaps played a larger part than normal in Isabeau's religious experience, such as going on pilgrimage, collecting devotional literature and making pious bequests; and third, what can be seen as largely original to Isabeau, and consequently of most value to the historian as evidence of her spirituality.

From the earliest days of her marriage, Isabeau of Bavaria was served by her own chapel staff as part of a household structure independent from that of Charles VI. The lack of any queen's accounts surviving from before 1393 leaves a relative lack of information for the first eight years of Isabeau's time in France, but we can still glean many pieces of information about her early practices from

---

[12] Anne Crawford, 'The King's Burden? – the Consequences of Royal Marriage in Fifteenth-Century England' in *Patronage, the Crown and the Provinces in Later Medieval England*, ed. R.A. Griffiths (Gloucester, 1981), p. 33.

the accounts of the king's *argenterie* – the private royal treasury, roughly equivalent to the Wardrobe in England. For example, from payments made through the king's *argenterie* in 1389, we know that the personnel of the queen's chapel comprised six priests and two *sommeliers*, who were responsible for transporting equipment, and two clerks.[13] The accounts of Isabeau's *argenterie* throughout her reign list additions and repairs to what was described as the queen's chapel – the hangings and plate transported around with Isabeau rather than any specific room that they adorned. The decoration of Isabeau's chapel was suitably lavish as befitted a queen, but the choice of ornament may be indicative of her personal tastes. One set of altar cloths, made up of forty panels of raised embroidery, showed *une histoire de la Passion brodée bien et richement de nues, estoille d'or et royes de soleil*. The canopy which hung above the altar had one of the four Evangelists in each corner and depicted the Last Judgement in the centre. The inner drapes of the canopy were embroidered with motifs of clouds, stars and sunbeams and the outer with the queen's arms. The plate included a gold chalice, a large silver-gilt cross decorated with cherubs and another with the Evangelists. The priest's robes were embroidered with scenes from the Passion as well as the queen's arms, while his official gloves were of blue leather, ornamented with ten *fleurs-de-lys*, in gold, silk and pearls.[14] From an account detailing the purchases of what are described as *menues plaisirs* between March 1416 and April 1417,[15] we know that Isabeau had a wooden oratory or small chapel which could be assembled and dismantled as required,[16] and that music was important to her at Mass. Eighteen shillings were given to Isabeau's chaplain, Jehan Pourcin *pour ses despens d'avoir esté dudit Saint-Germain au bois de Vincennes, querre et faire venir les orgues de la chappelle d'icelle dame*.[17]

The expenses of the royal household provide some information on the queen's piety: money given in offerings at daily masses, on feast days and special celebrations was accounted for in a separate category, and at each daily service,

---

[13] AN, KK19, f. 129v and f. 135.
[14] AN, KK41, f. 165v; KK45, f. 19v; KK48, f. 62.
[15] AN, KK49.
[16] Ibid., f. 45v.
[17] Ibid., f. 19v.

Isabeau gave twelve pence and her children four pence each, while on feastdays such as the Epiphany and Candlemas, the queen gave four shillings and four pence on each occasion. The *harnois* category, which accounted for purchases of wax for the queen's household, allows us to see which anniversaries Isabeau marked by special services. Obits were commonly celebrated for family members: in the account of 1 January to 30 June 1405, enough wax to make twelve one-and-a-half-pound candles was ordered for three obits to mark the anniversaries of the deaths of Queen Jeanne of Bourbon, Margaret de Mâle, duchess of Burgundy, and John II of France and to celebrate the feast of Corpus Christi on 18 June; while in the 1416/17 *menues plaisirs* account, requiem masses were ordered for Madame de la Granche and Annotte de Hallebroc, two of Isabeau's ladies-in-waiting.[18]

Possibly one of the most public expressions of piety in the Middle Ages was the dispensing of charity. In royal households this took two forms: customary alms, automatically dispensed on a regular basis, and individual acts of charity practised on the individual's own initiative.[19] Queens appointed almoners to handle these duties for them and there were two in Isabeau's service designated as such in her pension lists: Jean Mairesse, almoner and first chaplain from around 1398 to 1411, and Jacques du Boisherbert, almoner and first chaplain from around 1415 to 1417.[20] Despite it being an unexceptional practice, finding some record of the details of Isabeau's almsgiving is difficult: the only documentary evidence so far discovered is in the account for *menues plaisirs* for 1416/17.[21] In this account, donations are frequent, as one would expect from one of the wealthiest ladies in Europe: there are several gifts of eighteen shillings to *pauvres femmes*; eight shillings refunded to Boisherbert, the almoner, for

---

[18] AN, KK49, f. 30.

[19] *Letters of the Queens of England*, ed. Anne Crawford (Stroud, 1994), p. 16.

[20] Colleen L. Mooney, 'Queenship in fifteenth-century France' (unpub. Ph.D. thesis, Ohio State University, 1977), appendix I: 'List of Personnel at the Court of Isabeau', p. 369.

[21] The giving of alms is not accounted for in either the queen's household (*hôtel*) or personal treasury (*argenterie*) ledgers, so it must be assumed that charity of this kind was recorded elsewhere throughout Isabeau's reign. Unfortunately, the *menues plaisirs* account of 1416/17 is the only one of its kind in existence, so there is no real proof of the nature of Isabeau's almsgiving for more than the thirteen-month period that this record covers.

distributing to the poor at Lay on the eve of the feast of St John the Baptist; sixteen shillings to maintain a poor man in St Genevieve's prison; and four and three-quarter francs to clothe a mute child.[22]

References in the *argenterie* accounts to the purchase of devotional items for the private use of the queen and her children provide us with some information about their daily religious practices. In the very first account of Isabeau's independent *argenterie*, covering the period of May 1393 to June 1394, small, portable altars were bought,[23] while a regular expense was the purchase of what are described in the accounts as *tableaux d'or* – diptychs or single-panel sacred images, often engraved or enamelled on the reverse. As with the decoration of Isabeau's chapel, the subject-matter of these altar-pieces may tell us something of her religious preferences: one ordered in 1397 depicted the Trinity, a number illustrated the Holy Sepulchre, but the vast majority were dedicated to the Virgin Mary. The New Year's gift from Charles VI to his queen in 1390 must have been very special to her: it was a gilded, wooden diptych, showing Christ's tomb on one interior face and the Virgin and Child on the other, *esmaillié de blanc, garni de balais, d'esmeraudes et de perles*. On the exterior of one panel, the Virgin Mary was depicted and a mirror was attached to the other.[24] It is uncertain whether this dual use was common, but Isabeau's biographer Thibault considered the diptych to be the perfect gift for a young queen who was both devout and coquettish![25] The present was well-used by Isabeau – within a few months, expenditure on repairs to the hinges and to replace a few missing pearls is recorded in the king's *argenterie* account.[26] Quite small purchases also help to build up a picture of Isabeau's daily religious activities. In one account, for the period July 1394 to June 1395, the following items were bought: an ivory lantern for the queen's chamber, in which she could put a candle when she said her Hours in the early morning, so as to avoid dripping wax onto the pages of her book;[27] two travelling trunks to hold the plate of the

---

[22] These four in order are from AN, KK49, f. 3v; f. 14v; f. 37; and f. 39v.
[23] AN, KK41, f. 13v.
[24] AN, KK21, f. 90.
[25] Thibault, *Isabeau*, p. 170.
[26] Ibid.
[27] AN, KK41 (1 July 1394–30 June 1395), f. 66.

queen's chapel;[28] and various precious devotional objects for her children, including a *tableau* for the dauphin, a crucifix bought as a baptismal present for the baby Michelle and a *painachanter* ordered for Princess Jeanne in which to keep the Host.[29]

From early in her life, pilgrimage played a large part in Isabeau's religious experience. From donations recorded in her first will written in 1408, it is evident that she had visited the German shrines of Ramsdorf, Freisingen and Nordlingen during her childhood.[30] In his famous account of her arrival in France to be married to Charles VI in 1385, Froissart explains that, because of the delicate nature of the negotiations, the true purpose of the Bavarian expedition was kept secret and many thought that Isabeau and her uncle Frederick were in France only to make a pilgrimage to the shrine of John the Baptist at Amiens.[31] The fact that this was considered to be a plausible story seems to confirm a Bavarian chronicler's image of Duke Frederick as a man of pious reputation.[32] Isabeau's visits to French pilgrimage sites began within a few months of her wedding: on 6 January 1386, she made offerings at Nôtre-Dame-la-Royale at Maubuisson, a favoured abbey of the French royal house, founded by Queen Blanche of Castile in 1236, and the burial place of many Capetians.[33] In August 1387, she embarked for the first time on what was to become an almost annual summer grand tour of shrines, staying at the Benedictine abbey of Bon Pont at Pont-de-l'Arche and at Chartres, where she made an offering of cloth-of-gold *racamas*. In November, she travelled to Noyen and made similar donations of rich fabrics at Nôtre-Dame and at the abbey of Saint-Eloi.[34] Despite producing nine children by 1398, Isabeau made a local pilgrimage

---

[28] AN, KK41, f. 52v.

[29] Ibid., f. 55.

[30] BN, fond français 6544, n. 7.

[31] Jean Froissart, *Chroniques, II:ccxxxi* in his *Œuvres*, ed. Kervyn de Lettenhove (29 vols, Brussels, 1870), 10, p. 349.

[32] Jean Ebran de Wildenberg, *Chronicon Bavariæ* in *Rerum boicarum scriptores*, ed. A.F. Œfelius (Augsburg, 1763), 1, p. 312.

[33] AN, AB200, carton xix (collected notes, extracts and papers of the historian Lucien Douet-d'Arcq).

[34] AN, KK21, f. 183 and f. 228.

every summer or autumn throughout her twenties, especially favouring Chartres, Saint-Sanctin, Maubuisson and Pontoise.

Later in her reign, perhaps because ill-health, political preoccupations or wartime constraints on travel did not allow her to go in person, Isabeau performed pilgrimage by proxy, using 'professional' pilgrims, as was the common practice.[35] As with Isabeau's charitable activities, the main surviving record on this subject is the account of *menues plaisirs* for 1416/17: in this year Isabeau paid Gilette la Guilemette a total of six *écus* to make two novenas, one to Saint Fiacre and one to Saint Veronica.[36] Also in this account, a novena was organised for Saints James, Philip and Eutrope in the church of Saint-Gervais, the parish church in Paris, and novenas and quinzaines took place in the queen's name at the churches of Boulogne-la-Petite, Nôtre-Dame de Paris, and Sainte-Geneviève; at Saint-Antoine-des-Champs, Saint-Sébastian and Saint-Fabien de Paris, and elsewhere.[37] Other pilgrimages made for Isabeau by proxy during this period include that of a priest, Jehan Guerguesal, who went on pilgrimage on the queen's orders to Saint-Lomer, near Courcy in Normandy to make a novena to Saint Lomer; with the same aim, the queen's chaplain and her confessor's *aide* went to Saint-Christophe de Pontoise and Sainte-Geneviève de Nanterre respectively.[38] These pilgrimages and novenas were accompanied by gifts of candles such as the fifteen-pound wax candle offered at Avignon in honour of the saint-cardinal, Peter of Luxemburg.[39] As well as paying for pilgrims, Isabeau was also known to fast by proxy:[40] in 1416, Sister Jehanne la Brune, a nun at Saint-Marcel, fasted on behalf of the queen for thirty-six days, and was reimbursed for her pains by Jehan Cambrier, *aide* to Isabeau's confessor.[41]

---

[35] Elizabeth of York, well regarded for her piety, is also known to have employed a proxy: see Crawford, 'The Piety of Late Medieval English Queens', p. 52.

[36] AN, KK49, f. 4.

[37] AN, KK49, f. 8 ff.

[38] Verdon, *Isabeau*, pp. 232–3.

[39] Ibid.

[40] Verdon seems to find this practice particularly amusing, with his exclamation that *La souveraine jeûnait même par intermédiaire!*: see his *Isabeau*, p. 233.

[41] AN, KK49, f. 51v.

One of the best-documented areas of Isabeau's religious life is her collection of devotional literature. Throughout the Middle Ages, most educated noblewomen enjoyed a special relationship with their books which provided spiritual nourishment of a private and personal kind.[42] In her study of medieval female bookowners, Susan Groag Bell identified 242 laywomen as owning books before 1500; 182 of them (75 per cent) included books of piety in their collections and 145 (60 per cent) owned vernacular translations of pious works. In cases where only one book can be traced to an individual woman, it is almost invariably a devotional item such as a Gospel, Psalter, Lives of the Saints or, most often, a Book of Hours.[43] Of course, mere possession is no sure evidence of understanding, or indeed of reading: it may only reflect interest and this cannot be analysed perfectly, but possession is the only real guide we have to the importance of devotional literature.[44] Isabeau was particularly concerned for the preservation and safe transportation of her library when she moved around her favoured residences in the Île-de-France: from 1387 onwards, she travelled with a leather-bound wooden trunk to hold her books[45] and, at least from the time she received her own *argenterie* in 1393, one of her ladies, Catherine de Villiers, was charged with the care of her library. This collection would not have included the missals, breviaries and choral books which made up part of the furnishings of her chapel, but would have consisted of Latin devotional books, as well as romances and chronicles written in French. Most of the surviving queen's *argenterie* accounts – covering the period 1393 to 1407 – include some reference to the purchase or repair of books: her Little Hours of Our Lady seems to have been particularly well-used if the number of re-coverings and

---

[42] There is an expanding literature on female bookowners in the Middle Ages, but most recent research has been directed towards bookownership in England: see, for example, *Women and Literature in Britain, 1150–1500*, ed. C.M. Meale (Cambridge, 1993), and *Women, the Book and the Godly* and *Women, the Book and the Worldly: Selected Proceedings of the St. Hilda's Conference, 1993*, eds Lesley Smith and Jane H.M. Taylor (Cambridge, 1995).

[43] Susan Groag Bell, 'Medieval Women Bookowners: Arbiters of Lay Piety and Ambassadors of Culture' in *Women and Power in the Middle Ages*, eds Mary Erler and Maryanne Kowaleski (Athens, Georgia,1988), p. 160.

[44] R.N. Swanson, *Church and Society in Late Medieval England* (Oxford, 1989), p. 262.

[45] AN, KK18 (king's *argenterie*), f. 42v.

repairs to it are any guide.[46] The 1416/17 *menues plaisirs* account also includes payments for similar purposes such as six *écus* paid to Jehan Postie for buying materials to make up a new Book of Hours; three *écus* to Jehan Petit for a half-aulne of reinforced blue satin to make a cover for a Book of Hours; and ten shillings to Gilet Loy to make a lecturn of fine oak for the queen's oratory.[47]

Women's insistence on owning vernacular compositions and translations of Latin texts confirms female interest in both the spiritual and worldly importance of religious and secular literature, and provides evidence of their role as literary patrons.[48] In 1398, Isabeau commissioned for her own use *un livret de dévocions ou quel est contenue la Passion de Nostre Seigneur*.[49] There is no definite trace of the original work but its existence is confirmed by surviving copies. One such copy is the book catalogued by the Bibliothèque Nationale as *fond français* 7926, once owned by Marie of Cleves, third wife of the poet-duke Charles of Orleans: at the start of the text, after a dedication to God, the Virgin and the saints, the author writes that he has made the translation from Latin into French *à la requeste de très excellente et redoubtée et puissante princesse, dame Ysabel de Bavière, par la grâce de Dieu, royne de France*.[50]

---

[46] For example, in June 1399, the pages were cleaned, whitened and rewritten in certain places, then the whole book was newly bound in wood, covered in gold-embossed leather and the page-edges gilded: AN, KK42, f. 256.

[47] AN, KK49, f. 40; f. 34; and f. 42.

[48] Bell, 'Medieval Women Bookowners', pp. 149–50. As well as a translation of the Passion, Isabeau is very likely to have commissioned the copy of Christine de Pisan's *Œuvres* now in the British Library (Harley MS 4431), as argued by Sandra Hindman in 'The Iconography of Queen Isabeau de Bavière (1410–1415): an Essay in Method' in *Gazette des Beaux-Arts*, ser. 6, 102 (1983), pp. 102–3.

[49] AN, KK41, f. 185.

[50] BN, f. fran. 7926; see also, Auguste Vallet de Viriville, 'La bibliothèque d'Isabeau de Bavière, reine de France' in *Bulletin du Bibliophile* (January 1858), pp. 674–5, where the author concludes that this volume clearly did belong to Marie of Cleves, third wife of Charles, duke of Orleans. Marie's signature appears on the last page and there is a miniature on the frontispiece depicting the duke and duchess of Orleans in prayer which, from the costume and ages of the couple, Vallet de Viriville dates to around 1440. One could thus surmise that this volume is a copy made from the queen's original, or it may perhaps be the original commission, transferred to the Orleans library through the second marriage of her daughter Isabelle to Charles of Orleans on 29 June 1406. If this is the volume made for Isabeau of Bavaria in 1398, then Charles must have had it re-bound and further embellished before passing it to his third wife, perhaps as a wedding present.

Perhaps the most important, and certainly the most ubiquitous, reflection of medieval piety is the care taken in providing for post-mortem religious support, through testamentary bequests and chantries given in return for prayers and masses. Isabeau made three wills, only the last of which has been published: the first was written in April 1408, in the uncertainty following the assassination of Louis of Orleans and the triumphant return of John of Burgundy to Paris;[51] the second was produced in April 1411, with almost exactly the same format and bequests, but a completely different set of executors, which largely reflects the fact that the royal family was firmly under Burgundy's control.[52] The final will was written in September 1431, four years before her death, and is a good indication of her changed circumstances – the sums of money given are greatly reduced in line with her corresponding lack of income.[53] The common factor in all the wills is that most bequests go to religious institutions in return for perpetual services. The only exceptions to this are, in 1408, 10,000 francs were set aside to distribute among her household, while her clothing, linen and goods were to be given to poor brides, pregnant women and orphans, and to impoverished churches; in 1411, the legacy to her servants was absent but her material possessions were to be distributed as before; and, in 1431, all of Isabeau's goods and clothes were bequeathed to her daughter Marie, with only 260 francs set aside for alms. Her choice of religious institutions as recipients of gifts in return for prayers remained the same: Nôtre-Dame de Paris, Saint-Denis and Poissy are included in all three wills. In 1431, by which time the queen had no money but only her real estate, these three institutions were left an *hôtel* each in return for perpetual prayers, with provision for regular payments in alms to hospitals, and pensions to members of the queen's household such as her confessor.[54] In 1408 and 1411, when the queen had approximately 100,000 francs to spare after she had set aside money and

---

[51] BN, f. fran. 6544, n. 7.

[52] BN, f. fran. 6544, n. 1.

[53] BN, f. fran. 23024, f. 111–22. This third will is the only one of Isabeau's testaments in print, and can be found in *Histoire de la ville de Paris*, ed. Dom M. Felibien (5 vols, Paris, 1725), 3, pp. 553–8.

[54] Ibid., pp. 555–6.

property to pay her expected debts, her fortune went to churches and monasteries for funeral masses and perpetual prayers: Chartres, Senlis, and the Sainte-Chapelle in Paris were all left money to buy land worth ten *livres* annually in rent, to be used to keep an obit. Similar bequests to the Friars Minor and the church of Nôtre-Dame in Munich show that Isabeau had not forgotten her ties of birth. None of the practices discussed above was unusual, but they seem to have been performed by Isabeau with great vigour and frequency.

There is also a need to examine those aspects of Isabeau's piety that might be deemed to be more personal to her. There is plenty of evidence to indicate Isabeau's devotion to the Virgin Mary, in her role both as Queen of Heaven and as a mediator, but this should probably be seen as a reflection of a wide contemporary European practice rather than as something particular to Isabeau herself. Greater attention should be given to her choice of 'minor saints' as evidence of her personal devotional interests, the first being her name-saint. Isabeau's real name was Elisabeth, given to her in honour of Saint Elisabeth of Hungary, to whose family the house of Bavaria had allied itself by marriage many times. Elisabeth was the wife of Lewis of Thuringia but, when he died of plague while on crusade with Emperor Frederick II in 1227, she became a Franciscan tertiary and led a life austere almost to the point of masochism before dying in 1231 at the age of twenty-four. Elisabeth was a very popular name with the Wittelsbach family: Isabeau's grandmother was another Elisabeth of Hungary, while her great-aunt, paternal aunt and cousin were also christened for the saint.[55] There is no record of patronage by Isabeau of Bavaria to a church dedicated to Saint Elisabeth but this may be explained by the fact that the cult had not spread much beyond central Europe. A stained-glass window in the chapel at Saint-Denis where the joint tomb of Charles VI and Isabeau originally stood showed that the queen had a commitment to her name-saint as her natural intercessor with God: neither the window nor the grand mausoleum ordered in the king's will survived the desecration of Saint-Denis that took place in the aftermath of the French Revolution, but a description of them did, which tells us that there was: *une image du roy Charles VI a*

---

[55] BN, f. fran. 20780, f. 338–9; see also Thibault, *Isabeau*, pp. 20–1.

genoulx, ayant sa cotte fleurdelisée, presenté par un saint Louys. Et apres luy une Elisabeth de Baviere sa femme, présentée par une sainte Elisabeth, avec une robbe mipartie de France et de Baviere.[56]

A second royal woman favoured by Isabeau was another namesake, the Blessed Isabelle of France who, although not technically a saint, was at the centre of a relatively strong French cult.[57] Isabelle was a Capetian princess, the sister of Saint Louis IX; she became a Franciscan nun and a renowned ascetic before her death at the age of forty-five in 1270 at the abbey of Longchamps that she had founded. Isabeau of Bavaria's devotion to the saintly princess is expressed in her patronage of Longchamps, which had always been under the particular protection of the French royal house, especially its female members, who had developed the cult to its foundress. One of Isabeau's earliest official acts as queen, on 8 February 1389, was to place a formal ban on her household collecting the right of *prise* from lands owned by the nuns of Longchamps *pour la grant affection et devocion especiale* that she had towards them.[58]

Another saint favoured by Isabeau was Saint John the Baptist, whose cult was intimately connected with her marriage to Charles VI. When her father finally agreed to send her to France, it was on condition that no one, not even the prospective bride, should know the purpose of the visit in case she failed to win Charles' approval.[59] Thus, Isabeau, aged fifteen, left Bavaria in the spring of 1385, never to return, while under the vain impression that she was merely accompanying her uncle Frederick on a pilgrimage to the famous shrine of St John the Baptist at Amiens. The saint's head was believed to be preserved there – claims disputed by Rome and other shrines – and the visit of the Bavarians was leading up to the annual spring *fête* that centred on public worship of this relic.[60] Isabeau maintained her devotion to St John the Baptist's shrine for the

---

[56] Paris, Bibliothèque inguimbertine de Carpentras, MS 1791, f. 130; see also the commentary in Yann Grandeau 'La mort et obsèques de Charles VI', in *Bulletin philologique et historique, année 1970* (Paris, 1973), p. 158.

[57] Thibault, *Isabeau*, p. 117, n. 2.

[58] AN, K53, n. 79.

[59] Froissart, *Chroniques*, 10, p. 347.

[60] Vallet de Viriville, *Isabeau de Bavière*, p. 4.

rest of her life: in her first two wills, donations were made to *leglise damiens en laquelle monseigneur nous espousa*;[61] obituary masses were ordered from the cathedral chapter because of the reverence in which the queen held Saint John, who had witnessed her marriage; and charity was dispensed by Isabeau's almoner on the eve of the saint's feast-day.[62] It was claimed in the seventeenth century that the large gold platter ornamented with pearls and precious stones on which the relic of the saint's head rested was the young queen's wedding present to the shrine.[63]

The fact that there was a vernacular 'biography' of Saint Margaret within Isabeau's collection[64] implies a level of devotion to this saint who probably only ever existed in pious fiction but who was extremely popular in the Later Middle Ages. Saint Margaret of Antioch was the daughter of a pagan priest who was turned out of her home because of her Christian faith and lived as a shepherdess. The apocryphal promises that are credited to her contributed powerfully to the spread of her cult, especially among women: all who read her history would receive an unfading crown in Heaven; those who invoked her on their deathbeds would escape from devils, and pregnant women who invoked her name would escape from the dangers of childbirth. To an earthly queen who risked the dangers of twelve pregnancies, Saint Margaret seems an extremely suitable patroness.

Isabeau's choice of names for some of her twelve children is unusual and might be seen as evidence of the direction of her piety since a strictly limited range of names was usually given to children of the French royal family.[65] On

---

[61] BN, f. fran. 6544, n. 7 and n. 1.

[62] AN, KK49, f. 14v.

[63] Du Cange, *Traité historique du chef de saint Jean-Baptiste* (Paris, 1665), p. 134.

[64] AN, KK41, f. 185. *A Pierre Le Portier, escripvain de lettre de fourme demourant à Paris, pour sa paine et salaire d'avoir escript un petit livret, la ou est contenu la* Vie saincte Marguerite *et xxx suffrages de pluseurs sainz, et avoir quis le par chemin; pour ce, le xx jour de mois d'aoust, xxxii s.p.*

[65] For further information on Isabeau's family life, see Grandeau, 'Les enfants de Charles VI: Essai sur la vie privée des princes et des princesses de la Maison de France à la fin du moyen âge', in *Bulletin philologique et historique, année 1968* (Paris, 1971), 2, pp. 665–728, and A. Vallet de Viriville, 'Notes sur l'état civil des princes et princesses nés de Charles VI et d'Isabeau de Bavière' in *Bibliothèque de l'Ecole des Chartes* (1858), 19, pp. 473–82.

11 January 1395, at around eight o'clock in the evening, Isabeau gave birth to her seventh child, a daughter, and presumably the baptism of the child next day as Michelle, an unusual name for the time, was intended as a desperate plea for the intercession of the king's favourite saint, the archangel Michael. He was regarded as patron of the kingdom of France and had received the credit for the king's recovery from insanity in 1394, as shown by Charles VI's pilgrimage of thanks to Mont-Saint-Michel when he was well. What may now seem to us to be the rather morbid practice of naming a new baby after a sibling who had just died also occurred more than once in Isabeau's family: there are two Jeannes and three Charles among her twelve offspring.

Almost from conception, Isabeau's sixth child seems to have been designated as a living symbol of her mother's piety. During the spring and early summer of 1393, Isabeau *redoubla de ferveur dans ses exercises de piété et dans ses pèlerinages*, ordering an *Agnus Dei* to have with her during labour.[66] The fact that this baby was destined from birth for an unusual life was proved when, as the king again fell insane in June 1393, Isabeau promised to devote the child she was carrying to the Virgin Mary if Charles recovered, and approved of her vow.[67] On 22 August, around ten o'clock at night, she gave birth to a daughter at the château of Vincennes; the next day she was baptised Marie, a name chosen by Isabeau herself in honour of the Virgin and for an aunt of Charles VI, Marie of Bourbon, who was abbess at the royal nunnery of Poissy. Having been raised with her brothers and sisters up to the age of four, Marie entered the convent of Poissy on 8 September 1397 – the day of the Virgin's birth. She was escorted there by her parents, with a lavish entourage, before being admitted to the order.[68] Isabeau visited her daughter often, and there are records of frequent maternal letters, instructing the child to take great care of herself.[69] It certainly appears that Marie of France accepted and even approved of her mother's choice of vocation for her: when, in 1405, Isabeau and Louis of Orleans tried to persuade her to leave the convent in order to make an expedient marriage with the son of the

---

[66] Thibault, *Isabeau*, p. 221; BN, nouveau acquisitions latines 608, p. 203.
[67] Religieux de Saint-Denis, *Chronique de Charles VI*, eds L. Bellaguet (6 vols, Paris, 1839–52), 2, p. 95.
[68] Ibid., p. 555.
[69] For example, AN, KK45, f. 77–8.

duke of Bar, Marie declined to give up the veil, and ended her life as abbess of Poissy in 1438.

Isabeau's religious beliefs also affected her relationship with Charles VI, especially in the way that she reacted to his developing insanity during the 1390s.[70] Sceptical of the ability of the majority of the physicians who presented themselves to heal the king, she trusted mainly in God to come to her husband's aid, and her zeal to effect a cure did not waver for at least a decade. The Religieux de Saint-Denis tells us that she was overjoyed when an ascetic named Arnaud Guillaume promised her that he would be able to free the king from the sorcery that he was under,[71] but disillusionment soon followed with repeated failure, and she again took solace in prayer and ordered that all should contribute their pleas. In the winter of 1393, solemn processions were made in Paris on the orders of the queen and the council,[72] while a large number of prelates in France and the neighbouring lands heeded Isabeau's requests to make a novena for the king's health. She also made some particularly large donations in this period, including the foundation of a perpetual, daily mass at Senlis for herself and the king.[73] In January 1396, Isabeau sent instructions to bishops throughout France for processions to be organised and for prayers to be said *pour la bonne santé et prosperité de mondit seigneur*.[74] Froissart cites a copy of this letter sent to the bishop of Tournai, ordering three consecutive days of processing – in honour of the Holy Spirit on the Thursday; in remembrance of the Passion on the Friday; and in praise of the Virgin Mary on Saturday – to be performed barefoot, in pilgrims' robes, *ou en autre maniere, selon sa devotion*.[75]

---

[70] One of the better studies of Charles VI's madness is the first chapter of Famiglietti, *Royal Intrigue*, pp. 1–22. See also Françoise Autrand, *Charles VI* (Paris, 1986), pp. 271–345; Lizé, 'Description et nature de la maladie de Charles VI' in *Bulletin de la Société d'agriculture de la Sarthe XIII* (1872), pp. 345–57; and Jean-Claude Lemaire, *1380–1422. Le roi empoisonné: la vérité sur la folie de Charles VI* (Paris, 1977), pp. 153–74, who maintains that Charles' insanity was caused by long-term, systematic poisoning.

[71] Religieux, 2, p. 91.
[72] Ibid., p. 93.
[73] AN, JJ161, f. 21.
[74] Froissart, *Chroniques*, 15, p. 431.
[75] Ibid.

Perhaps hoping that their innocent prayers would have a better chance of being heard by an obviously dissatisfied God, in 1409 Isabeau sent her children to Mont-Saint-Michel, the shrine of the patron saint of the kingdom of France, to pray that the archangel would bring about their father's recovery as it was thought he had done in 1394.[76]

Two particular incidents in Isabeau of Bavaria's life have struck historians as evidence of the superstitious core to the queen's faith. In August 1390, when the king, queen, and the duke and duchess of Touraine were staying at Saint-Germain, a furious storm blew up during mass. The wind uprooted trees, tore the doors off their hinges and shattered the chapel windows. The pregnant Isabeau was terrified, and regarded this as divine anger against them because of heavier taxation that the council was thinking of instituting. When the storm abated, Isabeau threw herself at Charles VI's feet, saying that the people's suffering had roused God's anger and begging him to order the council to postpone the decision.[77] To calm her spirits, Isabeau went on a pilgrimage, leaving Saint-Germain at the end of August and passing through Paris on 26 August. By 1 September, she had reached Pontoise, visiting Maubuisson before going on to Saint-Sanctin and Chartres in October, and arriving at Villiers abbey in Ferté-Alais on 19 October, where she stayed for the rest of the month. As well as fearing possible physical retribution from God, there is evidence to indicate that Isabeau shared the fundamental belief in the power of relics. She personally owned a fragment of the True Cross[78] and a reference in her household accounts relates how, on 31 August 1398, when the queen was having difficulties during the birth of her ninth child John, she dispatched a courier to the Benedictine abbey of Coulombs in the Chartres diocese to beg one of the monks to bring her their prized relic of the infant Christ's circumcised foreskin in order to relieve her labour pains.[79]

In concluding this study of the devotional practices of Isabeau of Bavaria, it is

---

[76] AN, KK32, f. 24.

[77] Religieux, 1, pp. 685–7. Thibault interprets this intercession as influenced by the belief that she had escaped from peril by miraculous means: Thibault, *Isabeau*, p. 176.

[78] AN, KK41, f. 62v.

[79] AN, KK45, f. 16v.

important to bear in mind that religion was a social as well as a private affair during the later Middle Ages.[80] Devotions had the purpose of a status display and a fulfilment of public expectations, as well as being a personal expression of faith. This was especially the case for such a public figure as a queen whose pious practices, if not her inner beliefs, were on permanent display, and thus open to criticism if not considered a fitting expression of the kingdom's consciousness. Despite some of the more original and personal aspects of her religious lifestyle, Isabeau of Bavaria's practices are likely to have been similar to those of her peers. Along with the majority of her contemporaries, she placed great importance on the external trappings of late medieval Catholicism – chapel furnishings, religious imagery and relics – but this does not detract from, nor disguise, the depth of her underlying faith. Isabeau was never austere in her piety, like Cecily Neville, or her namesakes Isabelle of France and Elisabeth of Hungary, but it is very unlikely that lifestyles such as theirs would have been considered appropriate for a queen of France, or would have enhanced her contemporary reputation. However, Isabeau's religious practices did maintain their hold on her daily schedule and the direction of her life: she paid strict attention to the formal duties of her faith, and devoted a large amount of her time and income to those practices which especially appealed to her. In conformity with others of her social status, Isabeau of Bavaria did not baulk at using the advantages of her birth and position in the practice of her religion, but neither the visibility of her pious expenditure nor any doubts about the motivation behind her donations should detract totally from the merit of the actions themselves. The importance that she gave to pious practice in her life justifies, if not demands, the notice of any modern biographer.

---

[80] Crawford, 'The Piety of Late Medieval English Queens', p. 48

INDEX

Adys, Miles, goldsmith, 131n.
Agnes, 'doctrix puellarum', 147
Aldersey, William, 17, 20n
Alfonso V, king of Aragon, Naples and Sicily, 190, 191
Amiens, 207, 213, 219
Antwerp, Lionel of, duke of Clarence, see Clarence
Arneway, Sir John, mayor of Chester, 17
Arrowsmith, William, 63; Maria, his widow, 63
Arundel, John Fitzalan, earl of (d.1435), 170n; Richard Fitzalan, earl of (d.1376), 176; Richard Fitzalan, earl of (d.1397), 175; Thomas Fitzalan, earl of (d.1415), 169n, 174;
Arundel, William, 173n.
Asheton, Peter, of Acton (Ches.), 42
Ashton (Ches.), 75
Ashton, Richard, 57
Asthill, John, 57; Lawrence, 57
Aston family of Aston, 68
Aston, Thomas, 43; Margaret Vernon, his grandmother, 43
Avignon, 214

Barbour, William, priest, 147
Barton, Randolph, 86
Basset, Alderman. of London, 131n
Beauchamp, Thomas, earl of Warwick, see Warwick
Beauchamp, Sir John, Lord of Powick, 174
Beaufort: Edmund, duke of Somerset (d.1455); Edmund, duke of Somerset (d.1471); Henry, duke of Somerset (d.1464), see Somerset; Henry, Cardinal, bishop of Winchester, 184, 186, 188, 194n, 196n; Sir Thomas, duke of Exeter (d.1426), see Exeter
Beaumont, John, Lord, 173, 173n; John, Viscount (d.1460), 174
Bedford, John of Lancaster, duke of, (d.1435), 166, 170, 173; Enguerrand de Couci, earl of (d.1397), 165
Bedford, Richard, 34, 50
Betchton (Ches.), 43
Bingham, Sir Richard, 59
Bircheles, Henry, 69
Birchenshawe, John, abbot of Chester, 22, 24
Birkhead, William, 132n
Blanche of Castile, Queen, 213
Blundevill, Randle, earl of Chester, see Chester
Bodelwyddan (Flints.), 38n, 41
Bohun, Eleanor de, wife of Thomas of Woodstock, duke of Gloucester, 175n; Humphrey de, earl of Hereford (d.1373), see Hereford
Boisherbert, Jacques du, 211
Bold, Richard, 63
Bole, Richard, 199, 200
Bonville, William, Lord, 171
Booth, family, of Dunham Massey (Ches.), 68, 78–82, 90; Sir Robert, sheriff of Cheshire 56, 58, 67, 70, 79, 86; his great-grandson, Sir William 70
Booth, family, of Barton (Lancs.), 86; Sir Robert (d.1460), 81
Booth, John, of Twemlow (Ches.), 90
Booths, see Knutsford Booths
Bostock, Lawrence, 90
Botiller, Ralph, Lord Sudeley, 174
Boure, Thomas atte, 147, 148
Bourgchier, Henry, Viscount, 173, 173n; Isabel, his wife, 173n
Boydell, Geoffrey, 57, 67
Bracciolini, Poggio, 184–91, 195-6, 198-201, 203
Brereton, Sir Philip, 69; Randle, 41; Ranulph, sheriff, 48; William, 41
Brigg, John, of Newark, 37
Browdhurst, Hugh, 48; John, 48; Roger, 48
Brown, John, 34, 50
Bruni, Leonardo, 182, 189, 190n, 192-4, 200
Buckland, Joan (d.1462), 151
Bulkeley, Edmund, lawyer, 39
Burgh, Agnes, 151
Burghley, William, 63
Burgundy: dukes of, 155n; Charles 'the Rash', duke of, 158n; John 'the Fearless', duke of, 217; Margaret de Mâle, duchess of, 211; Philip 'the Good', duke of, 158n;
Burley, John, 162, 162n
Burley, Simon, 162, 162n, 163, 174, 178
Burnell, Hugh, Lord, 169, 169n
Busshell, John, 40
Butler, James, earl of Ormond, see Ormond
Butler, Thomas, baker, 9, 9n
Buxhill, Sir Alan, 162, 162n, 174
Byrom, Sir John, of Clayton (Lancs.), 74, 82n, 87n

Cambridge, Edmund of Langley, earl of (d.1402); Richard, earl of (d.1415), see York
Cambrier, Jehan, 214
Camoys, Thomas, Lord, 170n
Candour, Thomas, 201, 201n
Capell, William, 137n
Carrington, family of Carrington, 57, 68; Sir George, 69
Chamberlain, John, 135n
Champyn, Hugh, 46n
Chaplin, Thomas, clerk, 135n
Charlton, Edward, Lord of Powys, 169, 169n
Charles VI, king of France, 207-9, 212-3, 218-9, 221-3; his children, 208, 213, 217, 221–2
Chartres, 213, 214, 218, 223
Chaundler, Thomas, 203n
Chauntrell, William, serjeant-at-law, 50, 51n, 63, 64, 64n
Chester, 74, 79; abbey of St Werburgh, 19n, 21, 22, 24; abbot of, 19n, 22, see also Birchenshawe; archdeacon of, 12, 14n, 30; cathedral, 22; chamberlain of, see Stanley; Troutbeck; mayor of, 10, 17, 18, 19, 20, 21; see also Arneway, Gee, Goodman, Hanky, Lynett, Savage, Sotheworth
Chester: earls of, 12, 30, 31, 32n, 33, 35, 37, 51, 60, 74, 79n, 89; John 'le Scot', (d.1237), 79, 79n; Randle Blundevill, (d.1232), 13, 83, 83n; see also, Edward, the Black Prince; Henry V; Henry VI, Edward, his son; Edward IV, Edward, his son; Richard III, Edward, his son; Henry VII, Arthur, his son
Cholmondeley, Lady Mary, 56
Christine le Neetes, 113; John, her son, 213
Chrysostom, 186, 187, 201
Churche, Peter, Master, 150
Clarence, Lionel of Antwerp, duke of (d.1368), 165; Thomas of Lancaster, duke of (d.1421), 166
Clarke, Hugh, 19
Clerk, Richard, of Prestbury (Ches.), 83
Clifford, Lewis, 168
Coleman, Matilda, of Mourton, 102; Roger, her son, 102
Collins, John, mercer, 132n
Cook, Sir Thomas, 132n; Philip, his son, 132n
Corker, Peter, of Arclid (Ches.), 43
Cotiller, Robert, 114
Couci, Enguerrand de, earl of Bedford, see Bedford
Coulombs, abbey of, 223
Courcy, St-Lomer, 214
Coventry, city of, 21, 43
Cresewyk, William, 147, 151
Cromwell, Ralph, Lord, 175, 175n
Curbishley, Thomas, of Wilmslow (Ches.), 79

Dalton, Sir John, 106
Daniel, John, 57, 67
Daniel, Thomas, of Tabley (Ches.), 58
Davenport, family, of Henbury and Woodford (Ches.), 84, 85, 86; John (d.1350), 84
Davenport, Nicholas, 75, 80
Davenport, Thomas, of Welltrough, 84
Davenport, William, esquire, of Bramhall (Ches.), 75; Alice, his wife, 75
Decembrio, P. C., 189, 197n
Dedwood, John, 64, 64n
Delves, Henry, 35, 52; Richard, 47
Denny, William, 48
Despenser, Edward, Lord, 164; Thomas, Lord, earl of Gloucester, see Gloucester
Dodsworth, Roger (1585-1654), 86
Done (Donne), John, 35, 52
Downes, Roger, 39
Duncalf, family, of Foxtwist (Ches.), 84
Duncalfe, Sir John, vicar of Prestbury (Ches.), 83, 83n
Dunham Massey (Ches.), 57, 70, 79, 85, Dutton, family, of Chester, 12, 13, 68; Dutton, Sir Peter, 56, 69
Dutton, John, of Helsby (Ches.), 43
Eaton, Charles, 19
Edmund of Langley, earl of Cambridge,

INDEX

duke of York (d.1402), *see* York
Edward III, king of England; 157, 157n, 159, 165–7, 172–6, 179; sons of, 165; daughters of, 165
Edward, the Black Prince, 31, 164, 168
Edward IV, king of England, 32; Edward, prince of Wales, his son, 31, 32, 33, 39n, 51; Elizabeth, his daughter, 214n
Egerton, Philip, 35, 52
Egerton, Ralph, 47
Eland, Elizabeth, 146n
Elizabeth of Hungary, 218, 219, 224
Elizabeth of York, queen of England, *see* Henry VII
Erasmus, Desiderius, 192, 203
Erpingham, Sir Thomas, 162, 162n, 169n, 174
Everard, John, 98, 98n, 99, 110
Exeter, John Holland, earl of Huntingdon, duke of (d.1400), 177, 177n; Thomas Beaufort, duke of (d.1426), 169n, 174

Fastolf, Sir John, 75, 76n, 83n, 162, 162n, 170, 170n, 173n
Fawdon, Robert, 58
Felbrigg, Simon, 173n
Ferrers, Walter, Lord *see* Devereux
Finlow, Thomas, priest, 40
Fisher, Jane, nun, 140
Fitton, Robert, 79
Fitton, of Fernleigh, William (d.1523), 19, 82, 83
Fitton, of Gawsworth (Ches.), Sir Edward, 43; Sir Lawrence, 57, 69; Thomas, 66
Fitton, family, of Pownall (Ches.), 78, 79, 81, 81n, 85, 86, 87, 87n, 90; Ellen, 77; Margaret, 78
Fitzalan, earls of Arundel *see* Arundel
FitzHugh, Henry, Lord, 169
Foix, Jean de, earl of Kendal, *see* Kendal
Fortescue, John, 193
Fouleshurst, Sir Robert, 36
France, 49, 209, 219, 221, 222; kings of, 207, 208; *see also*, John II; Louis IX; Charles VI
Frederick III, Emperor, 218
Freisulngen, shrine of, 213
Frulovisi, Tito Livio, 188–93

Garrard, Elizabeth, 147
Gascoigne, Thomas, 63
Gawsworth (Ches.), 43, 81, 87;
Gee, Henry, mayor of Chester, 17, 19
Geryn, John, 34, 50
Gibbons, John, 75
Glasior, William, 43
Gloucester, Thomas of Woodstock, duke of (d.1397), 166, 175, 175n; Eleanor de Bohun, his wife, 175n; Thomas Despenser, earl of (d.1400); Humphrey, duke of (d.1447), 50, 166, 170, 171n, 173, 190–200
Glyndŵr, Owain, 169, 170n
Goodman, Christopher, 7, 7n, 18, 25, 26
Goodman, Richard, mayor of Chester, 20

Granche, Madame de la, 211
Gray, William, bishop of Ely, 191, 192n
Gresley, Sir John, 47
Grey, Sir John, 162, 162n, 170n
Grey, Thomas, Lord Ferrers, marquess of Dorset, *see* Dorset
Guerguesal, Jehan, priest, 214
Guilemette, Gilette de, 214
Guillaume, Arnaud, 222

Hallebroc, Annotte de, 211
Handforth, William, 80
Hanky, John, mayor of Chester, 18
Hardyng, John, 88
Harper, Thomas, 43
Harrington, William, 170n
Harware, John, abbot of Vale Royal (Ches.), 43
Hastings, Henry, earl of Huntingdon, *see* Huntingdon
Hastings, John, earl of Pembroke *see* Pembroke
Helsby, Henry, of Alvanley (Ches.), 43
Henry IV, king of England, 162, 165–9, 175–8
Henry V, king of England, 31, 166, 167, 169, 170, 176, 177, 184, 190, 190n; Katherine of Valois, his queen, 63
Henry VI, king of England, 31, 32, 160, 162, 164, 170–4, 178, 190–1 Edward, prince of Wales, his son, 31–2, 167; Margaret of Anjou, his queen, xvii, 32, 163n, 171, 174
Henry VII, king of England, 34n, 35, 46, 47, 188, 192; Arthur, prince of Wales, his son, 20, 22, 31, 32n, 37n, 39n, 51; Elizabeth of York, his queen, 214n
Hereford, Humphrey de Bohun, earl of (d.1373), 175, 175n; Eleanor, his daughter, 175n
Higden, Randle, 24, 25
Hilton, Walter, 141, 151
Hoccleve, Thomas, 152
Hogh, Alice, 47
Holes, Andrew, 197n
Holford, family of, 56; George, 56
Holand, John, apprentice, 146
Holland, John, earl of Huntingdon, duke of Exeter (d.1400), *see* Exeter
Holland, Robert, draper, 150-1
Holland, Thomas, earl of Kent (d.1400), *see* Kent
Holme, Randle, II, 86; his son, 86
Holt (Denbigh.), 29, 41
Holt, James del, 64–7, 75
Holynshed, Ralph, 48
Hoo, Thomas, Lord Hastings, 171
Hull, Sir Edward, 163, 163n, 179n
Hull, Dame Eleanor (d.1460), 140
Hungerford, Edmund, 179n
Huyde, Thomas, 40

Jankynson, John, weaver, 9, 9n
Jeanne of Bourbon, Queen, 211
John II, king of France, 211
John 'le Scot', earl of Chester, *see* Chester

Kardiff, Richard, 38
Katherine of Valois, queen of England *see* Henry V
Kemesyngg, John, goldsmith, 144
Kendal, Jean de Foix, earl of, 177
Kent, Thomas Holland, earl of (d.1400, 168, 168n, 172n, 173n, 176; Edmund his brother, 176
Kingsmill, William, scrivener, 147
Kinnersley, Mrs Rose, of Chipping Barnet (Herts.), 148
Kneesworth, Richard, 133n
Knighton, Henry, 143
Kyme, William, apprentice, 146
Kyriell, Sir Thomas, 171

Lancaster, John of Gaunt, duke o (d.1399), 165, 166, 168n, 169, 175 Katherine Swynford, his wife, 166
Latimer, William, Lord, 174
Lawrence, Honkyn, 57
Leftwich, Richard, 79
Legge, Robert, apprentice, 145n
Legh, family, of Adlington, 80, 82, 82n 84, 86, 87; Richard, 84; Robert, 47 Thomas, 82n
Legh, family, of Altrincham, 80n
Legh, John, of Booths, 57, 58, 65, 69 Anne, his wife, 65; Roger, his brother 57, 67
Legh, William, of Timperley, 57
Leland, John, 83, 89, 90
Letters, William, scrivener, 130n
Leycester, family, of Tabley, 69; John, 64 Sir Peter, 55, 86n
Lincoln, city of, 10
Lloyd, Fulk, 42
Lloyd, Robert, 43
London, 186, 199; city of, 21; guildhall o 145; Holy Trinity Priory, Aldgate, 15 house of Minoresses, Aldgate, 141, 152 parish of, All Hallows, London Wal 145n; St Sepulchre's, 132n; schools o St Martin le Grand, 141, St Mary l Bow, 141, St Paul's, 141
Longchamps, abbey of, 219
Louis IX, St, king of France, 219 Isabelle, 'the Blessed', his sister, 219 224
Lovell, Francis, 46
Loy, Gilet, 216
Lydgate, John, 152
Lymm (Ches.), 57, 67
Lynett, Sir Walter, mayor of Chester, 17
Lynne, William, grocer of London, 151 Alice, his wife, 151; his daughters 151, 152

Mainwaring, John, of Nantwich, 43
Mainwaring, family, of Peover, 68; Si John, 57; Randal, 57
Mainwaring, John, esquire, of Peover, 75
Mairesse, Jean, 211
Mansell, Rees, 41, 52
March, Edmund Mortimer, earl o (d.1425), 172, 176, 176n; Roge Mortimer, earl of (d.1360), 176n; Roge

INDEX

Mortimer, earl of (d.1398), 176n; Philippa, his mother, 176n
Mareflete, Maria, 'magistra scolarum', 147n
Margaret of Anjou, queen of England, *see* Henry VI
Markham, Sir John, 59
Massey, family, of Grafton, 78
Massey, Hamo, of Rixton, 64; William, 63; Joan, daughter of William, 63; William, esquire, 67
Massey, family, of Tatton, 65, 66, 68, 69; Thomas, eldest son of Sir John (d.1420), 57, 66, 67; Margaret, his widow, 57, 65, 66, 67, 69; Sir Geoffrey, (d.1456), 47, 57, 65, 66, 67, 69, 74; John, his heir, 74; Alice, his mother, 57, 66
Maubuisson, 213, 214, 223
Merbury, Richard, 38
Mere, family, of Mere (Ches.), 68; Matthew del, 69; William del, 69
Middleton, Henry, attorney, 136n
Milreth, Beatrice, widow (d.1448), 151; John, her son, 151
Minshull, Randal, 56; John, his son, 56
Minshull, William, 82
Mont-Saint-Michel, 221, 223
Montagu, John, earl of Salisbury (d.1400); Thomas, earl of Salisbury (d.1428), *see* Salisbury
Monte, Pietro del, 195–9, 202–3
More, Sir Thomas, 192, 203
Mortimer, family of, 173, 176n; Edmund, earl of March (d.1425); Roger, earl of March (d.1360); Roger, earl of March (d.1398), 176n *see* March
Mottershead, family of Mottershead, 78, 80, 84
Mottram, Sherd, Lord of, 84
Mottram St Andrew (Ches.), 78, 80, 84
Mowbray: John, earl of Nottingham, duke of Norfolk (d.1432); John, earl of Nottingham, duke of Norfolk (d.1461); Thomas, earl of Nottingham, duke of Norfolk (d.1399), *see* Norfolk
Mylburne, Wiliam, painter, 148

Nanterre, Ste-Geneviève de, 214
Needham, John, 30, 51, 67
Neville, Cecily, *see* York,
Neville, George, chancellor, 133
Neville, John, Lord, 174
Neville, Richard, earl of Salisbury (d.1460), *see* Salisbury
Newhall, William, 24, 25
Newton: family of Newton (and Pownall, Ches.), 77, 80, 80n, 82, 84, 85, 91
Niccoli, Niccolo, 185–8
Norfolk, John Mowbray, duke of (d.1432), 177; John Mowbray, duke of (d.1461), 173; Thomas Mowbray, duke of (d.1399), 173
Northumberland, Henry Percy, earl of (d.1408), 178
Nottingham, William, chief baron of the exchequer, 132n
Nougle, Katherine, 146n

Orléans, Charles, duke of (d.1467), 216, 216n; Isabelle of France, his 2nd wife, 216n; Marie of Cleves, his 3rd wife, 216, 216n; Louis, duke of (d.1407), 208, 217, 221
Ormond, James Butler, earl of, 165, 165n
Oxford, 117n, 191, 199–200
Oxford, Richard de Vere, earl of (d.1417), 177, 177n; Robert de Vere, earl of (d.1392), 164n, 173, 173n, 175, 178

Palmer, William (d.1400), 151
Paris, 141, 142, 208, 217, 222, 223; St-Antoine-des-champs, abbaye de, 214; St-Fabien de, 214; St-Geneviève, 214; St-Gervais, 214
Parker, Audrey, of Terling, 148
Parker, Will., tailor, 131n
Parre, Margaret, widow, 43
Paston, family, 76; William, 65; Agnes, his wife, 65; Edmund, his son, 65; John III, 149, 150
Pembridge, Sir Richard, 162, 162n, 174
Pembroke, John Hastings, earl of (d.1375), 165, 165n; Jasper Tudor, earl of (d.1495), 178
Penne, Mathilda, 150
Pierpoint, Henry, esquire, 59
Percy, family, 168n, 169; Henry 'Hotspur', 162n; Henry, earl of Northumberland (d.1408), *see* Northumberland
Perrers, Alice, 174
Perrette la Couppenoire, 141
Peterborough, abbey of, 187
Petit, Jehan, 216
Petrarch, Francesco, 197n, 200–1
Petronilla, 'scriweyner', 150
Petworth, Richard, 196n
Philip La Vache, 162, 162n, 173n
Pickering, Elizabeth, widow of Robert Redman, printer, 150
Pigot, John, 69
Pigot, Robert, of Butley (Ches.), 76
Plumpton family, 59, 76; Sir William, 69
Poissy, abbey of 217, 221; 222
Poklyngton, William, 146
Pole, John de la, duke of Suffolk (d.1492); William de la, earl and duke of Suffolk (d.1450), *see* Suffolk
Pont-de-L'Arche, 213
Pontoise, 214, 223
Ponynges, Sir Michael de, 106
Porter, William, clerk, 130n
Postie, Jehan, 216
Pourcin, Jehan, chaplain, 210
Pownall (Ches.), manor of, 77, 78, 81, 82; *see also* Fitton, family of; Newton (Ches.)

Radcliffe, Sir John, 162, 162n, 170, 170n, 176
Rameseye, Robert de, 144; Elizabeth, his daughter, 144
Redditch, John, of Dewysnape, 80
Rede, William, 132n

Rees ap Benet, of Vaynoll (Flints.), 41; Thomas, his son, 41
Reigner, Alice, 147, 148
Rempston, Sir Thomas, 162, 162n, 169n, 174
Richard II, king of England, 163, 164n, 165, 166, 168, 173, 174, 175, 176n, 177n, 180n
Richard III, king of England, 31, 34n; Edward, prince of Wales, his son, 31
Rigby, Under-sheriff, of London, 123, 132n
Ripley, Simon, abbot of Chester, 22
Rivers, Anthony Woodville, Earl (d.1483), 32
Robessart, Louis, 170n
Rogers, David, of Chester, 7, 14n, 21, 24; Robert, archdeacon of Chester, his father, 14n
Rokley, Thomas, 9
Roos, William, Lord, 169
Roucliff, Brian, 132n
Rous, John, 76, 88
Rous, William, mercer of London (d.1486), 148
Runcorn, John, 37

Saint-Denis, 217, 218; Religieux de, 221n, 222
Saint-Sanctin, 214, 223
Sais, William, 48
Salisbury, 96, 99, 101, 101n, 102, 110, 112, 114; bishop of, 103; 114; cathedral, 186;
Salisbury, John Montagu, earl of (d.1400), 168, 168n, 173, 173n; Thomas Montagu, earl of (d.1428), 177, 177n; Richard Neville, earl of (d.1460), 170n
Sarnesfield, Nicholas, 163
Savage, family, of Clifton and Rock Savage (Ches.), 68; Sir John (d.1450), 63, 69; his grandson, Sir John, senior (d.1495), 51; Sir John, junior (d.1492), 51; Sir John, mayor of Chester (d.1597), 18, 18
Scales, Thomas, Lord, 170n
Scrope of Bolton (Yorks.), William le, earl of Wiltshire (d.1399), 168, 168n, 173, 173n
Scrope of Masham (Yorks.), Henry, Lord (d.1415), 169, 176, 177, 178; Richard le, archbishop of York (d.1405), 176
Senlis, 218, 222
Sewster, William, 136n
Sexteyn, Johanna, 145n
Shakerley, Peter, 86, 87
Sharp, John, 132n
Shawe, John, vintner of London, 150; his daughters, 150
Sherborne, Robert, 35, 51
Shirley, John, 152
Shrewsbury, John Talbot, Lord Furnival, earl of (d.1453), 170, 170n; John Talbot, earl of (d.1460), 165, 165n
Silcock, John, 8
Smert, Peter, draper, 145; Margaret, his wife, 145n

INDEX

Smith, Richard, vicar of Prestbury, 39, 39n
Smith, Simon, Sheriff, 129, 136, 137n
Smyth, John, 9
Smyth, Piers, 37
Somerset, Edmund Beaufort, count of Mortain, duke of (d.1455), 166n, 170n, 173n; Edmund Beaufort, duke of (d.1471), 166, 166n; Henry Beaufort, duke of (d.1464), 166, 166n
Sonde, Reginald, 130n
Sotheworth, John, mayor of Chester, 10
Spicer, John, 144; Agnes, his daughter, 144
Stafford: Hugh, earl of Stafford (d.1386), 172n; Humphrey, earl of Stafford, duke of Buckingham (d.1460), 172
Stafford, Hugh, Lord, 164
Stafford, John, bishop of Bath and Wells, archbishop of Canterbury, 188n, 191, 191n
Stanley of Lathom (Lancs.): family of, 29, 30, 35, 64; Sir John (d.1414), 162, 162n; Sir John (d.1437), 50, 64, 65; Sir Thomas, 1st Lord Stanley (d.1459), 50, 63, 179n; Thomas, 2nd Lord Stanley, 1st earl of Derby (d.1504), 35, 37, 37n, 38, 51; his son, George, Lord Strange (d.1497), 30, 35, 51; Thomas, 3rd Lord Stanley, 2nd earl of Derby (d. 1521), 30, 35
Stanley, James, archdeacon of Chester, 30
Stanley, Sir William, of Holt, (d.1495), 29, 30, 34, 37, 38, 50, 51
Stanway, Henry, 43
Stillington, Robert, bishop of Bath and Wells, chancellor, 133
Stoke, Thomas, innkeeper, 114
Stonor, Sir William, 149; Elizabeth, his wife, 149
Suffolk: John de la Pole, duke of (d.1492), 46; William de la Pole, duke of (d.1450), 50, 63, 171, 174, 175, 177, 177n, 178, 179n; Robert de Ufford, earl of (d.1369), 164n; William de Ufford, earl of (d.1382), 172n
Swynford, Katherine, see Lancaster, John of Gaunt, duke of
Syon, abbey of, 140, 151

Tabley, William of, 58; Margery, his daughter, 58
Talbot: Gilbert, Lord, brother of John, Lord Furnival, earl of Shrewsbury (d.1453), 169, 169n, 170n; John, earl of Shrewsbury (d.1460), see Shrewsbury
Tatton, Robert, clerk, 75
Tatton, William, 37, 51
Thomason, Ralph, chaplain, 43
Thornton, Jane, 42
Tiptoft, John, earl of Worcester (d.1470), see Worcester
Townley, Robert, 69
Trafford, family, of Trafford, (Lancs.), 78, 81, 81n, 87, 90; Sir Edmund (d.1457), 75, 79, 81, 86; John, 75
Troutbeck, John, esquire, chamberlain of Chester, 48, 50; William, esquire, chamberlain of Chester, 48, 50, 63, 64, 64n, 65; Joan, his wife, 63
Tudor, Jasper, earl of Pembroke (d.1495), see Pembroke
Tytherington, Thomas, 39

Ufford: Sir Thomas, son of Robert de Ufford, earl of Suffolk (d.1369), 164; William de, earl of Suffolk (d.1382), see Suffolk

Vaynoll, see Bodelwyddan
Venables family of Bollin (Ches.) 79, 81, 86; William, Lord of Bollin, 81
Venables of Kinderton (Ches.), Sir Thomas, 34, 47, 52; William, esquire, escheator of Chester, 30
Venables, William, senior, 56; Eve, his daughter, 56
Vere, Richard de, earl of Oxford (d.1417); Robert de, earl of Oxford (d.1392), see Oxford
Vergil, Polydore, 83, 159n
Vernon, Margaret, 43
Vernon, William (c.1585-1667), 91
Villiers, abbey of, 223
Villiers, Catherine de, 215
Vincennes, château of, 221

Warburton, family, of Warburton, 68; David, 38; Geoffrey, 33, 33n; Sir Geoffrey (d.1448), 33n, 56, 63, 67, 70; Sir John, his grandson (d.1517), 70
Warde, Thomas, of Norbury, 40
Waren, Christopher, of Coventry, 43
Warren family of Poynton, 80, 87; Sir John (d.1518), 80
Warwick, earls of, 76; Thoma Beauchamp, earl of (d.1401), 172n 178
Weatherley, John, 129, 136, 137n
Weever, Thomas, 66
Werken, Theoderic, 199, 200
Whiksted, William, 43
Whitehead, Roger, 43
Whyteclyve, William de, 97–99
Wiche, Johanna, 145n
Willots family of Foxtwist, 80, 82n
Willoughby, William, Lord, 169n William, Lord, his son, 164
Wilmslow (Ches.), parish of, 79
Windsor, castle, 157n, 158; chapel of S George, 160, 161
Witham, Thomas, 132n
Woodhull, Thomas, 133n
Wittonstall, Oliver, 79; Thomas, 79, 82
Woodford (Ches.), 84, 80
Woodstock, Thomas of, duke of Gloucester (d.1397), see Gloucester
Woodville, Anthony, Lord Scales, Ear Rivers (d.1483), see Rivers
Woodville (Wydeville), Richard, Lorc Rivers (d.1469), 171, 171n
Worcester, Henry Somerset, earl o (d.1549), 52; John Tiptoft, earl o (d.1470), 191, 192n
Worcester, William, 75, 83, 88–90
Worth, John, of Tytherington, 39
Wyclif, John, 143

York, archbishop of, see also Scrope Richard le; city of, 5, 8, 8n, 10
York: house of, 173: Edmund of Langley duke of, (d.1415), 165, 166; his son Edward of Aumale, 166; Richard, earl o Cambridge, duke of (d.1415), 166, 168n 172, 176; Richard, duke of (d.1460) 170, 172, 173, 173n, 176; Cecily Neville his wife, 224, see also Edward IV Richard III

Zouche, William, Lord, 170n